# PETRIFIED

**Barbara Nadel**

headline

First published in Great Britain in 2004
by HEADLINE BOOK PUBLISHING

First published in paperback in 2004
by HEADLINE BOOK PUBLISHING

3

ISBN 0 7472 6721 9

Typeset in Aldus by Palimpsest Book Production Limited, Polmont, Stirlingshire
Printed and bound in Great Britain by Clays Ltd, St Ives plc

Headline's policy is to use papers that are natural, renewable and recyclable products and made from wood grown in sustainable forests. The logging and manufacturing processes are expected to conform to the environmental regulations of the country of origin.

HEADLINE BOOK PUBLISHING
A division of Hodder Headline
338 Euston Road
London NW1 3BH

www.headline.co.uk
www.hodderheadline.com

To all those wonderfully helpful people who prefer not to see their names in print. You know who you are and thank you.

Also to Ersin and Erdoḡan for another classic Istanbul experience. I'd also like to thank my editor at Headline, Martin Fletcher, and, as ever, my long suffering family.

# PROLOGUE

'Sir?'

The man sitting in the chair continued to look out of the window as if he hadn't heard. Could it be that whatever was happening in the streets of Kuloğlu was of more importance than the woman lying dead in the next room?

His pistol drawn, Sergeant İsak Çöktin turned briefly to look at the small squad of uniformed policemen behind him. But, from the expressions on their faces, they were just as clueless as he was about what to do in a situation like this. He returned his gaze to the motionless figure before him.

'Sir, I don't know what has happened here, but if you would just indicate that you have heard . . .'

The perfect poise of the figure robbed him of further speech. How could anyone be so still, so utterly statuesque? Çöktin had seen shock before but never this – catatonia.

Perhaps if Çöktin touched him, he might rouse him from his fugue. The man's hands were in plain sight, one to each side of his body, braced against the seat of the chair. In theory the man might dive one hand underneath that military blazer he wore and pull out a weapon, but was

1

that really likely? Or even really possible from a position of such utter immobility?

With one light movement, Çöktin allowed his hand not holding a weapon to take that risk. The man pitched forward into a foetal heap on the floor.

All of the officers moved to join Çöktin.

'Has he fainted?'

'Get him up!' Çöktin ordered.

One of the younger men, Constable Hikmet Yıldız, moved around the figure and took one of its wrists between his hands. It was perfectly, completely cold. Yıldız looked up into the piercing blue eyes of Çöktin and said, 'Sir, I think he's dead.'

Çöktin squatted down beside Yıldız and gently moved the chin of the man on the floor towards him. İstanbul was stewing in the humid, forty-degree heat of a midsummer afternoon but the man's skin felt as if it had just been removed from a refrigerator. Çöktin quickly took his hand away before easing himself down to look into the second dead face he'd seen that day.

However, unlike the first corpse, this one had its eyes wide open. They were violet, beautiful and startling. Çöktin found himself lost in admiration until he realised that they were not made of aqueous and vitreous humours but of coloured glass.

# CHAPTER 1

Çetin İkmen wiped one hand across his heavily sweating brow and sighed. He could fully understand why the elderly, fabric-swathed woman in front of him was weeping. In her position he would have come to exactly the same conclusion. But what she feared wasn't true, or rather proved – yet – whatever misgivings she or those around her might have.

'It is,' İkmen said, as he lit the latest in what had been, was always, a long series of cigarettes, 'my intention to return your grandchildren to your family alive. As yet we have no reason to believe that they—'

'But you are a homicide detective!' the woman wailed through her brightly coloured scarves. 'You bring justice only to the dead! Everyone in the city knows you and what you do! You are a great man Çetin Bey, you see things . . .'

'Yes, but I act for the living too, Mirimar Hanım,' İkmen replied gently, 'and on this occasion I have been assigned to search for your grandchildren because of my knowledge of this city and because of my many years of experience in the police force. We are taking their disappearance very seriously.'

'My daughter is like something already dead, Çetin Bey!

3

Neither eating nor sleeping, drifting about her business . . .
And Melih – he's no good to her, still working like one
possessed . . .' Overcome, she put her head down into the
folds of her clothes and wept once again.

The eight-year-old Akdeniz twins, Yaşar and Nuray,
had been missing for thirty-six hours. The children had
left their home in Balat on Saturday morning to go
and play out in the gentle early morning sunshine, had
never since returned and no one had seen them since.
The children had, seemingly, vaporised out of the steep
Balat streets as if by magic.

It was now fifty-five and a half years since Çetin had
been born to university lecturer Timür İkmen and his
Albanian wife, Ayşe, the famous witch of Üsküdar. And
although this thin, smoke-dried man had worked for the
İstanbul police department for all of his adult life, there
was a lot of his mother's magic underlying his well-honed
veneer of pragmatism. The woman before him should be
given only facts – even if those facts were things she'd
heard before. Mirimar Hanım was both of the age and
social class to nurture a deep, almost religious, respect
for Ayşe İkmen and her 'magical' policeman son. In
İkmen's experience, such people expected solutions to their
problems that were both out of this world and rapid.

'My officers are continuing to make enquiries in Balat
as well as in the surrounding districts,' İkmen said.

'Yes, but what if they have been taken away from
Balat?'

'To where?' İkmen shrugged his arms out to his sides in
a questioning motion. 'We haven't even finished checking
all the children's contacts in the district yet. I don't,

Mirimar Hanım, have any evidence that your grand-children have moved out of the Balat area. I have no leads or sightings outside of the district, and in a city of ten million . . .'

'Yaşar did tell me that Melih was taking them over to Sarıyer.'

'Yes, but clearly he didn't, did he, Mirimar Hanım?' İkmen stubbed his cigarette out in his ashtray and then lit up another. 'Both your daughter and your son-in-law were in bed when the children disappeared. Once he'd established that the children weren't with any of their friends, Melih called us, from Balat, late on Saturday morning.'

'Yes,' Mirimar Hanım shook her head helplessly, 'I know. I know. They are most likely close by. Even my daughter says that, and Eren is not one to entertain false hope.'

That the woman's son-in-law's name was not added to that of her daughter didn't surprise İkmen. No one, beyond Eren Akdeniz, that he had encountered so far had any great love for the children's father. But then that was often the way with famous people, doubly so if, like Melih Akdeniz, that fame was also allied to controversy.

A Balat boy by birth and still staunchly resident within the district, Melih Akdeniz was Turkey's wealthiest and most experimental visual artist. Though poorly educated in the conventional sense, Akdeniz had begun shocking art lovers both domestic and foreign in the late nine-teen seventies. His work, which was expressed through a variety of media, took modern, controversial themes and presented them in a traditional Turkish context. His most famous work, a series of carpets depicting stylised renditions of internal sexual organs, had been woven using human hair. This 'indictment of the myth of Turkish chastity' had, in places as diverse as New York and Ankara, earned him the soubriquet of 'genius' – which Melih Akdeniz believed with every fibre of his being. But in spite of his arrogance he was no doubt experiencing a great deal of pain since the disappearance of his children. Melih, in his own frenetic and work-obsessed way, had to be suffering just as much as Mirimar Hanım and her ghost-like daughter.

But then if the boy, Yaşar, had told his grandmother that he and his sister were due to accompany their father over to the Bosphorus village of Sarıyer, it was just possible that the children could have attempted to get there on their own. It wasn't the first time that İkmen had thought along these lines. He had indeed made enquiries to that effect, but no one in or around Sarıyer had any knowledge of the Akdeniz children. There was, of course, something further that he could do.

'Look, I'll send some of my officers over to Sarıyer,' he said, 'just to check it out.'

'Oh, thank you so much!' Mirimar Hanım replied. 'So, so—'

'I don't suppose,' İkmen said, cutting across her effusive and now tear-stained thanks, 'you know why the children and Melih Bey were going out to Sarıyer?'

'No.'

'Oh well, I will have to ask your son-in-law. He will know.' İkmen smiled.

'Yes.'

6

'Right.' He smiled even more broadly. 'Mirimar Hanım . . .'

'You want me to leave?' She lowered her eyes as she once again fastened the ends of her scarf around the back of her head. 'But of course. I know I have been a trouble to you.'

'Not at all. Not at all.'

As soon as she stood, so did İkmen, who then moved quickly to position himself beside his office door. Mirimar Hanım picked her large tomato- and bread-filled shopping bag up from the floor and walked wearily towards him.

'İnşallah, the little ones will return,' she said as she passed through the now-open door and into the corridor beyond.

'İnşallah,' İkmen repeated. 'We are all in the gentle hands of the Almighty, Mirimar Hanım.'

'Indeed, Çetin Bey, so very true.'

And then with other religiously inspired mutterings for company, Mirimar Hanım left.

İkmen, still leaning against the doorpost, raised his head upwards.

'Look, I know that You and I have our differences regarding religion, ethics, Your very existence,' he said wearily, 'but You know, these children are very young and even though we're doing everything we can, I would appreciate a little help . . .'

There had been a time when the idea of artists living in the district of Balat had been laughable. Run down, if hardworking, the district had always been a haven for refugees and those who were a little different. But not for artists.

7

Jews, as Nilufer Cemal knew only too well, had settled in Balat after their expulsion from Spain in 1492. Welcomed into the Ottoman Empire by Sultan Beyazıt II, the Jews had prospered in Balat – some, alongside more recent refugees from Kosovo, still remained. Living in great houses, their doorsteps littered with tiny gypsy children, were the old Jews – people with names like Levi, Baruh, Leon and Palombo. Nilufer's paternal grandmother had been a Palombo and when, back in the seventies, the old woman had died, Nilufer had inherited her deep brown wooden house, with its twisted, arabesque window grilles. What an excitingly eccentric location the house had provided for Nilufer's first studio! Her father had fretted. After all, who would want to go to filthy old Balat to buy or even look at an artist's work? However talented the artist, that surely was quite out of the question.

But Nilufer had faith. She bought her materials and set up her kiln in the small courtyard garden at the back of the house. She slowly and lovingly created the most exquisite ceramics, and at the same time made, rather more rapidly, artefacts the tourists would like to buy. Deals struck with various tourist outlets in the Grand Bazaar kept Nilufer in clothes, food and materials while her 'real' work – modern renditions of traditional Turkish ceramics – started to gain some attention from the artistic élite. One of her friends from university, another aspiring artist, moved, briefly, into the district afterwards and for a while Nilufer nurtured fantasies about an artists' colony in Balat.

When Melih Akdeniz first exploded on to the international art scene in 1979, Nilufer was ecstatic. The most famous artist in Turkey was living, had in fact always lived, in Balat. Her dreams of a colony buzzing excitedly around in her head, Nilufer went to see this so-called phenomenon in his great ochre house opposite the Greek Boys' School. And although his work was not to her taste, she appreciated it for its innovation and felt that as a statement it was extremely exciting. She never thought that Melih would really appreciate her work, but perhaps, like her reaction to his art, it would interest him in an academic sense. So Nilufer took one of her ceramics with her on her long, breathless climb towards the great ochre house and its almost unrivalled views of the Golden Horn.

When Nilufer arrived, Turkey's greatest artist was in the midst of one of what later became his legendary heroin binges. Drunk as well as delusional, he wasn't amused by the appearance of this sober, middle-class young woman carrying something he sneeringly derided as 'some tourist junk'.

But Nilufer wanted him to like her, wanted him to help her build up a colony, regenerate the area, bring Balat into the mainstream. And so she gave him her beautiful green and blue tile with its abstract images of Seljuk representational forms and he smashed it at her feet.

'This is shit!' he cried. 'Fucking gutless, Turkish virgin's shit!'

Both he and the two prostitutes he'd paid for that day laughed as Nilufer, tears streaming from her eyes, ran back down the hill to the safety of her own studio.

Not once during the twenty-three years since that event had Nilufer even so much as looked at the great

ochre house at the top of the hill. Until very recently
no other artists had come to join either herself or Melih
in their respective artistic isolation. Though always working, Nilufer had not lived up to her potential, and had
achieved little recognition in the intervening years, certainly nowhere near as much as Melih. It was, however,
Nilufer, as opposed to Melih, who knew the few but significant artists who had started to colonise Balat since the
beginning of the new millennium. The English writer who
had inherited his neat rose-coloured house from his native
grandparents; the couple who specialised in portraiture;
and Gonca, the big gypsy woman whose collages made of
equestrian and fortune-telling artefacts had been exhibited
in the Museum of Modern Art in Ankara. The colony,
or so it seemed, was finally happening, and without any
intervention from Melih Akdeniz, who, although now
married and a father, had not, it was said, moderated
his lifestyle in any significant way. Drugs and alcohol
still influenced both his work and his behaviour to which
Nilufer now, for the first time in twenty-three years, was
exposed once again.

'I was sorry to hear about your children,' she shouted
up to the shaggy-headed figure eyeing her suspiciously
from one of the second-floor windows of the great ochre
house. 'I hope they are found quickly, for their sake.'

'Who are you?' he responded sharply. Thinner and
more unkempt than Nilufer had remembered him, Melih
Akdeniz looked bad. 'Why do you care?'

'My name is Nilufer Cemal, a Turkish virgin,' she said
with an ironic smile. 'You destroyed a ceramic of mine
back in 1979. And I'm sorry not for you but for your

wife and the children themselves. Little ones like that shouldn't be separated from their parents, whoever those parents might be.'

Melih sniffed loudly – had he now perhaps taken to cocaine too? 'Keep your pity for your own lack of talent and leave me to continue my work.'

'As you wish, Melih Bey,' Nilufer replied evenly, 'but even your talent isn't going to bring the little ones back, is it? Not even you can do that, can you?'

For just a moment he stared, his long, slit-like eyes burning into her mildly amused and strangely immobile face.

'Bitch!' he spat as he yanked the window closed and disappeared somewhere deep inside his eyrie.

As soon as he had gone, Nilufer turned and made her way back down the steep cobbled hill. Her face impassive now, she didn't respond to the requests for money or offers of domestic services from any of the local children who clustered around her smartly dressed figure. Looking over their heads, she surveyed the shifting, watery vista before her, the Golden Horn and, beyond that, the Bosphorus. Massive and glimmering in the late afternoon heat, these waterways could be seen and perhaps in moments of delusion, commanded from Melih Akdeniz's vaunting house topped by its fantastic glass studio. She pictured him sitting there, up high, his drug-addled brain seething with new and even more shocking ways to express his genius. She had envisioned him like this many times before – an arrogant sultan just ripe for a fall, like a soft, wrinkling plum. Nilufer smiled. Well, now that fall had come and there was nothing Melih could do about it. The children, his creations, had gone and, just like Nilufer had been when Melih had smashed her lovingly created ceramic, he was completely powerless to do anything about it.

The doctor removed his glasses before minutely examining the blazer, frowning as he did so.

'This is part of no uniform I've ever come across, Sergeant,' he said. 'Looks quite old.'

İsak Çöktin leaned his head to one side; a lock of dark red hair flopped across his forehead as he did so. Still slightly shaky from his recent encounter with two dead bodies – one, the owner of the Kuloğlu apartment, the elderly Mrs Keyder, had been expected, but not the other one – being within the confines of the mortuary was not making him feel any better. Not, of course, that the pathologist, Dr Arto Sarkissian, was contributing in any way to Çöktin's sense of unease. Rotund and, despite his profession, unfailingly jolly, the doctor had worked for the İstanbul police for almost the whole of his professional life, which, given that he was now fifty-eight years old, was a long time.

'Do we know anything about the other body, Mrs Keyder?' Sarkissian asked as he shifted his attention from the outside to the inside of the blazer.

Çöktin shrugged. 'She attended St Anthony's church on a regular basis,' he said. 'It was the priest, Father Giovanni, who first raised the alarm. He tried to visit her, couldn't gain access – the kapıcı of that building is a lazy, useless creature who'd "lost" his key to the apartment – so Father Giovanni called us.'

'The woman was a Christian,' Sarkissian muttered as he continued to turn the blazer over in his hands.

12

'Yes.'

Although a secular country, the population of the Turkish Republic is ninety per cent Muslim. There are, however, minorities who follow other faiths like this Mrs Keyder and also like both Arto Sarkissian and İsak Çöktin. Not that the latter's faith, the native Kurdish religion of the Yezidi, was now or ever could be a topic of conversation. Sarkissian, however, like the recently deceased female body that lay in his laboratory, was a Christian. Unlike the woman, though like most of his fellow Armenians, he was Orthodox rather than Catholic.

Coming across a faded label on the inside pocket of the blazer, the doctor squinted to see what was written there.

'Do we know what Mrs Keyder's origins were, by any chance?' he asked. 'I assume from her surname that her husband was Turkish.'

'Most people who go to St Anthony's are Italian, aren't they?' Çöktin replied. 'Her first name was Rosita.'

'Which may well be Italian,' Sarkissian responded, his eyes still narrowed and fixed to the time-scarred label, 'but then it could be Spanish.' He looked just briefly up at Çöktin and smiled. 'It is Spanish that they speak in Argentina, isn't it, Sergeant?'

'I believe so,' Çöktin replied. 'Why?'

'Because this jacket, blazer or whatever it is was made in Buenos Aires.'

'We're not certain what if anything was the connection between Mrs Keyder and the dead man,' Çöktin said as he reached into his pocket for his cigarettes. 'Father Giovanni was, I know, of the opinion that the old woman lived alone.

That was why he was so concerned.' He sighed. 'In view of this new development, I'll have to go back and speak to him again.'

Sarkissian put the blazer down on his desk and looked up. 'I can't help you much until I've finished my examination,' he said. 'I'll be able to give you some more information about that tomorrow.'

Çöktin lit his cigarette. 'That's fine. Provided Inspector Suleyman doesn't need me, I'll go out and see Father Giovanni later this evening.'

'Inspector Suleyman is, I take it, busy at the moment?' Sarkissian said with a smile.

'My boss is always busy, Dr Sarkissian.' Çöktin exhaled on a sigh. 'You know some of the lads say that he's becoming more like Inspector İkmen every day.'

Sarkissian laughed. Çetin İkmen was currently the most experienced and successful detective in the İstanbul homicide division. Famous for his almost maniacal approach to his work, he was also Sarkissian's oldest and dearest friend.

'Well, Inspector Suleyman did work for Inspector İkmen for quite some time, you know, Çöktin,' he said, 'and Çetin Bey's "enthusiasm", I shall call it, is infectious.'

'Yes,' Çöktin allowed his head to droop down towards the floor, 'I know. But sometimes I wonder . . .'

'What?' Sarkissian, hearing the gravity in the younger man's voice, frowned. 'What do you wonder, Sergeant?'

'Well, it's not a criticism, you know, Doctor, but . . . look I'd do anything for Inspector Suleyman, he's been very good to me . . .'

'But?'

'But, well, you didn't hear it from me, but I know that he's got a Mafia boss in his sights. He's been after him for some time. There's information about this man all over his desk.' He looked up into the doctor's face. 'He's Russian.'

'Oh.'

Russians *en masse* had been coming to live and work in İstanbul ever since the disintegration of the old Soviet Union. Attracted to the relative affluence of the city, the Russians had almost taken over certain districts of İstanbul. And although the majority of these people wanted nothing more than just to make new and better lives for themselves in Turkey, some, like the pimps who sold their own women on the streets, had other, more criminal objectives. Others still, like the Mafia bosses who controlled sometimes vast and extremely wealthy crime organisations, moved to even blacker and more frightening rhythms. And although it was good that someone might finally be trying to tackle what had become an enormous problem for law enforcement in the city, the thought of it made both Çöktin and Sarkissian go cold. Just because the handsome Suleyman was an honest man didn't mean that everyone he came into contact with or even worked alongside was of a similar mind. Less than a year before, the whole department had been rocked by the activities of an Eastern European gangster, Zhivkov, who had possessed an informant inside the department. Taking on organised crime, even though Zhivkov was now dead, was not something to be done lightly, and although Arto Sarkissian had no idea upon what basis Suleyman was acting, he just hoped that he knew what he was doing. The doctor had over the years seen at first-hand what these people did to those who opposed them. Just the memory of these incidents made him wince.

'I'd better go,' Çöktin said as he first ground out his cigarette in the doctor's ashtray and then rose to his feet, 'leave you to your work.'

Sarkissian also stood up and started to move towards his office door. 'We will speak tomorrow, Sergeant.' He placed his fingers around the door handle and made ready to wish his guest goodbye.

'Yes. Thank you, Doctor.'

'Goodbye, Sergeant.' He opened the door out into the corridor.

However, instead of going through it, Çöktin stopped, his face suddenly grave as if something troubling had just struck him.

'Sergeant?'

Çöktin bit his bottom lip. 'Doctor, I assume that the man in the Keyder apartment must have been blind.'

'He had two glass eyes,' Sarkissian replied, 'and so I'd say that was beyond reasonable doubt.'

'But then don't you think it's very odd that he was wearing a military uniform? I mean, if he was blind . . .'

Arto Sarkissian sighed. He'd seen so much that was odd or out of the ordinary over the years that sometimes he almost missed certain, less obvious strangeness, like this seeming anomaly with the unknown man's corpse.

'Oh, I don't know, Sergeant,' he said wearily. 'People deal with situations in a variety of ways. Perhaps he used to be in the military and continued to wear the uniform after he lost his sight. Perhaps he couldn't quite get over not being in the military in Argentina or wherever he came from.' He shrugged. 'But then perhaps he just bought the blazer from a second-hand clothes stall. Maybe Mrs Keyder bought it for him. I don't know. Time will tell, or not.'

'I know,' Çöktin said as he moved past the doctor into the corridor beyond.

'İnşallah, all will be revealed in the fullness of time,' the Armenian concluded.

And with that expression so redolent of all things Islamic, the Christian and the Yezidi parted.

# CHAPTER 2

'I feel,' İkmen said as he leaned back in his battered leather chair and sucked hard on his Maltepe cigarette, 'that some clarification about why Melih Akdeniz was planning to take his children out to Sarıyer is needed.'

The attractive young woman sitting opposite, frowned. 'Why? They didn't go; they've not been spotted over there.'

'No, but I feel I'd like to know what was planned anyway. Where in Sarıyer they were going and who, if anyone, they were going to see are questions we need to ask Melih Akdeniz.'

The woman, Sergeant Ayşe Farsakoğlu, had worked directly for İkmen for just over six months. Prior to that she'd been in uniform, and had worked on operations he had commanded. She'd known about him outside of work through her previous sergeant, who had once been her lover. Not that she liked to dwell on the late Sergeant Orhan Tepe for too long these days. Since Orhan's death she'd thrown herself wholeheartedly into her career, which was why, she assumed, İkmen had chosen her to be his deputy. He was, however, as Orhan had always said, an odd character. Details, like this Sarıyer business, something that on the face of it meant very little to the investigation, bothered him. But then sometimes, as Ayşe knew from past experience – particularly with İkmen – these details were often crucial to the resolution of an investigation.

'Do you want me to call Akdeniz and let him know we're coming?' Ayşe said as she made to pick up her telephone.

'No,' İkmen replied, 'let's surprise him.'

'He might be out.'

'No, he won't be.' İkmen rose from his chair and put on his jacket. 'The wife goes out, remember? Prostrate with grief she might be, but Eren Akdeniz is still the one who goes out to get the bread and cigarettes. Melih's "great" work must continue . . .'

'You don't like Mr Akdeniz very much, do you, sir?'

İkmen smiled. 'As a professional, Ayşe, I don't "like" or "dislike" anyone. But as you've so rightly observed, although my experience of Mr Akdeniz is as yet slight I know he's not exactly my type of person. I can sympathise with the state his various drug habits have plunged that awful body of his into. I mean, he makes me look fat and healthy! But the "art" that has been fuelled by the drugs, well . . . I'm sorry but it does nothing for me, and as for his insistence that "the work" carry on in spite of the disappearance of his children . . .'

'Some people deal with stress like that.'

'Yes, I know,' İkmen said, 'and I expect that if he were a traditional calligraphy artist or a Greek monk painting an ikon, I'd feel entirely different. But I'm afraid I find it difficult to appreciate the value of carpets depicting the inner workings of the scrotum or that "mosaic" of Tarkan.'

'The one made of . . . ?'

'Condom wrappers, yes.'

'It's a very good likeness,' Ayşe said as she fought to suppress the laughter this work of art evoked in her. Tarkan, monumentally successful pop star, was practically worshipped by his teenage fans. Vast numbers of young girls screamed and fainted at his concerts, as she well knew, having been on duty at a few of them. Tarkan rendered in condom wrappers was an irony she could see only too easily.

'I admit it's a good likeness,' İkmen said as he took his car keys out of his pocket and then picked up his lighter. 'Akdeniz has talent. I can even appreciate some of the statements he's making about society and culture, what I object to is the money art collectors and galleries give him for spending an afternoon gluing some bits of tinfoil on a sheet of paper. And all the nonsense the critics write about it. But then I'm old, what do I know?'

Ayşe didn't reply. İkmen was always a bit tetchy and had been particularly agitated for the past few months. She wasn't sure why although there were rumours. His already bulging apartment – five of the nine İkmen children still lived at home – had recently swelled to accommodate another relative. And then there was the 'problem' of his daughter Hulya, who was in love with a young Jewish boy. Although İkmen himself didn't care for or practise his religion, his wife was, apparently, a devout Muslim and both she and the boy's father, an old colleague of both Ayşe and her boss, opposed the relationship. All that on top of the job had to be stressful.

'Well, let's get over there,' İkmen said, opening the

office door and allowing Ayşe to pass into the corridor. 'I'd like to have a stroll around some of the streets lower down the hill while we're there too. I know the men are doing house-to-house, but that's intimidating,' he smiled. 'It's cooling down now, let's see if we can engage some of the locals in a little off-the-record conversation.'

They walked side by side towards the stairs.

'I haven't worked in Balat for some years,' İkmen continued. 'I was still working with Inspector Suleyman at the time. In some ways the place has changed. Fewer Jews, more migrants, not as run down.'

'Well, the houses are very beautiful,' Ayşe said. 'The Akdeniz house is stunning. If I had enough money I'd buy a house in Balat and restore it.'

Although quite how, İkmen wondered, this beautiful policewoman would fit in with either the working-class locals or the eccentric artists he couldn't imagine. But he kept these thoughts to himself as he followed Ayşe down the stairs and out to the car park.

Father Giovanni Vetra, unlike some members of the foreign clergy, liked Turkey and the Turks, and had bothered to learn their language. Based at the church of St Anthony of Padua in Beyoğlu for the past twenty years, he delighted in both the history and vibrancy of İstanbul. He had many friends in the city, one of whom had been Rosita Keyder.

'I don't know exactly when Rosita came to this country,' he said as he passed the tiny cup of espresso coffee to Çöktin. 'I know it was in the nineteen fifties, but when . . . ?' He shrugged.

Çöktin looked down at his cup and smiled. Turkish

21

coffee was good but real Italian espresso, well, that was a treat. He took one glorious sip before moving to his next question.

'Did Mrs Keyder ever talk about Argentina?'

'Not often,' the priest said as he leaned back into his metal patio chair and looked up at the now darkening sky. 'By the time she met me, it was already a very long time ago. She spoke about it more in her early days here, to Father Carlo.'

'He was your predecessor?'

'Yes. Father Carlo knew the Keyders well – Veli, the husband, as well as Rosita. Unfortunately by the time I arrived to take over from Father Carlo, Veli was already dying. Poor Rosita has been alone now for nineteen years. There is a sister-in-law who lives in one of the Bosphorus villages, I believe, but I don't think there's anyone else. Rosita never had children and to my knowledge she never went back to visit any relatives she might still have had in Buenos Aires. She came to church and I visited her once a week.'

'You never saw anyone else in her apartment when you were there?'

'No. Why?'

Çöktin looked down at the warm terracotta-coloured floor of the courtyard before replying. 'Look, sir, this is at present confidential—'

'Of course.' The priest smiled. If nothing else he had to be accustomed to confidences.

'We found another body, aside from that of Mrs Keyder, in the apartment,' Çöktin said. 'That of a young man. There was no ID on the body.'

'A young man . . .' Father Giovanni shook his heavy Roman head. 'No. She never mentioned, certainly not to me, any other relatives apart from her sister-in-law, who was or is single. She had a few acquaintances at church, elderly ladies. This young man couldn't have broken in to her apartment?'

'We don't think so.' Çöktin finished his coffee and placed the empty cup on the table beside him. 'He was wearing clothes we think Mrs Keyder may have given him and we believe he was blind.'

'Oh, how—'

'The body has glass eyes.'

'Oh.'

They sat in silence for a few moments after that, Çöktin, in a state of static agitation. Catholic priests, or so his boss, Mehmet Suleyman, had told him when Çöktin had spoken to him earlier, were privy to their parishioners' innermost secrets during confession. Things said in confession were between the priest, the parishioner and God. This was, so Suleyman had said, absolute. His wife was a Catholic so he should know. But then if that were the case, perhaps Father Giovanni may know more about Rosita Keyder than he had offered so far. But how was Çöktin ever going to extract that information if it was told during confession?

'Father Giovanni,' he said, 'I know this might be difficult for you, but—'

'You want to know whether Rosita ever told me anything in confession,' the priest smiled. Although neither handsome nor young, his face had a sort of hawkish, battered nobility that was easy to warm to. 'No, she didn't, Sergeant. And before you start wondering whether I'm lying to protect her, please remember that by lying I would be committing a sin. Had she told me anything pertinent in confession I would tell you that had happened. But she didn't.' He shrugged. 'Rosita's "sins" revolved around events like cursing a stubbed toe.'

'I see.' The priest's statement, on the face of it, just added to the notion that nothing untoward had indeed happened in the Kuloğlu apartment. If both Rosita Keyder and the young man died from natural causes the only problem the police would have would be one of establishing the latter's identity. But that wasn't criminal work and wouldn't therefore concern Çöktin.

As if reading the young officer's thoughts, the priest asked, 'Do you know yet how Rosita died?'

'No, not yet, sir,' Çöktin replied.

'And this man . . . ?'

'No.'

Father Giovanni put his hand down to one of the numerous potted plants that filled the floor of the courtyard and gently stroked its leaves. 'Let us hope that God took them naturally,' he said softly, 'and without pain.'

'It would be nice to think so,' Çöktin replied.

The priest looked up into the young officer's face and said, 'İnşallah, as you Turks so rightly say.'

'Yes . . .'

'Putting all things in the hands of the Almighty is not a bad way to live,' Father Giovanni continued. 'I've often thought how both attractive and sensible your Islamic philosophy of total submission to and reliance upon God is. You learn acceptance, which is a hedge against both greed and disappointment. The trouble with Christianity and I think with Judaism too is that we're encouraged to believe that we can influence our own destinies, which is most dangerous. The older I get the less I believe in the freedom that desire and choice are alleged to bring. We can't be anyone we want to be or have anything we want to have any more than we can stop ourselves from dying.'

Çöktin, who had toyed with the idea of mentioning that not every Turkish citizen was Muslim, decided against it. How did one explain the Yezidi faith to others? They were branded devil worshippers by those who knew no better, their philosophical stance on the nature of Satan, a deity they called the 'Peacock Angel', being entirely unique. He did, however, have to say, 'I don't disagree with you, sir, but I must say that I think that some Turks can be just as greedy and anxious as anyone from Western Europe.'

But Father Giovanni didn't reply. Now looking really rather sadly at the vine-covered wall in front of him, he just finished his coffee and then sighed.

'I must leave you now, sir,' Çöktin said as he rose from his seat. 'Thank you very much for your help and the delicious coffee.'

The priest looked up and then rose to his feet.

'You're very welcome, Sergeant. I'm sorry I haven't been able to be of more assistance. Had I had Veli's sister's address . . .'

'That won't be difficult to find,' Çöktin said. 'If, as you say, she isn't married, she must have the same name as her brother. Anyway, we're still looking through Mrs Keyder's things.'

'Mmm. And there is, of course, her funeral to consider.'

Father Giovanni opened the door that led back into his house. 'I know she would want a Catholic funeral.'

Çöktin entered the priest's living room. 'Yes, although we'll have to try and contact her sister-in-law and any relatives she might still have in Argentina first. The story will hit the newspapers tomorrow. That may jog somebody's memory. But I'll tell our doctor to keep you informed.'

They walked through the building, past many pictures and statues of saints, to the front door.

'It's fortunate, under the circumstances, we don't have any time limits on the burial of our dead,' the priest said as he opened the door on to the street. 'You Muslims have to be in the ground within twenty-four hours, don't you?'

'Yes, although in circumstances like this that isn't always possible,' Çöktin replied as he stepped across the threshold. 'Thank you again, Father Giovanni, for your help and your hospitality.' He smiled. 'Your courtyard is delightful. It's like being in a little corner of Italy.'

Father Giovanni laughed. 'Yes,' he said, 'it's designed to be. I love it here but I do miss my home – if you can understand that.'

'Yes,' Çöktin said, 'I understand that.'

And then he left, his mind suddenly possessed by images of his village home that he could only dimly remember. A place where everyone was Yezidi and there were no silences where the truth should be. But there wasn't, then or now, any work, any money or any hope. Only the strange and harsh beauty of eastern Turkey and the certainty of the closeness of the Peacock Angel, the

Yezidi image of the miraculously restored and benevolent Satan.

They were not an overtly unusual couple. Lots of men and women had sex in doorways and deserted courtyards after dark in this part of the city, especially Russian women – like her. Voluptuous and blonde, she was quite different from the man whose hands were on her. He was obviously local. He wasn't, however, her usual type of customer. Tall, well groomed and very handsome, he looked like a lawyer or a doctor, someone who could afford far better than her. He curled his long arms round her back and whispered in her ear.

'Why should I believe you, Masha? There's no body. For all I know Vladimir could just be a figment of your imagination.'

'But he isn't!' she hissed. 'I told you, Inspector Suleyman, he was my love and now he's gone. Killed by that animal Rostov! I want, I need justice!'

Inspector Mehmet Suleyman took his head away from her ear and stood straight and tall in front of her. There was no one about: he could afford to be a little less cautious, just for a moment.

'Look, if Vladimir came into the country illegally, I can't even prove that he was ever here,' he said. 'Beyond your belief that Rostov's heavies tied him into a sack and threw him into the Bosphorus, I've got nothing to go on.'

'Yes, but Vladimir said he feared they'd kill him just before I saw him for the last time!' Masha said, her hands resting pleadingly against Suleyman's chest. 'And drowning is how Rostov kills people. If you cross him or

27

take what's his, he drowns you. There's so much water here, it's easy.'

Suleyman sighed. Valery Ivanovich Rostov was one of several incredibly powerful Russian Mafia bosses who had settled in İstanbul since the fall of the old Soviet Union. A known, if unproven drug baron, Rostov had friends in high places amongst the local crime families and, it was alleged, within the Turkish Establishment. A bachelor, Rostov surrounded himself with violent but attractive young Russian men, which led many to suspect he was homosexual. And if this Russian prostitute was to be believed, her boyfriend, this Vladimir, had been one of Rostov's boys – even though she claimed he'd never shared the boss's bed. He'd just carried Rostov's drugs to wherever they were 'needed' until the temptation of what he was holding became too much for him – or so she said. Suleyman knew he had to be careful. Russians like Masha who'd spent most of their short lives in İstanbul almost always worked for one or other of the mobs. It was very probable she actually worked for Rostov. It had, after all, been she who had sought him out that first time and not vice versa. Just like now, she'd pulled him into a doorway – he was going to arrest her for unlawful soliciting – until she mentioned Rostov – the man he'd been after for nearly six months. How had Masha known? But then if she wasn't on the level, Suleyman couldn't as yet work out quite what game she was playing or to what end. However, if she were telling the truth . . .

'There must be something of Vladimir's in Rostov's house,' Masha said mournfully. 'He was always there in recent months. There has to be an item of clothing or . . . I could identify anything of his, I remember it all.'

'No,' Suleyman flicked his head back to indicate his disagreement, 'it would be your word against his and that's not good enough. Rostov is too well connected. I need independent proof that this Vladimir existed.' Then, hearing voices approaching down the alleyway opposite, he said, 'Kiss me!'

He reached down and took her lips between his. Horribly, even with her cold junkie's eyes looking over his shoulder, it felt really good. And although he did manage to stop himself from reaching out towards her almost naked breasts, he couldn't prevent the erection that made itself very obviously apparent. Once the small group of late-night revellers had passed them by, Masha took her lips away from his and placed her hand on the front of his trousers.

'I can make that feel so much better,' she said as she toyed provocatively with his zip.

For just a fraction of a second, Suleyman hesitated. He loved his family, adored his wife, but ever since she'd given birth to their son nearly a year ago sex had been uncomfortable for her. And even though he knew exactly what this Masha was . . .

'No,' he pushed her hand away roughly, 'I can't search Rostov's house on a pretext as whimsical as this.'

'So what do you need, Inspector?' she said provocatively as, yet again, she placed her hand over his crotch. This time he didn't stop her.

'I need some proper evidence of Vladimir's existence and of his involvement with Rostov. So many young men come and go from that house . . .' He looked down just as she slipped her hand inside his zip and took his penis between his fingers. 'I . . .'

'You're a very big, attractive man, Inspector,' she pouted. 'I can give you so much pleasure.'

'No!' He tore her hand from his penis and pushed himself away from her. 'No.'

'What?' She shrugged, watching bemused as he fastened the front of his trousers. 'I don't understand. I'd do you for free. You're hot and, anyway, you're helping me, aren't you? I have to give you something.'

Suleyman breathed deeply. 'Not that,' he said thickly, 'information. If you're serious about wanting to avenge this Vladimir's death then you have to give me something I can work with.'

'But—'

'Look, I've got this feeling I'm finding very difficult to shake off that you work for Rostov.' He moved back towards her once again. 'I know, I can tell that you're addicted to heroin. We have good reason to believe that Rostov gives his girls heroin. Now if you can take me to that—'

'No!'

'Masha!'

'No!' She looked up, her eyes glazing into his. 'No, look, all right, I do work for Rostov – how else would I have met Vladimir? But I'm not prepared to go on record with that, and as for drugs, I can't give you . . .'

Suleyman moved away. 'Well, then I can't help you,' he said. 'Don't bother me again. If you do I'll arrest you.'

He turned and began to walk towards the light emanating from the still busy Yeniçeriler Caddesi.

'But what if I can get you what you want? What if it could be possible for me to get closer to Rostov for you? Maybe sometime in the future . . . ?'

He resisted the temptation to turn back and look at her. He knew all about her long blonde hair, thick lips and even thicker breasts.

'If it's information I can substantiate, then maybe,' he said, flinching as one of the city's thin street cats ran across the front of his shoes.

'Maybe I'll get it then,' she called. 'For Vladimir I'll perhaps take that risk. And for you.'

Impulsively he turned back, just to see her cheap sexiness one more time. But she had gone, leaving only the sound of her voice drifting down the stillness of the hot, dark alleyway.

'I've always wanted to fuck a prince,' it said.

Suleyman put one hand into his jacket pocket and shakily took out his packet of cigarettes. How did she know that? Not that he was a prince, but he was the grandson of a man who had been. Like Rostov, Suleyman's ancestors, the Sultans of Turkey, had tied those they didn't like into sacks and thrown them into the Bosphorus. But then perhaps that was why Masha had ascribed that particular method of execution to Rostov – so it would be familiar to Suleyman, so he'd feel something about it. Allah, but these people, like Rostov, had eyes in every place, even, seemingly, his own bedroom. To tempt his sex-starved body with that full, luscious body! Oh, it had to be! She couldn't possibly be serious about this

'Vladimir' – girls like that didn't love anyone. It had to be a set-up.

But then this wasn't the first time he'd thought this way. Before, on the first and only other occasion she'd pulled him into a doorway to whisper stories of Vladimir into his ear, he'd been convinced she was lying. And yet he'd gone back for more. He'd arranged to meet her here tonight. Nothing she said could be substantiated. Why had he come?

He lit a cigarette, inhaled and then exhaled slowly. He'd nearly ejaculated in her hand when she'd reached inside his trousers. The thought of it now made him want to be sick. He, a married man with a son, with a wife, not to mention a career. Masha was a junkie, one of Rostov's junkies, and she was setting him up for something. Somehow, Rostov and who knew what other crime bosses – there seemed to be so many of them now – had learned that Suleyman, İkmen and another colleague, İskender, had taken it upon themselves to tackle the gangs whenever they could. This was not police policy. When Zhivkov, the all-powerful Bulgarian boss and his men had been dealt with, that had, officially at least, been the end of the matter. But since Zhivkov's death a lot of people had come forward as contenders for his crown. Rostov, renowned for his intelligence as well as his brutality, was one of them. Miserably Suleyman wondered who Rostov had 'bought' in his department and just how close that person was to him. It had to be someone who knew how vulnerable he was at this time, someone who had detected his unhappiness. He hadn't after all told anyone about his personal problems, not even İkmen.

Perhaps it was written on his face, that growling, inner hunger?

One thing that was for certain was that he had to forget all this now. Rostov wasn't going to allow himself to be offered up easily and so Suleyman had to go back to what he'd been doing before Masha appeared: gathering evidence, such as it was, and waiting. He was, he thought bitterly, as the vision of his wife, Zelfa's, face flashed briefly into his mind, good at that.

The great ochre house belonging to Melih Akdeniz had been owned by his family since long before anyone could remember. And although they were, if somewhat unenthusiastically, a Muslim family now, it was accepted that, like so many of the other original residents of Balat, their ancestors had been Jews.

Originally arranged over three floors plus cellar, the already tall house had gained much from the enormous glass studio Melih had built on the roof back in the nineteen eighties. And not just because of the views that it afforded. The thing itself, with its ornamental stained-glass windows and warm wooden roof, was – just like the rest of the house – stunning. The large number of antique items of furniture plus the truly gorgeous carpets and kilims were totally in keeping with what was a property of considerable age and stature. The works of art that Melih had embellished the place with were, to some minds at least, another matter.

'There's a sculpture in the bathroom that's going to give me nightmares,' Constable Roditi said to İkmen when the latter joined him in the courtyard beside the house.

İkmen sat down next to him at the table where, presumably, the Akdeniz family ate during the summer months. 'What is it?' he asked.

'Well, he,' Roditi tipped his greying head in the direction of the house, 'says it's the Mother Goddess, whoever she is. Looks like a lump of dough with breasts, if you ask me. And it's got no head.'

'Idols similar to that have been discovered at Hittite settlements like Çatal Höyük,' İkmen said as he pulled another chair out for Ayşe Farsakoğlu. 'I imagine in that work he was exploring ancient pagan themes.'

'Well, I think it's weird,' Roditi continued. 'He's weird.'

'Akdeniz?'

Roditi shook his head as if confused. 'He's been up there in that studio all day, doing things with great lumps of material. Not been out to look for those children. He had a row with some woman who came to sympathise with him this afternoon. Shouting out of the window at her as she stood in the street—'

'The bitch had come to gloat,' a thick, slightly hysterical voice interjected.

All three of the officers looked round to see a tall, thin figure silhouetted against the light pouring across the courtyard from the kitchen.

'And which "bitch" was this, Mr Akdeniz?' İkmen asked.

'I don't know her name,' Melih replied scornfully. 'Some woman who fancies herself as an artist.' He laughed. 'I upset her once, years ago. I said her work was shit, which it is. When she heard about my children she used the opportunity to come here and abuse me personally.'

He joined the officers at the table, sitting down slowly as if in pain. Melih Akdeniz had not aged well. At forty-seven he was thin, wrinkled, and his hair, which reached down to just beyond his shoulders, was almost completely grey. He put a cigarette that İkmen at least hoped was just a cigarette between his nicotine-stained teeth and lit up.

'There are several so-called artists in Balat now,' Melih continued, 'all wanting to present traditional artwork in new and original forms. They think that if you make a copy of an İznik tile and skew the pattern thirty degrees to the left you're making a statement. Wankers!'

He looked down at the ground with an intensity so fierce that for a moment all three police officers were rendered speechless. Although still hot, it was now, despite the light from the kitchen, almost completely dark – a condition that only served to heighten the ghostly paleness of Melih's face. Active or not in the search for his children, the artist was obviously a very distressed man. With this in mind, İkmen, notwithstanding his obvious antipathy for the man, proceeded gently.

'Sir, if we may return to Saturday for a moment,' he said, 'you were due to take your children over to Sarıyer.'

'Yes, to eat fish.' Melih's head was still down, crooked over what had turned out to be, mercifully, only a cigarette. 'They like fish.'

'Was that you and your wife and the children?'

'Yes.'

'Why?'

Melih looked up. 'What do you mean?'

'I mean,' İkmen said as he lit up a cigarette, 'that you're

35

not a person who, it seems to me, goes out a great deal. You like to work . . .'

'I have to work!' the artist corrected. 'Someone has to shake this fucking country out of its stupor!'

'Yes, but what I meant—'

'You meant that I'm a bad father!' He pointed his cigarette into İkmen's face. 'That I don't care!' He lowered his voice. 'If only you knew. I care for my children more than you will ever know or understand.'

They all sat in silence for a few moments in the wake of this outburst.

Then with a sigh, Ayşe Farsakoğlu said, 'Mr Akdeniz, I'd like to take another look at the children's bedroom, if I may.'

'You know where it is,' Melih murmured tightly.

'Thank you.'

She rose and made her way towards the back door.

'Just don't wake my wife, she's only just finally managed to sleep,' the artist added. 'She's in our bedroom.'

'I'll be quiet,' Ayşe said as she disappeared into the house.

As soon as she'd gone, İkmen sent Roditi over to the stables, which were on the western side of the property. Until Melih had built the glass extension on top of his house, the old stone stables had served as his studio. Now defunct, they were still full of old materials and abandoned works of art, things that two young constables and now Roditi were attempting to search through. Houses as old and complex as this could have any number of forgotten rooms, cellars, et cetera, into which people, particularly children, could conceivably disappear. They'd already searched the cistern on the eastern side of the garden. That had yielded a chamber that had probably been bricked up in the nineteenth century.

İkmen put his cigarette out and immediately lit another. 'My colleague and I walked up here today,' he said; 'took a stroll through the streets.' He smiled. 'It's a long time since I've worked in Balat. It's not a troublesome district.'

Melih threw his cigarette end on to the ground underneath the table and then stamped on it. Tiny sparks of orange ash pierced the darkness.

'It's always been a friendly place,' İkmen continued, 'with a strong sense of community.'

The artist, his expression contemptuous, trained his eyes on İkmen's face. 'I don't join communities,' he said. 'I don't need to. I am Balat, I'm not some incomer. People here know me and I know them and that's where it stops. I neither want nor need their ill-informed opinions of me or what I do.'

'They're just Balat people, like yourself—'

'They're ignorant and small-minded.'

'But they're not stupid,' İkmen said, 'nor are they unobservant.'

Melih's eyes narrowed. 'You mean they've got their eyes in everyone's business.'

'I mean I'm surprised that no one saw your children on Saturday morning,' İkmen smiled. 'It's obvious to me from the few conversations my colleague and I have had with some of your neighbours today, that you are not exactly liked.'

'Oh really?' Melih smirked unpleasantly. 'You do surprise me.'

'But Yaşar and Nuray are liked and do have friends,' İkmen said. 'Now I know that you said the children got up at what you describe as early . . .'

'I told you I heard their door open at six.'

'Yes, when a lot of people are up and about their business. This is a hard-working district, Mr Akdeniz.'

Melih crossed his arms over his chest as his face assumed a confrontational expression. 'What are you trying to say? That I'm lying? About this?'

İkmen sighed. This man was so tense it was like trying to hold a conversation with a volcano. 'No, I'm not. But what I am saying is, could you be wrong about when the children left the house? If they left in the middle of the night then it's highly unlikely they would have been seen.' He made himself look into Melih's hollow and suspicious eyes. 'What I'm trying to do here is to open up other possible lines of investigation. If somebody did see something unusual on Friday night, an unknown vehicle or—'

'They left the house at six. I know this, I heard them. I can't help it if the people of Balat are blind and deaf.' He turned away to concentrate on the thick tangle of bindweed that was threatening to choke one of his grape-vines.

'If you're sure,' İkmen said with a shrug.

'I am.'

And after that all conversation ceased until Ayşe Farsakoğlu returned.

'Seen anything new and significant in my children's bedroom?' Melih asked sourly when the young woman sat down beside him.

'No, although it does help me to get more of an idea of what Yaşar and Nuray might be like,' Ayşe replied.

İkmen looked up, 'Oh?'

'They obviously take after you, Mr Akdeniz,' she said, looking at the artist with a small smile.

'What do you mean?'

'You are, I believe, critical of the current state of Turkish society. You express this in your art work.'

'You know that I do. What of it?'

İkmen, wondering just where this was leading, frowned.

Ayşe shrugged. 'I just think it's very interesting, given what you do, that Yaşar and Nuray are so obviously fascinated by Karagöz and not besotted with Tarkan or Britney Spears like most children now.' She paused to allow Melih to answer. But he remained silent and so she elaborated, 'What I mean is that in Ottoman times Karagöz shadow puppet plays were used as artistic vehicles for social criticism.' She turned to look at İkmen. 'The puppets are stuck on the children's walls, sir. No Türkpop stars, just the two main shadow play characters Karagöz and his adversary, Hacıvat.'

'Really.'

'Yes.' Melih rose from his seat and raked a hand through his hair, 'I believe in educating one's children properly.' He looked up into a darkened sky, covered with stars. 'Give them Tarkan and they'll grow up thinking tiles with skewed designs are art. Expose them to deep archetypal figures like those in Karagöz and just maybe they'll understand something about what it means to be an artist and the responsibility that comes along with it.

39

Young minds and bodies are materials just like clay, paint and fabric – we have a responsibility not to contaminate them and to treat them with respect.' And then he looked down at the officers, his eyes full of tears. 'I love my children,' he said. 'I love them more than my life.'

# CHAPTER 3

The post-mortem on the body of Rosita Keyder revealed that her death had been entirely natural. Already the victim of a minor stroke, which her doctor had told Arto Sarkissian happened back in 1990, Rosita Keyder had died of an aneurism, that sudden rupturing of a weakened artery. Death had been almost instantaneous. There were not, as far as Arto could tell, any suspicious marks on the body or any clues in the apartment that might lead him to believe she may have been unlawfully killed. Only the young man he was now looking at laid out straight, almost militaristically, on his operating table sounded a discordant note in this seemingly ordinary saga of elderly demise.

İsak Çöktin, rightly or wrongly, had assumed that this unknown man had died at round about the same time as Rosita. Somewhat, in Arto's opinion, simplistic traditional police-style thinking, but justified in this instance. After all, if the man had died before the woman she would have called the relevant medical services. Had he died after her he, surely, would have done the same for her prior to his demise. But no doctors or ambulances had been called. So to assume that they had died at roughly the same time was reasonable. There was, however, a problem.

41

Rosita had died, Arto reckoned, at the most, three days before. The condition of the corpse was consistent with this time frame given the current very hot temperatures. The other body, however, the man's, had only just started to degrade. This seemed to indicate that he had died after she did. That his corpse had been stone cold when it was discovered was odd. Bodies began to rot quickly at the height of an İstanbul summer and Arto would have expected at least some liquefaction. But that hadn't happened. With his violet-coloured glass eyes wide open and his erect bearing, the young man looked as if he were resting rather than deceased. Indeed, as Arto raised his knife in preparation for cutting into the body he felt quite nervous lest his 'patient' cry out in pain.

Whimsically, he put his instrument down. Although not exactly overwhelming, Arto recognised that he was experiencing something of the old desecration anxiety that had afflicted him in the early days of his practice. Always fascinated by the inner workings of the human body as well as curious about how and why people came to die, he had nevertheless never quite managed to shake the idea that what he did was an act of defilement. What had once been human was cut up, taken apart and closely examined by him. And in spite of the fact that Arto wasn't and never had been a religious man, there was still that faint notion always at the back of his mind that what he was doing was breaking an ancient taboo.

But usually he managed either to ignore or suppress such thoughts. Quite why he couldn't in this case he didn't know. But whatever the reason for this was, it was growing, which was alarming. Could it be that if this feeling persisted he wouldn't be able to perform a post-mortem on this corpse? Could it be that perhaps he wouldn't be able to operate on any corpse?

The idea that perhaps he was losing his nerve caused Arto to reach reflexively for his scalpel. The cold glass violet eyes looked on. So very, very dead and yet seeming so very alive at the same time. Watching ... Perhaps if he could get rid of them and their vigilant influence over him he would feel more able to continue. But then without any reason to remove the eyes that, surely, had to be desecration. And he had no reason to remove them, did he?

He went for the left eye first. He told himself it was OK because he'd probably need to dissect out the head anyway. He'd put it back later when he closed up. As he'd anticipated the eye came out easily, plopping coldly into his latex-covered hand, just like a marble. Large and round and clean – which was how it would have stayed had Arto not dropped it on the floor.

Removing the eye was one thing, but looking into the socket behind it was quite another – especially if what was there was unexpected. Arto just stood staring into the socket as the violet eyeball first bounced and then shattered across the floor.

'I'll have to speak to Estelle about this,' Zelfa said as she reached into the back of the car to remove her child from his baby seat. 'She's supposed to look after him at her apartment, not keep exhibiting him here like some fairground attraction.'

'You know that's not what it's about,' her husband said.

'Do I?' She moved backwards out of the car and when she was clear she shuffled the beautiful brown-eyed infant on to her hip. 'What's that then, Mehmet?'

Inspector Mehmet Suleyman sighed. He'd had this conversation with his wife several times over the past few weeks. Estelle Cohen, their baby Yusuf's nanny, had taken to visiting her friend Fatma İkmen with the child in tow. Through their policemen husbands, the Cohens, the Suleymans and the İkmens all knew each other very well. Estelle and Fatma were born within a year of each other and despite the former being Jewish and the latter a Muslim, they shared a lot of interests, many of which revolved around the home, children and other things decent middle-aged ladies should like. Zelfa Suleyman was, however, another matter.

Though just a few years younger than Estelle and Fatma, Zelfa had been married to her handsome 'toyboy' husband for only eighteen months. That their child had to have been conceived a long while before their marriage was well known but accepted. Zelfa was, after all, both a foreigner and a doctor and so could therefore, to Estelle and Fatma's way of thinking, be forgiven. What the ladies didn't know, however, was that Zelfa didn't really like this current arrangement and that actually delivering the baby to Fatma's as opposed to Estelle's apartment was the last straw.

'Having Yusuf around really cheers Fatma up,' Mehmet said. 'Her brother's dying—'

'Yes, around my baby!' Zelfa spat, and then slipping

into her native English she said, 'Christ knows what it'll do to his mind! Having those yellow hands touching his cheek, the smell of death and morphine . . .'

'Talaat will be going into hospital soon. He's not going to die in front of Yusuf.'

'Oh, you know that, do you?' She walked towards the entrance to the İkmens' apartment block, her blonde head held high and petulant.

'As far as I'm aware the doctors have said—'

'And what do they know?' She turned to look at him, her eyes hard.

'You're a doctor,' Mehmet said smoothly as he wrestled to maintain control over his temper.

'I'm a psychiatrist,' his wife retorted, 'a good, Irish psychiatrist who sees a lot of people whose problems are basically physical. Many of these have come about through bad practice by Turkish doctors. Unless they've been trained abroad, they're useless. Do you know—'

'No, I don't know whether Fatma's brother's doctor has been trained abroad!' Mehmet raked his hands nervously through his hair. 'For the love of Allah, Zelfa!'

'I'm not going to have my baby taken over by Turks.' She paused just briefly to look and smile at her child, who happily gurgled back at her. 'I'm Irish . . .'

'Your mother was Irish.'

'I was born and brought up there; it's my home.' Zelfa cleared her throat. 'I don't want an exclusively Turkish life for Yusuf. Estelle on her own is fine, but together with Fatma it's all boncuks, evil spirits, Maşallah . . . Christ, I've agreed to have my child raised as a Muslim, what more do you want?'

'I—'

'Oh, apart from sex, of course,' she said bitterly.

'Zelfa!' Instinctively Mehmet looked around to see whether anyone was listening.

Zelfa raised her eyes impatiently up to the sky. 'I'm speaking English, Mehmet,' she said. 'No one can understand.'

'Unless, of course, Çetin is still at home,' Mehmet said as he pointed up towards the İkmens' top-floor apartment.

'Afraid İkmen'll find out you're not getting fucked?' She turned and started walking towards the apartment building again, cooing at the child as she went.

Stung by her words, Mehmet didn't follow. He'd always loved her so much, but this sexual problem she was experiencing was straining their relationship. She'd always had problems living up to what she perceived was his superior physical attractiveness. Not that he'd ever seen it that way. But what had started as low self-esteem had become poisoned by the physical discomfort during sex that she, or so he felt, had almost wilfully failed to address. Instead of consulting one of her medical colleagues she had just simply railed at him about other women she imagined he was going to run to for sex. Now in a sense she was almost pushing him to do that. The previous evening he had almost complied. Mehmet sighed. The only thing he could do for the moment was concentrate on his work – on Rostov and his cohorts. There had to be a way to make the Russians commit some error that would lead to their arrest and conviction. But then that would have to come without the intervention of young Masha . . .

He watched as Zelfa handed Yusuf over to Fatma, who had come down to greet them. Contact with the child seemed to, at least temporarily, remove some of the strain from İkmen's wife's face. Poor woman. How Zelfa could want to deny her a little light in the midst of her dark world, Mehmet couldn't imagine. Watching someone you loved die had to be awful; he couldn't imagine how he'd feel if his brother were terminally ill. One always hoped that oneself would go first . . .

'And let him play with his leprechaun,' Zelfa said as she handed over the strange green and red doll her uncle in Dublin had sent for Yusuf.

Fatma, a little taken aback said, 'A doll . . .'

'It's a leprechaun,' Zelfa corrected. 'It's called Sean. Make sure he has it. He loves it.'

'OK.'

Yusuf started crying as soon as the leprechaun was placed beside him. He always did. But then with Zelfa becoming more Irish by the minute there was no point arguing with her.

She walked back towards the car and got in without another word. Mehmet smiled tiredly at Fatma, who was attempting to encourage the now screaming Yusuf to wave at his parents, and then slid down into the driving seat.

On reflection, İkmen could have done with a day outside the city. Melih Akdeniz had mentioned the fish restaurants on the waterfront at Sarıyer where he and his family had been due to go and eat on the morning of the boys' disappearance. Ayşe Farsakoğlu had gone over there to check out them and other possible connections

Melih might have with that district. İkmen, as was only right and proper, remained in Balat to supervise operations and also to make connections. One of these had turned out to be a large gypsy woman called Gonca. Like Melih Akdeniz, Gonca was an artist who, although not nearly so successful, exhibited her work all over the country. Unlike the famous man, however, Gonca was very sociable, particularly with other artists. When İkmen called she was entertaining her friend Nilufer Cemal.

Framed in a doorway draped with many brightly coloured sequined fabrics, Gonca was quite a sight. Probably in her mid-forties she was extremely dark, tall and excessively curvaceous. Every part of her silk-swathed body that could be covered with jewellery was, and her hair, which was the very densest black, hung down to no more than a few centimetres from the floor. A fat dark cigar between her very white teeth completed an ensemble that brought back many happy childhood memories for İkmen. His mother, the Albanian 'Witch of Üsküdar', had been very partial to visiting the gypsies in the district of Ayvansaray, which borders on Balat. There she would treat her children to dancing bears, the wailing music of the zurna and the sight of, to İkmen, the very 'forward' gypsy girls dancing barefoot and bejewelled in the street. While all of this was going on his mother would talk of tarot cards and movements in the heavens with the elder ladies of the tribe – large, scary women, just like Gonca.

When she'd heard why İkmen had come, Gonca led him into her studio where Nilufer Cemal was already taking tea and eating something that looked sticky from a small terracotta pot.

'It's zerde,' Gonca said, flicking her wrist in the direction of Nilufer Cemal's food. 'We generally make it for wedding feasts, but I like it so I make it all the time. Would you like some?'

'Yes, thank you,' İkmen replied. He didn't actually like the saffron-coloured sweet at all but he knew that gypsies, just like his own people, tended to favour those who ate their food.

'OK, please sit,' Gonca said, sweeping one long arm across a vast rank of brightly coloured cushions. 'This is my friend Nilufer, Miss Cemal, she's a ceramicist. She's been here longer than I have. I'm sure she won't mind talking to you about our illustrious neighbour. Nilufer, this is Inspector İkmen, from the police.'

She drifted off into what İkmen assumed was the kitchen.

'I suppose this is about the poor Akdeniz children,' the very respectable middle-aged woman at his feet said.

İkmen pulled up the material around the knees of his trousers and lowered himself down on to a vast magenta-coloured cushion.

'I'm trying to find out whether Mr Akdeniz has any enemies,' he said.

Nilufer laughed. 'Well, that should keep you busy for a while!' she said bitterly.

'I must admit that he doesn't appear to have many friends,' İkmen said, 'but whether or not that means he has actual enemies . . .'

'Melih Akdeniz enjoys his notoriety,' Nilufer said. 'He has no respect for or appreciation of other people's work. He thinks everyone apart from him is absolutely talentless

49

and treats people with contempt and rudeness. Some say it stems from the fact that his family were Jews – Nabaro – they changed their family name to Akdeniz when they converted to Islam. It is said that Melih was originally shunned by the art world because of his background, but I think that's unlikely. Artists are, in my opinion, very liberal. I think it's more likely Akdeniz chooses to feel put upon and aggrieved. He's so bitter at the world! Many years ago he smashed a ceramic piece I gave him as a gift – in front of my eyes! He's an awful man.'

İkmen sighed. So this was the woman Melih had called a bitch. 'Well, yes, most unpleasant. But what I suppose I'm looking for is a deep enmity of either a personal or professional nature.'

'You don't think it's dreadful to have your work destroyed in front of your face?'

'I, er . . .'

'Nilufer, as well as having been insulted by Melih, also hates his work, Inspector,' Gonca said as she placed the small pot of zerde and a spoon she had retrieved from the kitchen into İkmen's hands.

'He's just using the power of shock to sell his trash,' Nilufer said disgustedly. 'I mean, why else would anyone want to buy a urine-soaked canvas unless it's to shock people? He's always making some "statement", using his notoriety to persuade stupid people to part with vast amounts of money to buy the stuff.'

'In some cases, maybe,' Gonca said as she bonelessly lowered herself down to the floor, 'but I'm still enthralled by his early stuff, the hair carpets, the sex magic pieces . . .'

'Sex magic.'

Gonca turned her huge black eyes on İkmen and smiled. 'Melih used to perform sex acts with women on large canvases. He'd paint the resultant stains in the astrological colours associated with the time and date of each act. Sometimes he'd adorn the staining with jewellery. I like the sex magic pieces, they're very organic.'

'Yes, you do,' Nilufer said darkly. 'I just can't see where the skill comes in.'

'Then perhaps we should track down those women and ask them,' Gonca said with a thick, mucoid laugh in her throat. 'I mean, the things Melih is supposed to be able to do . . .'

'Gonca!'

İkmen, confused, turned to the gypsy with raised eyebrows. She reached out and put one large hand on his knee.

'Melih Akdeniz is reputed to be both a very big – if you know what I mean – and a very skilful man, Inspector,' she explained. 'It was said, although I doubt whether this holds today, that Melih always pleasured two women at a time, one with his penis, the other with his mouth.'

She licked her thick red lips, squeezed İkmen's knee just once and then took her hand away, smiling around her cigar.

İkmen plunged his spoon into the zerde and quickly ate a mouthful. 'So your art . . .'

'My medium is collage,' Gonca said. 'I work with tarot cards, tea leaves, oil and equestrian equipment, horsehair, horse sweat, flies. Stuff that is traditional to my people.' She pointed towards what looked, to İkmen, like a large, hair-covered screen in the corner of the room. 'That's my

51

latest piece,' she said lazily. 'The hair comes from my father's stallion and from the heads of my ten daughters.' She moved in close to him and added, 'I call it the *Tree of Life*.'

'Ah.'

'A lot of us, including Melih, although his work is more abstract, like to invoke Kabbalistic images and themes here in Balat,' Nilufer said, a trifle primly, İkmen thought. 'The Tree of Life is the centre point of that magical system. I represent it myself in many of my works too. I suppose it must be an echo from Balat's Jewish past.'

'Yes.' İkmen smiled. He knew something about Kabbala, the ancient Jewish scheme of correspondences. It was, after all, the cornerstone of all Western magical systems. 'But to get back to Melih Akdeniz . . .'

'You want to know whether we know of anyone who might wish to harm him? Or whether indeed we would harm him by taking his children ourselves?' Gonca asked with an obvious and visible twinkle in her eyes. 'Inspector,' she said, 'I have twelve children of my own. I'd have to absolutely loathe Melih to want to add yet more mouths to my table. And I don't loathe him, I quite like his work.'

İkmen, father of nine children, could all too easily follow this line of reasoning – even if, as he well knew, some of the most prolific gypsy families made a lot of money by performing multiple kidnappings for various city gangs.

'And until I spoke to him yesterday, to express my sympathy for his plight, I hadn't so much as walked past his house for over twenty years,' Nilufer said.

İkmen turned to look at her. 'But you dislike Mr Akdeniz . . .'

'Oh, I hate the man!' Nilufer said without embarrassment. 'But I only feel pity for his children, having him as a father, and would wish them no harm.'

Unless, İkmen thought, you're so sorry for them that you've taken them somewhere, maybe even put them out of their misery . . . There was something he didn't like about this small, seemingly prudish woman. Not that he had a bad feeling about her – he didn't. But there was or didn't appear to be any generosity in her soul. Unlike Gonca . . .

'Unfortunately for you, Inspector,' Gonca said with a laugh in her voice, 'there are so many candidates for the "who hates Melih the most" title that your job is going to be very hard. There are his in-laws, for a start. He seduced their then unmarried daughter, made her pregnant. But then,' she shrugged, 'as the son of Ayşe of Üsküdar, you do have recourse to, shall we say, rather more unconventional methods than most of your peers.'

İkmen looked into her fathomless black eyes and smiled. 'You know . . .'

'I'm a gypsy, Inspector, I know everything.' She laughed fully and raucously. 'You're a famous man, always in the newspapers and, besides, gypsies of my mother's generation knew the Witch of Üsküdar. She was very good with cards. Are you good with cards, Inspector, or do you just have feelings?'

'My methods are quite my own,' İkmen responded with a smile, 'as I'm sure you know from the newspapers, Gonca Hanım.'

'Yes . . .' Her face suddenly became serious. 'And so what have your "methods" informed you about the Akdeniz children, Inspector?'

'What do you mean?'

'What do you think may have happened to them?'

İkmen frowned. 'I don't know.'

'No, but what do you feel,' Gonca said, as she moved once again closer in upon İkmen, 'deep down in that place where emotion becomes truth? That place that the cards and the leaves and the oil speak to. In the dark . . .'

The room telescoped, becoming small around him. Far away or so it seemed, Nilufer Cemal finished what remained of her zerde and left to go to the kitchen – a small figure and background to the gypsy's large hair-draped face. Had İkmen been unaccustomed to similar such experiences he would have been frightened, but he'd been having them since he was a child and so he knew where he was even if he didn't know why. His mind, nudged by the gypsy, had entered that realm where his mother and certain members of his existing family were wont sometimes to venture. Some called it magic, others an 'altered state'. He preferred 'insight' himself.

But then suddenly there was such a crushing dread upon him that İkmen gasped for breath. Although he could neither see, hear, nor even in the conventional sense know anything out of the ordinary, the fear he experienced was suddenly overwhelming. Gonca saw it too.

'They're going through hell aren't they,' she said as the room resolved itself back to its normal state around her, 'the Akdeniz children?'

'I don't know that.' İkmen dropped his gaze.

Gonca's hand whipped across and fastened itself on to his chin, forcing him to look into her eyes. 'Don't lie! Not to a gypsy!'

Nilufer Cemal, who had just walked back into what was an alarming tableau, cried out in order to stop her friend from getting herself arrested, 'Gonca!'

'Tell me, İkmen!' the gypsy continued. 'I know what you saw.'

'Then you don't need me to tell you, do you?' İkmen said as he tore himself away from her grasp and jumped to his feet.

'No . . .'

She looked into his eyes and he looked back. He had to get out of this place and now, before the darkness inside came out of him and swamped this place of cheap glitter and soul-stealing tarot cards. That he and, yes, the gypsy knew also, was bad enough. But the other woman didn't know and shouldn't.

İkmen walked towards the studio door and out into the house. Gonca, her large hips swaying provocatively beneath her long silk dress, followed. When he reached the front door, İkmen turned and, after looking to see whether Nilufer Cemal had followed her friend, he said, 'You will speak about this to no one. Not even your friend.'

Gonca raised one eyebrow, and taking the single card she had in the bosom of her dress, she held it up for İkmen to see. He turned away from it and, his face grey, let himself out of the house without another word.

Constable Hikmet Yıldız knocked smartly on Inspector Suleyman's office door and then waited to be allowed in. It wasn't actually the inspector he'd come to see, it was Sergeant Çöktin, whom Yıldız knew was alone at present.

A light, young voice called, 'Come in.'

Yıldız entered. The office Çöktin shared with his superior was small but bright. Like Suleyman himself it was generally tidy and, although some ashtrays and food and drink detritus were in evidence, there was a feeling of control within the room. Not too messy, things in their place, not too many smoking requisites . . .

Çöktin, who had been searching for something in one of the filing cabinets when Yıldız entered, looked up.

'Constable Yıldız,' he said with a smile. He rather liked Yıldız, he was a bit like himself a few years back. 'And what can I do for you?'

'I was just wondering whether you've heard anything about that body we found yesterday, Sergeant,' the young man said.

Çöktin closed the filing cabinet drawer and moved towards his desk.

'The elderly woman, Mrs Keyder, died of an aneurism,' he said as he sat down and then switched on his computer screen.

'What about the man?' Yıldız asked. 'What did he die of? When did he die?'

'I don't know,' Çöktin replied as he stared intently at the start-up sequence of his machine. 'Dr Sarkissian has yet to get back to me.'

'Why?'

'What do you mean?' Çöktin looked up into a face that was obviously more than a little troubled.

Yıldız shrugged. 'I mean why if he knows what killed the lady doesn't the doctor know what killed the man. They were found together, at the same time.'

'I really don't know, Constable,' Çöktin said with a sigh. 'Perhaps he just hasn't got around to the man yet. Dr Sarkissian's always so busy.'

'Sergeant . . .' Yıldız sat down in the chair opposite Çöktin's desk and removed his cap. It was very hot and his brow was sweating heavily underneath his headgear.

'Yes?'

Yıldız wiped his face with his smooth, brown forearm. 'Did you think there was anything odd about that man's body?'

Çöktin, who had found unsettling the fact that the body had two glass eyes that were also the most vivid purple, just simply grunted. Odd or not, there were no facts known about the corpse at the present time and so to ascribe strangeness to something that could be most ordinary was not a thing he wanted to do. It certainly wasn't what Suleyman would do, or rather did. Always measured in his responses, the proud Ottoman could be counted upon to explore each and every possibility – when he was around. Ever since he had taken upon himself the task of bringing a small group of men suspected of involvement in organised crime to justice, Suleyman had become a distant, almost shadowy figure. One that his deputy was finding increasingly hard to reach.

'The man was blind – it's what we've told the press – what of it?' Çöktin said.

'Well, yes, but . . . not that, exactly . . .'

'So what then?'

Yıldız sighed. 'I have a feeling, an uneasy feeling.'

'Inspector İkmen has those,' Çöktin said with a smile. 'His generally prove valuable.'

'Yes, I know. His mother was a witch.'

'Perhaps you should talk to him about this then, Hikmet. Maybe he might be able to help you put what you're experiencing into words.'

'Mmm.'

The ringing of Çöktin's telephone brought their conversation to a halt. He picked up the receiver and stated his name. Yıldız stood up and made ready to leave.

'Ah, Doctor,' Çöktin said as he waved the younger man back into his seat. 'Yes, I've just been talking about that with Constable Yıldız . . . Yes . . .' As he listened his face, which at the beginning of the conversation had been relaxed, resolved into a frown.

'Are you sure?' Çöktin asked. 'I mean . . . Well, yes, of course I have to bow to your medical knowledge, Doctor, but . . .'

Yıldız, who had been watching Çöktin ever since the call came in, began to feel slightly sick. Whether it was as a result of the grave expression that was now etched on the sergeant's face or whether something else was at play here, he didn't know. But he felt what he could only describe later as 'tingly', as if all the hairs on his head and body had suddenly stood up straight.

'OK,' Çöktin said on a sigh, 'I'll be over straight away. I still can't believe . . .' He shrugged. 'OK, Doctor, I'll be there. Yes.'

His conversation over, Çöktin replaced the receiver and then rubbed his face with his hands.

'Inspector İkmen will be very proud of you, Hikmet,' he said as he took his jacket off the back of his chair and then rose slowly to his feet. 'Seems your feeling was right.'

'Oh?' Yıldız, aware that the more senior man was now on his way out, also stood up. 'So was that man murdered?'

'No.' Çöktin made his way over to his office door and opened it. 'It's far stranger than that, Hikmet,' he said. 'Murder I can kind of understand but this . . .' He shrugged.

'What?'

'Why don't you come with me over to the mortuary and find out?' Çöktin said. 'You were the one who, after all, kind of anticipated this.'

'What?'

'I'll have to let Dr Sarkissian explain,' Çöktin said as he made his way out into the corridor, 'because I'm afraid, Hikmet, that I just can't.'

He then made his way towards the stairs, bearing a young man who felt very 'tingly' again in his wake.

# CHAPTER 4

'I think he was probably about twenty when he died,' Arto
Sarkissian said as he pulled the sheet back to reveal the
unknown man's head and shoulders.

'But, let me get this right, you don't know when that
might have happened?' Çöktin asked.

'No.'

Briefly the two men stared into each other's eyes.

'As I told you on the phone, Sergeant,' Sarkissian
continued, 'this body has been embalmed.'

Yıldız, who had been watching the proceedings from
behind Çöktin's shoulder, looked confused.

'An embalmed body is one that has been treated and
preserved,' Sarkissian expounded. 'It's something that
Muslims don't do,' he smiled. 'You're in the ground
within twenty-four hours, but to some extent Christian
bodies are preserved. Not like this but—'

'What do you mean?'

The Armenian sighed. Although just as distressed by
death as their Christian and Jewish neighbours, Muslims
were, in Sarkissian's opinion, much more pragmatic and
practical about it. People died, you buried them and then,
after all the frenetic activity around the funeral was over,
you mourned. Debates about the immortality or not of the

soul didn't impinge until the body was in the ground. That was and always had been important.

'Christians wait to bury their dead,' the doctor explained. 'Even in very modern countries, like the USA where most bodies are now cremated, there is a delay. There are numerous reasons for this. In some countries, especially Eastern European and Latin states, there exists a traditional anxiety with regard to premature burial.' He looked up into two horrified faces. 'Oh, it used to happen,' he said, 'and although it shouldn't happen these days some people are still anxious about it. As well as that, Christians do like to view their dead.'

'You mean like when the Greeks carry their priests through the streets after they've died?' Yıldız asked.

'Yes. The body is displayed and people come to pay their respects to it. But there is, of course, a theological reason too.'

Çöktin frowned.

'We, or rather Christians,' Sarkissian said with a smile, 'believe that when Christ comes again to redeem the world the dead will rise from their graves. Embalming keeps them in a condition to render this possible.'

'Yes, but surely if they're in the ground,' Çöktin began, 'with all the worms and the bugs . . .'

'Oh, it's far more of a tradition and a cosmetic exercise than a practicality,' the doctor said as he looked down at the corpse, 'in most cases.'

Yıldız, who was once again experiencing an unpleasant feeling, shuddered.

Sarkissian took the dead man's head in his hands and moved it gently to one side.

61

'But not this one,' he said gravely. 'This one is different.'

'What do you mean, Doctor?' Çöktin asked. 'Different in what way?'

'This one, I believe, has been subjected to a far more sophisticated version of the embalmer's art.' He moved the head again. 'It has movement, suppleness and it is as far as I can see only just now starting to degrade.' He looked up sharply. 'What I mean is that he is almost totally preserved, even down to the remnants of the tumour that killed him. I've never seen anything like it.'

They all stood in silence for a few moments until the doctor, suddenly mindful of the unknown man's dignity, covered his head and shoulders with the sheet once again.

'But he died naturally?' Çöktin said as soon as the three of them started to move away from the corpse.

'Yes,' Sarkissian replied, 'cancer. Nothing I can see of a suspicious nature – except, of course, the fact that I can't even guess at when he died.'

'Why not?'

Sarkissian stopped and then leaned against one of his long steel benches.

'Because I think this body might have been what morticians call maintained,' he said and then, in response to the policemen's confused expressions he added, 'This man's body is, if you like, in a state similar to that of Lenin in his mausoleum in Moscow. Maintained – I think – to keep it looking fresh. I've found some evidence of the skin having been treated with an emollient, but I've got to take advice on this, and so I've left a message for Yiannis Livadanios, who is an undertaker.'

'And so this Mr Livadanios—'

'Will be able to tell me whether my assumption is correct and also who might be performing this task.' Sarkissian made his way out of the laboratory and back into his office. 'Yiannis employs embalmers himself. And so if one of them is keeping the young man fresh, he will presumably know who our mystery man is, which will allow you, Sergeant, to bring this bizarre affair to an end.'

The doctor sat down behind his desk, offering seats to the two policemen as he did so.

'Mrs Keyder's body can now be removed,' he said, 'provided there is someone to do that.'

'There is a sister-in-law we now know lives out at Sarıyer,' Çöktin replied. 'I sent Constable Roditi out there first thing this morning but apparently, so her neighbours say, Miss Keyder is away at the moment and isn't due back home until tomorrow. They don't know where she is.'

'I see.'

'I've also been in contact with the Argentine Consulate, although what that might yield I don't know,' Çöktin sighed.

'Why?'

'Rosita Keyder changed her nationality back in the fifties. The Consulate didn't know of her. I'm hoping that her sister-in-law will be able to tell us what her maiden name was so that we can at least give the Argentines some sort of lead. It will, unfortunately, Doctor, take some time.'

Sarkissian shrugged. 'Oh, well,' he said, sinking comfortably back into the grim humour so common to those in his profession, 'she at least won't need embalming while she's in my refrigerator.'

'No . . .'

Constable Yıldız, who had, up until this time, been really very quiet, spoke.

'But, Doctor,' he said, 'what I don't understand is why this old woman had that man's body in her apartment.'

'Neither do I,' Sarkissian replied. 'I haven't a clue.'

After that the three of them sat in silence for a few moments as some of the implications of what they had been discussing began to sink in.

It wasn't the extent so much as the blatancy of their wealth that so sickened him. The men, Russians, Chechens, Azerbaijanis, all dressed in the 'mobster' uniform – leather jackets, whatever the weather, and far, far too much gold. Their bottle-blonde women, in their ill-fitting designer dresses and, again, mountains of gold, complemented them perfectly. When, Mehmet Suleyman wondered as he strolled between the closely packed booths that made up the central area of the Grand Bazaar, the İç Bedesten, had this become 'normal'?

There had always been gangsters in the city, there always would be. But the disintegration of the old Soviet Union had unleashed what seemed to be a flood of totally amoral people on to the streets. Instead of concentrating on just one or two 'businesses', for example, drugs and prostitution, these men did everything – including contract killing. Without feelings or conscience, they pleasured themselves with drugs, hard-faced women and with spending their considerable fortunes. They were doing that now, in the İç Bedesten, where the most precious items of jewellery, both modern and antique, were sold.

As he threaded his way through the knots of tourists that gathered around every glittering, antique-stacked window, Suleyman was careful to keep Rostov, two of his heavies and the small dark Central Asian-looking man that accompanied them at a distance. Although he and Rostov had never actually met, Suleyman knew that the gangster, one of whose women was the lovely Masha, knew him. Rostov was not the first and certainly wouldn't be the last mobster to 'buy' one of Suleyman's colleagues. Indeed, it was still less than a year ago that Çetin İkmen's former deputy, Orhan Tepe, had fallen for the promises of Zhivkov the Bulgarian. Tepe had paid for that mistake with his life.

Whilst watching to see what Rostov did and where he went, Suleyman found that his eyes were drawn to the booths of the İç Bedesten. Ottoman military medals, inscribed in the old Arabic script few could now decipher, sat next to fabulous examples of art deco jewellery from the nineteen thirties. One booth even had a crown, a small one admittedly, which, so Suleyman felt, had to be made from paste rather than real jewels – but it had probably been a treasure to the family that once owned it. Such a thing would be meaningless to a person like Rostov, who would just buy it to sell on. Ostensibly an antiques dealer, Rostov knew as much about history as Suleyman did about childbirth.

But then Suleyman knew that he had a personal interest

in what happened in this particular part of the bazaar. His father, Muhammed, frequently sold things to the dealers in the İç Bedesten – when he couldn't pay a utility bill or when he had a suit made that he couldn't afford. Muhammed Suleyman or 'Prince' Muhammed, as some called him, came from an aristocratic family related to the Ottoman sultans. His two sons both worked and regarded themselves as ordinary men, but the old prince still lived an entirely other kind of life. Even though his palace on the Bosphorus had been sold many years before, Muhammed's existence was punctuated by dinners at expensive restaurants, bespoke suits and quality cars. Now devoid of money and too old to work, he supported himself and his wife by selling off what remained of his inheritance. It was why Mehmet tried not to look too closely at their wares for fear of recognising some of them.

Why Rostov couldn't buy the ordinary glittery baubles they sold on Kuyumcular Caddesi, Suleyman didn't know. The type of customer he attracted wouldn't know the difference. Perhaps someone had told Rostov that Ottoman antique goods were now in vogue. Perhaps he'd even worked it out for himself. He was obviously a clever man – he had to be because he was still walking free. Even with, possibly, police 'protection', knowing what he was involved with, that was quite a feat.

Rostov had just disappeared into a booth specialising in art nouveau jewellery when Masha appeared at Suleyman's elbow.

'If you meet me tonight, I'll give you the information you need,' she said.

She looked quite small and ordinary in daylight and, in this very public place devoid of dark and squalid corners, he felt nothing for her. Perhaps it was just simply the glamour of the forbidden that attracted him. Maybe like some of his more debauched ancestors he possessed an overwhelming curiosity about how the 'lower orders' conducted themselves during sex. Perhaps that was why, in the past, he had felt the need, briefly, to take a mistress.

'You know that Rostov is here, don't you?' he said as he looked quickly at the booth into which the Russian had disappeared.

'Yes. He's buying jewellery.'

'For whom?'

She shrugged. 'I don't know. To sell. Maybe for his men. He gave Vladimir a gold and diamond ring. He's very generous to his men – sometimes.'

'But not his women?'

Masha shrugged, glanced at the booth and then said, 'So? Tonight?'

Suleyman took his cigarettes out of his pocket and lit up. 'Only if the information is good.'

'It is!'

Her face, pleading, looked desperate. Someone had obviously promised her a lot of money to set him up like this.

'Where and when?'

'Tonight, after eleven o'clock. I work at a pavyon on Camekan Sokak. All Russian konsomatris,' she smiled. 'Turkish punters, you see, they like that.'

Unbeknown to Masha, Suleyman knew the area around

Camekan Sokak intimately. After his separation from his first wife, Zuleika, he'd spent several years renting a room in the district known as Karaköy from his old colleague Balthazar Cohen. Pavyons, like the one Masha worked in, and gazinos, places dedicated to the twin vices of drinking and leering, were what the district was famous for – that and the rather more honest brothels or genelev. Men went to gazinos and pavyons in order, they hoped, to have sex, but they were required to pay a lot of money for drinks offered to them by the konsomatris or 'hostesses' first. Russian bosses, like Rostov, were known to be very active in the pavyon business. In Suleyman's opinion these places were more insidious and corrupt than regular brothels.

'How will I find this place?'

He knew better than to ask the name of the establishment – places like this didn't have names.

'It's in the basement of a Turkish genelev.' She wrinkled up her nose as she said the word 'Turkish'. Like a lot of Russian girls she felt herself to be far superior to the often quite naïve Anatolian girls the state-run and legal Turkish brothels employed. 'The doorman has long blond hair and there's a string of red and green lights around the door. You can't miss it.'

'So what do I do?'

Masha smiled. 'Leave that to me,' she said lasciviously. 'I'll take care of you.'

'I just want the information.'

'Yes, and you'll get it,' she said. 'We will get Rostov. Trust me.'

And then she walked away. Suleyman looked back

towards the booth where Rostov was, presumably, still involved in buying, and then walked over to it. It was empty. Somewhere during the course of his conversation with Masha, Rostov had slipped away. All of this was so obviously a set-up and yet he had to see it through just in case something useful could be gleaned from it. That or sex with Masha . . .

Suleyman shuddered. No. No, that couldn't and wouldn't happen. He'd have to share this with either İkmen or Metin İskender – he'd have to get support, another pair of eyes to watch what he and those around him at the pavyon did. Now, suddenly, set-up or no set-up, here was a chance possibly to call Rostov's bluff. Using himself as bait there was just a chance that he could get close enough to the operation to work out what, over and above Masha's 'stories', was really going on. What did Rostov want of him or want him to do? The only problem was that his boss, Commissioner Ardiç, was unlikely to sanction such a dangerous move. Suleyman was already in far further than the commissioner knew about or would approve. Using informants like Masha was notoriously risky, which was why İkmen and İskender and only they could know. The three of them had, after all, committed themselves to making sure that no one ever became powerful enough to take over where Zhivkov had finished. But Rostov was getting there. He had to be stopped.

In the meantime, however, if he was going to go to a pavyon and look like a proper punter he'd have to go to a cash dispenser and get some money. Masha, whatever her motivation might be, would want him to pay for his drinks. And if a very distressed American who'd recently been stung in this way was to be believed, it could cost him several hundred dollars.

In spite of his very long and quite grey beard, the monk wasn't by any means an elderly man. With his unlined and very blue eyes, he was probably, İkmen thought, fifty at the most.

'You're sure you saw this vehicle on Friday night,' İkmen said.

'Oh, yes,' the monk replied, 'definitely. It's stuck in my mind because I've never seen these gates open before.' He looked up at the tall and ancient metal gates he and İkmen were standing in front of. 'Some of these old Jewish places have such lovely gardens,' the monk continued, 'and what with this one being the residence of Melih Akdeniz, I looked in.'

'Which was when you saw the blue van.'

'Yes. The engine was running, quite smoky as if it wasn't very well maintained. The smoke meant that I couldn't really see anything of the garden and so I just walked on.'

İkmen offered the monk a cigarette, which he took with a smile.

'So what time was this, Brother Constantine?'

The monk looked up into the cloudless blue sky and pursed his lips. 'It had to have been nearly midnight,' he said. 'I'd been visiting my sister – she lives down near the Daphnis Hotel. She made me some dinner and then we talked; she's just got divorced and is very unhappy. After that I left.'

'You work at the High School?' İkmen said as he tipped

his head towards the large red-brick building at the top of the street.

'Yes,' Brother Constantine answered. 'Over twenty years now.'

'So are you acquainted with Mr Akdeniz in any capacity?'

'No,' Brother Constantine frowned, 'Mr Akdeniz is something of a recluse and has been for many years, I believe. The children are nice, polite little ones.' He shrugged. 'But then to be honest with you, Inspector, I would never have sought Mr Akdeniz out. I know he's our most famous and controversial artist, but his stuff isn't for me. I like to look at a picture and know what I'm seeing.'

İkmen laughed. 'You and I concur there, sir,' he said. 'I'm sure Mr Akdeniz is very clever, but . . .'

'Indeed.'

Their conversation was briefly interrupted by the sight of Melih Akdeniz dragging what looked like a bolt of cloth out of his kitchen and into the garden. It was obviously giving him some considerable trouble because he puffed and gasped as he moved.

When he saw the policeman and the monk framed in the open gateway to his property, the artist put the cloth down and stood up straight, hands on hips.

'What does he want?' he called across to İkmen, pointing rudely at the monk.

'I'll tell you in a minute, sir,' İkmen replied.

'I don't like Christians,' Melih said. 'Fucking torturers!'

İkmen turned to face the artist full on. 'I told you I'd speak to you in a minute – sir,' he said acidly. 'At the moment I'm talking to this gentleman, who has never, as far as I'm aware, tortured anyone.' He turned back to Brother Constantine and smiled. 'I apologise for him,' he said. 'Now would you be willing to make a written statement about what you saw last Friday?'

'Yes, naturally,' the monk said and then, smiling, he continued, 'You know it is said that Mr Akdeniz's family were originally Jews. They came here from Spain and Portugal because they suffered the most appalling persecution at the hands of Christians in those countries.'

'Yes,' İkmen said, still with one eye on Melih Akdeniz, 'but that was all a very long time ago. People should move on. These old enmities do nobody any good. We're all guilty of it from time to time, but we shouldn't do it.' And then moving forward a little to see Akdeniz more easily he said, 'What is he doing?'

The monk narrowed his eyes. 'I don't know.'

They both watched as the artist, sweating heavily in the intense midday heat, strung what appeared to be a huge canvas across the entire width of the garden.

Ayşe Farsakoğlu took the ferry back to the city from Sarıyer. It fitted the sort of day she'd had: slow and fruitless.

The local constabulary had been friendly and welcoming, and had quizzed her at some length about the 'excitement' she must experience working in the city. But with regard to information on the missing Akdeniz children they hadn't been any help. As usual the district was quiet and ordered, and everyone obeyed the law from behind their very tasteful front doors.

'This is a fishing village,' one of the younger constables, called Said, had remarked. 'People concentrate only on the catch. İnşallah it will always be so.'

'We also have the rich folks,' an older colleague put in, adding darkly, 'some of whom are foreigners these days.'

Ayşe had asked what sort of foreigners the district tended to attract.

'Oh, those with a lot of money,' the older man, Rifat, had said, 'mostly from up there.' He tilted his head northwards, which Ayşe interpreted as from somewhere in the old Soviet Union.

'But they don't cause any trouble?' Ayşe had said.

'Not as yet,' Rifat had replied, 'and it's not up to me to worry myself about where they might have got their money from. You need a lot to buy one of the old yalıs these days, but then that's their affair. Provided they don't start having their gang wars here or parading their Natashas in our streets . . .'

It was ridiculous to think that the wealthier mobsters wouldn't reach a place like Sarıyer. As soon as they made enough cash they left places such as Beyazıt and Beyoğlu in favour of one or other of the villages. And although they still conducted their business in the city, with their swarms of prostitutes – the Natashas – and their various drug and human traffic cartels, they didn't seem keen to sully their own hearths. Hence the police in Sarıyer, Yeniköy and other smart Bosphorus villages had little trouble with them. Ayşe had, however, taken a list of these people's names from the local cops to show to İkmen. It was probably a waste of time like the rest of her trip. There was no reason to think, as yet, that the children had been taken by mobsters. They always demanded money, and so far no one had contacted the artist, much less asked him for money. But it had been a very pleasant day in spite of her lack of success. Wandering around very attractive fish restaurants asking about whether Melih Akdeniz was known there had been hot but enjoyable work. Everyone she asked knew of him, but no one knew him personally. Not that Akdeniz had ever said he and his family ate in Sarıyer often. All he'd actually said was that his children liked fish, and that they had planned to go out to Sarıyer on that particular occasion.

'Hello, Ayşe.'

She looked up into a pair of large, dark eyes.

'Hulya. What are you doing here?'

Hulya İkmen, seventeen and sweetly pretty in her thin summer dress, sat down beside her.

'We've just been to visit Berekiah's aunt at Rumeli Kavaği,' she said as she brushed a great swathe of black hair out of her eyes.

Ayşe had decided to sit outside in order to smoke. What Hulya was doing out in the warm but strong wind she couldn't imagine. One could just as easily admire the view from inside the ferry, far away from the wind and occasional splashes of spray.

'Berekiah's just coming. He wants a cigarette,' the girl said in reply to Ayşe's inner musings.

'Oh.'

Berekiah Cohen was a nice young man. The son of Ayşe's old colleague Balthazar Cohen, he worked for one of the better jewellers in the Grand Bazaar. As he walked somewhat unsteadily towards the two women,

74

Ayşe noticed how his gold Star of David medallion smacked against his face in the wind. She wondered how that went down with Hulya's mother, whom she knew to be a very devout Muslim.

'So you're not with my dad today,' Hulya said as she watched Berekiah sit down and then took one of his hands in hers.

'No,' Ayşe replied, 'I had business in Sarıyer.'

'Oh.' Hulya, like the good policeman's daughter she was, didn't push for any further details.

Ayşe looked across at Berekiah and smiled. 'How's your father, Berekiah?'

The young man smiled sadly. 'Oh, as well as we can expect,' he said. 'He's going to try false limbs soon. He's never wanted to before, but he's so restless.'

Balthazar Cohen had lost both of his legs from just below the knee in the hideous earthquake of 1999. Unable to work either in or out of the police force since, he had existed on painkillers and a seemingly endless stream of gossip supplied to him by his friends and family. It was said that he strongly disapproved of his son's relationship with Hulya and had even fallen out with İkmen, whose philosophy stated that if people loved each other they should be allowed to be together, because of it. Perhaps he now wanted legs so that he could, literally, stand up to the Inspector.

'I do hope that he gets on well with them,' Ayşe said.

'Thank you.'

Berekiah lit his cigarette and then leaned back against the ferry cabin to admire the view. They were passing Yeniköy now, with its pretty waterfront characterised by pastel-coloured nineteenth-century villas. The young man breathed in deeply and then exhaled on a sigh.

'I love it up here,' he said as he closed his eyes with pleasure. 'It's so clean.'

'Maybe we'll live here one day,' Hulya said. 'It certainly would be nice.'

'Yes.'

Ayşe turned away to light a cigarette of her own. Much as she liked them both, she didn't want to get involved in their future-planning conversations. Such things were private and, besides, with these two, they were contentious also. The Jewish boy and the Muslim girl ... OK, it happened but not usually to old Balat families like the Cohens. They were fiercely proud of their heritage, and even though she knew that Fatma İkmen and Cohen's wife, Estelle, were firm friends she also knew that the last thing they would want was to be related.

However, this line of thought led to another. Melih Akdeniz's family had, so it was said, converted to Islam from Judaism. When, she didn't know but perhaps that was where Melih's isolationism had stemmed from. Neither Jew nor 'real' Muslim, maybe as a youngster he had been rejected by his peers. It was well known that he had been a very odd and lonely child. Maybe his 'difference' was what had spurred him on to prove himself so dramatically in the art world. Perhaps that was why he didn't seem to like or admire anyone except himself. Low self-esteem. She remembered a talk she'd attended some months ago about crime and mental illness. It had been given by Inspector Suleyman's wife, Dr Halman. She'd made a list, Ayşe recalled, of those traits that could indicate a vulnerability to mental ill health. Low self-esteem and self-isolation were two of them.

But then it probably wasn't wise to read too much into her memory of one distant lecture. If she'd paid complete attention to it then maybe, but she had, as ever, spent most of her time looking at Dr Halman's husband. She'd loved Mehmet Suleyman once, but now that was over – for him, at least.

Ayşe put her head back and dismissed that unhelpful thought from her mind on a sigh.

By the time Yiannis Livadanios managed to get over to the mortuary, dusk had arrived. A dapper and immaculate man, he had only recently taken over the family business from his father who, at ninety, had finally decided to retire to his villa on Burgazada in the Sea of Marmara.

'I'm sorry I couldn't come before,' he said as he shook Arto Sarkissian's hand, 'but we've had two interments today and I had to go back to the families' homes,' he smiled. 'So much ouzo! Must be why Papa has lived so long – preserved in the stuff!'

Arto laughed. 'Talking of preservation,' he said as he led the undertaker through into his office, 'that is, of course, why you are here, Yiannis.'

'Yes. Your message was very intriguing,' Yiannis said. 'A young man found in an apartment . . .'

'In what I think might be a most advanced state of preservation,' Arto said as he handed Yiannis a white coat and a pair of latex gloves.

'So a sagging but recognisable mummy then,' the undertaker replied.

'No.'

Yiannis frowned. 'No?'

'Put your coat and gloves on and follow me,' Arto said as he moved towards the door of his laboratory. 'You'll see.'

The body, which was laid on a table in the centre of the laboratory, was covered with a white sheet. Only the feet could be seen, strangely supple-looking things. Arto stood to one side of the table and instructed Yiannis to stand opposite. He grasped the top of the sheet and then said, 'I believe he's about twenty years old. See what you think.'

The Armenian folded the sheet down to the top of the dead man's hips. And for just a moment there was nothing – no sound, no movement, barely even a breath.

'My God!' The Greek placed a hand up to the tautly sculpted face, and then just gently he palpated the flesh.

'That's supple,' he said as he looked up into Arto's eyes. 'It's very good, starting to degrade a little now . . . Are you sure he isn't recently deceased?'

'Yes,' Arto sighed. 'I wish it were that simple. But even I, with my rudimentary knowledge, know when a body has been preserved over a considerable period and this one has. The arterial formaldehyde solution used was in strong concentration and we've got glycerol and ethanol present. In addition the glass eyes have been fixed with mortuary paste.'

'So when did he die?' Yiannis said as he still gently touched other parts of the man's body.

Arto shook his head sadly. 'I have no idea,' he said, 'but I think some time ago.'

'Mmm,' the undertaker sighed, 'that is possible. However, if you found him, outside of a controlled environment, there has to be something else present too.'

'What do you mean?' Arto enquired. 'Like Lenin in his mausoleum?'

The Greek threw his arms dismissively in the air. 'Lenin? Pah! That body doesn't need a germ-free environment, it's ninety per cent wax dummy! They've been shoring him up for decades!'

'So . . .'

'There needs to be some sort of barrier between the skin and the atmosphere. Internal treatment can only do so much. If insects get into the skin they will destroy it.' He bent down to look closely at the dead man's face. 'And this is just starting to happen, so whatever that barrier was, it's degrading. What was he wearing, if anything, when he was brought in?'

Arto, unsettled that they were talking over such a disturbingly live-looking subject, pulled the sheet back up once again.

'A military uniform,' he said. 'It was one that neither I nor the policeman who brought him in recognised. My assistant investigated and we discovered that it dated from the nineteen fifties.'

'So maybe he or his relatives favoured antique clothes,' Yiannis said with a smile. 'A lot of young people wear very bizarre things these days. Was there anything actually on the skin? Perhaps polythene or cream . . .'

'There are traces of an emollient.' Arto took his gloves

off and threw them into one of the rubbish bins. 'A grease, I'm not sure quite—'

'An emollient could provide the necessary barrier,' Yiannis replied. 'It would have to be a good one if he'd been unattended in that apartment for some days because he's only just now beginning to degrade.'

'Mmm. How often would such an emollient have to be applied then, Yiannis? In order to maintain perfect preservation?'

'Oh, daily.'

'Across the whole skin surface?'

'Yes.' He shrugged. 'Provided an appropriate emollient was used, anyone could do it. What just anyone couldn't do is apply the occasional injections of disinfectant that would be needed to keep this young man wholesome – that and do the odd little bits of restoration to the facial tissues. Also the emollient would have to be excellent. Something produced, again, professionally.'

'OK,' Arto started moving back towards his office, 'so a professional must have been involved in his care?'

'Undoubtedly.' The Greek threw his gloves into a bin as he joined Arto on his way out of the laboratory. 'But not any of mine.' He looked back at the now covered corpse and smiled. 'I'd know about something like him,' he said, and then cleared his throat. 'So, this military uniform, did you find out what it was?'

'Yes. My assistant did an Internet search, which is why we know that it dated from the fifties.'

'So what was it?'

'A lieutenant's uniform. Argentine. The woman we

found this body with was originally Argentinian. She came to İstanbul in the nineteen fifties.'

It was only when he had finished speaking that Arto realised that Yiannis was no longer following him. Confused, he looked back at the figure of the undertaker, which was perfectly still in the middle of the room.

'Yiannis?'

'Are you sure that the uniform was Argentine?'

'Yes.'

'One hundred per cent?'

'Yes, what . . . ?'

'Give me another pair of gloves,' Yiannis said. 'I have to look at him again.'

Wordlessly, Arto reached on to one of the benches and retrieved a pair of gloves, which he gave to the undertaker.

'Have you thought of something or—'

Yiannis hurriedly put the gloves on and then scuttled back to the body on the table. He pulled away the sheet with a flourish like a conjurer and then stood back and looked at the body with a fierce intensity.

'Yiannis . . .'

'Arto, I can't be certain, and so I will have to take advice from colleagues but . . . but I think you may have something absolutely extraordinary here.' He looked up into the Armenian's eyes and then licked his now bone-dry lips. 'The police don't happen to have found the emollient that was used on this boy, do they?'

'Not that I know of. Why?'

'Because if it's the same emollient Ara used on Eva, then . . .' The undertaker took his gloves off, flung them to the floor and walked up to Arto, took his shoulders between his hands and kissed him on the cheek. 'Then that means your boy could be older than you, and we could be in the presence of a miracle,' he laughed.

Arto, confused, looked from the dancing eyes of the animated undertaker to the corpse on the table and then back again. OK, so the boy was wearing clothes from the nineteen fifties, but for that body to be older than his own was surely not truly possible. However, if Yiannis was talking about miracles . . . So the man had been dead for a very long time . . . But then if that were so, why had he been preserved so well when Lenin, who had to have been attended by the best embalmers in the business, had needed wax to keep him together?

# CHAPTER 5

Uncharacteristically for İkmen, he decided to have an early night. After a dinner of mixed vegetables and bread and a couple of games of tavla with his brother-in-law Talaat, he made his way wearily into his bedroom and lay down.

Today was one of those days – the days when he noticed things, became aware of thoughts and feelings in his own head. Talaat's hands had been thin and yellow for some time, but today was the first time he'd seen them shake. Hardly able to lift the counters off the tavla board, sometimes even dropping them. It wouldn't be long now – they'd be playing tavla on his hospital bed, Talaat's arms and hands riddled with needles hooked up to tubes connected to machines dispensing drugs . . .

Poor Fatma. Both her parents had been dead for years, and although she still had two sisters and an older brother, it was her little brother Talaat who had always been her favourite. It had been Fatma who had to all intents and purposes raised him – bathing and feeding him while that monstrously fat mother of hers lay on her bed slowly killing herself with a mixture of lokum and sherbet. Somehow he'd have to make time to care for Fatma properly, with something approaching full attention, once Talaat had gone. But if he were honest with himself it wasn't either Fatma or Talaat that was on his mind at the present time. It was the Akdeniz twins.

In one of the pictures Melih had given the police of Yaşar and Nuray, they looked so alive; sitting in their garden, playing with puppets and laughing at the antics of the local cats. İkmen wanted, more than anything else, to find them, to bring them back unharmed. He could even see it in his mind, the children running into the garden, into the arms of their tear-stained mother. But as tears started to rise in his own eyes, he knew it was only a vision, it wasn't true. The truth was much darker than that, something that damned gypsy had leeched from inside his body. The children were in torment. As sure as the sun rose in the east and set in the west . . . The card had confirmed it. People could say as many fluffy things as they liked about modern interpretation of tarot, about the 'Lightning-Struck Tower' card representing change . . . But the turn of a single card that showed the ruined tower, its occupants flung down from heaven into hell, meant only one thing. After all, as his mother had always said, the possibility of a descent into hell, whether metaphorical or physical, is always a risk, and if a person can't face that then that person shouldn't be looking at cards. Not, of course, that İkmen had actually wanted to look at cards on this particular occasion.

But then if the Akdeniz children were being tortured, in whatever sense of the word somewhere, shouldn't he be acting? In a way, through the card they were crying out to him.

But where to start? He couldn't say anything about his intuitions to any of his colleagues; they would think he was insane. How could he proceed with more rapidity? He needed to move fast. Not that there was anything to proceed with. House-to-house had yielded nothing, ditto interviewing known child molesters. Ayşe had come up with nothing useful in Sarıyer . . .

All they had was the children's home, their personal things and the unsubstantiated contention of Melih and Eren Akdeniz that the children had left the house at 6 a.m. on Saturday morning. They, well-known and gregarious children, had been seen by no one at that time. In fact the only out-of-the-ordinary incident that had occurred had been the appearance of the blue van Brother Constantine had reported seeing at the house late on the Friday night. Melih Akdeniz, a non-driver himself, had explained this quite satisfactorily. Late on Friday night his brother-in-law, Reşad, had visited to pick up a canvas for one of Melih's many wealthy admirers. Roditi had phoned to check this out with the brother-in-law, and it had held up. There was no reason to doubt anything the Akdeniz couple had done or were saying. But İkmen did.

Of course they wouldn't, couldn't harm their own children. Akdeniz was an odd man, to say the least, but he was obviously very upset and anxious about what was happening. His wife, a sleepwalking figure, existed almost exclusively on tranquillisers – or so it appeared. No, it couldn't be them, but there was something . . . Something else they knew, something they were burying . . .

The house. Solid and immutable, packed with everything, strange or not, that the children had ever known.

İkmen picked his mobile telephone up off the floor before he had a chance to change his mind. He punched a number in and waited for the recipient to answer. When she did she sounded a little surprised.

'Oh, hello, Inspector,' Ayşe said. She wasn't yet accustomed to his ways, which included phoning his inferiors out of hours, sometimes at very peculiar times.

'Ayşe, I'm going to order a full forensic examination of the Akdeniz house.'

'Why? Do we think the parents are suspects? How could they have kidnapped their own children? Where would they be hiding them? Melih Akdeniz never goes out.'

'In an evidence vacuum like the one we're in at the moment, everyone has to be a suspect,' İkmen said, 'including you and me.'

'Well . . .'

'Taking it a bit far, I know,' he said with a smile, 'but working on the premise that the last person to see a murder victim alive is the person most likely to be his killer . . .'

'Yes, but we're not talking about murder, are we?'

'No, but if we extend that premise to abduction . . . Look, I've always been and I remain very dubious about this idea that the children left the house at six a.m. on Saturday morning. People get up early in places like Balat; they would have been seen. I'm not saying that Melih Akdeniz is lying. Mistaken, maybe . . . But the gates to that house were open that night so that Eren's brother could load his van with one of Melih's pictures. How do we, or they, know that someone didn't get in?'

'We don't.'

'Which is why we need full forensics on the whole house. Had I known that the gates had been open on the

86

Friday night, I would have ordered it sooner, but Melih didn't bother or want to tell me.'

'You really, really don't like him, do you, sir?' Ayşe said with a smile.

But İkmen ignored her. 'Forensics will go in as soon as I get approval,' he said. 'We'll need to speak to Mrs Akdeniz's brother too. Oh, and by the way, I do apologise for disturbing you, Ayşe.'

But before she could answer he pressed the end button and threw the phone back down on to the floor. It was far too late to listen to her lie to him about how his call hadn't inconvenienced her in the slightest.

İkmen lay in the dark completely still and awake.

'Every profession must have its legends,' Yiannis Livadanios said as he leaned across the table towards Arto Sarkissian. 'For embalmers, it is Dr Pedro Ara.'

Arto placed his glass of Coke down on the table and leaned back into his chair. Yiannis wasn't drunk but he did smell strongly of rakı which, no doubt, was proving an interesting addition to all that ouzo he'd drunk earlier.

'So he was Argentinian . . .'

'No, Ara was a Spaniard.' Yiannis paused to signal for the waiter to bring him more water for his rakı. 'He went to Argentina, I don't know why. But anyway, while he was there he was asked by the dictator Juan Peron to preserve the body of his wife, Eva.'

'Evita Peron.'

'Yes.'

Arto took some pistachio nuts from the bowl in front of him and shelled them into the ashtray. Even though he didn't drink himself, he really enjoyed coming to these little Bosphorus-side bars.

'I vaguely remember hearing that her corpse was very well preserved,' Arto said.

'Well preserved! Well preserved!' Yiannis gulped down what was left of his drink and then poured himself another, adding just a touch of water at the end. 'It was a miracle!' he said. 'I've only seen photographs, you understand, but I tell you . . . A "liquid sun" is how Ara himself described it. Supple, ageless – a masterpiece, just like that boy would be if the treatment were continued.'

Arto threw a couple of naked pistachios into his mouth and chewed. 'So how did he do it? Preserve them so well?'

'Dedication, time, skill, the right combination of chemicals and, most importantly,' Yiannis said conspiratorially, 'a barrier balm, an emollient applied daily, something entirely of his own, to stop the contamination getting in. You know, he once embalmed a ballerina, a beautiful girl, and posed her on full pointe. The Russians wanted him to put things right with poor old Lenin, but he wouldn't go. No amount of money could persuade him.'

'But he worked for Peron.'

Yiannis beckoned Arto towards him. The Armenian inclined his head across the table.

'It is said that Ara was besotted with Evita,' the Greek hissed. 'It is said that he may have had "knowledge", if you know what I mean, of that corpse.'

Arto, despite having come across this sort of thing before, cleared his throat in an embarrassed fashion.

'I see,' he said. 'But going back to the boy from Kuloğlu . . .'

'Ara could have done it,' Yiannis said. 'Like I said, it is possible that body could be older than you. I will have to consult with my colleagues.'

'But if Dr Ara embalmed the body of Eva Peron then he must be really quite old now,' Arto said.

The Greek laughed. 'Oh, Ara was a sad middle-aged man when he was in Argentina.' He took a sip of rakı and then coughed. 'He died sometime in the nineteen seventies.'

'Without, I assume from what you've said, imparting his secrets, of the balm, for instance, to others.'

Yiannis looked up from his glass, his face suddenly and strangely sober.

'That's right, or, at least, that's what I always believed,' he said. 'Ara wasn't just a clever anatomist, an inspired preserver of bodies; Ara was a genius. Somehow, we don't know by exactly what means, he could actually imbue his subjects with life.'

'You make him sound like Dr Frankenstein.'

'Which is what, in a way, he was,' Yiannis replied. 'He practised a kind of reanimation.' He looked across at the deep, black waters of the Bosphorus before continuing softly, 'He fought to capture the spirits of them, with chemicals and balms. Wrestling decay for years . . .'

'Yes,' Arto said, 'although if what you say is correct he can't have "wrestled" with my boy for many years. Certainly not on the daily basis you have suggested.'

'No, and so someone else, someone who knows Ara's

techniques very, very well, must have been maintaining the body.'

'Yes, but if, as you say, Ara's exact method isn't really fully understood . . .'

The Greek smiled. 'Ah, yes,' he said, 'or so it has always been thought. But what if I'm wrong? What if there is someone who knows *exactly* what he did, who knew Ara maybe?'

'Yes, but—'

'An Argentine connection has been established. The police will find a jar or a tub of something in the apartment where he was found. Maybe that dead woman, the *Argentine* woman you found with him, applied the stuff. Perhaps she knew Ara, or the person he passed his secrets on to. I would urge you to investigate this,' Yiannis said. 'Although the person isn't likely to be a Turk, is he?' he laughed. 'They like their dead really dead and rotting.'

Arto thought about the small and elderly body of Rosita Keyder and frowned. Not a strong candidate for a professional embalmer. But appearances, as Arto knew only too well, could be deceptive. He'd need to speak to Sergeant Çöktin again, after the policeman had interviewed Rosita Keyder's sister-in-law. He hoped that conversation would shed some light upon what was shaping up to be a most bizarre situation.

Metin İskender was almost completely unrecognisable. Indeed, when Mehmet Suleyman looked around the cheap, smoke-sodden room he found it very difficult to locate his colleague. He looked so like them – the hard, leather-clad gangsters who habitually patronised places like this. But for all of his acquired polish, Metin was a boy from the slums. Letting his voice revert to rough tones, talking too loudly and swearing with gusto came easily to him. Not that Suleyman was trying to be like that himself. He didn't need to. If Masha knew who and what he was then so did a lot of other people in this place. As the target of whatever game the whore and her master were playing with him, he needed only to play along until the end – wherever that might lead him. The trick was to try to outwit Rostov, which was why Metin İskender had turned up at this ghastly place of expensive, desperate flesh and barely drinkable alcohol. It wasn't as if anyone but Metin really knew what Mehmet was doing. İkmen was too involved in his own case and Suleyman's deputy, Çöktin, didn't need to know the finer details. Like this . . .

Suleyman looked about him – at men buying cheap champagne at two hundred dollars a bottle for women who looked like inflatable sex dolls. Their faces bloated with drugs and alcohol, the women whispered both their areas of sexual expertise and their prices into the ears of the men who never, ever smiled. Later, the men would go to the back of the premises with their choice or choices for the night and relieve themselves into various orifices. To his horror, just the thought of it made him feel aroused. He was determined that nothing like this was going to happen to him. Metin İskender had come along specifically to prevent any harm coming to him. Metin, as Mehmet knew that he would, had insisted upon it.

'You can't go to a place like that on your own,' he'd said when Mehmet had told him about his encounter with Masha in the İç Bedesten, 'especially without Ardiç's knowledge. These types could murder you and have your body burned to dust by morning. No one will talk – it will be as if you'd never been in the place. At the very least this tart, if she says you've had sex with her, could compromise what you're trying to achieve here. I know it's her word against yours, but even a hint of sexual impropriety would destroy what you've done.' It was all true . . .

The 'tart' pushed her way through the greasy, beaded curtains that led, Suleyman imagined, to unmentionable rooms at the back of this terrible place and walked towards him, smiling.

'Come to the bar and have a drink with me,' she said as she slipped one of her arms through his. 'I like champagne, what about you?'

'Does it matter what I like?' he said as he forced something resembling a smile on to his features.

'No,' she laughed, and then barked something at the blond barman who brought her a bottle sporting a label covered in Cyrillic characters.

Russian champagne – even the thought of it made Suleyman's stomach turn. If it was anything like the stuff he'd had before it was probably a mixture of low-grade Georgian grapes and glycol. Masha led him to a nicotine- and ethanol-scented booth in the corner of the room and placed the bottle, together with two large glasses, down on the table. A small young man whose face was almost as hard as his heavily gelled hair watched Masha and her 'mark' sit down with interest. It was a revelation just how seedy Metin İskender could look in this context.

Masha poured 'champagne' for them both and immediately started sipping from her glass. It was said that stuff like this could make a person go blind, which was why Suleyman contented himself with just looking at his glass. Even the bubbles looked greasy and unnatural. He looked away from the glass and into Masha's greedy, sexual face. He had to get out of here and soon.

'So,' he began, in a low voice, 'this information you have for me.'

Masha looked around nervously. 'You don't think I'm going to give it to you here?'

'Well, you suggested that I come to this place.'

'Yes,' she drew closer to him, placing one of her hands firmly on his thigh, 'to meet.'

'But—'

'We can only talk in my room,' she said as she took a large swig from her chipped champagne saucer. 'It's too risky out here.' She smiled. 'And, anyway, in my room who knows what may happen?'

'What will happen is that you will give me the information that I need to avenge your friend,' Suleyman replied sternly.

'You know you'll have to pay to make it look—'

'I'm not stupid!' he hissed as he pushed her hand roughly from his leg. 'I've got money for you and for this filthy stuff too.' He nodded in the direction of the champagne bottle.

Masha frowned. 'I like it,' she said.

'Well, you can drink it then,' Suleyman replied. 'Now can we get on with this business? I want to leave this place as soon as possible.'

'All right! All right!' She smiled again, a dull-eyed heroin grimace. She reached for his hand as she rose

93

slightly unsteadily to her feet. 'Come on then, my eager prince,' she said, as she led him past the hard little Turkish gangster who seemed so very taken with her friend Raisa.

Masha's room was obviously not her home – if indeed someone like her had a home.

'Where can I sit?' Suleyman asked as Masha shut the door behind them.

'On the bed,' she replied.

He did as he was told, turning just in time to see her remove both her dress and the bra beneath it.

'Masha . . .'

The strained expression on his face made her laugh. He could try as hard as he liked to fool himself that he didn't want sex, but he couldn't fool her.

She walked over to him and then lowered herself quickly into his lap.

'The information . . .'

Her hand moved swiftly to the front of his trousers, and began massaging what was already hard.

'I thought you'd like some of this first, Inspector,' she said as she raised one of her large breasts up to his face.

'No . . .'

'Oh, come on,' her hand was moving now, slowly, expertly, 'you can come inside me.'

'No . . .'

She was a cheap, heroin-addicted tart – a creature from and of Rostov. Probably riddled with disease, maybe even HIV positive. And yet when one of her heavy nipples touched his lips, when he looked at her pubis moving rhythmically towards the penis in her hand . . .

It had been such a long time, such a long frustrating time . . .

He took her breast into his mouth as she slipped him inside her. It felt so good. As she rose and fell with his ever-increasing thrusts, she even gasped with what could be pleasure. He shouldn't be doing this! This was dangerous! He should, had to push her away, get the information and get out of this place . . .

'I think I'm in love,' Masha murmured into his ear.

And even though he knew that it wasn't, couldn't be true, that statement moved him on to a place of no return. Just the relief of that moment made him scream.

# CHAPTER 6

Melih Akdeniz looked, with a critical eye, at the huge swathe of material stretched tautly between the two largest trees in his garden. The morning sun shone strongly on its blank whiteness, causing the artist to squint as he considered it.

'I'm wondering whether it will be big enough,' he said, before tipping the liquid from a small brown bottle in his hands into the back of his throat.

The thin, black-eyed woman at his side looked dully on.

'I don't know,' she said, 'I don't know much right now.'

Melih handed her the bottle.

'Just drink, Eren,' he said without looking at her, 'drink deep.'

He walked over to one of the trees and adjusted the tapes holding the material so that it was stretched even more tightly.

Eren Akdeniz put the bottle to her lips and drank. Afterwards, her face wrinkled in disgust at what she'd just done, she threw the bottle on to the flagstones at her feet. It smashed into many sharp, tiny pieces.

The noise caused her husband to look round. 'What did you do that for?' he asked.

Eren sat down on the patio table, her eyes heavy and glassy. 'Because I shouldn't be doing that,' she said. 'I should be feeling—'

'Feeling is just what you shouldn't be doing,' Melih cut in sharply. 'Start that and Allah alone knows where it might lead.' He walked over to her, across the broken shards of glass and placed a hand on her shoulder. 'The work is all that matters,' he said earnestly. 'It's important, we agreed. It will stand for eternity, for us, for the children . . .'

At this, she looked up, her eyes filled with tears. 'I'm losing everything that I love.'

'No, you're not!' He took his hand roughly away from her. 'You're losing nothing, gaining everything – becoming part of everything. When we first met you were an ignorant art student – a dauber. Now you're on the threshold of reaching the stars! If you'd stop talking to that mother of yours and take my advice—'

'Like drinking your medication?'

Melih turned back to look at the material once again. 'We have always shared everything, Eren,' he said as he moved in closely to look at the details of the weave on the cloth. 'I am the greatest artist this country has ever produced. I took you, a child and made you my muse. I have given you everything.'

'I know,' she said. She reached out and touched him just lightly with the ends of her fingers. 'You are the owner of my soul. I would die in agony for you.'

'Your pain would be an exquisite thing,' he said as he turned again to face her. 'Just your grief inspires me.'

She stood up and leaned into his arms. They kissed,

unaware for several seconds that they were being watched.

'I'm sorry, I let myself in,' İkmen said as he, followed by Ayşe Farsakoğlu, made his way up the steps from the main gate.

Melih tore his face away from Eren's, frowning. 'What do you want?'

'I'd like to know why you're standing on broken glass,' İkmen said, shaking his head at the sight of Melih's feet, bleeding over the shards of smashed bottle.

Both Melih and Eren looked down and, although her eyes remained rooted to the gory sight, the artist glanced away almost immediately. 'That isn't your concern,' he said. 'I repeat, what do you want? My wife and I are busy.'

İkmen, now level with the artist, surveyed his thin features sternly. 'I want your co-operation, Mr Akdeniz,' he said.

'In what?'

'I want to perform a full forensic examination of this property.'

'Why?'

İkmen sighed and lit a cigarette. 'Because I want to find your children, Mr Akdeniz,' he said. 'As I'm sure you're now aware, I'm not convinced that your children left this property at six a.m. last Saturday.'

'But I told—'

'Yes, I know what you told me, sir,' İkmen said, 'and I do believe that you believe that to be true. But I'm not convinced. I think it's possible that someone may have entered this property sometime during the course of Friday night and—'

'Abducted my children?' Melih laughed. 'How? Even if Eren and I didn't hear these "abductors" the children wouldn't have just allowed themselves to be taken.'

'No,' Eren agreed, 'they're not babies.'

'No, but if they were drugged or restrained in some way . . .'

Melih laughed. 'This is fucking ridiculous!' He moved in close to İkmen's face. 'You're mad.'

İkmen smiled. 'Maybe,' he said, 'but if I am, then so are my superiors.'

'We'd like your willing compliance with the investigation, Mr Akdeniz,' Ayşe Farsakoğlu added, 'even though we don't actually need that.'

Melih and Eren's eyes met briefly before the artist brought his thin hands up to his face and groaned. 'I'm working. I must work.'

'The forensic team will work around you.'

Melih tore his hands away from his face and yelled, 'If they damage any of my works, either completed or in progress, I will sue everyone involved, including you!'

There had been a time when even the rich and powerful would have balked at suggesting the notion of legal redress to a senior Turkish policeman. But times had changed and this wasn't the first time İkmen had been threatened in this fashion. His response was both practised and typical of him.

'Well, sir,' he said, 'you are at liberty to do that, should damage occur. Legal action against my department is—'

'Oh, do whatever the fuck you like!' the artist shouted, throwing his arms in the air as he stumbled his way back towards his house.

İkmen, Ayşe Farsakoğlu and his own wife watched Melih go – his long hair joining his arms, flailing in the hot, still air. İkmen noted that Melih seemed immune to the wounds on his feet. With what he hoped was a reassuring expression on his face, he turned to Eren Akdeniz and said, 'I will also need to speak to your brother in due course, Mrs Akdeniz. He was, I understand, here on Friday night collecting one of your husband's art works.'

Eren Akdeniz first regarded him blankly, then her face lost all of its colour and she sat down slowly on one of the garden chairs.

On both the European and Asian shores of the Bosphorus sit many yalıs – summer houses. Although anyone with the money to do so may now own a yalı, traditionally these residences were occupied by Ottoman royalty and dignitaries. In Tarabya and Büyükdere the yalıs belonged to the European ambassadors, in Kuruçeşme to the wealthy Ottoman Armenians and Greeks. The large wooden yalıs of Sarıyer were, however, and still remain, the most prestigious. These tall, ornate properties, now priced well beyond the reach of anyone but the most wealthy, were the summer residences of the Ottoman princes. As İsak Çöktin entered the oval-shaped central area of the yalı, a space known as the sofa, he wondered whether this was the type of building Mehmet Suleyman, his boss, had been raised in. There was a common concensus that Suleyman had been born in a palace – maybe he spent his childhood summers in a place like this. Yalıs, even Çöktin knew, had been, to those who possessed them, rather downmarket, slightly amusing places for the over-privileged to spend a few months in the summer playing at being 'rural'. Çöktin smiled as he recalled an old photograph he'd once seen in a tourist shop of a group of Ottoman princes lounging around in silk şalvar trousers and heavily embroidered waistcoats, being peasants. Such a long way from his own experience: the sight of his uncle in dung-stained şalvar trousers and the thin, hungry looks on the faces of almost everyone in sight.

The current owner of this, the Pembe Yalı, was the late Rosita Keyder's sister-in-law. Tall, thin and dressed in a most severe shade of grey, Miss Yeşim Keyder was an unsmiling woman in, what Çöktin calculated, was probably her early seventies. She was not, he quickly discovered, a woman either well versed in or approving of the traditional Turkish niceties.

'Sit there,' she said, pointing to a brown chair over by the door which led out to a landing stage.

Çöktin sat, his eyes directly in line with a black and white photograph of a graceful dancer snapped in mid-step. Not, he felt, the grim Miss Yeşim Keyder as a girl.

'So you said you had some bad news for me,' Yeşim Keyder said as she lowered herself down into an identical chair across the other side of the sofa. 'What is it?'

Çöktin, uncomfortable with the vast amount of space between himself and this woman, leaned forward.

'I'm afraid I have to tell you that your sister-in-law, Rosita Keyder, has passed away,' he said. 'I'm—'

'When?' Both the thickness of her voice and the sudden blanching of her face told Çöktin that Yeşim Keyder hadn't been expecting this. She obviously hadn't read the newspaper reports.

'Our doctor has recorded last Wednesday as the date of Mrs Keyder's death, Miss Keyder,' Çöktin said. 'She died from something called an aneurism, which is—'

'I am fully aware of what the word "aneurism" means,' the woman snapped, 'and it's Dr Keyder, not Miss Keyder, for future reference.'

'I'm sorry . . .'

'So what happened? How did you get involved?'

Çöktin told her about how Father Giovanni had raised the alarm and when and why he himself and his officers had entered the Kuloğlu apartment. Through all of this Yeşim Keyder looked on impassively, regarding him coldly with her pale blue eyes across the vast wastes of the sofa.

'Of course, Father Giovanni would like to bury your sister-in-law after the Christian fashion,' Çöktin said, 'but he, and ourselves, are aware that Mrs Keyder may still have relatives in Argentina, who may want her body to be returned to that country.'

Yeşim Keyder sighed. 'I don't think so,' she said tightly. 'Rosita was an only child. By the time she married Veli her father was already deceased. Her mother died sometime in the nineteen sixties.'

'Yes, but if we knew the family name . . .'

'Arancibia.' It was, to Çöktin, a strange, foreign word, but it was one Yeşim Keyder said without hesitation. 'My brother met her in Buenos Aires in nineteen forty-nine,' she continued. 'Rosita Arancibia.' She spelled the word out for him, lapsing afterwards into silence.

102

Çöktin smiled. 'So how did they meet,' he asked, 'your brother and Mrs Keyder? I mean, she was a Christian Argentinian and he a Muslim Turk. In those days surely—'

'My brother was a scientist,' she replied, 'a biologist – religious differences meant nothing to him. There was a scientific convention in Buenos Aires, he went – he stayed with one of our uncles who emigrated there – and met Rosita.' She scanned her surroundings haughtily. 'My father fought alongside İnönü in the War of Independence. Quite correctly for a family possessed of both nationalistic fervour and intelligence, we have done well.'

'I see.'

'As far as I am aware, Rosita corresponded with no one in Argentina,' she said.

'I will check this name out with the Argentinian authorities.'

'That's up to you. But as far as I'm concerned her priest may bury her. She had, I believe, some friends at St Anthony's. They may wish to attend her funeral. Rosita and Veli were childless and so the property will revert to me. I will call my advocate.'

There was no emotion. It was impossible to tell whether or not Yeşim Keyder had been close to the dead woman. Given her tone, one could be forgiven for thinking she was only interested in what she might gain materially from Rosita's death.

'Father Giovanni was always of the opinion that Rosita lived alone after your brother died,' Çöktin said.

'Yes, she did.'

Çöktin took a deep breath. Quite how he was going to

broach the subject of the young man's body he hadn't really thought through. During the pause in which he pondered this, she looked at him quizzically.

'I have to tell you that we found another body in your sister-in-law's apartment,' he said, 'that of a young man.'

Yeşim Keyder remained motionless and silent.

'We've no idea who he was.'

'Maybe he was an intruder.'

'No.'

She looked down at the floor. 'If you don't know who he is, how do you know that?'

Çöktin wasn't sure just how much or how little he should tell this woman. Given what Dr Sarkissian had said about the body, its embalmed state, the sergeant didn't feel confident getting into such bizarre territory with a family member before he knew a little more.

'There are indications that this person might not have been unknown to Mrs Keyder,' he said. 'I can tell you there are no signs of foul play. He died naturally.'

'In that case, I can't see why I need to be involved in this,' Yeşim Keyder responded harshly. 'As far as I am concerned, Rosita lived alone. And, if as you say, this man died naturally, I would suggest that you bury his body with all haste.'

As a Muslim, particularly in the height of summer, it was logical that she should suggest such a sanitary move. Although she knew that he was nameless, Yeşim Keyder didn't know how important it was to discover this man's identity. Probably Argentine, definitely embalmed some long time ago, whether he had been murdered or not was almost immaterial. What he needed was a name, a nationality, a religion and, ideally, an 'owner' to put an end to what seemed to Çöktin a most peculiar state of death within a simulacrum of life. Displayed by that window in Kuloğlu, the young man reminded Çöktin of one of those Ancient Egyptian mummies on display in the Egyptian Museum in Cairo.

There was no point going any further with this at the present time. Yeşim Keyder knew nothing about the unknown man and cared, apparently, little for her deceased sister-in-law. And so Çöktin decided to leave her to call her advocate in peace. She saw him to her front door and then shut it behind him with alacrity – probably because she didn't want him to see what she did next. But he heard her anyway, bitterly weeping her way back into the sofa. As he got into his car, Çöktin thought about how wrong one can be about people and found himself feeling sorry for the strange, stiff old woman rattling around in her great, lonely yalı.

'Valery Rostov is going to take possession of twenty kilos of heroin tonight,' Suleyman said as he stood, almost to attention in front of his superior, Commissioner Ardiç.

Metin İskender, who was standing next to his colleague, cleared his throat.

Ardiç, who was a large and, in this heat, red and sweaty man, removed the enormous cigar from his mouth and viewed his officers with a harsh eye.

'That's a huge amount. Very tempting. Where did you get this information?' he said. 'The Rostovs of this world are not above starting a gun battle, I'm not prepared to commit officers unless this is going to be worth it.'

'It's very possible that the heroin drop is a bluff, sir,' İskender said as he looked sideways at a very slightly reddening Suleyman. 'The informant is one of Rostov's prostitutes, so this could well be a set-up.'

'What we're proposing, sir,' Suleyman continued, 'is to stake out both the drop site and follow Rostov himself. If, as I suspect, his "work" takes him somewhere other than the location I've been told, we will be in a position to see why he's hoping to divert our attention elsewhere. I've had contact with this informant for some time and I believe her "mission", if you like, is to try and lead us as far away from Rostov's business dealings as possible.'

Ardiç leaned back heavily in his considerable chair and looked into Suleyman's eyes. 'Why you?' he said. 'Why contact with you?'

In the absence of any cohesive departmental plan with regard to the gangs since the demise of the dreaded Zhivkov organisation, it was a fair question. It wasn't, however, that easy to answer. There were several possibilities, including the notion that Masha had received her information about Suleyman from someone inside the department. Someone who could have knowledge about what Suleyman was involved in investigating. In addition, there had been some gossip about his marriage. His wife was, after all, a lot older than he.

Masha said she loved him, which had to be a lie. And yet . . . She'd thrown herself into his pleasure with abandon. Even when he'd finished, she'd continued; stroking, sucking, winding her body in an almost desperate fashion around his. The relief had been amazing, or at least it would have been had he not felt so guilty.

'Inspector Suleyman?'

The harsh words of his superior brought him back to himself.

'Er, I suppose Rostov must have discovered, somehow, that certain officers, including myself, have an interest in trying to control organised crime. Inspectors İkmen, İskender and myself have had some success in this area. If you recall, sir, last year—'

'The subtext,' Ardiç interrupted, 'is that some of my officers are paid by and loyal to people like Rostov.'

'Sir . . .'

'I know you don't want to actually come out and say that, Suleyman,' he continued, 'but you're not telling me anything I don't know. Some of my officers are in the pay of mobs,' he shrugged, 'I know that. I don't know their names, but I know my department has leaks. If you know this is a set-up, you will also know that men at the drop site could be in considerable danger.'

'Yes, sir.'

'There is also the possibility of a double bluff,' Ardiç looked at both of his officers in turn, 'that Rostov wants you to go to the drop site and follow him while whatever it is he wants to conceal from us takes place elsewhere.'

Suleyman looked at İskender who shrugged. 'We had considered that too, sir. But we need to make a decision. We don't have much time.'

'I don't like getting involved in anything at short notice,' Ardiç said. 'I like to be given time to plan, which is not, of course, what Rostov wants us to do. He wants us to react. The question is, do we play his game and see what, if anything, we can achieve by that, or do we take the safe option and do nothing?'

He leaned back into his chair and puffed thoughtfully on his cigar. The two officers in front of him remained silent while they waited for Ardiç to answer his own query.

# CHAPTER 7

There were strange, unearthly figures moving around Melih Akdeniz's house and garden. Creatures, whose sex was indistinguishable, covered from head to toe by thick white overalls. Also present were İkmen, and the beautiful policewoman he always had with him, the two of them serious and hot in their stuffy-looking business suits. Seemingly oblivious to the activity was the artist himself, who was in his garden, sitting in front of a large sheet stretched tightly between two trees. He was sewing what looked like a small jacket.

Although the people of Balat had been told by the police to move away from outside Melih's house several times, a considerable number of them persisted in returning. Mainly old people and children, this group also included the tall and exotic figure of Gonca the gypsy, who was there with the youngest of her daughters, six-year-old Ceylan. Half hiding from what she called 'the spacemen' behind the folds of her mother's skirt, the little girl looked gravely at the artist as he pushed and pulled his sewing needle through several thicknesses of plum-coloured velvet. He was a man that Ceylan knew, not a friend of her mother's but someone who would sometimes come to the house, sometimes at

109

night in order to share her mother's bed. Other men did that too . . .

'What's he doing?' the child asked her mother, pointing at Melih's downturned, shaggy head.

'He's sewing,' her mother replied.

'Is sewing art?'

Gonca smiled. 'It can be,' she said. 'Many things can be art. Walking along the street can be art if it's done in the right way.'

Ceylan frowned. 'Do you paint a picture with your feet?'

'In a sense,' Gonca said, and then she too frowned as she watched Melih Akdeniz break off from his labours to drink from the small brown bottle that she knew to be always at his side. Instinctively her eyes flew to İkmen, who had also been watching the artist at work.

Would he, obviously confused about the purpose of the little brown bottle, now go over to Melih and ask him about it? Well, even if he wanted to do so, he didn't. He just stood with that slim and attractive girl and looked on, unsmiling.

Gonca, who knew only too well what the significance of the little brown bottle was, could have told the policeman all about it. But she didn't. If İkmen was half what her mother had told her Ayşe İkmen had been, he'd know soon enough.

Melih reached down and picked up something that was familiar to Gonca from the ground beside him. He held it up just as one of the white overalled forensic technicians passed in front of him obscuring the gypsy's view. But Gonca knew what it was anyway, and when the technician had moved away, she looked at it again and smiled. That brought so many childhood memories flooding back.

She'd come to see him, she said, because she thought they might go to lunch together. He knew she was lying. Lunch for her was a cigarette. She'd come to check up on him. It wasn't the first time. But he smiled anyway, sent out for kebabs and settled down to the idea of entertaining his wife for half an hour.

'So, you're all alone in here then,' Zelfa said as she looked around his office with critical eyes.

'I am at the moment,' Suleyman replied. 'As you know, Çöktin shares with me.'

'But not today?'

'No.'

'So you're alone today?'

'Yes.'

If the lack of sex hurt him physically, the constant questioning damaged him psychologically. In fact, the questions and the implications behind them hurt him more. The distrust, the suspicion – none of it justified – until Masha, of course. Suleyman looked down at the desk in front of him lest his eyes reveal what his mind had just recalled.

'So are you always busy like this or do you get to actually go out to lunch sometimes?'

'Not generally,' he replied, still with a smile. She was fishing to see whether he would own up to having lunch with another woman. When had their conversation descended into this?

'Oh.'

Couldn't she see that by doing this, by pushing him away physically and by dwelling on her own insecurities, she was actually precipitating the event she was most afraid of? She was a psychiatrist, she had to be in contact with people like herself from time to time. Not, of course, that any of this excused his behaviour with that whore. Middle-aged insecurity allied to sexual problems wasn't exactly an unknown phenomenon – lots of men had it and experienced it from their wives. Lots of men didn't look elsewhere. He'd have to tell her.

'Zelfa . . .'

Catching, if misinterpreting the pleading tone in his voice, she snapped at him in English. 'If you're going to start on about my consulting a colleague, you can save your breath.'

'No . . .'

'Sex isn't everything, you know, Mehmet,' she said. 'Sometimes women have problems and men have to fucking wait.'

'Yes, I know, Zelfa, and I haven't bothered you.'

'No, although whether you've "bothered" any other females . . .'

His patience, together with his brief desire to confess, cracked. 'I don't have to dignify that with an answer!'

As if stung, Zelfa jumped to her feet. She leaned across the desk and pointed one finger into Suleyman's face, 'Oh, that's a good answer, Mehmet,' she said. 'Getting out of it while saying fuck all! Christ, man, you should have been a psychologist. You've got all the skills for it!'

'The skills maybe,' he countered, 'but not the knowledge!'

'Well, of course you haven't!'

'Because if I did then maybe I might be able to work out why you don't love me any more!'

For just a moment Zelfa remained motionless. Then, as the implication of what he'd said sank in, she pushed herself away from his desk and sat down again.

'But I do love you, that's why—'

'You persecute me, Zelfa!' He pulled himself up straight in his chair and lit a cigarette. 'With your constant suspicions, with your outbursts of self-hatred, with your contempt for anything to do with this country—'

'I don't want my son to forget that he's Irish!'

He flung his cigarettes and lighter across the desk at her. 'But he won't! Yusuf is fine. He's a very happy child. I too would be happy if you would just let me back in . . .'

'To my knickers!' Zelfa took a cigarette and lit it. She then threw the packet back at her husband.

'No!'

'Ah!'

'No, I mean,' he screwed up his eyes as the effort of trying to express himself properly took its toll, 'of course I want to make love to you, but I want to feel that you love me.'

'Oh, I love you, it's just you're—'

'Ah, yes, of course, because I am such a huge adulterer, aren't I? I . . .' he took a breath, preparing himself to tell her what he knew would, despite all her protestations to the contrary, shock her to the core.

And then his office phone rang.

'Allah!'

Under the toxic gaze of his wife, Suleyman picked up the receiver and mumbled his name.

'Sir, it's Hikmet, Constable Yıldız.'

'Yes?'

'Sir, I'm out at Atatürk Airport. I was meeting a relative, but then I saw Rostov . . .'

'Rostov?' The Russian's home had been watched since dawn. How and when had he got out? Suleyman took a pad of paper out of his desk drawer and grabbed a pen.

'Yes, sir,' Yıldız continued. 'I know you've an interest in him at the moment. I thought you'd like to know he's picked up a very big trunk.'

'From the airport?'

'Yes. There's several flights just landed. One from St Petersburg.'

'So did this trunk come off that flight?'

'I don't know, sir; couldn't get close enough to see.'

'So where is he now then, Yıldız? Rostov?'

'He's still here, sir, with some airport official and this trunk. I expect it's antiques. That's his business, isn't it?'

'Yes.' Officially it was. However, in view of what was supposed to be happening later on that evening, this could possibly be an important development. 'Are you able to follow him, Yıldız?'

'Well, I suppose I could put my uncle in a taxi . . .'

'Do so,' Suleyman said, 'and keep in touch.'

'OK. But what if Rostov and the trunk part company? What do you want me to do?'

Suleyman frowned. The trunk was tempting, but in view of the fact that they now had Rostov back in their sights, he was loath to let him go.

'Follow Rostov,' he said. 'As I said, keep in touch and if the trunk goes elsewhere, I'll arrange to have it tailed. I'll relieve you myself as soon as I can.'

'Yes, sir.'

Suleyman then cut the connection.

'I'm sorry, Zelfa . . .'

But she'd gone and he hadn't even noticed, so caught up had he been with Rostov and those around him. Inwardly Suleyman winced, and when his and Zelfa's kebabs did finally arrive, he was too miserable even to think about eating.

It was his wife, Maryam's, birthday in two days' time and so Arto Sarkissian used his lunch break to go and look for a suitable gift. And although he knew that Maryam would probably prefer something from one of the new shopping malls like Galleria, he found himself, purely out of self-interest, driving in the direction of the Kapılı Çarsı. Not only had he grown up going into the Grand Bazaar on a regular basis, often with Çetin İkmen, he had friends there who he knew would help him to choose wisely.

As soon as he entered Lazar's gold shop, Arto was enveloped in a cocoon of familiar affection. Ever present behind his gold-encrusted counter, the tiny old goldsmith smiled with impish pleasure as he regarded the corpulent figure of the pathologist easing itself uncomfortably into his little kingdom.

'Doctor!' Lazar cried as he first pushed his spectacles up on to his nose and then raised his arms in greeting.

'Lazar.'

Due to his size, Arto couldn't possibly get behind the

counter to get to Lazar. But the goldsmith knew this and so he came to him. And after embracing and listening to Lazar's usual selection of traditional Ottoman greetings, Arto told him why he had come and allowed Lazar to take him through to the room he reserved for his 'special' guests, behind the showroom.

'Çetin Bey hasn't bestowed honour on this humble business with his presence for some time,' the old man said, referring to Çetin İkmen.

'No.' Arto sat down on one of the red velour settees that Lazar kept solely for his guests and took off his jacket.

The goldsmith bent low in order to speak quietly to him. 'I understand there are some problems,' he said conspiratorially. 'Fatma Hanım's brother,' he shook his head sadly, 'cancer.' He lit a cigarette and sighed. 'A terrible thing.'

'Yes, it is.'

'Of course, I do see quite a lot of the inspector's daughter, Hulya,' the old man continued, 'which is a worry for him also.'

Arto, who knew something of what was going on romantically between İkmen's daughter and Lazar's assistant, Berekiah Cohen, just inclined his head to show that he'd heard, knew what it was about but had no answers.

'So it's a brooch for Madame Maryam this year,' Lazar said, rapidly turning to more commercial matters. He patted Arto affectionately on the shoulder. 'You wait here, Doctor. I'll get Berekiah to bring a tray of our very best pieces to you.'

'Thank you, Lazar Bey.'

The old man waved a dismissive hand as he slowly made

his way back to the showroom. 'It's nothing,' he said airily. 'Neither these old legs of mine nor my useless grandson, off, so his mother tells me, with some American woman, nor even God himself can stop me from providing the very best gold to the Sarkissian family.'

Arto smiled. Lazar 'the Jew' as both his own and Çetin's father had called him, had indeed served the wealthy and well known of İstanbul for over fifty years. Quite how old he was, no one seemed to know, but Vahan Sarkissian, Arto's father, had frequently described Lazar as an 'old' man and Vahan had died in the nineteen fifties.

'We all appreciate everything you do, Lazar Bey,' Arto said as he watched the old man's bowed back slip through the curtains that separated the hospitality room from the showroom beyond.

A few minutes later he was joined by a smiling young man carrying a tray of gold brooches in a variety of colours and styles.

'Hello, Dr Sarkissian,' he said. 'How are you?'

'I'm fine, Berekiah,' Arto replied, purposefully omitting to mention what he knew had to be a growling gall bladder problem.

'Lazar Bey tells me you want to purchase a brooch for Mrs Sarkissian,' Berekiah said. 'Do you know whether she would like something of modern design or . . . ?'

'I'm afraid I know little beyond the fact that my wife likes jewellery and loves gold,' Arto said with a smile. 'You'd think that after thirty years I would know these things.'

Berekiah placed the tray down on the table in front of Arto and sat down. 'Women do keep a lot of things to themselves,' he said, Arto felt, a little gravely. 'They can be most puzzling creatures.'

'Do I detect an element of recent experience in your voice, Berekiah?' Arto asked.

The young man looked up at him and smiled. 'It's stupid for us to behave as if you don't know . . .'

'About you and Hulya? Yes, I know.'

'And what do you think? About Hulya and me?'

'What I think is immaterial,' Arto said, adding quickly, lest the boy misunderstand, 'And I don't mean that unkindly, Berekiah. It just isn't my business.'

'I know.'

A moment of silence passed, during which Arto glanced briefly at the brooches before him.

'But you see,' Berekiah continued, 'I thought that I was doing the right thing by asking Hulya to marry me. We'd talked about being together and she seemed to want that, or so I thought. But then when I asked her to marry me, she said no.' He looked up into Arto's eyes. 'She said she wanted us just to live together.'

Arto, for whom all of this was very fresh news, sighed. 'Well, I'm afraid,' he said, 'that as well as dealing with a woman, you are, in this case, Berekiah, also dealing with one of Çetin Bey's daughters.'

'Yes,' the young man responded gloomily.

'A very strong-minded and independent group of people,' Arto said as he lifted a small red gold brooch from the tray and turned it over in his hands.

'I've thought that perhaps it might be a form of protest,' Berekiah said. 'Mrs İkmen and my parents are very much against our being together and so Hulya wants to really upset them by living with me. Our mothers, it's true, would be scandalised . . .'

At that moment, Arto's mobile phone began to ring and so, with apologies to his young friend, he answered it. It was İsak Çöktin.

'I'm just coming back from Miss Keyder's house in Sarıyer,' he said. 'I thought I might call in, if you're not too busy, Doctor.'

'I'm not actually at the lab at the moment, Sergeant,' Arto said, 'I'm in a shop.'

'Oh . . .'

Berekiah, who was a veteran of slipping away during confidential telephone calls, did just that, leaving Arto alone with Çöktin.

'It's OK now, we can talk,' Arto said as soon as the youngster had left. 'Did Miss Keyder have any idea who our young friend might be?'

'No, but she was shocked by the whole event,' Çöktin replied. 'Outwardly she was very cold, talking about how she might now take possession of her brother's property, but I could see she was disturbed.'

'What about relatives in Argentina?'

'Miss, or rather Doctor, Keyder doesn't think there are any, but we'll have to see what the Embassy come back with.'

'Yes.' Arto put the red gold brooch down and picked up a white one in the stylised shape of a palm frond. 'Actually, I'm glad you've called, Sergeant, because there is going to be a meeting at my office, about our young friend, at five and I think you might like to attend.'

'Oh?'

'I had a meeting with the undertaker Yiannis Livadanios last night,' he said, 'which was most interesting. I won't go into detail now, only to say that he called me this morning to arrange the further meeting at five. He wants some of his colleagues to see our boy.'

'Why?'

'I can't go into it here,' Arto said, 'it's far too complicated. Why don't you and I meet at my office at four, before they all arrive?'

'The undertakers?'

'They're actually professional embalmers,' Arto said, cringing, knowing that Çöktin would be disgusted. 'Two Greeks, one Armenian and a Spaniard who, apparently, serves the Roman Catholic deceased here in the city.' There was another reason why Señor Orontes had been invited along with his more indigenous colleagues, which had more to do with the fabled Dr Pedro Ara than with the Spaniard's current practice. But to go into all that phantasmagorical stuff with Çöktin at this stage would only serve to confuse him. And so once Çöktin had agreed to the meeting, Arto said goodbye and went back to looking at brooches once again.

After a while Berekiah returned. Smiling, he asked whether the doctor had found anything that was to his liking.

'I rather like this white palm frond,' Arto said, pointing to the modern piece that had caught his eye while he was on the phone.

'Yes, that's nice, isn't it? Shall I gift-wrap it for you?'

'Yes, Berekiah, thank you.'

The young man opened a drawer and took out a sheet

of tissue paper and a piece of ribbon. 'I do hope that Mrs Sarkissian likes it,' he said.

'I'm sure that she will.' He wasn't. Beyond the plastic surgery to which his wife was addicted, there was little that she ever expressed open interest in. It was the reason why Arto, though at heart a kind and moral man, sometimes went 'elsewhere' for female company.

'Doctor . . .'

'Yes?'

Berekiah looked up from the ribbon, which he was twisting into a bow and said, 'I'm sorry but I couldn't help overhearing.'

'What?'

'You talked about somebody having relatives in Argentina.'

Arto narrowed his eyes. 'Yes, Berekiah, what of it?'

'It's just that, well, a lot of our people, İstanbul Jews, went to Argentina and Brazil and places like that years ago. My dad had an uncle in Argentina – you can ask him.'

'The people I'm talking about aren't Jewish, Berekiah.'

'Are you sure?' He placed the brooch gently into a little velvet pouch and then proceeded to wrap tissue paper around it.

'I don't think so.'

'I only say this because there are some of our people, generally from poor families originally, who live as others, shall we say, change their names, their religion.' He tied the piece of ribbon around the little package so that the bow was uppermost. 'I think in the wake of the Holocaust in Europe some people, even here, became anxious. It might be worth checking out,' he said as he handed the

121

finished present over to Arto. 'It might help, I don't know. Some years ago, I think in the fifties and sixties, Argentina was a favoured destination.'

'Yes,' Arto smiled, 'I'll give it some thought, Berekiah. Thank you.'

Once he had paid – the discounted price for a friend, of course – Arto left. The strange occupant of Rosita Keyder's apartment was causing the doctor to move in some very odd directions. Embalmers, famous Spanish embalmers no less, Peron and his wife and his vicious corrupt regime, now South American Jews – maybe. Well, he recalled, the young man was, after all, circumcised.

'He's drinking with some associates in the bar at the Pera Palas,' Suleyman said as he lit both his own and İskender's cigarettes. 'Perhaps he finds the whiff of Cold War subterfuge that still hovers over the place amusing.'

The rather hard-faced young woman who stood in front of the two officers looked blank.

Suleyman, who was not unaccustomed to this sort of response in his inferiors, cleared his throat. 'Well, just watch and follow, Gün.'

'I don't understand why Constable Yıldız can't carry on,' Halide Gün said miserably. 'These gangsters live in a man's world. I'll stick out—'

'Yıldız is the one who's "sticking out" at the moment,' Suleyman responded sternly, 'solely because he is a man – a young and attractive one.'

'Rostov likes them like that,' İskender interjected.

'So why—'

'Yıldız came upon Rostov and his men at the airport simply by chance,' Suleyman said. 'I would never have assigned him to that duty because of the Russian's proclivities. As soon as you take over, he'll be much more comfortable and you'll be quite safe.'

'Stick with him, report where he goes and who he sees and you'll be relieved at six,' İskender added.

'So what happens after that?' Gün asked as she slipped her mobile telephone into the inside pocket of her jacket.

'That isn't your concern,' Suleyman said.

Gün shrugged. She was a constable and as such she was used to being kept in the dark about many and various things. As soon as she had gone she knew that the two men would talk about whatever it was they were all doing, which they did.

'So what about this trunk Rostov picked up at the airport?' İskender asked.

'A couple of his men drove it straight back to his house.'

'I wonder what's in it.'

Suleyman sighed. 'Probably antiques, knowing Rostov. I doubt even he would be so obvious as to bring anything "hot" through the airport. Not when the land and sea borders are so much easier.' He cleared his throat. 'So when are you and your men going to move into the area?'

'At seven,' İskender replied. 'The drop is supposed to happen at eleven, which will give us good time to get our bearings, see what's happening, come and go from the actual site.'

'There'll be five of you?'

'Yes.'

123

'At least you know, even if nothing does happen, where you're going and what you're looking for.' He stubbed his cigarette out in his ashtray and then lit another. 'I have no idea where I might be at eleven o'clock tonight. I could be at Rostov's house, I could be halfway to Bulgaria.'

'You wanted to pursue it, Mehmet,' İskender said – a trifle harshly, Suleyman thought.

'Ardiç agreed,' he responded defensively. 'I'm being set up, we know that. We have to see where this is going to lead.'

İskender sat down in what was usually Çöktin's chair. 'It's all a bit clumsy, though, don't you think? I thought Rostov was supposed to be one of the cleverer mobsters.'

'He is.' Suleyman turned and made his way over to the seat behind his desk.

As he moved the chair backwards, İskender sighed. 'You know,' he said, biting nervously on his bottom lip as he spoke, 'and don't misinterpret this, but you were with that Russian girl for a very long time . . .'

'She had a lot to tell me,' Suleyman smiled, 'and besides, we had to make what we were supposed to be doing look real. I mean, I know she was only playing a game, but I had to go along with it.'

'She and Rostov must know that you were just playing along.'

'Maybe.' Briefly, but to İskender, significantly, Suleyman averted his eyes.

He had been with that whore an awful long time. İskender himself had almost had to go with one of her fellows just to make his presence there plausible. It was something Suleyman should have taken into account. But then when he'd come out of the woman's room, he hadn't looked as if he were taking much of anything into account. He'd looked ruffled, flushed, in fact just like some of the 'real' punters that İskender had seen coming and going from those awful greasy rooms at the back of the pavyon. The thought that Mehmet would, could go with such a creature had to be ridiculous – and yet it wasn't an idea that was going away easily. And indeed, the more he looked at those still slightly averted eyes, the more the possibility of it grew inside his head. Mehmet hadn't been happy, in his personal life, for a while. In spite of the privacy of his nature, a lot of people had deduced that Suleyman had problems – the rows he had with his wife, who made no secret of her marital dissatisfaction when she came to the station to see him, were legendary. However, to confront his colleague head on about his conduct was not, İskender knew, the way forward. Whatever had or had not happened, Suleyman would deny involvement with the girl. All that İskender could hope was that if anything had happened, Suleyman had been careful – in every sense of the word.

'If no actual deal takes place but Rostov's men appear for another purpose, you have the right to question them about their activities,' Suleyman said, breaking through into his colleague's secret but, both of them knew, suspected thoughts. 'We are, after all, acting upon information received.'

'And if no one appears and nothing happens?'

'Then you stand your team down,' Suleyman said. 'I'll be in contact with you. By that time my men and I may know what's really happening.'

'I still think that Rostov's counting on us to be there,' İskender said, frowning. 'This "deal", if it's happening at all, could be taking place in a completely different part of the city. Like Ardiç said, a double bluff.'

'That will become apparent.'

'I just hope we're not wasting our time – or worse.'

Suleyman frowned. 'What do you mean, "or worse"?'

'Walking into some sort of elaborate trap,' İskender said gravely, 'something we might have to pay for with blood. We know these people are armed. And if you remember what happened with Zhivkov and his men, we also know they have no compunction about using those weapons. These people, Mehmet, don't give a shit that we're the Law. Their own loyalties override everything.'

# CHAPTER 8

'They've been in there a very long time, Doctor,' Çöktin said as he watched the small group of dark-suited men through the laboratory window.

'They're trying to come to some sort of conclusion,' Arto Sarkissian replied, as he too watched the men through the glass.

There were four embalmers currently in Arto's laboratory, looking at the unknown corpse, studying X-rays and carefully considering the data the pathologist had supplied about the chemical composition of the body fluids. And although Yiannis Livadanios, his brother Spiros and the Armenian undertaker Hagop Balian were obviously skilled at their craft, it was very clearly the Spaniard, Orontes, who was taking the lead. Shunning conversation, which generally proceeded in Turkish but sometimes in French, the Spaniard favoured looking at and touching the body as opposed to talking about what its appearance might mean.

'I am told Señor Orontes is an enthusiastic expert on Dr Pedro Ara's work, familiar with what is known about the mechanics of his technique,' Arto said. 'He comes from Madrid, where Ara himself was originally based, and has studied examples of the great man's work in that city.'

'You mean dead bodies,' Çöktin observed sourly.

'Yes.'

The Yezidi sighed. Even though Dr Sarkissian had explained why and how Christian people were so keen on preserving the dead, he still found the whole thing incomprehensible. Dead things were, well, dead things. One could and did mourn the passing of loved ones, often bitterly, but to try to hang on to them in corporeal actuality was weird. It wasn't hygienic – or natural. Some people, for obviously desperate reasons that were entirely beyond Çöktin, did things with corpses. Dr Sarkissian had even intimated that this Ara person had 'done things' with the corpse of Eva Peron – an idea that made viewing Ara's admirers lurking around the Kuloğlu boy's body a particularly grisly tableau. But then suddenly, and with what Çöktin imagined was a typically Iberian flourish, it was over. Orontes flung open the laboratory door and, without even so much as looking at his colleagues, invited Arto and Çöktin back inside.

'It is my considered opinion,' the Spaniard said without preamble, 'that what you have there is a corpse that has been preserved according to the technique of Dr Pedro Ara.'

'But not by him,' Arto said.

The three other embalmers had now come to huddle respectfully around their leader, hanging on his every sibilant syllable.

'I believe,' Señor Orontes continued haughtily, 'that it is possible this man's corpse was originally treated by Dr Ara. It is a brilliant example of the embalmer's art, quite exceptional.'

'Well, at least I suppose that makes it unlikely that our man was a Turkish citizen,' Arto said with a sigh. 'The body being possibly old enough to have come from elsewhere. But quite what I'm supposed to do with him now . . .'

'First find the balm he was treated with or allow me to apply an emollient to stop any further disintegration. He must be preserved. There are many, many museums and university departments both in Spain and South America who would be delighted to possess such an exhibit,' Orontes said with a smile. 'I could put you in touch—'

'Until we know who he is and who he "belongs" to, if you like, "we" can't do anything,' Arto replied with some vigour. 'In my opinion, he died naturally.'

'And there is still a public health issue,' a grave-faced Çöktin put in.

'Indeed,' Arto concurred. 'Unless he is claimed by a foreign national and transported to that person's country, eventually he will have to be buried.'

Orontes' eyes blazed. 'No!' he cried. 'No, that can't happen!' And with a wide sweep of his arm in the direction of the corpse, he said, 'This is art, Dr Sarkissian!'

'No, it isn't,' Çöktin snapped, 'it's a dead body and it needs to be given a decent burial!'

Orontes said something in Spanish which, at least to Çöktin's ears, sounded particularly venomous. And although the other embalmers didn't understand any more Spanish than Çöktin or Arto Sarkissian, they all nodded their agreement with whatever Señor Orontes had said.

It was clear to Arto that the situation between the

Christian embalmers and the Turkish policeman was about to become critical. In theory, now that they'd done their job, he could just throw the undertakers out into the street. But then there were several very good reasons why that wasn't a bright idea. First, he'd need Orontes' report to back up his own findings and, secondly, people as obsessed by death and the accoutrements of death as the Spaniard did tend to veer in the direction of the very odd. If, as he'd said, Orontes looked upon the Kuloğlu corpse more as a work of art than a dead body, who knew what he might do to try to save it from the black clutches of a deep Turkish grave?

Smiling through a hideous picture that had just flashed into his mind of Orontes in ecstasy over his 'artwork', Arto put his hand on to the Spaniard's shoulder and led both him and his colleagues through into his office.

'But all of these issues are for the future,' he said as he shot a reassuring glance towards Çöktin. 'For now we all just need to digest for a while what has been discovered so unexpectedly in our great city. I have a little brandy and a few cigars we can enjoy. Now, about this balm . . .'

Seeing and appreciating what the doctor was doing, Çöktin smiled as he followed the dark-suited men back into Arto's office. About a year ago, his boss, Inspector Suleyman, had told him that one of the doctor's ancestors had been a physician at the court of the spendthrift and permanently enraged Sultan Abdul Aziz. Very few people around that particular monarch, especially towards the end of his life, had lived to tell the tale. However, that one of this rare group had been a Sarkissian was not surprising given the doctor's talent for diplomacy. As he watched Arto pour out drinks and light cigars for the embalmers, Çöktin wondered at what a diplomat the man was – and what an outsider. Like Çöktin himself, accommodating, getting around things, flattering – playing the part of the loyal servant. How different they both were from the confrontational Suleyman, with his iron-clad opinions and his direct and certain commands. But then he was an aristocrat, an Ottoman, and although Turkey had now been a republic for over seventy-five years, that ruling mindset was still deep inside his bones. It was what made the man go after truly terrifying gangsters with so much confidence and panache. Çöktin had heard that something might be on with regard to Rostov that very night. He hoped that if things became difficult, Suleyman would remember what he'd seen of Arto Sarkissian's diplomacy and attempt to employ his methods.

Reşad Kuran was a small man of about forty-five. Like his sister, Eren Akdeniz, he possessed the deep-set, heavily shadowed eyes of one who is always weary – that or the effects of many years of narcotic abuse.

'This vehicle is very clean, sir,' İkmen said as he peered into the back of the battered blue Renault van.

Reşad Kuran lit a cigarette and looked up into the darkness of the sky. 'I take pride in my work,' he said. 'I take care.'

Tepabaşı was not the sort of district in which one would expect to find a close relative of a celebrity – narrow, washing-draped streets, perpetually dusty in summer and mud-choked in winter. It existed a few short minutes away from the bustle and glitz of İstiklal Caddesi, to the north of the traffic-swamped Tarlabaşi Caddesi, which led down, ultimately, to the Atatürk Bridge, which spanned the upper reaches of the Golden Horn. Now, at the height of summer, this populous and underprivileged district smelled of overripe fruit and cheap tobacco, its crumbling façades resounding to the sounds of babies crying and men shouting at women who had long since given up all of their girlish dreams.

'So who do you work for, Mr Kuran?' Ayşe Farsakoğlu asked. There was, she recalled, a Syrian Orthodox church somewhere in this area, a huge white place with chandeliers and paintings decorated with coloured lights inside. She'd been there once to the wedding of a girl she'd been at school with – a very dark girl; no one had even known she was a Christian until she'd married a man who not only wore a cross around his neck but looked like an ikon of Jesus.

'For anyone who needs goods transported,' Kuran replied with a shrug.

'Including your brother-in-law, Melih?'

'I work for Melih, yes.'

'You went to his house to pick up a work of art last Friday night.'

'Yes, I've told one of your officers this already. I took it over to some place in, er, Yeniköy – I don't remember. Some rich collector.'

'Rather an odd time to be doing a delivery, isn't it?' İkmen said. 'At night?'

Kuran shrugged again.

'So while you were at your sister's house, did you see either your niece or nephew?'

'No, they were in bed.' Kuran's eyes narrowed into a frown. 'You don't think that I had anything to do with their disappearance, do you?'

İkmen smiled. 'I don't know, sir,' he said. 'You tell me.'

Even by the weak light from the streetlamp, İkmen and Farsakoğlu could see that Kuran's face instantly flooded with blood.

'I didn't,' he said as he waved his cigarette high up into the air to emphasise his point. 'Why would I? I'm their uncle! I love them!'

'I'm sure that you do, sir,' İkmen replied as he took his mobile phone out of his jacket pocket, 'but I'm afraid that my job dictates that I take nothing on trust and so I'm going to have to ask you to allow me to subject your vehicle to forensic analysis.'

'What!'

'Look, if you've nothing to hide, you've nothing to fear,' İkmen continued. 'I need to check your vehicle for possible evidence.'

'Those children have never been in my van!'

'Then you've nothing to worry about.' İkmen walked over to Kuran, punching a number into the phone as he went. 'Now are you going to give us permission?'

'But my business . . .'

'I'm sorry.'

'Oh, so I can't refuse, is that what you're saying?'

'No,' İkmen said as he placed the phone up to his ear, 'you can't. But I do always like to ask first. It seems, somehow, just that little bit more pleasant. Oh, and don't leave the city, will you, Mr Kuran, not until we've cleared this matter up?'

As her superior turned away to speak into the mobile, Ayşe Farsakoğlu smiled. How typical of İkmen to be both tough and polite at the same time. So few officers had that knack, and she felt it had to be better than the usual shouting, strong-arm stuff one generally witnessed at such times. Not of course that Reşad Kuran was looking particularly comfortable in spite of İkmen's low-key approach. He just stood rooted to the spot, his eyes roaming nervously over the surface of his van.

The church of St Stephen of the Bulgars was a quietly extraordinary building. Standing just back from the shore of the Golden Horn, between Balat and Fener ferry stages, the church looked traditional enough – a dirty white, Eastern-influenced Gothic, typical of some nineteenth-century ecclesiastical buildings. To those unaware of its history, it appeared to be an ordinary building in every way. It was only when one realised that rather than being constructed from stone, St Stephen's was actually made of cast iron that the uniqueness of the place began to seep into the consciousness. Cast in sections in Vienna where the building was designed, the various parts were individually shipped down the Danube to be finally assembled and erected in İstanbul in 1898.

Ever since that time, St Stephen's had serviced the small Bulgarian community's needs via a succession of Orthodox divines, none of whom had ever attracted the attention of the police. And, in spite of what Suleyman's

informant had told them about the corrupt priest of St
Stephen's and his involvement in the drugs trade, Metin
İskender was not inclined to believe that anything rotten
had invaded the place. According to the sultry Masha, at
11 p.m. that night one of the Fathers would come out of
the church to take delivery of a large quantity of heroin
from an associate or associates of Rostov. It was now
10.45 p.m., and there was not so much as a whisper
from the building beside which İskender and his four very
ordinary 'friends' were sitting. It was, after all, summer,
the park beside the church afforded uninterrupted views
of the Golden Horn and the men were all chatting and
smoking and, occasionally, laughing. Men did such things,
particularly working-class men, which is what this group
appeared to be.

'The fact that there's a light on in there,' the skeletal
head of Constable Güney inclined towards the church,
'would seem to suggest that someone's in.'

'Not necessarily,' İskender said, his throat a little tight
now, partially strangled by rising anxiety. 'Christians
often leave candles burning in their churches for their
dead, I believe.'

'Overnight?'

İskender shrugged. 'They place them in sand usually.
It's perfectly OK.'

'Audi in front of the gates,' a thickset officer called
Constable Avcı slid effortlessly into the conversation.

In line with received practice, only İskender turned to
look at the car that had moved so quietly into the orbit
of their operation. The three-tiered wedding-cake tower
of the church loomed palely over the dark vehicle like an

impassive Russian hit man. For several seconds there was, with the exception of İskender's hammering heartbeat, perfect stillness.

And then without the slightest attempt at subterfuge, the double entrance doors to the church spread wide to reveal a tall, black-robed figure.

'This could be it,' İskender said, his head down as he took a light for his cigarette from his sergeant, Alpaslan Karataş.

The black-robed figure ran down the steps from the church into the surrounding gardens and over to the tall, wrought-iron gates. Someone, the officers couldn't see whether it was male or female, got out of the Audi. As the priest began unlocking the gates of St Stephen's the five police officers started to make their way slowly up towards Demirhisar Caddesi, a route that would take them directly in front of the church. Still chatting in low tones they glanced occasionally at what was happening over by the church until the owner of the car produced a large box from somewhere inside the vehicle. The cleric came forward, smiling, to take possession.

'OK, I think that's enough,' İskender said as he led his men purposefully over to, by virtue of the clothes the pair wore – one a cleric's robes, the other a gangster's leather jacket – the odd-looking scene that was unfolding under the bell tower.

Drawing their weapons as they surrounded the area, İskender's men covered him as he moved to show his identification to the priest and his thick-lipped, bullet-headed friend.

'Police.'

The cleric gasped. 'Police?' His voice, as well as being heavily accented was also tremulous with fear. 'What do you want?'

'Open it.' İskender tipped his head in the direction of the box in the priest's thin, white hands.

'But it's only—'

'Open it!'

Later, İskender wouldn't be able to recall whether he'd actually seen or imagined Rostov's creature smirk as the priest opened the box and released that unmistakable smell into the night. But whether he did or not, it was at this point that all the bad feelings he had about this operation became reality.

As soon as the lid of the box landed on the ground, İskender plunged his hands into the sweet-smelling cones within with a desperate intensity. Dozens of them spilled out on to the pavement, breaking into powdery nothing as they fell.

'What do you want with our incense?' the priest wailed as he looked on horrified at the policeman's seemingly insane antics. 'It's a gift—'

'From Rostov?' İskender looked up sharply.

'Valery Ivanovich is a very pious and kind—'

The priest's flattering homily was cut short by the sudden opening of one of the Audi's rear doors. Four handguns moved to line up what emerged from the vehicle, which was soon revealed to be a most attractive middle-aged woman.

Smiling as she approached an increasingly nervous İskender, she held a small card up for him to see by the light from inside St Stephen's.

'Betül Ertüg, *Radikal*,' she said, smiling as she mouthed the name of her newspaper. 'Now what's all this about the İstanbul police and their harassment of the Christian minorities?'

Inwardly cursing Rostov to hell, İskender breathed in deeply in order to give himself some time to think of a response.

'I believe it takes a certain type of mentality to find any humour in what has happened tonight,' Suleyman said as he looked down into the deeply satisfied face of Valery Ivanovich Rostov.

Although seated himself, Rostov hadn't offered chairs to any of the three officers who were now standing before him in his gaudy, whiskey-perfumed salon. Probably in his early forties, Rostov, though not good-looking was so well groomed and pristine in his appearance that he almost pulled off the illusion of being handsome. Those around him, however, were another matter. There were five other men in the room, besides Rostov, Suleyman and Yıldız, four of whom were young, tall, muscular and, in the opinion of the only female present, Officer Gün, heartbreakingly handsome. The fifth man, seated beside Rostov on a couch that screamed its lack of taste unashamedly to the world, was a lot older than anyone else. Probably about sixty, if a badly preserved example of that age group, this man, Lütfü Güneş, was the source of the alcoholic miasma that currently infected the room. He was also, as Rostov had been very quick to point out as soon as the police arrived, his lawyer.

'I don't find the idea of you guys harassing honest

Christians funny,' Rostov replied as he lazily crossed one dark-suited leg over the other.

'Information received had led us to believe that Father Alexei might be involved in illegal activities.'

'Yes, but he wasn't, was he?' Rostov leaned forward and took a cigarette box from the coffee table in front of him, which he offered to his lawyer. 'You were wrong about him just as you're wrong about me.'

There was no arguing with the first part of Rostov's statement. Father Alexei, of everyone involved in the débâcle İskender had facilitated, had been totally innocent. Rostov, good Orthodox boy that he was, frequently donated incense and candles both to St Stephen's and to St Mary Pammakaristos up in Fener. That such goods were delivered by men who looked like professional killers had never so much as entered the innocent divine's head. Not that Father Alexei had made any trouble for İskender. He'd fully understood that İskender and his officers had to be vigilant with regard to contraband items and had said that he didn't actually feel in the least bit harassed. That word had only been used by Ms Ertüg who, as far as Suleyman knew, was still with İskender and his officers. Only Allah, unfortunately, knew what she and her *Radikal* bosses would eventually decide to put into print.

'Father Alexei is, so my colleague Inspector İskender has informed me, a very pleasant and innocent man,' Suleyman said. 'He is obviously devoted to a simple life of prayer and meditation, far removed,' he looked very pointedly around the expensively awful room, 'from the things of this world.'

'Just because I have things, doesn't mean that I'm not a good guy,' Rostov said.

'That depends how you came about such things, doesn't it, Mr Rostov?'

The lawyer, Güneş, who had up until that time simply looked with sagging, red-rimmed eyes at the officers, spoke. 'But all of this is beside the point,' he said through the smoke from one of Rostov's green cocktail cigarettes. 'That you're here at this property now is something I need explained to me.'

'We're here, sir,' Suleyman said, 'to act on information received—'

'From the same source as that about the priest?'

'I'm not at liberty to discuss—'

'Two Christians – three, including Mr Rostov's associate – two infringements of personal privacy, in one night? There are no issues of national security at stake here, Inspector. And if that is so, as you must know, a private citizen has a right to his or her privacy.' Güneş shrugged. 'It doesn't look good, Inspector Suleyman. It looks like harassment. It could even be racial, especially given that you are a member, are you not, of the House of Osman?'

'My past—'

'Your ancestors, Muslim monarchs, ruled this country for over five hundred years, did they not?' Güneş turned to Rostov. 'There are still royalists about, you know, Valery,' he said. 'You see them hanging around the Royal Tombs on Yeniçeriler Caddesi, worrying about whether the Russians and other Orthodox have designs on Aya Sofya. It's pathetic.'

Rostov turned back to face Suleyman and laughed. In response to the unusual amount of sweat that was pouring down the side of Suleyman's face, both Gün and Yıldız moved a little closer to their superior.

'You – gentlemen – and your friends know a lot about me, don't you?' Suleyman said, the raised cords in his neck only hinting at the fury that was building inside him. Rostov raised his eyebrows just a fraction and smiled. If and when Suleyman eventually found the person or persons inside the department who had been so free with information about him, a crime scene would quickly follow.

Suleyman took his mobile telephone out of his jacket pocket and held it up for Rostov and the others to see.

'In a minute,' he said, 'I'm going to ask Inspector İskender to release a couple of his men to join me here.'

Well, it was the only way Suleyman, Gün and Yıldız were going to get assistance this night. Asking Ardiç for more men, whether or not he knew what was currently happening over at St Stephen's, was pointless. The only way forward with what was going to be a big job – Rostov did, after all, have an enormous house – was to involve İskender yet again.

'I do hope this doesn't mean that you're planning to continue your imposition upon Mr Rostov,' Güneş said with ill-concealed menace.

'Oh, I'm afraid that it does,' Suleyman replied as he indicated to his officers that they should sit down. 'It means that we're going to be here for quite some time.' He looked behind him, identified a seat and sat down.

'But on what grounds . . . ?'

'We have received intelligence,' Suleyman said as he keyed İskender's number into his phone, 'that has led us to believe that this house may contain illegal substances, Mr Güneş. The law, as you know, empowers me to search for and if necessary remove those substances.'

As he put the phone up to his ear, he watched Rostov's face drop into a scowl. Güneş, meanwhile, laughed.

'Well, you're going to be very disappointed then!' he said. 'There are no "substances", to use your word, in this house.'

Suleyman, given the décor and the men in front of him, would have begged to differ on that point. If this place hadn't been built on drug money, he would be surprised to say the least. Long since convinced that a search for Vladimir, lover of Masha, was a thing of pure imagination, narcotics and, maybe if he were very fortunate, weapons too were now his target. He'd get Rostov for every knife his men had strapped to their ankles, every tiny trace of cocaine on his carpets, if necessary. He'd come this far, he wasn't going back now, whatever it might cost him.

# CHAPTER 9

Some men like to share certain details about their romantic successes with others. Unlike women, they rarely, only when they are very young, joke about such things. But they will talk anyway in a stilted, limited kind of way. Other men, however, are completely closed books when it comes to love and sex. İsak Çöktin was a case in point. As yet unmarried, he knew that it was only a question of time before that changed. At some point his parents would travel back to the tiny cluster of villages they came from and then return with a girl, probably illiterate, certainly a nervous virgin, who would become his wife. A nice Yezidi girl whom he would care for and have children with in order to perpetuate his ancient culture and religion. He may even come to be quite fond of her – in time. One thing that was certain, however, was that he would never love her in the way that he loved Döne, his secret and passionate Turkish lover. Even looking at her across the cat-infested kitchen, cooking him a breakfast of eggs with bread, made him smile. Döne's usually sad dark eyes lightened when they connected with his.

'There's a newspaper on the chair,' she said, tipping

143

her head towards the seat beside him, which was currently occupied by a large white cat. 'It's underneath Osman Paşa.'

The cat didn't want to move, but after a little gentle goading he was persuaded to do so. Çöktin took the paper and placed it on the table in front of him. He liked a paper in the mornings, a paper and breakfast to start the day, quietly and slowly. Döne, for all her independent, liberated-woman stance, always did these things for him whenever he came to visit her at her little ground-floor apartment in Balat. One of the relatively new influx of artistic types who had come to the district in the past few years, Döne, who was a writer, lived the kind of life that, had she not been so discreet by nature, would have scandalised the majority of her neighbours who were still, for the most part, conservative. However, with İkmen working up at the Akdeniz house less than a minute from Döne's place, Çöktin had taken a considerable risk in spending the night with her at this time. Not of course that İkmen, if he found out, would actually say anything about it to him. It was the others he was nervous about – Roditi, Avcı, Güney – bluff types who would drive him crazy with their prurient questions if they knew he had a girlfriend.

Çöktin opened the paper at the arts pages. There was going to be a general election in October and, although he knew he should give the very serious issues around this event the attention they deserved, he was almost as bored and exhausted by this topic as he was by the endless accounts of celebrity marriages, affairs, divorces, et cetera. So he looked at the pretty pictures on the arts pages – until, that is, one name leaped out at him from the text.

'Yeşim Keyder,' he muttered under his breath, '*Dr Yeşim Keyder.*'

Döne, a plate of eggs in one hand and a loaf in the other, came over and placed the food down in front of him. As she did so, she first kissed the top of his head and then looked at the paper spread out in front of him.

'Oh,' she said, 'Yapi Kredi are having a retrospective of Melih Akdeniz's early work. That's interesting – given his current situation.'

Çöktin looked up.

'With his children having gone missing,' Döne elaborated. 'Quite unfortunate that the bank should choose to exhibit him, what with all the stuff in the papers. But then maybe it was planned a long time ago.'

'Maybe.'

Çöktin looked back at the photograph of a Melih Akdeniz work – a furious swirling of blues and reds – entitled *Love*, and read once again the card beneath it, which said it had been 'Kindly loaned by Dr Yeşim Keyder'.

'Just try and eat something,' Fatma said as she placed a plateful of bread, cheese and honey in front of the jaundiced man at the head of the table.

Talaat Erteğrül smiled by way of reply.

Fatma, a little sad-eyed, smiled too as she walked out of the kitchen, leaving the two men at the table to their breakfasts.

İkmen, for whom breakfast was always four cigarettes

and a cup of coffee, pushed his plate to one side as soon as his wife had gone.

'I know I shouldn't encourage you,' he said as he offered his packet and lighter to his brother-in-law, 'but . . .'

'But the dying should have everything they want,' Talaat finished as he helped himself to a cigarette and lit up.

'I didn't—'

'No, I did.' Talaat smiled at his usually strident brother-in-law's obvious discomfort. 'I don't mind talking about death, my death. It's going to happen, Çetin, and when it does that will be that. And so if I don't smoke, laugh, drink and think wicked thoughts now, I'll lose the opportunity.'

'Strange the way religious belief seems to be limited to the women in your family,' İkmen said as he lit his cigarette and leaned back in his chair.

Talaat laughed. 'Yes, Ali, Father and I were always in awe of the way mother and the girls believed in all of that perfumed garden after-life stuff. Mother was convinced that it was going to be sherbet, lokum and chocolate all the way for good Muslims. She always saw everything in terms of food – even death.' He frowned. 'But I just couldn't see it. Still can't.'

'You believe that death is the end.'

'Yes.' He looked up into İkmen's smoke-wreathed face. 'I know that you have other ideas, Çetin, things you got from your mother . . .'

'The witch.' İkmen laughed, a thick bronchitic sound. 'You know, Talaat, I sometimes think that my mother taught me too much.'

'What do you mean?'

What İkmen actually meant involved things that he couldn't say, not to his brother-in-law, not to anyone. Yaşar and Nuray Akdeniz were caught up in a horror beyond understanding. What form this torment might take and who might be doing it to them, he didn't know. But just as one look into Talaat's yellow-tinged eyes told him that this brother-in-law would be dead by the end of the week, so that brief glimpse into Gonca the gypsy's heart had revealed the truth about the Akdeniz twins. There had to be a connection, between Gonca and the children or their father – probably the latter. Gonca had had sex with Melih – of course she had – Gonca would and did have sex with many men. Her blood had mixed with his and his with hers . . .

'You know it's at times like this I can all too easily understand how you confuse my sister.'

İkmen, only just roused from his musings, said, 'What?'

'You with all your background in the occult,' Talaat said. 'Your oblique references to things that others, people like Fatma and me, couldn't understand. Just now you said that your mother taught you too much.'

'She did.' İkmen put his cigarette out and then immediately lit another.

'Yes, but what?'

'It's not important.' İkmen looked down at the floor, smoking in a concentrated fashion.

'Ah, but it is, though, isn't it?' Talaat replied. 'In fact, it's so important, so frightening even, that you have to lock us out, keep it to yourself.'

İkmen looked up and regarded his brother-in-law sharply.

Now lined with pain, humbled and shaded with death, Talaat Erteğrül, one time beach bum and lothario, had finally arrived somewhere close to understanding.

'You know I used to wonder why you chose to specialise in murder,' Talaat said as he too put his cigarette out and then, like İkmen, immediately lit another.

İkmen frowned.

Talaat moved his chair closer to İkmen so that he could easily whisper in his ear. 'I know you have experience of what it is to die, what men go through,' he said, 'and I know that sometimes you know when it is coming, as it is for me.'

'Talaat . . .'

'Just don't tell my sister when it's her turn – that's all I ask.'

İkmen turned away, just as he always did when he got the feeling that he might see death or pain in someone that he loved.

'And don't tell her that the perfumed garden for the good Muslims doesn't exist.'

'What makes you so sure that it doesn't?' İkmen said, and then in response to a ring on the doorbell he got up and left the kitchen.

Mehmet Suleyman rubbed a hand across his tired, greying features and sighed.

'So nothing,' he said to the small equally weary group of officers standing in front of him, 'you've found nothing. Not even in the trunk they brought from the airport?'

'No, sir,' Hikmet Yıldız replied.

'You've been everywhere? Searched everyone?'

'Almost. There's two enormous kitchens in the basement.'

'Then get down there,' Suleyman said as he looked out of the window at Rostov's garden, a lush oasis now flooded with sunlight. It had been a long, hot and frustrating night.

As the officers left the salon, Rostov and his lawyer, Lütfü Güneş, returned. Although the two men hadn't actually followed the police around as they searched they had remained awake and, in Rostov's case at least, obviously attentive to what was happening.

'I thought they'd finished,' the Russian said as he tipped his head towards the retreating officers.

'We still haven't searched your kitchens, Mr Rostov,' Suleyman said.

'And what do you hope to find there?' Güneş smirked. 'A small amphetamine production plant—'

'There's nothing but food in my kitchens,' Rostov cut in. 'I don't want it spoiled.'

'I can understand that. Why don't I just go and make sure that my people don't damage anything,' Suleyman said with a smile. 'Would that put your mind at rest?'

'I'll come with you,' Rostov snapped.

'There's no need . . .'

'It's my house!'

'I'd let them get on with it if I were you Valery,' Güneş said as he relaxed back on to one of the tasteless sofas. 'You and I both know that there's nothing . . .'

'Mind your own business, Lütfü,' Rostov said as he fixed his eyes on Suleyman's. 'I wish to go with the inspector.'

149

'Then so you shall,' Suleyman, still smiling, replied. And then as he extended one arm towards the salon door, he said, 'Shall we?'

Valery Rostov, his eyes mobile with what could have been fear, moved slowly forward.

Nurettin Eldem knew that, from a professional point of view, it wasn't a good thing to have either favourite or hated clients. Although it was difficult not to like a pleasant person more than a miserable one, as a lawyer he had to try at least to remain impartial. There were, however, exceptions. The thin, grey woman sitting in front of him now was a very good example. Rich as well as charmless, Dr Yeşim Keyder was, Nurettin thought silently to himself, a grasping old hag.

He put on one of his grave, concerned smiles and said, 'Unfortunately you won't be able to gain access to the apartment until the police have finished their investigations.' He shrugged. 'I know it's inconvenient—'

'It's incomprehensible,' the woman replied hotly. 'Both Rosita and this other character they apparently discovered with her died of natural causes. I can't see why they're still involved.'

'They do have to check with the Argentine authorities,' Nurettin said, 'and if the identity of this other body is in question—'

'Rosita's family are dead,' Yeşim Keyder said tightly, and then added under her breath, 'thanks be to God. And as for this other body, well, as I said to that officer, Çöktin, that has nothing to do with me or my family.'

Although Nurettin had always known that the Keyder

150

family were not religious people, he was still a little taken aback by her use of 'God' instead of 'Allah'. Maybe it stemmed from being around Rosita for so many years. And, of course, she had spent some time in Argentina with Veli when he met Rosita all those many years ago.

'Yes, but then whatever we may think, Dr Keyder, there is nothing we can do until the police have finished. I've tried to impress upon them the importance of not damaging what will be your property.'

'Yes, but they will, won't they?' she retorted. 'It's what they do, stamping around in their great, oppressive boots, stealing things they take a fancy to.' She looked up into Nurettin's fat, jowled features. 'I do know what goes on, Mr Eldem. I am under no illusions about the trustworthiness of our legal institutions.'

'Dr Keyder!'

'And don't think that just because your father was my lawyer before you, I trust every utterance that issues from your mouth,' she continued coldly. 'I know that a few words in the right ear can utterly transform situations like this. I'm rich . . .'

'Yes, Dr Keyder,' Nurettin, stung, cleared his throat, 'which is why I can't quite understand why you are so anxious to take possession of the Kuloğlu apartment. Although I don't suppose it will be long now, Mrs Keyder's body hasn't even been released to you as yet.'

'I told the officer Çöktin that as soon as it's ready, the priest Vetra can take care of it,' she said with a dismissive wave of her hand, 'and if I am, as you say, Mr Eldem, "anxious to take possession" of the Kuloğlu apartment, then that is my business. In addition, I believe that my brother and his wife gave you some documents for safekeeping.'

'Yes, but—'

'You and I both know, Mr Eldem, that the Kuloğlu apartment belonged solely to my brother Veli. As his only living relative, that, together with all contents not personally belonging to Rosita, now automatically reverts to me.' She fixed the lawyer with a hard-eyed stare. 'This, according to my understanding, also includes Veli's and Rosita's joint documents.'

'I would have to—'

'Which I would like to see now, please,' Dr Keyder said coldly.

Many years ago, just shortly after Nurettin had taken over the practice from his father, Dr Veli Keyder and his attractive Argentinian wife had given him a selection of sealed envelopes for safekeeping. Young and rather awed by the academic status enjoyed by Veli Keyder, Nurettin hadn't even thought to ask him what these documents were. The unpleasant Dr Yeşim might know, however, and if the gravity of her already severe features was anything to go by, they were really rather important. Nurettin just briefly played with the idea of getting to them before the woman who was, it was true, their rightful owner.

'If you'd like to make an appointment, Dr Keyder,' he said, 'I can arrange for the safe to be opened . . .'

'I'd like my property now, please, Mr Eldem,' the woman replied coldly.

'Yes . . .'

Dr Yeşim, despite her age and the intense midday heat,

stood up quickly. 'Take me to the safe, and let's get this part of your duty to me, for which I pay you handsomely, over with.'

Deep in the basement, and insufficiently ventilated, Valery Rostov's kitchens were very unpleasant places to be at the height of summer. Even the sartorially immaculate Inspector Suleyman had removed his jacket in order to supervise the hot and uncomfortable search.

However, Rostov's freezer cabinets were another matter. Suleyman had chosen Yıldız and Gün to search those. There were two, what were in reality, small rooms, full of sheep carcasses, fish, chicken and large quantities of dairy products, all covered with thin layers of plastic wrapping. The inspector had told them that every item had to be looked at and, if necessary, unwrapped. In contrast to the rest of the team, Yıldız and Gün were both blue with cold. Unwrapping, wrapping up again, searching through the innumerable layers of polythene for the small bag containing cocaine, the oilcloth-shrouded pistol . . . And then there was Rostov. Shaking with cold, he'd stood there in the doorway, his lips a grim shade of purple, watching Yıldız's every move.

As he peered through several layers of plastic at three plucked chicken carcasses, Yıldız tried to decide whether Suleyman was punishing Gün and himself by putting them in the freezers, or whether, on this very hot day, it was an act of kindness. Either way, Yıldız's initial sense of gratitude towards his boss was beginning to pall. Sergeant Çöktin, with whom Yıldız was developing a very friendly relationship, worshipped the ground Suleyman walked on. Quite why, the young constable didn't entirely understand. Suleyman, though generally fair, wasn't the easiest man to be around. Unlike İkmen he never joined the lower ranks for the occasional drink and, these days at least, his face rarely moved out of its tense, scowling expression.

Yıldız put the chickens down and began to tackle what looked like a side of mutton. Wrapped in plastic bags as opposed to polythene, this object was going to take him some time to get into. He slipped one hand underneath and dragged, he couldn't possibly lift, the object to the side of the shelf on which it rested.

'Put it down.'

Yıldız, surprised by the sound of a voice, especially the glowering Rostov's, looked up.

'Inspector Suleyman has given instructions that every item—'

'Put it down!'

'Sir—'

'Touch it again and I'll fucking kill you!' the Russian shrieked.

Yıldız placed his one free hand over his gun holster. The Russian's pale eyes, motionless through the swirling vapour from the ice, reminded Yıldız of the still glass eyes of the strange dead boy of Kuloğlu. The memory of that image made his throat tighten and he had to swallow hard in order to be able to speak again.

'Inspector Suleyman,' he called. 'Sir . . .'

'I've told you—' Rostov began as he moved towards Yıldız.

'Inspector!'

Yıldız removed his gun from its holster just as Suleyman entered the cupboard.

The senior officer could see instantly that something was very wrong.

'What's going on here?' he said as he too removed his weapon from its holster. 'Yıldız?'

'Mr Rostov doesn't want me to unwrap this piece of meat,' Yıldız said as he attempted to tear his gaze away from Rostov's snarling features.

'I told you I wanted to see everything, didn't I, Rostov?' Suleyman said and then, looking again at Yıldız and the very large piece of meat on the shelf in front of him, he continued, 'Open it.'

Rostov's head whipped round violently so that now his eyes blazed at Suleyman. 'No!'

'That's an order, Constable,' Suleyman reiterated quietly.

Yıldız replaced his gun in its holster and then slipped his fingers underneath one of the outer plastic bags.

The sound that came from Rostov as he launched himself at Yıldız was more animal than human. Fingers bent, he clawed at the young officer's face with such ferocity that even when Suleyman, who had been quickly joined by Avcı and Karataş, did eventually manage to pull him off, the damage was already done. Leaving the other two to restrain the still screaming Rostov on the floor, Suleyman went over to Yıldız and took his chin in his hands.

'Constable Gün!' he called as he surveyed the tattered side of the young man's face.

'I thought he was going to rip my eye out!' Yıldız said as the shock of the incident set in and he began to tremble uncontrollably. 'I thought—'

'Sssh!' Suleyman, who was accustomed to the effects of shock, put his arms around the young man until Gün arrived to attend to him.

'Call an ambulance,' he said as he placed Yıldız into her care. 'Go with him.'

'Yes, sir.'

When they had gone he turned to look at Rostov, who was still being held down on to the freezing floor by the other two officers.

'So what's in the package, Mr Rostov?' he said with what the others knew was frightening calmness. 'I'm going to look anyway so you might as well tell me.'

'If you take her out of here, I'll kill you!' the Russian screamed.

Both Avcı and Karataş looked up at Suleyman with questions in their eyes.

'Her?'

'Some woman's body, must be,' Karataş said as he turned back to look into the pale face of the Russian. 'Some tart he did away with.'

'No!'

And then suddenly all the rage seemed to drain out of him and Rostov began to cry. Suleyman, still not trusting, but nevertheless affected by this development, squatted down on the floor beside the Russian.

'So what . . . ?' he began.

'It's my daughter!' Rostov shouted through his tears. 'My daughter is wrapped in those bags!'

# CHAPTER 10

Ayşe Farsakoğlu replaced the telephone receiver on its cradle and looked across at İkmen.

'Reşad Kuran isn't answering his phone,' she said wearily.

'Have you tried his mobile?' her superior asked.

'That is his phone, sir,' Ayşe replied. 'He's only got a mobile.'

İkmen looked up. 'One of us should go round,' he said. 'He can't have gone far without his van.'

Ayşe lit up a cigarette. 'He could have got on a bus.'

'Yes.' Of course he could. People did it all the time, traversing the vast tracts of Anatolia on cheap and, more importantly in this case, plentiful public transport.

'Am I right in thinking that you've got a bad feeling about this, sir?' Ayşe said as she attempted to catch the dark, hooded eyes of her superior.

İkmen lit a cigarette of his own, inhaled deeply and then sighed. 'There's something, I don't know what, not right about that family, including Kuran,' he said.

'You mean like the way Melih Akdeniz just carries on with his work?'

İkmen waved a dismissive hand. 'No, no. He's an artist, it's what he does. It's odd to us, but art is, if I'm not much

157

mistaken, an obsessive vocation for those who are involved in it. No, it's . . .' He looked up at the ceiling as if searching for the right words on its cracked, nicotine-stained surface. 'I didn't like the way Melih walked across that glass without feeling anything. He always carries that bottle around with him. Medication, I assume, but what for? We know he used to be a junkie. And there's his wife . . .'

'What do you mean?'

'She's obviously distraught,' İkmen said, 'but what I don't get is how she can carry on assisting Melih under these circumstances. She was once, I believe, his student, but she's got no career of her own now. What's her motivation? Is Melih, his work, or both more significant to her than her own children?'

Ayşe shrugged. 'Some women do love their husbands more than their children. It's not that uncommon.'

İkmen smiled weakly. 'I suppose not.'

'Some men actually expect their women to be more attached to them than to their children.'

'True.' He wanted to ask her whether she was speaking from experience, but then decided against it. At thirty Ayşe was both beautiful and single. She'd had affairs – most significantly with her own predecessor, İkmen's former sergeant, the now deceased Orhan Tepe – which had been at times somewhat complicated. Men had, İkmen knew, used Ayşe badly and although she didn't have any children of her own, he could imagine men from her past asking her to sacrifice things that were meaningful to her for them. How lucky he and his wife were by comparison. Without doubt still completely in love, Çetin and Fatma İkmen nevertheless had identical views when it came to their children – they were absolutely paramount. Even that troublesome Hulya and her Jewish boyfriend . . .

'And if you're worried about what might be in Melih's bottle,' Ayşe cut into his thoughts, 'then why not ask him?'

'Oh, I'm not exactly worried about it,' İkmen said, frowning over his heavily burning cigarette. 'I'm not bothered if Melih's moved on to some oral opiate or whatever it is. No, it's not what it might mean that bothers me.'

'I'm not with . . .'

'To artists like Akdeniz everything they do, say and think has added meaning,' İkmen said as he rose from his chair and began slowly to pace the room. 'Everything is a statement. He's always got that bottle, he's seen me watch as he drinks from it. He could assuage my curiosity with one sentence. But he doesn't because he's an artist; it's part of the performance that is his life. And as for all that pompous stuff about Karagöz . . .'

'Karagöz?' Ayşe laughed. 'It's satire.'

'For the masses, yes. A bit of state-sanctioned and harmless social comment,' İkmen said. 'I know why Melih's mentioned it.'

'Why?'

'Because he's planning to perform a Karagöz shadow play himself,' he said. 'That's why he's stretched that material across his garden. He's going to light it from behind and use those things he's sewing as props. Very innovative,' he added sourly.

Ayşe shrugged. 'Should be fun.'

'Or not,' İkmen responded gloomily. 'I can't stand Karagöz myself. It gives me the creeps.'

Perhaps, Ayşe thought, it was because of what the puppet show was associated with. Karagöz has always traditionally been performed during the Holy Month of Ramadan, when adult Muslims fast between sunrise and sunset. It is also sometimes performed as part of the celebrations following sünnet, the male circumcision ceremony.

İkmen's reasons, however, were nothing to do with either of those events.

'You know that the two central characters in the plays, Karagöz the peasant and Hacıvat the Ottoman were once real people,' he said. 'They worked as artisans at the Great Mosque in Bursa during the reign of Sultan Orhan.'

Ayşe shrugged. 'If you say so.'

'And because the two men joked and gossiped so much it irritated the Sultan and so he had them executed. Later when the guilt started to roll in, one of Orhan's more obsequious subjects designed the now familiar Karagöz screen and puppets so that, in a way, the executed men could live again. The Sultan was delighted.' He sat down again and sighed. 'So what people have laughed at for centuries was born out of state-sanctioned murder. And, well, I always think that's maybe why we're only ever allowed to see the characters in shadow.'

'Why's that?'

'Because in the shadow you can't see the reality, the blood, the sag of the skin as the life retreats from it. It relegates reality to an illusion. Everyone's dead but they're still moving and criticising the status quo so that's OK.

160

It's comfortable and cruel at the same time. By presenting the shadow play as a 'statement', Akdeniz is only inviting his audience to a funeral of dead, toothless ideas. After all, who takes dead men, djinn, gypsies and all the other Karagöz regulars seriously?'

It was strange that İkmen, who had worked with death almost all of his adult life should suddenly sink into such deep and reflective melancholy. But then it was said that his brother-in-law was dying, which had to have an effect upon him. And also he was no longer young. Perhaps he was feeling the weight of years piling up on him, as his children grew, as his wife's hair turned from black to white as, perhaps, he felt his own powers of deduction shake beneath the weight of responsibility of looking for missing children – such a heavy load. Ayşe impulsively cut across rank and status and put her hand out to him. İkmen took it between his fingers with a small smile.

'What do you mean, she's your daughter?'

Suleyman, his officers and Rostov were now in the main body of the kitchen, away for the moment from the strange and contentious package in the freezer.

The Russian drew on his cigarette before replying. 'I mean that what is left of my daughter, her body, is contained within those plastic bags,' he said.

'But I thought . . .'

'That I was gay?' Rostov smiled, not only at Suleyman but also at the two astounded officers who stood on either side of his chair. 'I do like young men, yes. But it wasn't always so. When Tatiana was born things were very different. I lived and worked in Moscow; I had a wife.'

Suleyman glanced briefly back at the freezer before asking, 'So when was, er, Tatiana born?'

'Nineteen ninety-two.'

'And her death . . . ?'

'She died in nineteen ninety-nine.' The Russian's face visibly sagged at the memory of it. 'Leukaemia – and what is laughably called the Russian health service.'

'So why's she in your freezer?' Karataş, not a man known for his empathy, asked. 'Why haven't you buried her, like a decent person?'

Rostov, who until this moment had appeared to be mollified, reddened to the ears.

'Have you ever lost someone,' he hissed, 'someone whose face you can't bear to see disappear into a muck-filled hole?'

Nobody answered. Somehow, although Suleyman could barely now remember the sequence of events involved, they had got from Masha and her tales of lost Russian boys and tantalising amounts of heroin, through gifts of incense to old priests, to this – a dead child, cold as the reputation of her mobster father's heart.

'The law demands that the dead must be buried,' Suleyman began.

'Your laws, yes,' Rostov replied, 'but I am not Turkish.'

'I'm sure that Russian law—'

'She stays where she is!'

'But what for?'

All of them turned to face the source of the question, the large figure of Constable Avcı.

162

'It's not like you can look at her, all through those plastic bags and ice is it?' he said. Not known for his intelligence Avcı nevertheless, on this subject, had a point.

Suleyman turned back to look down into the pale face of Valery Rostov.

'Well, Mr Rostov?' he said. 'Can you give me any good reason why I should flout the laws of my own country and allow your daughter's body to remain in this house?'

Rostov looked briefly at the two junior officers before returning his now concentrated gaze to Suleyman's face. He was obviously considering something, a course of action designed perhaps to mollify these hostile foreign policemen in some way.

After a few moments, during which Suleyman successfully held his gaze, Rostov said, 'I'd like to speak to you alone, Inspector.'

Suleyman considered the request for a few moments before saying, 'All right. I'll give you five minutes.'

'Sir!'

'It's OK, Avcı,' Suleyman said. 'I—'

'I won't do anything!' Rostov snapped. 'Not with you lot crawling all over my property!'

Suleyman told Avcı and Karataş to leave and then seated himself down opposite the Russian.

'So, Mr Rostov . . .'

'I can make you rich beyond your wildest—'

'I think this conversation just came to an end,' Suleyman said as he rose smartly from his chair.

'What about the bad press you're going to get from last night's event up at St Stephen's?' Rostov said as he watched Suleyman move towards the door.

Suleyman stopped. According to İskender the woman from *Radikal* was proving problematic, to say the least. And besides, if Rostov did actually admit that Betül Ertüg had been accompanying his man not, as he had originally said, to observe an act of Russian generosity but to set up the police, then who knew what else he would admit to? Masha's involvement in all this perhaps? The name of the person inside the department who had told Rostov so much about Suleyman's personal life? Obviously that poor little body in the freezer was Rostov's weakness. He hadn't wanted anyone to find it; he'd already fought to protect it once. For him as well as the police, things had not gone to plan.

Suleyman came back and sat down once again. 'So you sent Betül Ertüg—'

'No I didn't,' Rostov replied, averting his eyes as he spoke. 'She was invited along to observe what my organisation is doing for the Orthodox community. She just happened to be there when you—'

'Nonsense!'

'Well, whatever the truth of it, I do have, shall we say, some influence with Miss Ertüg.'

'You mean she's a junkie.'

Rostov held both hands aloft. 'I didn't say that!'

'You didn't have to.'

'Did you find any drugs in my house?' Rostov shrugged. 'No! I don't deal drugs, I'm an antiques dealer.'

'That's not what I've been led to believe.'

'Then you've been misled.'

'What about Masha?'

The Russian took in a deep breath and then let it out slowly through his nose.

'You know,' Suleyman said as he leaned forward in order to get closer to his quarry, 'the whore you sent to set me up? The woman who told lies about Father Alexei, who knew I'd find only a paragon of virtue here in this house.'

'I don't know what you're talking about,' Rostov replied. 'I'm gay, I don't know whores,' and then, suddenly looking Suleyman straight and coldly in the eyes, he said, 'I don't know anyone of that name, Inspector. No one of that name exists.'

All the hairs on the back of Suleyman's neck stood on end. He'd got rid of her! But, of course, if she didn't exist, tracing the leak at the department back to Rostov was going to be next to impossible. Suleyman wanted to scream but he managed somehow to prevent himself from doing so. However, his throat was dry and so he had to swallow hard to lubricate it. Rostov saw this and, Suleyman fancied, he smiled just faintly.

'So if I were to contact Miss Ertüg . . .' Rostov began.

'If you—'

'Provided you agree to leave Tatiana where she is I can do that,' the Russian said as he took a mobile phone out of his pocket.

Suleyman looked first at the instrument and then at Rostov.

'I'll need to think about that,' he said.

'Well don't think for too long.'

'No.' Suleyman took his cigarettes out of his pocket and, with a shaking hand, he lit up. 'No, but while

I am thinking, why don't you tell me about your daughter?'

Rostov's face darkened with suspicion. 'What do you mean?'

'I can't believe you just simply intend to keep her here for the rest of your life. I mean, I've heard of this cryogenic process—'

Rostov laughed, mirthlessly. 'Which is the biggest con going! Bringing people back to life at some time in the future – my ex-wife believed in it which is why my daughter is in the state she's in now. I paid those people millions of roubles,' he said. 'No, Tatiana is only to be embalmed, Inspector.'

Suleyman frowned. 'Yes, but surely you could have had her embalmed in Russia? Years ago, I imagine.'

'Not so she'd look like she was when she was alive,' Rostov replied on a sigh. 'That's only possible here. That's why I finally persuaded my ex-wife to send her to me. The most skilled embalmer in the world lives in İstanbul,' he said, his eyes now lighting up as he enthused. 'Bodies that look as if they're about to move; sitting up in chairs, books in their hands! I've seen things that would take your breath away.'

Suleyman frowned. 'But why?'

Rostov smiled. 'Because they are beautiful. This is art, Inspector. Your loved ones, eternally with you as works of art!' His eyes shone. 'People pay millions of dollars for this. People come here from all over, especially from back home. There is even a trade in these works of art, people collect . . .'

'So you have consulted this embalmer?'

'Not directly, no,' Rostov said. 'I'm still negotiating, through a third party – one of my countrymen has put me in touch with someone associated with this practitioner. The embalmer is always busy, everybody wants the embalmer's work.'

The strange image of an assortment of Russian gangsters sitting contentedly at home with their lifelike but very dead relatives passed briefly across Suleyman's horrified brain. He knew about what he considered to be the essentially Christian practice of preserving the dead as much as was possible – Zelfa had told him some very odd stories. However, for such things, admittedly with Christians involved, to be happening in a predominantly Muslim city seemed very out of place – if not unprecedented. He now remembered, vaguely, about Çöktin and the strange little investigation he had become involved with while Suleyman ran around after Rostov. Not a victim of crime, Çöktin's apparently preserved body of a man was, Suleyman had heard, the subject of an investigation into his 'ownership'. After that, of course, 'he' would have to be buried for reasons of hygiene and public safety – as would Tatiana. But then perhaps it might not be wise to bring that subject up with Rostov yet, not until he had managed to get some more information from him.

'All right,' he said as he slowly nodded his head in agreement. 'Make your call to Betül Ertüg and Tatiana can stay where she is for the time being.'

Rostov reached across to pick up his phone. Suleyman put his hand across the gangster's and looked him gravely in the face.

'However,' he said, 'if you want me to help you protect her in the future, you're going to have to help me now.'

He was lying, of course: Tatiana would have to be buried in the end whether Rostov liked it or not. But it was obvious from the Russian's face that he either had no knowledge of this or didn't want to allow himself to think about it.

'I want you to talk me through your supply routes, Mr Rostov,' he said now with a smile on his face. 'We know that most of the local heroin originates from Afghanistan . . .'

'You've found no drugs! I don't—'

'Oh, please, do not insult my intelligence any more!' Suleyman snapped. 'Think of Tatiana. Think about what might be more important to you.' He leaned back in his chair, suddenly and horribly enjoying the sight of Rostov's seemingly painful confusion. 'Oh, and while I'm here, you might as well tell me the name of your contact to the embalmer also,' he said. 'A friend of mine needs some help in that direction.'

Döne said that some people in the district reckoned that Melih Akdeniz's house was haunted. It had something to do with, Çöktin recalled, the original occupant, Akdeniz's ancestor, who it was said had died mourning the loss of his Spanish homeland. Çöktin hadn't intended to come this way but he was here now and so because he was a little curious about the home of the famous Melih Akdeniz, he did allow himself to peer around the open metal gates at the back of the building. He'd imagined a rather pleasant garden of some sort, perhaps like Döne's, which had a small fountain in the centre. And it could have been that the artist's garden did indeed possess such features – it was just difficult to tell with an enormous swathe of white material stretched across almost the entire space.

Çöktin sighed. In spite of everything Döne had ever told him about modern art, it still left him cold. That a pile of bricks, some weird blob made of clay and spit or, in this case, seemingly, a blank sheet, could constitute a 'statement' about the world or religion or whatever was beyond him. Smiling at what he considered to be the absurdity of the 'exhibit' he was about to walk away when the sheet rippled to reveal what looked like a figure behind it. Someone, perhaps even Akdeniz himself, was doing something . . .

Çöktin moved forward on to the little path that led into the garden and looked more closely. Now he could see that there were actually two figures – elbows jutting through cloth, heads moving, first one way and then the other as if searching for contact. Up in what little he could see of the house he spotted the profile of a thin, anxious-looking woman, a telephone up to her ear, looking, frowning down at the same scene that Çöktin was experiencing – or rather the other side of it. From behind the screen came the familiar grunts and gasps of passion. The woman on the telephone visibly flinched and Çöktin wondered whether Akdeniz or whoever was behind the screen with what, from the sound of its voice, had to be a female, knew that she was there. Watching.

Suddenly aware of and uncomfortable with his own presence at this scene, Çöktin left.

As he made his way down the steps that ran from the top of Balat to the Demirhisar Caddesi below, his mobile phone began to ring. He took it out of his pocket and placed it against his ear.

'Hello?'

'Hello, İsak?' The familiar voice of his boss, Inspector Suleyman asked.

'Sir.'

'İsak, are you still involved with that, er, preserved body situation?'

'Yes, although we do know there's no criminal—'

'He was embalmed, wasn't he, the man you found in Kuloğlu? Expertly so I've heard.'

Instinctively, Çöktin looked across the Golden Horn towards the new, 'European' city, to Kuloğlu. 'Yes, Dr Sarkissian called in some undertakers who were very impressed,' he said as, even now in this stifling heat just the thought of what Dr Sarkissian secretly called 'the men in black' made him shudder.

'So do you know who embalmed the body yet?' Suleyman asked.

'No. A few theories, some of them rather odd, but nothing concrete.' Although quite what interest Suleyman could have in the Kuloğlu boy, Çöktin couldn't imagine. 'Why?'

'Because I think I may have a lead for you,' Suleyman said. 'Apparently there is some sort of master embalmer in the city who has performed this grisly task for various Russian heavies.'

'Oh?'

'Yes,' Suleyman replied. 'Valery Rostov is, apparently,

in need of this person's services for a relative. It's all most strange.'

'Ah, so do you know his name then, sir, this embalmer?'

'No,' Suleyman said, 'although Rostov has named his contact, a Dr Keyder.'

'Dr Keyder!'

'Yes, an elderly woman, I believe, who . . .'

But Çöktin was no longer listening Yeşim Keyder. Dr Keyder. Well, what sort of doctor was she? He'd never asked. Were embalmers, if indeed that's what she was, doctors? No, that was ridiculous, she was an old woman, she . . . But then embalmer or not, that had to mean, surely, that she must have known about the boy in Rosita, her sister-in-law's, apartment. She must, therefore, have lied.

'Sir,' he said, cutting Suleyman off in mid-flow, 'would it be possible for me to speak to Rostov?'

Quite a long period of silence passed before Suleyman replied.

# CHAPTER 11

'There's very little point in your being here now, Inspector,' the technician said as she stared down at him through her bottle-bottom-thick spectacles. 'I've harvested samples, but the analysis will take some days, as I'm sure you know.'

'Yes, but hair is one of the samples you have retrieved?' İkmen reiterated.

'Yes,' the technician replied, exhibiting now just a little of the irritation she was feeling. 'As I told you earlier, human hair is just one of the materials we've retrieved from the inside of the van. Some of it is long, some short.'

'So some of it could be female?'

The technician, Miss Göle, shrugged. 'Yes, it's possible, although until we have completed our tests—'

'You're not prepared to make any sort of judgement, I know,' İkmen said with a dismissive wave of his hand. And then as he moved, apparently deep in thought towards the door of the technician's office, he did just briefly murmur 'thank you' as he left.

Once out in the corridor he made his way quickly down to the front of the building. The Forensic Institute always smelled odd, not in a pleasant way but in a sort of artificial, formaldehyde kind of fashion. It made him want to heave, that and the interminable duration of some of these forensic processes rendered him quite weak. Fucking scientists, everything seemed to take for ever with them. Not that there was anything one could do about it – that was the problem. Science took time, everybody knew it, especially those who practised it and, so İkmen felt, played upon its protracted nature in order to avoid setting helpful deadlines.

Once out in the open but stifling air, İkmen breathed in deeply before lighting a cigarette. Ayşe Farsakoğlu, who had been waiting for him on one of the benches outside the building, walked over to join him. İkmen couldn't help noticing that one side of her face had caught the sun rather more profoundly than the other. But he averted his eyes from this ruddiness, which Ayşe either hadn't noticed or was choosing to ignore.

'Nothing yet?'

'No,' he replied wearily, 'but then it was unlikely anything significant would come to light so quickly. They know they've got human hair, but . . . So Reşad Kuran wasn't at his apartment.'

'No,' Ayşe said, 'according to a young girl who lives across the road, he left, carrying a sports bag, just after the van was removed.'

'Anyone else see him go?' İkmen asked.

'No one who would admit to it,' Ayşe replied cynically. 'I've tried calling the Akdeniz house a few times but the number is always engaged. I looked Reşad Kuran up: he's got a record, attempted sexual assault.'

'Oh dear.' İkmen took his mobile phone out of his pocket and pressed the button that unlocked the keypad.

'Have you got Reşad's number with you, Ayşe?' he asked.

'Yes. Do you want it?'

'Yes.'

She brought the number up on her own phone and then read it out to him. İkmen, pressing the digits into his handset, said, 'While I'm doing this, try the Akdeniz house again.'

Several seconds passed before they both terminated their unanswered calls.

'Well, Mr Kuran's phone is now on, but engaged,' İkmen said frowning.

'The Akdeniz' number is engaged too,' Ayşe said as she replaced her phone in her handbag. 'Could just be a coincidence, sir.'

'It could, but I'm going to ask for a trace anyway,' İkmen said as he punched another number into his phone. 'If Eren is on the phone to her brother we may be able to find out where he is.'

'Oh, of course!' Ayşe said enthusiastically. 'Triangulation of the signal.'

'I don't know what it's called,' İkmen said as he put his phone up to his ear. 'Technology and myself are almost total strangers,' he smiled, 'it's a magical system I have yet to study.'

'But then if Mr Kuran has nothing to do with the children's—'

'Oh, but he does,' İkmen said.

'What, just because he's got a record? Or is it because—'

'That's where my particular brand of magic, as I'm sure you're aware, comes in,' he said gravely. 'I know, as I've asserted before, that he's involved in some capacity.'

\* \* \*

It was such a pitiful attempt at breaking and entering that the solitary young officer who had been assigned to guard the Kuloğlu apartment could barely contain his amusement. The 'criminal', an elderly Spaniard who had tried to open the door first with a length of wire and then with a credit card, was for some reason that was lost on Constable Akçura, demanding to see the pathologist Dr Sarkissian.

'If you call Dr Sarkissian, all will be explained,' he said as he looked with some distaste down his nose at the officer's hand upon his forearm. 'My reasons for wanting to gain access to this place are totally about the furtherance of knowledge.'

'You tried to break the lock,' Akçura responded tartly. 'You damaged someone else's property.'

'Call Dr Sarkissian—'

'What's this?'

The voice, though obviously female, was as hard as it was expressionless. Both the policeman and the Spaniard turned.

'Madam,' the officer said as he observed the grey severity of the figure before him. 'What can I—'

'You and this – person,' she replied as she looked scornfully at the Spaniard, 'can do little for me besides moving away from the door of my property.'

The policeman, in line with what he'd been told about the place, started to talk about how the apartment had belonged to a Mrs Keyder, but . . .

'I am Mrs Keyder's sister-in-law,' the woman said as she removed her ID card from her handbag, 'Dr Yeşim Keyder, the legal owner of this property.'

'Ah,' the Spaniard's eyes lit up, 'then if you are a doctor, an educated person, you will fully understand why I have to gain entry to this apartment.'

Yeşim Keyder looked at the man so sharply her gaze could have been construed as hatred. Even the policeman shrank from its viciousness.

'Who are you?' she spat. 'What are you doing?'

'My name is Fernando Orontes,' the Spaniard said. 'I am an academic, a man of science.'

'What do you want?'

'There is something in your apartment, madam, a chemical substance of great value—'

'What kind of scientist are you?' she asked. 'What do you mean?'

Señor Orontes drew himself up before saying, 'I am an embalmer, madam, a master anatomist. There is, I believe, a substance somewhere in this apartment—'

'You're mad!' Yeşim Keyder vomited the words as close as she could get to the Spaniard's face.

'No! It is, this substance, something, I believe, will preserve the dead indefinitely and imbue them with life, suppleness—'

'Get away from my property!' she hissed, and then, turning on Akçura, she said, 'I want to get into my apartment.'

'It's still under investigation,' the young man said, as he tried to avoid directly telling this fierce old woman that she couldn't go in.

'It is my property!' she said as she reached into her handbag and removed a sheaf of papers from its depth. 'Here, my brother's papers, proving—'

176

'I can't let you in, madam.'

'If you would just call Dr Sarkissian,' Orontes interrupted.

'If you think I'm going to let you into my apartment to
look for some "substance", then you are very much mistaken,' Yeşim Keyder said as she turned once again to the
Spaniard. 'Quite how you knew that I was coming—'

'He didn't,' Akçura said and then added more to distract
this vicious old woman than to actually damage Orontes,
'I found him trying to break in.'

'Oh, did you?' she snarled, her eyes now moving from
the cringing Orontes towards Akçura's face.

'You may wish, madam, to—'

'Charge him with attempted burglary!' Yeşim Keyder
said as she moved to get behind the officer and into
the apartment. 'Take him away and let me into my
property.'

'But I can't do that madam, as I explained . . .'

Trying to keep hold of Orontes while at the same time
attempting to block access to the apartment was proving
difficult. The old woman was intent upon getting in and,
by the look on her face, she didn't care too much about
what she had to do in order to achieve that.

'Now look here, young man . . .'

'Just please call Dr Sarkissian the pathologist, he's
my friend!' Orontes cried. 'And he is in charge of the
body . . .'

'Madam, if you don't move away, I'll have to arrest
you along with him!' Akçura said as he tipped his head
in Orontes' direction. 'This apartment is at present the
subject of an investigation into the death of an unknown

man. Until we know who he is, I can't let you in!' He narrowed his eyes just a little as he awaited the full force of her furious outburst.

Strangely, however, particularly considering that Akçura was alone, this didn't come. She just very deliberately, looking at Orontes the whole time she did so, replaced her papers inside her handbag and then, after what looked like several seconds' thought, she cleared her throat.

'Oh, well,' she said, 'I suppose you are just doing your job.'

Akçura signalled his assent by inclining his head to one side.

'And I suppose I will be given access as soon as that is possible,' Yeşim Keyder continued.

'Yes.'

Moving away from the door now, Yeşim Keyder shrugged. 'Maybe,' she said, 'I should go.'

Strangely, and with alarming rapidity, she walked towards Orontes and took one of his hands in hers. The Spaniard visibly cringed.

'Madam?'

'Oh, and you might as well let this mad fellow go too,' she said as she looked across at a now very confused Constable Akçura. 'He's obviously in need of some sort of intervention and I am a doctor.'

'Oh, you're a psychiatrist?'

'I think that maybe you should come with me,' Yeşim Keyder said to a now heavily sweating Orontes, 'tell me about this substance that is supposed to be in my brother's apartment.'

'Well . . .' Orontes began and launched into the tale

he'd told Arto Sarkissian about the perfectly preserved boy, about Pedro Ara and about the mysteries that still surrounded his methods. As he spoke, Yeşim Keyder watched as Constable Akçura's expression veered between disbelief and disgust. Seemingly enjoying both the officer's discomfort, as well as Orontes' effusive exposition, she smiled.

Rostov had asked to be interviewed in his own home. This had been granted and Çöktin was currently with him in his office. Suleyman and İskender, relaxing as much as they could in the Russian's salon, were waiting for him to finish.

'You know that even if he has done something to Masha, Rostov won't tell you,' İskender said as he bent down in order to light his colleague's cigarette.

'He will if I threaten that thing in the freezer,' Suleyman replied grimly. 'He'd do anything to protect that.'

'I disagree,' İskender said as he sat down on one of Rostov's overstuffed armchairs. 'He's dealt with the lovely Betül Ertüg, he's talking to Çöktin about that bizarre embalmed body of his and we hope that at some point some of his contacts in the drug trade may be sacrificed too. Personally I think that in view of the fact we've never actually found any drugs on Rostov or his associates, that is a long shot. But Masha? He'd have to own up to all sorts of things if he admitted to her existence.'

Suleyman shook his head, his eyes narrowed. 'He's done something to her. I could see it in his face,' he said. 'Maybe if I tried to contact her . . .'

'Maybe if you tried forgetting her.' İskender leaned

179

forward towards Suleyman and lowered his voice. 'I don't know what went on between you and that tart, and quite honestly I don't want to know—'

'Nothing!' Suleyman's face reddened instantly. 'Nothing happened!'

'Well then, leave it!' İskender hissed. 'Forget about her and concentrate on what we're going to do about Rostov.' He leaned back in his chair again and sighed. 'We can't leave that child's body in that freezer,' he said. 'We only have Rostov's word that she's his daughter. She could be anyone. She could have been murdered, for all we know. We need to get her out of here, thawed out,' he raised his eyes incredulously towards the ceiling, 'and get a post-mortem performed.'

'But once she's out of here, our chances of getting anything out of Rostov—'

'Once Çöktin has finished with him, you and I had better attempt to persuade Mr Rostov that it would go better for him and his "daughter" if he gave us some useful information,' İskender replied. 'If she is his daughter, if we really have found his Achilles heel, then that might perhaps work. I doubt it, but . . . If, however, she was some junkie he's killed and was preparing to ditch, we'll have to do some work to prove it.'

Suleyman shrugged. 'Either way we should come out of this with something.'

'If not quite the enormous drugs haul Ardiç was anticipating,' İskender responded bitterly.

'No.' Suleyman lowered his eyes. The thought of what Ardiç would say and do when he learned that this costly operation had yielded nothing beyond the frozen body of a child in the Russian's freezer, was not comfortable. Of course, things could be worse – if the *Radikal* journalist had indeed written up the Father Alexei incident, for instance. But it wasn't good and İskender was absolutely right to be doubtful about the eventual outcome. If only he himself could concentrate fully on the task at hand! If only he could forget about Masha and about the malicious light that had danced in Rostov's eyes when he denied all knowledge of her existence. After all, the girl was only, as İskender had said, a tart. She'd had sex with him, which is what tarts do. So what?

So, first she'd relieved the sexual frustrations of months and she'd done it, or rather he had, with no protection. Because he'd been so deprived for so long, it had all happened far more quickly than it should have – he hadn't had time to make preparations. He hadn't meant to do it at all – especially not with a woman he knew was a junkie. Almost as soon as it was over, he'd started to worry about what she may or may not have given him in terms of disease. But then at the end she'd said that she loved him – Zelfa hadn't said that for such a long time. Poor Masha, if she were indeed dead, in a way he'd killed her . . .

Çöktin entered the lounge and sat down in the chair next to İskender. Suleyman, roused from his thoughts by the appearance of his deputy, looked up.

'So?'

Çöktin shrugged. 'Rostov says that he learned about the existence of this amazing embalmer some months ago,' he said. 'From what I can gather, some other Mafia types here have used this person's services for their dead wives, mothers, dogs, whatever. These bodies are quite the "must have" item. So when Rostov heard about it, he wanted it too. His daughter had, as I think he told you, been cryogenically preserved back in Russia. But somehow he managed to persuade the kid's mother that this was a better option so "Tatiana", still in deep freeze, turned up here yesterday.'

'How?'

'In that trunk he picked up from the airport.'

'That didn't have anything on it denoting human remains.'

'This is a Russian gangster we're talking about, sir. They have friends everywhere, including the airport,' Çöktin said with a grim little smile. 'Apparently preservation of the dead is very important to Russians. They like to keep the departed around, they always have. Saints, Rostov said in the old days, and more recently politicians too.'

'So did he tell you who this master embalmer is?' Suleyman asked.

Çöktin sighed. 'No, sir,' he said wearily, 'not exactly. A friend put him in touch, as you know, with Dr Keyder, who assured him Tatiana would be dealt with in due course. Now whether that was by her or—'

'Do you believe him?'

Çöktin shrugged. 'I can't see why he'd lie, sir. If that body downstairs is his daughter, then he must want to know exactly what is going on as much as I do.'

'Then all you have to do is go and see this Dr Keyder,' İskender put in.

'Yes, sir,' Çöktin replied, 'I will. However, if she is reluctant to tell me . . . I mean, embalming isn't a crime, is it?'

'No. But if Rostov was recommended to this embalmer by other Mafiosi then they, surely, would know.'

'Yes, well, he's named several people who've used the service.' Çöktin took his cigarettes out of his pocket and lit up.

'As I said before, they will know, won't they?' İskender said.

'Yes, although that does mean owning up to possessing unburied bodies,' Çöktin said darkly. 'There's also another secret, possibly a very lucrative one, involved here,' he continued wearily and then he told his colleagues about his meeting with the embalmers at the mortuary, about Pedro Ara and about the possible existence of miraculous techniques and balms.

İskender, shaking his head in disbelief, said, 'It's all quite beyond me, especially in view of the fact that both the Keyder woman and the boy died naturally. I can't see why you're still involved, İsak.'

'If we knew who the boy was, I wouldn't be,' Çöktin replied, 'but we don't. We asked Dr Keyder if she knew who he was. She said that she didn't. She must have lied.'

'The bodies of the Russians who have already been embalmed must have been delivered to this embalmer in some way,' Suleyman said.

'Dr Keyder, apparently, arranged for them to be picked up,' Çöktin said.

'By whom?'

'Rostov doesn't know. Dr Keyder didn't tell him much about the process because it was still a way off. Nothing about how Tatiana might be maintained after treatment.'

'What do you mean?' İskender asked. 'Maintained?'

Çöktin gave his superiors a brief résumé of the possible course of this process and then said, 'It's very intensive. If several bodies are involved, the embalmer must have to have help.'

'So you think there might be other people working with or for this embalmer? The person providing the transport perhaps?'

'Maybe.'

'You said he named some of the other Russians who've already had their loved ones preserved?' Suleyman said as he put his cigarette out in his ashtray.

'Yes, I've made a note of them, sir,' Çöktin said. 'Three very big names, if you know what I mean. But then if their bodies, like mine, weren't unlawfully killed . . .' he shrugged. 'I mean, I suppose that if people want to get this done . . .'

'Keeping a dead body in a private residence is a public health issue,' İskender said as he rose thoughtfully to his feet. 'The dead should be buried and if they are not being disposed of properly we need to investigate.' He looked down at Suleyman and smiled. 'We could gain access to the homes of some people we've been watching for a while, Mehmet.'

Suleyman looked up. 'Yes,' he said, 'although I still want to talk to Rostov first.'

'Of course,' İskender replied, 'but bear it in mind. We've got to capitalise on this situation, weird as it is. I mean, there's a real trade we had no idea about going on here. And if they can bring bodies in without detection what can they bring in with or in those bodies, eh?'

'What do you mean?'

'Well, if some Ivan's dead mother can come across the Black Sea or on a plane without hindrance, then why not insert a kilo of heroin into her for good measure? It makes excellent business sense and the old woman is hardly likely to complain, is she?'

Çöktin looked across at Suleyman, who shook his head a little as if trying to dislodge this unpleasant image from his mind.

'I think this is all a bit more kind of to do with their beliefs and their aesthetics, sir,' Çöktin said.

'Nonsense!' İskender retorted. 'The people we're talking about here are murderers and drug dealers, they use every opportunity, however personal, to maximise their profits.'

Suleyman leaned back in his chair and briefly closed his eyes. İskender was so much more dispassionate than he. In Metin's world things were good or bad with very little in between these polarities. The Mafiosi were bad and so of course they would, if possible, use their departed loved ones to courier drugs. Masha was a tart and so one didn't have anything to do with her, however sexy she was. One certainly didn't have sex with her, enjoy it, fantasise about repeating the experience, risk the integrity of one's career . . .

Suddenly, and with an urgency he hadn't experienced for some time, Suleyman felt the need to speak to İkmen.

# CHAPTER 12

Estelle Cohen watched with sad eyes as Zelfa Halman Suleyman left the apartment holding her baby, Yusuf, in her arms. The psychiatrist wasn't a happy woman. Everything seemed to irritate her these days. Estelle took the baby round to Fatma's for the morning and she didn't like that – this time she'd stayed at home in Karaköy with him and that was, seemingly, unacceptable too. Perhaps it was because Fatma was with her? Estelle had always thought that Zelfa liked Fatma. Maybe it had to do with what her friend was doing? Not that she was engaged in anything Estelle felt was unusual.

'Thank you for these,' Fatma said as she took another leech out of the jar and laid it against one of the swollen veins on her leg. 'These have been agony lately.'

'The leeches should get them down.'

'İnşallah. Not that she approved,' she said as she tipped her head in the direction of the front door.

'Zelfa?' Estelle sat down opposite her friend and leaned back in her chair. It had been, as usual for this time of year, a hot and tiring day. 'She's a doctor, probably finds it a bit old-fashioned.'

'And foreign,' Fatma added darkly. 'I don't think that Dr Halman has ever adapted to living here, not properly.

But now that she's married Mehmet she's made her choice.'

'Yes.'

Estelle knew that Fatma had never really approved of Mehmet Suleyman's marriage to Zelfa Halman. She was older than he, a foreigner at least in part and, more importantly, she wasn't a Muslim. Fatma, as Estelle also knew, disapproved of marriages that crossed religious boundaries. Although they'd never discussed it, Estelle knew that her friend was even more opposed to the liaison between her Berekiah and young Hulya than Estelle's husband, Balthazar.

'Well, at least little Yusuf is being raised in your faith,' Estelle said airily.

'Yes, but only because Zelfa doesn't practise hers,' Fatma responded sharply. 'If that child had been born in her country with all those relatives she has in the Church, things would be different.'

Estelle shrugged. 'Maybe.'

Religion had never been a large part of Estelle Cohen's life. Her parents, Yuda and Hanna Şaul, had been more interested in politics than religion – except, of course, when it came to their daughter's marriage. On one level the middle-class Şauls hadn't been particularly pleased when it became apparent that the scruffy policeman son of the alcoholic Haim Cohen was interested in Estelle. But on the other hand Balthazar was a Jew and so the match, for better or worse, was approved. And in truth, it hadn't been all bad. They'd never had much money, but the children, Yusuf and Berekiah, had been a consolation. It wasn't Balthazar's fault that Yusuf's mind had broken during the course of his military service. Estelle could, however, have done without her husband's incessant infidelity. Had he been at home instead of at the apartment of one of his many mistresses when the earthquake hit İstanbul in 1999 he wouldn't be crippled and useless now. She looked towards the door of their bedroom where her husband now lay asleep, and sighed. There had been another boy once, long ago, a Turkish lad called Ersin. At times like this she wondered what he might be doing now and whether he was happy. She hoped so. Happiness was important – it was something that she wished for her son Berekiah more than anything else in the world. She looked across at her friend and wondered how she was coping with her daughter at this time.

'Fatma?'

'Yes?' Still engrossed in the application of leeches, she didn't look up.

'Fatma, about Berekiah and Hulya.' She said it in a rush, lest she lose her nerve.

The other woman stopped what she was doing and looked up.

'We do need to talk,' Estelle continued, 'at some time.'

'Not now,' Fatma's eyes had suddenly taken on a hardness that Estelle didn't particularly like.

'But—'

'I have spoken to my husband, told him what I think,' Fatma continued stiffly. 'It's for him to discuss whatever needs to be discussed, which is nothing in my opinion, with your husband.'

'They are serious.'

'And foolish!' Fatma looked back down at her leech-covered leg again and grimaced. 'It's up to us to guide them correctly.'

'Yes—'

'Estelle, we are friends,' Fatma said as she looked up again. 'I don't want that to change. And anyway,' she shook her head slightly in agitation, 'I can't think about anything beyond my immediate troubles right now. My dear brother is the whole of my life at this time.' And her eyes filled with tears.

Estelle, in spite of her own feelings, reached across to take Fatma's hand in hers. Poor woman. Her brother was dying, a situation she was having to deal with largely on her own – obviously she didn't need any more problems at this time. However, when Talaat had gone, the issue of the youngsters would have to be addressed. They were, she knew, 'intimate', if not actually engaging in sex, as yet. She'd come home from her mother's early one day and seen them through the half-open door to Berekiah's bedroom. Although clothed and only kissing, it was obvious they were both aroused – and in love. She recognised the scene well, from long ago, when she and Ersin had kissed like that in the old stable at the back of her parents' house.

'Let's make sex magic.'

Eren Akdeniz lay down naked at her husband's feet and stretched her arms sensuously out above her head.

Melih, who was sitting on a chair in the middle of his studio, put the piece of camel skin he was stitching down beside him and took a long swig from his medicine bottle.

When he'd finished, he wiped one hand across his mouth before resuming his work once again.

'I haven't got the time or the energy,' he muttered without so much as looking at his wife's performance at his feet.

'You had enough time for that gypsy slut this morning,' Eren returned acidly.

'Gonca?' Melih frowned. 'I was creating,' he said, 'you know that. Sometimes I need it then. Anyway, you were on the phone.'

'You fucked her.'

'I've been fucking her for years,' he said lightly. 'I needed sexual input then, it was essential. She understands me.'

Eren sat up, her small breasts sagging to her ribs as she did so. She put one hand on his knee, felt him flinch under her touch.

'I know you better than she does, Melih,' she said. 'I'm so lonely without the children.'

'The children will return.'

Eren pushed herself up using Melih's knees to support herself. 'Melih, please, it won't take long.'

Melih exhaled impatiently and shoved the medicine bottle towards her. 'Drink this, Eren.'

'No!' She pushed the bottle away. 'I don't want that!'

'I don't feel strong enough!' Furious now with her pleading, Melih Akdeniz threw his work down on to the floor and leaned forward, staring into her face. With one shaking hand he pushed her back down on to the floor.

'Your stupid brother has taken fright at a couple of

policemen and you want me to stop my work to service you?' He picked the piece of camel skin back up off the floor and started sewing again. 'I haven't got time.' His face became grave. 'I feel it very close now. I feel like I'm liquefying inside.'

Eren, momentarily subdued by his words, sat up again and remained quiet for several seconds. As she placed one tentative hand on his knee, she cupped the other around one of her breasts.

'Why don't you watch,' she said softly, 'me, with myself?'

At first Melih didn't respond. But, after several moments' thought, he looked up and nodded his assent.

Eren closed her eyes and skimmed her hands lightly across her body.

Someone knocked at the studio door.

'Tell them to go away!' Eren breathed.

'Who is it?' her husband yelled.

A short but heavy cough preceded the word, 'İkmen.'

Eren's eyes widened with fear.

'Come in,' Melih said with amusement, if the smile on his face was anything to go by.

'Melih!'

There was nothing for Eren to cover herself up with. But even if there had been, it would have been impossible for her to do so now that Melih, suddenly springing lightly from his chair, had dragged her to her feet.

İkmen entered the studio just in time to see Eren Akdeniz's naked figure stretched before him. The artist had pinned her arms behind her back. The woman's eyes screamed with humiliation and fear.

'The female form in performance,' Melih said joyfully. 'What do you think, Inspector?'

İkmen wasn't often lost for words but this was one of the few occasions when he was.

Melih, revelling in both İkmen's discomfort and his wife's shame, laughed.

'Ah, but she's a little worn now, isn't she?' he said as he carelessly let his wife drop back down towards the floor and resumed his seat. 'Wrinkled tits.'

Eren, who had now crawled into a heap of paper underneath one of her husband's easels, began to cry.

İkmen cleared his throat.

The artist, who had resumed sewing something that looked much like a house to İkmen, muttered, 'What do you want? Do you have my children?'

'No, Mr Akdeniz, I don't,' İkmen said as he attempted to avert his eyes from the pathetic sight of the humiliated woman on the floor. 'I do, however, or at least I will have in a few hours' time when he is transferred over here from Bursa, Mr Reşad Kuran, your brother-in-law.'

'Reşad?'

İkmen was immediately aware of a cessation of weeping.

'What are you doing with him?'

'I want to ask him why he ran away just after we took his vehicle for forensic analysis.' İkmen looked around the room at the various pieces of art in progress. A lot of it appeared to be made of that translucent camel hide that was used in traditional shadow plays – except that these pieces were much bigger than usual. 'I would,' he continued, 'also like to ask him what he and your wife were discussing on the telephone this morning. Did you, Mrs Akdeniz, know that your brother left for Bursa last night?'

'Well,' Eren, several pieces of paper clutched to her chest, sat up. 'I . . .'

'Your brother was,' İkmen said sternly, 'as far as we know, the last person to visit this house before Nuray and Yaşar disappeared. This and his recent behaviour makes him a very strong candidate for your children's abductor.'

'No!'

'Yes.' İkmen held one finger up in order to silence the artist. 'He had the means, the opportunity and, as my sergeant discovered earlier today, a past record too.' He turned back towards Eren and smiled. 'You must remember, surely, Mrs Akdeniz, that your brother was accused of attempted sexual assault twice in the nineteen eighties.'

'Yes, but he was cleared!' Eren retorted, her face flushing with anger. 'Those girls lied!'

'Did they?' İkmen put a cigarette in his mouth and lit up. 'We'll have to see about that, won't we? Why don't you get dressed and come with me to the station to welcome Reşad home.'

'I don't like your tone . . .'

'Oh, but I thought you'd be pleased that we might have a break in this case,' İkmen said as he picked up Melih's medicine bottle and read what was written on the label. 'Mmm, well, well. Now look, if Reşad is hiding them somewhere, we might have them back to you tonight, Mr Akdeniz. Your children. Those people you love more than your own life.'

'Yes . . .'

İkmen put the bottle down and made his way back towards the studio door.

'So get some clothes on and come with me.' Turning just before he exited, he added, 'And bring your medication, Mr Akdeniz. I can see from what it is that you must need it a lot.'

Melih and Eren Akdeniz looked at each other, their faces damp with cold sweat.


He didn't need this now. The police had just brought in a body that had been washed up on the shore at one of the villages on the Bosphorus. In cases like this time was always of the essence – if for no other reason than to get rid of the inevitable stench.

Arto put his hand on the excited Spaniard's shoulder.

'Señor Orontes . . .' he began.

'I have been talking to Dr Keyder, we met and . . .'

'I am very busy right now, señor . . .'

'Yes, but Dr Keyder is the late Mrs Rosita's sister-in-law. It is just possible that she might know the identity of your boy.'

Arto Sarkissian started to walk back in the direction of his office. 'She has denied all knowledge of him,' he said.

'Yes, I know,' the Spaniard replied nervously, twisting a handkerchief between his fingers as he did so, 'but she feels that just to be certain . . .'

'I don't know! I don't know!' Arto said as he opened his office door and began to move inside. 'I'll have to speak to Sergeant Çöktin.'

'Yes, but—'

'Come back later,' Arto said as he attempted to close the door behind him.

'When?'

'I don't know! Oh, in three hours, maybe,' the Armenian responded tetchily, pulling a time out of the air. He then shut the door behind him, leaving the Spaniard outside.

A few moments later, the person who had been lurking at the other end of the corridor during the course of his conversation, caught up with him.

'So what did he say?' Yeşim Keyder asked coldly.

Señor Orontes lowered his eyes, as if in deference. 'He said he can't do anything now, but if we come back in about three hours—'

'That will do,' the old woman replied and turned to make her way back down the corridor once again.

Orontes, at her heels, looked like a small, dark ape.

Judging by the state of the ashtrays as well as the overpowering smell of sweat in the place, Interview Room No. 4 had seen a lot of action during the course of the day. And even though it was now dusk outside, the room had not yet even started to cool down. Ayşe Farsakoğlu caught a rivulet of perspiration as it rolled down her forehead, and wiped it away with a tissue. Her eye make-up had all but melted in the heat but there was no point in making it any worse. Steadily, almost as a form of meditation, she stared at the clammy, bloodless face before her. Reşad Kuran, like her and the constable over by the door, waited for İkmen in perfect silence.

Casually, Ayşe wondered what Melih Akdeniz's brother-in-law might be thinking. Was he regretting having left the city after his van was taken away for analysis? Was he, as an innocent party, angry at having been dragged back to İstanbul against his will? Were images of his 'old' crimes, fiddling with a nine-year-old girl in a cinema and then hassling another youngster to masturbate him in Gülhane Park, coming back to haunt him? It was difficult to tell from a face as expressionless as Reşad's. And yet, if İkmen were convinced he was a possible contender for the abduction of the Akdeniz children . . .

A knock at the door heralded the arrival of the inspector who, once the usual preamble was over, went straight to the point.

'Why did you leave İstanbul, Mr Kuran?' he asked. 'I distinctly remember telling you not to do so.'

'I had business in Bursa,' Kuran replied.

'Then why didn't you tell me that when we spoke originally?'

'Something, came up . . .'

'Rather sudden, wasn't it?' İkmen said. 'Rather odd too, considering that you told me your profession was delivery driver. Working, without your van, can't have been easy. What did you do, Mr Kuran, carry the goods hamal-style on your back?'

Reşad Kuran looked down at the floor. 'If you are arresting me—'

'No.' İkmen suddenly and, Ayşe always thought, dazzlingly smiled. 'No, I'm not ready to do that,' he said, 'I just want to know why you left the city.'

'I told you.'

'Yes. But I do need a few more details, Mr Kuran, before I let your sister and brother-in-law take you home.'

Kuran looked up, frowning. 'Eren and Melih?'

'Yes, they're here, Mr Kuran,' İkmen said and paused briefly in order to light a cigarette. 'Once we had established your location, I felt I had to go round to tell them. After all they had indirectly helped us to do that – or rather your sister, via her long telephone conversation to you, had.'

Reşad Kuran had in the time it had taken for the Bursa police to transfer him across to İstanbul, learned rather more than he'd ever wanted to about the lack of security surrounding the use of mobile telephones.

Ayşe Farsakoğlu emptied the ashtray to stop the ash from İkmen's cigarette destabilising the already towering pyramid of butts.

As she sat down again, Kuran began speaking. 'Look,' he said, illustrating his speech with heavy, measured hand gestures, 'I lied, all right? I . . . look, I have this woman friend in Bursa, she lives in Muradiye district . . .'

'Woman or girl?' İkmen asked.

'What?'

'Two incidents,' Ayşe Farsakoğlu interjected, 'from the nineteen eighties, two young under-age girls.'

Kuran closed his eyes and sighed. 'That was a long time ago,' he said wearily. 'I don't do that now. It was a mistake then . . .' He opened his eyes again and said, 'Look, my friend, this woman, she's thirty-seven.'

'Name?'

'What?'

'Her name, your friend,' İkmen said tartly. 'The Bursa

197

police picked you up in a khavehane. I want to know that this woman, this thirty-seven-year old exists.'

'She's married . . .'

'I don't care,' İkmen shrugged. 'All I'm interested in is whether or not you're telling me the truth, Mr Kuran.' He leaned forward across the table. 'Your van is currently being analysed for traces of material that might have come from your nephew and niece.'

'But—'

'You were at the Akdeniz house late on the Friday night . . .'

'Picking up some art work for one of Melih's clients.'

'Yes.' İkmen leaned back in his seat and smiled once again. 'Someone whose name appears to have completely slipped Mr Akdeniz's mind. In view of what has happened to him of late maybe I can understand that. But you?'

'What?'

'I asked you before and I'll ask you again, who did you deliver the art work to, Mr Kuran? Where did you take it?'

Reşad Kuran threw his arms petulantly into the air. 'I don't know! I can't remember!'

'You must be able to!' İkmen shouted. 'You're not a fucking idiot, are you?'

'No!'

'If any of the samples inside your van match the children's DNA we've gathered from the Akdeniz house, then you are looking at a lot of trouble. As you told us yourself, Mr Kuran, they've never ever been in your van, have they?' İkmen said menacingly. 'Now you told us that you took that work of art out to Yeniköy. Where in Yeniköy?'

Kuran lowered his head. 'I don't know,' he said, 'some wealthy place.'

'What do you mean, "wealthy place"?' İkmen, who was becoming increasingly impatient with this man, snapped, 'A palace? A yalı? A yacht, perhaps? What?'

'I don't know!'

'You keep on saying that, but you do, Mr Kuran,' Ayşe Farsakoğlu said. Taking one very calm breath she continued, 'It's very simple. You took this art work from Balat to . . . ?'

'What's Melih's art work got to do with the children? What does it matter where I took it?'

'It matters, Mr Kuran,' İkmen said emphatically, 'because if Yaşar and Nuray, with or without your knowledge, were in your van at the time—'

'But they weren't!'

'How do you know?' Ayşe Farsakoğlu asked. 'If you don't know where you went then how can you be certain about what you were carrying?'

Reşad Kuran put his head down into his hands.

'You must have been drunk or on drugs,' İkmen said with what sounded to Kuran like an iron certainty.

'No! I'm clean, I never . . .' Realising, suddenly, what the implications of what he'd just said were, Reşad Kuran looked up.

'So if you're so clean, why can't you remember, Mr Kuran?' İkmen said. 'Do you perhaps have some sort of medical condition that affects your memory?'

Reşad Kuran, who was now sweating even more heavily than he had been before, cleared his throat. 'I want a lawyer,' he said.

İkmen nodded his assent. 'Very well.' As he rose to leave the room, he added, 'I'll tell your sister and her husband to go home. I think that might be for the best.'

The guard opened the door to allow İkmen to leave.

# CHAPTER 13

'I don't know why Çetin recommended you come to me,' Arto Sarkissian said as he folded his white-coated arms across his chest. 'It's my brother you really need to see.'

Suleyman sighed. 'Perhaps our friend, quite correctly, assumed that because I don't really know your brother, I might be more comfortable approaching you first, Doctor.'

The younger man's face was, the Armenian noticed, quite grey with tension. That wasn't surprising, given what he had just told him. To admit to infidelity was bad enough, but to further admit to unprotected sex with a prostitute – that was something else.

'The best thing to do would be for me to call Krikor and make you an appointment at the clinic,' Arto said as he reached across his desk to retrieve his telephone.

'Yes, but . . .'

'What?'

Suleyman lowered his gaze. 'But I mean I don't want my employers to know.'

'My brother is the soul of discretion, I can assure you,' the Armenian responded kindly and, seeing that Suleyman wasn't quite ready to hear himself discussed on the telephone, he put it down again. 'Look, Mehmet,' he said using, unusually for him, the policeman's first name, 'you can be tested for hepatitis B now. The result, whatever that might be, will be conclusive.'

'And Aids?' The word flashed fear into his eyes.

Arto sighed. 'Krikor will, of course, go into more detail than I can,' he said. 'Addiction and diseases of addiction are his speciality. But what I do know is that early testing for HIV, just after sexual or blood contact, isn't conclusive. If you take a test now, you'll have to have another one in three months and, maybe, I'm not sure, another one after that.'

Suleyman rubbed his face wearily with his hands. 'I can't believe I've been so stupid!'

Arto too found it difficult to credit. He'd been aware of Mehmet Suleyman for, he reckoned, fifteen years. He'd known him well for ten of those. To him, Suleyman was an honest and honourable man. Not that that had changed. A dishonourable man wouldn't be this mortified. Because of the personal risk to his health and also because of the guilt and shame that he was exhibiting.

The Armenian reached out and placed a hand on his shoulder. 'You'll get through this,' he said.

'Will I?'

'Yes.'

Suleyman stood up and raked his hands nervously through his hair. 'With my life and my marriage intact?'

'That I don't know,' Arto replied, 'but I know I don't have to tell you that you must protect Zelfa now.'

'I must tell her! Although, how . . .'

'That I can't help you with, I'm afraid,' Arto replied. 'That's something I suggest you discuss with Krikor.'

'Yes. Yes.'

Suleyman sat down again and lit a cigarette.

'I'll call him now,' Arto said as he once again took hold of his telephone, 'make that appointment as soon as possible.'

'Yes.'

Once everything was settled, Arto led his guest out into the corridor. It had been a very tiring evening; first that bloated drowning victim, now this dreadful situation with poor Mehmet Suleyman. How awful and how dangerous desire could be.

'Dr Sarkissian!'

Oh, yes, and of course there was also Señor Orontes.

Arto sighed. 'Yes?'

'You said that Dr Keyder might be permitted to view your unknown boy.'

'I should really ask Sergeant Çöktin first,' Arto interrupted. 'That boy is, after all, his responsibility at the present time.'

The severe woman at Orontes' side sniffed unpleasantly.

'I take it you are Dr Keyder,' Suleyman said to her with a smile. So this was the woman who may or may not be Çöktin's embalmer. Obviously the Kurd hadn't managed to speak to her yet. This could be interesting.

But Suleyman's charm, which was legendary amongst most women he came into contact with, didn't have the slightest effect upon Yeşim Keyder. 'Yes,' she responded coldly, 'I am. And you are?'

'I am Inspector Mehmet Suleyman,' he said. 'Sergeant Çöktin is my deputy.'

'You know about my deceased sister-in-law?'

'Mrs Rosita Keyder. Yes. May your head be alive, Dr Keyder,' Suleyman said, repeating the old formulaic response to one recently bereaved. 'I have been working on something else myself, but I am aware of some of what Sergeant Çöktin has been doing.'

'It might, we thought, be a good idea for Dr Keyder to see our boy,' Orontes said as he turned his attention entirely on to Suleyman. 'She might recognise him.'

'Sergeant Çöktin was under the impression that you knew of no young man who had any involvement in Mrs Keyder's life,' Suleyman said to the woman.

Yeşim Keyder failed to respond.

'So, can we see him?' Orontes began.

'I don't—' Arto began.

'It's all right, Doctor,' Suleyman said as he turned to the Armenian with a smile. 'I'll take responsibility on behalf of Sergeant Çöktin.'

'If you think it will be all right . . .'

'Yes.'

Arto started to make his way back into his office, followed by Suleyman and the others. Pandering to Orontes' unnatural interest in the Kuloğlu boy's body seemed to him wrong. Yet it wasn't Orontes that interested Suleyman, but Dr Yeşim Keyder. This woman was the only connection they had to the embalmer. It would be interesting to see what her response to the corpse, which Çöktin had said she had to know, would be. As he put on the white coat Dr Sarkissian gave to him prior to entry into the laboratory, Suleyman, now temporarily distracted from his own problems, began to frown.

\*    \*    \*

'What do you think your brother might say?'

Eren Akdeniz stared into the darkened garden outside the window, her eyes fixed and empty. 'I don't know,' she replied. 'I've no idea.'

Melih stopped applying paint to the piece of canvas in front of him and wiped away the sweat on his brow with his forearm. 'I must finish,' he said breathlessly. 'If I don't it's all been for nothing. The work is the only thing now.'

Eren turned to look at him. 'And if the police come?'

'I will deny everything!' He took his medicine bottle out of his pocket and took a long draught from its neck. When he'd finished he wiped his hand across his mouth and placed the bottle down beside his canvas. 'They've searched the house several times. If we get Yaşar and Nuray back here now—'

'But they're not ready!' Eren said, tears of frustration springing into her eyes. 'They won't be ready yet!' She moved across to where her husband was standing and stood in front of him. 'I won't have my babies mistreated like this! I want what's best for them!'

'What's best for them is if the work proceeds,' her husband responded in a low, menacing tone, 'which it won't if this fucking cancer takes me away or if the police get that necrophiliac to say what he shouldn't.'

'Don't use that word!' Eren screamed. 'Not with my babies. He wouldn't touch them!'

'No, but you know as well as I do exactly what Reşad is,' Melih said as he lowered himself wearily down into a chair and lit a cigarette. 'At least this way he's no longer fucking the living,' and then briefly he laughed. 'I'm sorry, Eren, that was glib. It's just my way of dealing with stress.'

'I thought that was fucking other women,' Eren responded sharply.

Melih smiled. 'You've never really come to terms with my need for other women, have you, Eren?' he said quietly. 'You've pretended, joined in when I've wanted you to, said you've understood. But you've never really approved. Prudish . . .'

'Shut up, bastard!' She turned away and walked back towards the window once again.

'Eren, if my work is to—'

'Fuck your work!' she screamed, her tearful eyes now beginning to drip with water. 'Fuck you, Melih, with your ideas and your ego and that vicious thing inside you, eating . . .'

'Eren!' Slowly, and amid much pain, Melih rose from his chair, walked towards his wife and, once he was opposite her, he slapped her face with the full force of his hand.

Eren didn't so much as whimper.

Several seconds passed in silence before she reached out to him and, tenderly taking his head in her hands, kissed him full on the lips. They embraced, again tenderly, Eren stroking Melih's back like a mother gently patting her infant.

'Melih . . .'

'We have to get them back, Eren,' he said sadly. 'I've put too much into this to watch it fail now. I've worked, planned, done deals with devils. To a purpose, yes. This will be the greatest, most innovative artistic statement the world has ever seen.' And he turned to her, his face drawn and stained with fear. 'I hope that we might be able to trust Reşad, but what if we can't?'

She took her head from off his shoulder and moved back so that she was looking at him. 'But, Melih, they're not ready.'

'I know!' He sighed, a jerky ill little sigh. 'I know. But what can we do?'

Eren shook her head. 'I don't know.'

Melih took his mobile phone out of his pocket and dialled a number on the keypad. 'All we can do is get the children back,' he said.

'So that the show may begin?' Eren said hollowly, looking out into the blackness of the garden once again.

'Yes,' her husband said as he placed the telephone up to his ear, 'and we'll all be together again.'

It was 10 p.m. by the time the lawyer, a Miss Korcan, finally sat down opposite İkmen in Interview Room No. 4.

'As I understand it,' she said, fixing İkmen with clear and motionless eyes, 'there is no physical evidence which connects Mr Kuran with the possible abduction of Nuray and Yaşar Akdeniz.'

'No, although his van is currently under analysis at the Forensic Institute,' İkmen replied, 'and Mr Kuran did leave İstanbul just after the vehicle was taken and against my expressed instructions.'

'Yes, he went to visit a Mrs . . .' the lawyer looked at her client for clarification, 'Edip?'

Reşad Kuran nodded his agreement.

'A Mrs Edip in Bursa, as I believe he explained to you, Inspector.'

'Yes,' İkmen said, 'although quite why he would do such a thing . . .'

'Oh, Inspector.' Miss Korcan smiled a little, the policeman felt, shyly. 'When one is in love . . .'

'He's hardly a besotted teenager, Miss Korcan!' İkmen countered angrily. 'And at thirty-seven Mrs Edip can't exactly qualify for that status either!'

'No.'

'And besides,' İkmen continued, 'as Mr Kuran knows only too well, my real concern is not with Mrs Edip or any of these other details that have come to light since the disappearance of Nuray and Yaşar. What fascinates me, Miss Korcan, is why your client appears to be incapable of remembering where he went and what he did on the night the children disappeared.'

'Ah, but the children didn't disappear on the Friday night, did they, Inspector?' Miss Korcan smiled. 'Mr and Mrs Akdeniz assert that the children were still in the house in Balat on the Saturday morning.'

'An assertion that is completely unsubstantiated,' İkmen put in.

'Yes. But why would they lie, Inspector? Mr and Mrs Akdeniz are the children's parents. They love their children.'

From everything that Melih and Eren had ever said to him and from his own observations of them too, İkmen had to agree with this. And yet something wasn't right. Kuran had left İstanbul for a reason, which had, he knew, everything to do with his van.

'I would still like to know where you went after you visited the Akdeniz house on the Friday night,' İkmen said, addressing Reşad Kuran. 'You picked up a painting . . .'

'Mr Kuran's memory of that night is somewhat hazy,' the lawyer interrupted smoothly, 'as an insulin-dependent diabetic' – İkmen looked across at Ayşe Farsakoğlu who just shook her head very slightly – 'Mr Kuran cannot always be counted upon to recall every detail of his daily existence.'

'So if your memory's that bad, how do you get and keep business, Mr Kuran?' he asked. 'If I wanted someone to deliver goods for me I'd want to know that person would know where he was going to, what he was doing and what he'd done.'

'If you ask my brother-in-law—'

'Your brother-in-law can't remember either,' İkmen cut in tartly. 'I suppose that when you're pouring morphine down your throat all day long, the world does tend to get a little indistinct. Given his past, I assumed at first that his use of the drug was recreational, but I believe it is prescribed. He must be very ill, our greatest living artist.'

'I didn't have Nuray or Yaşar in my van that night,' Kuran leaned forward, speaking emphatically. 'You can search my apartment, ask my neighbours.'

'Yes, yes,' İkmen said as he ran one hand through his sweat-soaked hair, 'I agree that we may not find anything of value in either your home or your transport. But that doesn't detract from the fact, Mr Kuran, that I can't understand how you can be so sure you don't know where you went that night when you are, apparently, absolutely certain that Nuray and Yaşar were not with you. Does diabetes affect only parts of the memory? Please tell me because I'm interested.'

Concerned if unfazed by the look of confusion on her client's face, Miss Korcan said, 'But in the face of only circumstantial evidence, all of this is irrelevant at this time. My client has admitted that he was in error when he went to Bursa to visit Mrs Edib and has agreed to stay in İstanbul until your investigations are at an end, Inspector. He has, despite the fact Mrs Edib is a married lady, given you her details in order that you may verify his story. I don't see what may be achieved by keeping him here at this time.'

She was right. Beyond İkmen's belief that Kuran had to be dissembling, there was nothing more to be said without embarking on the same circular argument they had been having for hours. Kuran couldn't or wouldn't explain why he didn't know where he'd been on the Friday night in the apparently clear knowledge that the children weren't with him. And until something came to light to force that issue they were at an end. Reluctantly, İkmen agreed to let Kuran leave.

Miss Korcan, pleased with what was for her a most successful night's work, led the way. However, just before Reşad Kuran got up to follow her, İkmen leaned across the table towards him and said, 'Where are they, Reşad? Where are Nuray and Yaşar?'

'Wh—' As if shocked by electricity, Reşad Kuran's head jerked backwards, robbing him temporarily of speech.

'I will find them, you know,' İkmen hissed as he watched the man in front of him stumble as he got up from his chair, 'and then I'll come for you.'

Reşad Kuran turned and ran, his jacket hanging limply from his hands, into the corridor after his lawyer.

When the room had returned to silence once again, Ayşe Farsakoğlu went over to İkmen and stood in front of him.

'Why did you say that, sir,' she asked, 'about the children?'

İkmen lit a cigarette before replying. 'To shock him . . .'

'But what if he is telling the truth?' she said. 'What if he really can't remember what he did? People are frightened of the police, it's quite natural. He may have left the city simply because he was spooked.'

'I take your point,' İkmen said as he sat down wearily in the chair that Reşad Kuran had recently vacated. 'But he's a kiddie fiddler and I'm afraid I believe that once a kiddie fiddler always a kiddie fiddler. Nuray is a little girl . . .'

'Yes.' Ayşe, sitting opposite now, sighed. 'And Reşad is her uncle. Surely Mr and Mrs Akdeniz would have known something. Surely, for the sake of their daughter, they would have brought Kuran to our attention before?'

İkmen shrugged. 'He's Eren's brother.'

'Yes, I know. But surely her maternal feelings for her children would override her feelings for Kuran.'

'I don't know,' İkmen said. 'To be honest with you I can't make either Melih or Eren Akdeniz out. They live in a world that is beyond my understanding. The only thing I'm sure of is that those children are suffering in some way . . .'

'What?'

'Oh, it's one of my, you know,' İkmen gesticulated

in order to get his point across to her, 'I see things in my mind.'

'Yes, Orhan,' she lowered her eyes as she spoke of İkmen's previous, deceased deputy, Orhan Tepe, 'used to talk about it sometimes. He said that when you have these very strong pictures in your mind, you're always right.'

İkmen smiled. 'Sometimes. But then going back to Kuran, what did you make of his exit from here in the wake of my remark, Ayşe? What do you think, if anything, his response means?'

Ayşe drew heavily on her cigarette before replying. She was dealing with a range of emotions right now – sadness at the sudden mention of Orhan's name, and pleasure because İkmen was now obviously beginning to trust and confide in her.

'The fear was all over his face like a tattoo,' she said.

'So what do you think he'll do then, Ayşe?' he said. 'What would you do if you were him?'

He reached across the desk and picked up the receiver of the interview room telephone.

'Well,' Ayşe said, 'assuming he has the children or knows where they are, I'd keep as far away from them as I could, if I were him. Maybe that was what he was doing when he went to Bursa.'

'Maybe. But if he knows we're on to him and the kids are out there somewhere, he'll also know it's only a question of time before we find them.'

'Yes.'

'Well, I think if I were him I might try to hide them more securely or even kill them,' İkmen said as he dialled a number into the telephone keypad, 'which is why I'm going to have him followed.' As he waited for someone to answer he added, 'Oh, and tomorrow I think we might go and see how Mr Akdeniz is getting on with his new exhibit. If he is as sick as his intake of morphine would seem to suggest then I expect he's keen to finish soon.'

Yeşim Keyder walked around the body three times before she finally came to a halt and nodded her head. When she spoke, however, her cold, pale eyes remained on the young boy's face.

'His name is Miguel Arancibia,' she said. 'He was Rosita's brother.'

Orontes, who was leaning over, peering at the side of the corpse's head muttered, 'Degradation. Oh, we must do something . . .'

Suleyman hadn't seen the boy's body before. He was both fascinated and repelled. That it could be as much as fifty years old was abominable. Death was hard to bear but he had been brought up a Muslim and so he believed that if Allah willed a thing to be so then that was that. The dead had gone, what possible function did their empty shells perform?

'If you knew who he was, why didn't you tell Sergeant Çöktin?' Arto Sarkissian remarked with some heat in his voice. 'We've been labouring under the misapprehension that we were dealing with a mystery here.'

Yeşim Keyder looked up from the corpse with hard eyes. 'I didn't want to get involved,' she said coldly. 'Most people in this country don't understand or are against embalming. This absurd belief that the soul of the deceased cannot rest until the body is buried doesn't help.'

'That is a traditional Turkish belief.'

'Yes, it's ridiculous.'

Suleyman cleared his throat. 'So what then has changed your mind, Dr Keyder?' he asked. 'Why share this information with us now?'

'I went to see my lawyer today,' the old woman responded briskly. 'Apparently I cannot take possession of my late brother's apartment in Kuloğlu unless I arrange for Rosita and Miguel to be buried together. My sister-in-law added that caveat to that will without my knowledge.'

Señor Orontes looked up, frowning.

Suleyman sighed. He was going to have to take this further which – given the old woman's level of hostility – wasn't going to be easy.

'I need to talk to you, Dr Keyder,' he said as he motioned for Arto to re-cover the corpse. 'May we use your office please, Doctor?'

'Of course.'

'Look, all I want to do is to arrange for the priest Vetra to come and take Rosita and Miguel away . . .'

'All in good time, yes,' Suleyman said as he started to move towards the laboratory door, 'but there are some questions that I need to ask you first, Dr Keyder.'

'What questions?' She hadn't moved. She was still motionless beside the corpse, Señor Orontes at her side.

'I think if we go to the office . . .'

'I'd rather you said whatever it is you have to say here,' Yeşim Keyder snapped. 'If I'm not under arrest for anything, which in view of the fact that I've done nothing wrong I assume I am not, then I would rather not be questioned in a formal manner.'

Arto looked across at Suleyman with nervous eyes. The younger man simply shrugged by way of reply.

'Very well,' he said, 'but I don't feel that it is entirely appropriate that this gentleman,' he gestured towards Orontes, 'is present at this time.'

'Oh, but—'

'I agree.' Yeşim Keyder turned her cold eyes on to the Spaniard and continued, 'You can go now, Señor Orontes.'

'Ah, but—'

'I'll be in touch,' she concluded. Turning away from him entirely she said to Suleyman, 'Well?'

Suleyman waited until Arto Sarkissian had shown the Spaniard out and then returned before he began. He had a feeling that it might be useful to have a reliable witness, like the Armenian, to what he felt was going to be a somewhat unusual conversation.

'So,' he said as he lowered himself down on to one of the stools that were littered around the edges of the laboratory, 'let us begin at the beginning, shall we? Do you know who embalmed this body, Dr Keyder?'

The woman remained standing. 'Dr Pedro Ara,' she said flatly, 'a master—'

'We know who Dr Ara was, Dr Keyder,' Suleyman said as he looked across at Arto Sarkissian. 'I have only just found out about this, but Dr Sarkissian and Sergeant Çöktin have done a considerable amount of research on Dr Ara and his methods.'

'Then you'll know he was a genius,' Yeşim Keyder said. 'You'll know about Evita.'

'Yes,' Arto Sarkissian put in, 'we do. However, she was the wife of a powerful dictator. This boy . . .'

'Rosita's family were prominent within the Peronist movement – military people.' Yeşim Keyder finally sat down. 'When Miguel died in nineteen fifty-one, Rosita's mother engaged Ara to preserve the boy.'

'That was a year before Evita died.'

'Yes,' she smiled. 'Veli always used to say that Ara was only engaged by Peron because he had seen the miracle that was Miguel Arancibia.'

'Veli being?'

'My brother,' she said. 'He married Rosita Arancibia in nineteen fifty.'

'In Argentina?'

'Yes.'

Suleyman folded his arms across his chest. 'Why was your brother in Argentina, Dr Keyder?' he asked.

She looked him straight in the eyes. 'My brother was a biologist. An academic. An uncle of ours had emigrated to Buenos Aires some years before. He managed to get Veli invited to a conference there and then helped him to secure a very good position in a university department.'

'And you went with him.'

For just a moment she appeared to be slightly taken aback. 'What makes you think that?'

'Well, somebody must have been, what's the word,' he looked across briefly at Arto Sarkissian, 'maintaining this corpse since it came to this country in . . .'

'Nineteen fifty-five,' the woman interjected coldly, 'and in answer to your implied question, yes, I did study under Dr Ara. I was privileged to be in receipt of his methods and formulas and, yes, I did and have maintained Miguel ever since Rosita and Veli removed him from

Argentina in 'fifty-five.' She looked from Suleyman's face to Sarkissian's and back again, 'When the Peronistas were overthrown everything connected with that regime was in peril,' she said earnestly, 'including Miguel.'

'You helped to smuggle his body into the Republic.'

Yeşim Keyder shrugged. 'If that's the way you want to put it. Rosita's family wanted Miguel to be safe. Veli hoped he could obtain work back here in İstanbul. I would look after Miguel. He is, after all, probably the finest example of Dr Ara's art.'

'Which you are now prepared to bury in the ground,' Suleyman observed.

'Now I don't have a choice.'

'But if you did, you'd keep him?'

'Of course.' She raised her head haughtily up on its thin neck. 'Ara wasn't just an embalmer, he was an artist,' she said.

'And do you consider yourself,' Suleyman asked, 'to be an artist also, Dr Keyder?'

She looked at him steadily and without expression.

'Because,' he continued, 'having established, as I believe we have, that you possess the requisite skills to enable you to preserve the dead, I would further suggest that some people in this city consider you to be without equal.' He leaned forward towards her. 'Eastern European clients, Dr Keyder, people with a lot of money, and a profound interest in something they look upon as art.'

'The preservation of a corpse isn't a crime,' she said with a look of distaste on her features.

'No,' Suleyman agreed, 'it isn't. However, possessing a corpse in a private home . . .'

'What people may or may not do with one of my subjects is not my affair,' she said with a petulant toss of her head. 'I am by profession an anatomist. I have every official piece of paper and permit to allow me to practise.'

'But you maintain these bodies, don't you,' Suleyman asked, 'in people's homes?'

Arto Sarkissian, for whom the whole connection between Çöktin's dead boy and Suleyman's investigation into the activities of Valery Rostov was still a mystery, looked confused.

The look in Yeşim Keyder's eyes was one of restrained hatred. 'Yes,' she said, 'I do. What of it?'

'What, you mean apart from the public health issue?' Suleyman responded coldly. 'Now look, I don't know whether or not you are aware of what type of people you are dealing with here, Dr Keyder. If you are then you will know that they generally make their money via illegal means.'

'That isn't my affair,' she said with a dismissive wave of her hand. 'I produce works of great beauty for bereaved people. I continue the work of my mentor.'

'If I'm not much mistaken,' Arto Sarkissian put in, 'some of your colleagues, like Señor Orontes, would be very interested in your methods and formulas.'

'I'm sure they would,' the old woman replied unpleasantly, 'but they're not getting them. I apply my balm to a considerable number of my subjects on a daily basis. Some of my clients, including Rosita, I trust to do it themselves. But I would never allow another professional to come into possession of my balm.'

Suleyman, his mind now fixed upon Rostov, rubbed his

chin thoughtfully. 'So where are these "subjects" then, Dr Keyder?'

'Oh, I was under the impression that you knew,' she answered bluntly, 'but if you don't, then that's my affair. People come to me in confidence.'

'Yes, I know.'

Yeşim Keyder rose to her feet with remarkable speed. 'And so unless you intend to arrest me for something, I would suggest that—'

'Dr Keyder, I can force you to let us see your records,' Suleyman said. 'Or I can have you followed in order to see which houses you enter.' The look of disgust on her face only encouraged him to continue. 'Your co-operation . . .'

'Don't threaten me, young man!' Yeşim Keyder leaned towards him and hissed, 'What I'm doing is no threat to national security. I've committed no crime. You'll need to get authorisation. But do it if you must.' Looking across at Arto Sarkissian, she said, 'I will call the priest to make arrangements for Rosita and Miguel.'

'Yes . . .'

'And now I am going,' she said as she picked her handbag up from the floor, 'home.'

'Don't leave the city, will you, Dr Keyder,' Suleyman said as the woman turned towards the door.

Without even looking back she replied, 'It's not possible for me to go far without endangering the integrity of at least some of my subjects as well you know.'

With that she left. Suleyman and Arto Sarkissian, now deprived of her presence, looked blankly at each other and then at the sheet-covered corpse that still lay, like a traveller from the past, in the centre of the laboratory.

# CHAPTER 14

Constable Ali Güney was bored. Ordered by İkmen to follow some man called Kuran, he was now in a dark and silent street in Balat sitting in his car outside a very tall, old house.

His instructions had been simple. Follow Kuran and report on where he went and what he did. Well, so far Güney had seen Kuran's lawyer drop him at this house and then drive off. Kuran had gone inside and for well over an hour now that had been that. Dull.

Güney lit yet another cigarette and leaned back into his seat. Balat had always been known as a Jewish district. One of the men he'd trained with, Cohen, had apparently originated from Balat. But over the years a lot of the Jews had gone – to better parts of the city, to Israel and sometimes to places even further afield. Other migrants, from Anatolia and from places like Albania had since come to take their place. As if to underline this thought, two heavily veiled women passed in front of the car, their eyes averted from Güney's vaguely curious gaze.

A few lights were on in the house. There wasn't any noise, however. Not that this was unusual in this upper part of Balat. Apart from this house and the Greek school, there wasn't actually much in the area. A couple of other big, old Jewish houses – places surrounded by thick, high walls, crouching behind heavy metal gates. Now home to quiet, pious families from places like Hakkari, Mardin and Kars. Sun-baked eastern towns where the lack of almost everything threw the inhabitants back onto their religion like exhausted castaways. Hard lives they have out there in the east, the city-born-and-bred Güney thought vaguely. Once, years ago, he'd been 'out there' to Mardin, a town not far from the Syrian border. It had been appalling. Full of arrogant soldiers, it had been hot beyond endurance and the only entertainment available, the local brothel, had been inhabited exclusively by women of over fifty. Some people complained about İstanbul, but when you compared it to other places it was like paradise.

A sharp, metallic sound from the direction of the house he was supposed to be watching made Güney sit up. It sounded as if something heavy was being flung down on to concrete ... But before Güney could really begin to speculate what the sound might mean, something else happened that took all of his attention.

From somewhere inside the walled-in compound that comprised the house and garden, a great light came on. So bright, that, if Güney hadn't known better, he might have thought that the sun had somehow come out at night. 'Allah!' he exclaimed, softly underneath his breath, just in case some unnatural or demonic thing might be at work in this silent old quarter of the long-gone Jews.

'. . . so, as you can see, Doctor,' Suleyman concluded, 'the connection between the late Miguel Arancibia and my Russian mobster is both significant and fortuitous.'

The Armenian, who had been listening open-mouthed to Suleyman's account, shook his head.

'You know,' he said slowly as he leaned forward in order to light the end of his guest's cigarette, 'whenever one thinks that one has experienced the most strange thing it is possible to experience, along comes something else. Like this.'

Suleyman smiled. 'Superior embalming.'

'Your loved ones, seemingly, preserved as in life, for ever.' Arto Sarkissian leaned forward on to his elbows. His desk creaked beneath his weight. 'And, if as you say there is also a vogue for these bodies, then Dr Keyder must be making a lot of money out of this.'

'Yes,' Suleyman dragged on his cigarette and frowned, 'which makes you wonder why she was so keen to get her hands on the Kuloğlu apartment.'

'Indeed,' Arto agreed. 'She has a yalı out in Sarıyer,' he shrugged, 'but then maybe it wasn't always so easy.'

'What do you mean?'

'I mean,' the Armenian said, 'that perhaps the Keyder family were not always so fortunate. Maybe their roots lie in one of the less affluent districts of the city. Something a young friend of ours, Berekiah Cohen, said the other day, about how some poor Jews from here went to South America years ago . . .'

'Yes, but the Keyders aren't Jews and anyway they returned.'

'Only because they had to.'

Suleyman sighed. 'I'll check it out.' He rubbed the side of his face with his hand. The stubble on his face rasped against his palm. 'Leaving the dead unburied is an offence,'

222

he said wearily, 'but where we stand in relation to the activities of the embalmer is less certain.'

'Are you going to attempt to gain access to her records?' Arto asked.

'In the morning. When I've had a chance to speak to Çöktin, I'll go to Ardiç. The possibility of finding unburied corpses should be enough to get access. We can cross-reference those records with the names Rostov gave us. It may even give us legitimate access to some properties we've been wanting to look into for a while.'

Arto glanced down at the watch on his wrist and was shocked to find that it was already 1 a.m.

'You don't think Dr Keyder might destroy her records before you get there?' he said gravely. 'If, as you say, she's involved with gangsters, then they must be relying upon her to protect their anonymity. Whatever the position may be with Dr Keyder, her clients are holding their corpses illegally.'

Suleyman shrugged. 'I don't know,' he replied. 'Maybe she'll excise the names. But surely she'd have to keep scientific records for her own reference.'

'True.'

'And we've always got Rostov's information to fall back on. Well, at least while his daughter is in that refrigerator.'

'It was odd the way Orontes and Dr Keyder came here together,' the Armenian frowned at the memory of it. 'He said that they met, but he didn't say where or how.'

Arto shook his head as if to dislodge an unpleasant thought from his mind. 'He's a strange, unsettling man,

Orontes,' he said. 'I don't feel that I would want to trust him with a deceased relative.'

Exhausted by what had been a very busy and emotional night, both men lapsed into temporary silence. Staring, seemingly at nothing, they both remained silent and motionless for some minutes.

It was Arto who made the first move. Rising smartly, if shakily from behind his desk he said, 'Well, Inspector, I think that we should return to our respective homes and get some sleep.'

Suleyman smiled weakly.

Arto reached around the back of his chair and retrieved his jacket. 'I had to work on a woman your men dragged out of the Bosphorus earlier this evening,' he said wearily. 'Even now I find water-logged bodies extremely troubling.'

'A woman? How old?'

'Early twenties.' Arto stooped down in order to pick up his briefcase.

'Blonde?'

The Armenian moved upwards, smiling. 'Peroxide. Why?'

Suleyman stood up slowly and sighed, his hands braced against the back of his chair. 'I think I might need to take a look at her, Doctor,' he said. Looking up into Arto's drawn and exhausted features he added, 'I'm sorry.'

Ever since Güney had called him to tell him about the light, İkmen had been unable to sleep. It had unsettled him. That and the disturbed groans and shuffles that continually emanated from Talaat's bedroom. The sound of a mind and body locked in mortal combat with a deadly, growing foe.

In order to get away from the stifling heat inside the apartment, İkmen had come out on to the balcony. Below on the normally bustling Divanyolu thoroughfare, not a soul save a few straggly cats, moved. Across the road, the brooding bulk of the Sultanahmet Mosque, now in the dead hours of the morning, un-illuminated and sombre, loomed over the Hippodrome, that once bloodied centre of the distant Byzantine Empire. How many, İkmen wondered as he drew on yet another Maltepe cigarette, had perished in that place for the purposes of entertainment? He'd never understood the word games as applied to the activities that used to take place in the Hippodrome. How could anything that killed people be a game? And yet over the years he had, from time to time, come across those who killed for their own entertainment. Mercifully they were rare. Generally they were fairly inadequate people possessed of little power and influence – which as Suleyman's wife had once told him was why they took pleasure in the death of others.

Sometimes, however, such people did attain power and influence – Hitler, for instance. And some, notably the American government, had placed the Iraqi Saddam Hussein also in this category. It was being said that the Americans, having failed to secure the arrest of the man they believed had mounted the 11 September attack on the World Trade Center in New York, were going after Saddam and his lieutenants. It could mean war. İkmen frowned at the thought of it. The Turkish Republic, a member of NATO, a friend to America and a neighbour of Iraq. Not being involved wasn't going to be an option, either for him or for his country. And his son Bülent was due to be conscripted into the army in less than six months.

İkmen put his cigarette out and then lit another. He looked across the darkened rooftops and monuments of Sultan Ahmet once again and sighed. The Akdeniz children, Nuray and Yaşar, were out there somewhere, lost, alone and, he knew, in pain. If only, may Allah forgive me, İkmen thought, that image were not so fixed in my mind. If only I wasn't experiencing a growing conviction that they are probably dead . . .

'Talaat is very restless tonight.'

The familiar female voice roused him from his reverie.

'Fatma, what . . . ?'

'I can't sleep in this heat,' she said as she lowered herself into the chair beside her husband. A hank of her long black and grey hair flopped over on to his shoulder as she sat.

'Worrying about everything probably isn't helping either,' İkmen said as he reached out to take one of her plump hands in his.

'I can't help that,' Fatma said bluntly. 'There's a lot to worry about. What with Talaat, Hulya – not to mention all these rumours about the Americans and Iraq.'

İkmen raised an eyebrow. Fatma didn't generally pay much heed to world affairs.

Seeing the surprise on his face, made her smile. 'You'd be surprised what I pay attention to,' she said a little caustically. 'Politics affects housewives just as much as it affects policemen.'

226

'Fatma, I've never been in any doubt about your intelligence.'

'In the current climate for a Muslim girl to be marrying a Jewish boy . . .' She shrugged. 'I know you think my disapproval is all about my faith, but it isn't.' She turned to look her husband straight in the face. 'It's also about my fears – for both of them. The world gets less tolerant every day, or so it seems to me. What hope can there be for Hulya and Berekiah with all this hate?'

İkmen shook his head. 'I don't know,' he said on a sigh, 'but if they get some comfort from being together . . .'

'They won't be very comfortable if someone takes against them.'

'Life is risk. Every day could be our last. You could walk out of the house and get run down by a car, we could all perish in an earthquake.'

'Do not remind me of that!' She closed her eyes against the images that still, nearly three years after the last great quake in 1999, persisted in haunting her mind.

İkmen lit a fresh cigarette from the smouldering butt of his last smoke. 'I'm not going to oppose Hulya and Berekiah. I won't be a hypocrite, Fatma.'

'I didn't think that you would be,' she sighed. 'Much as it pains me in this case, you wouldn't be the man that I married if you went along with my opinions. You know, I think that Estelle might share your views, Çetin.'

'That wouldn't surprise me,' İkmen smiled. 'Her family were never religious. That Balthazar is so adamant is beyond me. I've never seen him go near a synagogue and the only thing his father ever worshipped was rakı. But he's got this thing about his Jewish heritage.'

'Perhaps it's because Berekiah is the only child he has now,' Fatma said, referring to the fact that Cohen's eldest son, Yusuf, was an inmate of a psychiatric institution. 'Maybe it's all that much more important now.'

'Maybe.'

İkmen placed an arm across Fatma's shoulders and hugged her to his thin chest.

'Perhaps I'll go and talk to him,' he said wearily, 'not to try and change his mind, just to let him know that I do understand. I don't like being his enemy. I'm not his enemy.' He smiled. 'Disgusting old gossip that he is, I have a lot of affection for Cohen. He gave Mehmet Suleyman a home and a family when he needed all the support he could get. I know he's had his problems with women and—'

'Problems!' Fatma pulled away from him quickly, her eyes wide with amazement. 'Balthazar Cohen has slept with every loose woman in this city and countless foreigners.'

'I know. I know.'

'Estelle has cried for days.'

'Yes . . .'

'Men!' She shrugged her hands upwards as if appealing for inspiration from above. 'You talk so glibly of such things! And to think of my daughter married to the son of such a man.'

'Berekiah isn't like that, Fatma!'

'You think,' she tutted petulantly, 'but my mother used to say the same about Talaat! Oh, he's a good boy, she'd say, not at all like your Uncle İsmet. You know Uncle İsmet?'

'The one who had a mistress in İzmir.'

228

'A whore in Gaziosmanpaşa and some Italian woman who used to visit him every July. But Talaat was worse than that,' she exclaimed, 'with his foreign beach girls and the sophisticated women from Ankara . . .'

'Yes, well, now he's got cancer, all that's at an end, isn't it?' İkmen said acidly. Weary now of his wife's tirade against significant men, he added, 'Talaat had a good time in the way that he wanted to.'

Fatma lowered her head and looked down at her hands. 'And now he's dying.'

'Yes.'

Her eyes filled with tears, which glistened in the light from the streetlamps as she raised her head up to look at her husband once again. 'Oh, Çetin!'

He put his arms around her and kissed the top of her head. 'We all die, Fatma,' he said gently, 'time runs out.'

'And then we go to Paradise.'

'Maybe,' he shrugged, 'I don't know. One thing that I do know, however, is that we should try to be happy while we're here.' He looked down at her and smiled. 'Which is why I will help Hulya and Berekiah in any way that I can. After all,' he said as he lifted one hand to stroke his wife's thick hair, 'I would be a miserable old bastard if I denied them what we've had all our married lives.'

'And what is that, Çetin?'

'True love,' he responded simply.

Fatma reached up and pulled his face down towards hers. Soon dawn would come, the hour of prayer bringing with it the muezzin's earnest call – a time when base urges like those she felt now should be washed away from the minds of all the Faithful.

# CHAPTER 15

Commissioner Ardiç leaned back into the softness of his new swivel chair and observed the younger, slimmer man in front of him with a critical eye. 'In view of what you believe might have happened, I've decided to assign İskender to liaise with Rostov,' he said. 'I feel it's best.'

'It was definitely my informant, sir,' Suleyman said, as he shook his head slowly and wearily from side to side. 'She was drowned.'

It had been the prostitute herself who had told him about how Rostov disposed of his enemies. Like the Sultans of old he favoured drowning. What was it Rostov had said so coldly when Suleyman had asked him about Masha? *I don't know anyone of that name, Inspector. No one of that name exists.*

He'd killed her. Used her in some game with the police first – a game that none of them as yet, or so Suleyman felt – truly understood. Surely there had to be more to what had happened over the past two days than the search for some mythical boy called Vladimir followed by the clumsy discovery of Tatiana's body? However clever Rostov was, it was really suspicious that they hadn't found anything incriminating at his home.

'Yes, but we don't know whether it was Rostov and

his men who did that, do we?' the Commissioner cut across Suleyman's thoughts with blunt practicality. 'What is more to the point,' he continued, 'is whether this disgusting trade in preserved bodies might give us access to other mobsters' houses. In view of the fact that you discovered nothing of any interest at Rostov's place . . .'

'It could be that we only find bodies at the other locations, sir,' Suleyman put in. Perhaps it was all some sort of elaborate plot hatched by all of them. Maybe there were no other bodies?

'Yes, it could, but then if that is the case at least we'll be able to remove these ghastly corpses,' Ardiç responded tersely. 'There is a moral and a health issue here.' He looked down at the cigar sticking out of his mouth and re-lit its extinguished end. 'And who knows what else we may find during the course of a very thorough search of Sergei Vronsky's home and who's that other gangster . . . Malenkov?'

'Yes, sir.'

'All of which may prove very fruitful.' He looked up, frowning. 'Now, Dr Keyder, the embalmer.'

'I think it's very likely, sir, that she may wish to conceal or even destroy records that relate to this work. If she's any awareness of how these people operate, she'll know that one doesn't give information about them to us.'

'Mmm.' Ardiç puffed heavily on his cigar for a few moments. 'But then if we have Rostov's testimony . . .'

'I don't think he'd be very happy if he knew we were going in to, say, Malenkov's place, solely on his advice,' Suleyman said.

'Do we care?'

'If such a situation could start a gang war, then yes.'

Ardiç sighed. 'But if we have, effectively, taken possession of his daughter's corpse . . .'

'Oh, we currently have a hold over him, yes, sir. He's very concerned about what may or may not happen to that corpse.'

'Mmm . . .' Ardiç put his hands together in front of his chin and grunted. 'All right, Inspector,' he said gravely, 'get over to Dr Keyder's place and see what you can find.'

'Yes, sir.' Suleyman moved his chair back from his superior's desk and stood up.

'I'll authorise a search but don't intimidate the woman, she only treats these bodies, she's not a criminal and, besides, in the wake of your little misunderstanding with the Bulgarian priest the last thing I need is for the Keyders to get involved.' He paused in order to let the memory of the Father Alexei incident sink in. He hadn't exactly savaged Suleyman about it. His response in view of the rumours about another possible Middle East crisis, was very restrained. Incidents with minorities, particularly those of a non-Muslim persuasion, like Father Alexei and Dr Keyder, were not what Ardiç wanted.

'What do you mean, sir?' Suleyman said frowning. 'How can Dr Keyder be "involved" with Father Alexei?'

'She isn't.' Ardiç, annoyed at his inferior's seeming lack of grasp, sighed. 'There are all sorts of rumours going around, as I'm sure you're aware, about another conflict brewing in this region,' he said. 'The Americans want to have another go at Saddam Hussein. That and the up-coming election is making me a little tense about our public image. I've told you to be careful of Yeşim Keyder because I feel it would be unwise to upset our Jewish population.'

'She's Jewish? Dr Sarkissian thought she might be.'

'Oh, yes,' Ardiç responded breezily. 'Her brother, Dr Veli Keyder, was a famous biologist, served in the army with one of my cousins. Born in Balat, the Keyders. Poor family, apparently, got to where they wanted to be through sheer hard work. Can't understand why the sister became an embalmer, though.' He shook his head confusedly. 'I always thought she was an anatomist.'

'It would seem that the time they spent in South America had a great influence on her.'

Ardiç looked up. 'Through this Dr Ara. Yes.' He shook his head slowly. 'South America. What a place that is,' he said. 'You know that the Aztecs or the Incas, can't remember which, practised human sacrifice? They used to cut hearts, still beating, from their "offerings". Then they'd mummify what remained – Allah alone knows why. Barbarians!'

'That was a very long time ago, sir,' Suleyman responded. 'I don't think that Aztec practices have anything to do with the preservation of dictators' wives or the children of gangsters.'

Ardiç, who didn't appreciate being disagreed with, simply grunted.

Suleyman took his jacket off the back of his chair and put it on. Later on he would have to explain to his wife why he had been so late home last night. How he had needed to spend time at the mortuary with Dr Sarkissian and his corpses, but not why. He wouldn't mention how he had stared and stared at Masha's corpse until his eyes felt like they would crack. Not a word would he speak about the test the Armenian was going to perform in order to discover whether the girl had been HIV positive. That, together with the appointment Dr Sarkissian had made for Suleyman with his brother, Krikor, was not for Zelfa's consumption. Not yet.

'Sir, I'd like to take three officers with me out to Dr Keyder's yalı,' he said as he made to open the door out into the corridor.

'As you wish,' his superior responded. 'Just make sure that one is female. We don't want Dr Keyder getting upset.'

'No, sir.'

'Very well.'

And with a wave of one hand Ardiç dismissed him.

Once out in the corridor, Suleyman pondered on what he'd just been told. So Yeşim Keyder was Jewish, was she? He wasn't aware that they routinely practised embalming, but perhaps they didn't; perhaps her interest only came about because of Argentina and her experiences in that country.

Suleyman lit up a cigarette. Amazing that Dr Keyder, who now lived, according to Çöktin, in a very luxurious yalı had been born in Balat. Many years before, when he was still a sergeant, Suleyman had worked, with İkmen, on a case involving an old Jewish communist up in Balat. It was, he recalled, a picturesquely shabby place. Funny that its name should come up again and at the same time as İkmen was involved in looking for the Akdeniz children up in Balat. Synchronicity. Suleyman smiled. But then, if İkmen was to be believed, maybe not. I do not, he recalled İkmen saying once, many, many years ago, hold with synchronicity, Suleyman, and neither should you.

Eren Akdeniz left the house at ten thirty. Alone, she carried nothing except a handbag and hadn't, at least not within Constable Gün's hearing, bade farewell to anyone inside the house. And since neither Melih nor Reşad Kuran had been spotted by Güney during the night it was probably safe to assume that the two men were still sleeping.

As she descended the steep flight of steps that led down into the centre of the district, Eren threw a patterned scarf over her head. Gün, who was out of uniform for this particular assignment, was similarly attired. It wasn't a mode of dress that she liked but she could appreciate why it was necessary. In spite of its smattering of artists and its recent application for World Heritage Site status, Balat was still essentially a working-class district and as such its people, particularly the women, tended to dress modestly.

When the woman first left the house, Gün, whose orders had been to follow Kuran, had wondered what to do. A brief phone call to İkmen had confirmed that she was to follow Eren and report her movements. Another female officer, Sibel Yalçin, daughter of one of the department's oldest and admittedly slowest detectives, had been ordered to take her place. Once she'd finished the call, Gün put her mobile back in her handbag and followed the artist's wife down the steps.

It was already very hot and the air had that sticky,

humid quality that characterises high summer in İstanbul. As Gün looked out across the tops of the old Greek and Jewish houses towards the Golden Horn, her vision was blurred by the heat haze that hung like a tacky rug over the great waterway. She didn't like summer in the heart of the city. But unless one happened to be very wealthy one was more or less stuck with it. The rich could escape to summer houses in one or other of the Bosphorus villages. Gün, her eyes once again pinned to the back of Eren Akdeniz's pattern-wrapped head, wondered idly whether Inspector Suleyman's family still retained one of these places.

At the bottom of the steps the artist's wife turned right on to some nameless street where little bits of activity were taking place around a general store and a barber's shop. A group of middle-aged and elderly men stood outside the latter, their hair just slightly overgrown, smoking. They spoke in low voices, each one waiting his turn to sit in the barber's chair and have the short, neat standard Turkish haircut. As Eren, a plain and also headscarfed woman passed, they didn't so much as flick their eyes in her direction.

More surprisingly, she was also ignored outside the general store with its knot of headscarfed women and their many bags of shopping in tow. Groups of thin, excitable children played around them like insects, occasionally stopping to berate their mothers for not buying them this or that in the shop. Like a small patch of darkness she passed beside them, and two tiny white kittens flew from in front of her feet as she went.

A little further up the road, on the opposite side of the street from a vast, vine-covered mansion, the sound of hammers on metal signalled the existence of a copper-smith's workshop. Entered via a fenced yard at the front, it was typical of the small-scale artisan businesses that had always characterised Balat. Without looking to either left or right, Eren entered the courtyard and, by the time Gün had caught up, she had disappeared from sight. The hammering inside the building stopped.

Reluctant actually to follow her into the ramshackle little workshop, Gün stood beside the opening into the yard and surveyed the area. Large cauldrons, some of which were obviously there to be repaired, lay carelessly on the ground outside the workshop, which was little more than a wooden shed. At the back of this building there was a wall, to which it appeared to be attached or at least leaning against. The wall, Gün observed, was old and crumbling in places, but that wasn't unusual in this area. Long ago it had probably been part of something – a house or maybe even a church or synagogue.

When, a few moments later, the hammering started up once again, Gün moved slightly back on to the street and waited for Eren to reappear. But seconds passed into minutes and with no Eren in sight, Gün decided to go in and see what was happening.

The workshop, which was stacked from floor to ceiling with copper – pots, pans, plates, kettles – only supported one workman. Small and elderly, he sucked heavily on a home-made cigarette as he brought a small hammer down on to a currently very misshapen plate. He seemed, from the look of wrapt concentration on his brown weathered face, to be contented in his solitude. However, when he saw Gün he stopped what he was doing and looked up.

The policewoman could see at a glance that there was no one with him.

'Good morning, uncle,' she said to the old man. 'Did a lady come in here just now?'

'Yes,' the old man replied, 'Eren Hanım. But she's just gone.'

'No.'

'Yes.'

'But, uncle, I didn't see her leave. I've been outside in the street.'

The old man smiled, his eyes almost disappearing into the heavy lines that surrounded them. 'She left by the back door,' he said as he waved a hand towards a rough-looking plank in the back wall, 'out on to Mürsel Paşa Caddesi.'

Without even asking if she could do so, Gün sprang forward and pushed the plank roughly to one side.

'Young lady!' the old man said disapprovingly as he watched her make a most unladylike exit.

There was a small piece of rough scrubland just beyond the door which fell away sharply towards the fast-moving Mürsel Paşa thoroughfare and the glittering Golden Horn beyond. On the side of the road, standing beside a now stationary yellow taxi stood a woman in a patterned headscarf. As Gün struggled to maintain her footing on the powdery scrubland the woman turned just before getting into the vehicle. Eren Akdeniz first said something to the driver and then, with a smile directly at Constable Gün, she got into the vehicle and sped away in the direction of the Atatürk Bridge.

\* \* \*

'People who purchase my expertise pay me a lot of money,' Yeşim Keyder said as she placed a large buff folder into Suleyman's hands. 'They expect me to operate in legal and sanitary conditions. You'll find everything pertaining to my conformation with City and Government regulations in this file.'

'I have never questioned the legality of your practice, Dr Keyder,' Suleyman said as he briefly glanced through the documents in the folder.

'Just its morality,' she returned sharply.

'You weren't exactly forthcoming about your profession when Sergeant Çöktin first spoke to you about Miguel Arancibia.'

'I feared the lack of understanding you are exhibiting so graphically now, Inspector,' Dr Keyder retorted. 'I work, as I'm sure you can appreciate, in a very discreet and confidential world. It isn't, in general, Muslim practice to embalm the dead.'

'No.' He put the folder down on a bench, which looked very similar to those used by Dr Sarkissian at the mortuary. Dr Keyder's laboratory, which was situated in the basement of her yalı, was a somewhat unnerving place. Various instruments were visible, the function of which was only too easy to imagine. Çöktin, who had been given access to a filing cabinet in the corner, briefly looked up.

'I must confess,' Suleyman continued, 'that I find it very odd that you chose to practise in Turkey, Dr Keyder. Surely you could make a far better living in Western Europe or even back in South America.'

'Turkey is my home,' she said shortly. 'I left it once before, but now I'm too old to leave.'

Suleyman shrugged. 'I was only thinking that professionally—'

'I make a living, a good one, as you know,' she sniffed as if there were suddenly a bad smell under her nose. 'My work is without equal. People will pay almost any price. And anyway,' she added, her voice now just tinged with spite, 'some of my clients are Muslims. Not everyone is who he or what she seems.'

'No,' Suleyman replied, smiling, 'that's true. Some Jewish people for instance . . .'

'Look, if you're trying to make something out of the fact that my parents were Jewish then don't bother,' the old woman said as she lowered herself down into the chair behind her desk. 'Just because I don't publicise my origins that doesn't mean that I keep them secret. I am a Jew, I was born in Balat.'

'You told me when we first spoke,' Çöktin interjected from across the room, 'that your family had become wealthy because of their involvement with the Republican movement, that your father knew President İnönü.'

'No, what I said,' Dr Keyder corrected emphatically, 'was that my father fought with İnönü. Like many people at that time, my father was in the Republican army. I told you further that we had done well as a family, but by virtue of our intelligence and not because of some sort of favour from İnönü. My brother, Veli, was a brilliant biologist. Because of my involvement with Dr Ara, I am the world's premier embalmer.'

Suleyman leaned back against one of the benches and looked down at her. 'So do you have assistants?'

'I use those endowed with more muscle than brain

to assist in the delivery and placement of my subjects, yes.'

'But you perform the process?'

'Like Dr Ara, I work alone,' she answered shortly. 'The more people you have in a laboratory the more likely it is that contamination will be transferred to your subjects. Others bring them in, set them down here and take them out, but only I do the work, Inspector.'

'Quite stressful for—'

'An old woman?' she smiled. 'Ara taught me well. I know all the tricks, all the shortcuts, all the right ways in which to do everything. I need no one and nothing.'

'Except that you once needed Ara,' Suleyman said. 'I assume from what you've already told us that you met him through Rosita's family?'

'Yes. I went with Veli and the rest of Rosita's family to view what he had done with Miguel and,' suddenly she smiled, dazzlingly, 'it was magical. So perfect, so alive! Señora Arancibia, Rosita's mother, cried with joy. Dr Ara could bring back the dead, I could see that. I wanted to have that skill for myself.'

'Dr Ara didn't think it odd that—'

'I, a woman, should want to do such a thing? No.' She looked down, Suleyman felt, a little coyly. 'Pedro was a brilliant, fascinating man. An artist. We . . . we got on well. We shared a philosophy about the preservation of beauty. Beauty should never die. It's too precious and rare. That's why Pedro refused to work for the Soviets. Using his skills to preserve the likes of Lenin and Stalin was anathema to him.'

241

'And yet some of your subjects must be old and unat-tractive,' Suleyman said.

'I am not Pedro.'

'You know he was accused of necrophilia?' Çöktin put in.

Yeşim Keyder's eyes blazed. 'Don't talk about things you can't understand! Pedro Ara was my soul-mate. Everything he did was aimed at the preservation of beauty. Everything!'

'Dr Keyder!'

The three of them looked up towards the door at the top of the stairs leading into the basement. Roditi, corpulent and slovenly, stood in front of it, looking vaguely horrified at the scene below.

'You've got a visitor, Dr Keyder,' he said, 'a lady.'

'All right, I'll come,' she said, and then rose from her seat. 'Excuse me, gentlemen.'

She walked up the stairs towards Roditi, who escorted her out of the basement.

Suleyman, now that she'd gone wrinkling his nose up against the strong smell of formaldehyde that pervaded every part of the laboratory, walked across to Çöktin, who was still busy with the filing cabinet.

'Anything?' he enquired as he watched the younger man flick through the contents of a large green file.

'If you mean have I come across the names Vronsky, Bulganin and Malenkov, no I haven't, sir,' the Kurd replied. 'Most of these records are in excess of five years old.' He sighed. 'I don't suppose she's volunteered any names.'

'No.' He looked down at the floor, lost in thought for

a moment. 'I wonder if she gave them code names or numbers.'

'None of the other records are compiled like that; they're all very explicit,' Çöktin said. 'She must have destroyed them.'

'Is there anything recent? She works all the time.'

Çöktin sighed. 'There are records for Miguel Arancibia and for a male and female by the name of Nabaro.'

'Mean anything to you?'

'No, sir.'

Their conversation was temporarily cut short by the arrival of Constable Roditi. He was alone, and from the expression on his face he was somewhat troubled.

'Roditi?'

The constable drew rather nearer to his superior than he usually did and said, 'Sir?'

'Yes?'

He looked once over his shoulder towards the stairs before proceeding. 'Look, sir,' he said, 'it might not mean anything but . . . you know I've been working on that Akdeniz missing kids case with Inspector İkmen?'

'I didn't know you were working with him,' Suleyman said, 'but go on.'

'Akdeniz's wife has just come to see Dr Keyder,' Roditi said.

'Do you know why?'

'No,' he shrugged, 'they just went into the sofa together and Dr Keyder closed the door. I couldn't really insist that she keep it open, could I? I mean it's weird, this embalming stuff, but it's not like she's actually done anything wrong.'

'No,' Suleyman said frowning. 'No, you were quite right, Roditi. Thank you.'

'Sir.'

And then he left.

Suleyman turned to Çöktin. 'I wonder what Mrs Akdeniz can want with Dr Keyder,' he said.

'Maybe one of her relatives has died and she wants to use Dr Keyder's "service".'

'Don't you think that's somewhat odd in view of what is happening with her children? I don't think I'd be capable of attending to such a thing if I were worried about my son.'

'If this job and particularly this case has taught me anything, sir, it's that people are weird,' Çöktin replied, shaking his head from side to side as he spoke. 'As Inspector İkmen always says, life is infinitely variable and anything is possible.'

'Mmm . . .' Suleyman took his mobile phone out of his pocket. 'I think perhaps I should pass this information on to him, don't you?'

'Yes, sir.'

However, before he could bring İkmen's number up on the screen Dr Keyder returned carrying yet another folder which, this time, proved to be full of invoices. Rather oddly, she was smiling.

İkmen first looked down at what he'd just written in his notepad and then turned his attention to the red-faced young woman by his side.

'Right, so,' he said, 'the car was a Mercedes, it pulled in to the open gates at the back of the house . . .'

'Someone I couldn't see closed the gates,' the young woman put in breathlessly.

'And then, ten minutes later, the gates opened and the car rolled out.'

'Yes.'

'Could you see who was driving the car?' Ayşe Farsakoğlu asked.

The girl with the red face, young Sibel Yalçin, bit down on her bottom lip. 'Er . . . a man.'

'On his own?'

'Yes, I think so.'

'What was he like?' İkmen asked. 'Young, old, fat, thin . . . ?'

'Er . . .'

'You didn't get the licence plate number, Sibel,' Ayşe Farsakoğlu said, more as a statement than a question.

'Er . . .'

İkmen, suddenly infuriated beyond reason by the youngster's seeming lack of attention, said, 'All right, Constable, that will be all. Thank you.'

'Oh, but, sir, don't you want me to stay?'

'Allah forbid, no!' Realising from the hurt look on her face that he had gone way too far for her delicate sensibilities he moderated his tone. 'No, thank you, Constable. That will be all for today, thank you.'

'Sir.' She saluted, sloppily, but with conviction – something that wasn't lost on İkmen, who duly saluted back. Both İkmen and Farsakoğlu watched as the young woman trudged grimly back down the hill and away from the Akdeniz house.

Once she was out of earshot, İkmen said, 'You'd think

wouldn't you, Ayşe, that someone like Ardiç would have learned his lesson with that girl's father.'

Ayşe, a little embarrassed to be discussing another senior officer with one of his fellows, simply looked down at the ground.

'I mean poor old Hüsnü Yalçin has always been a liability. Allah forgive me, I mean him no harm, but wouldn't you think that Ardiç would draw the line at employing the old man's idiot daughter? She sees nothing, hears even less . . . The only thing she can ever be counted upon to do is wander around after Inspector Suleyman whenever he's in her vicinity.'

'Sir . . .'

'Oh, well,' İkmen shrugged, 'at least I suppose we can be grateful that she noticed the car. I would have liked a licence plate – even a colour would have been nice – but . . .' He placed a cigarette firmly between his lips and looked up into the seemingly sightless windows of the Akdeniz house. 'OK, Ayşe, let's see what Mr Akdeniz is up to today.'

# CHAPTER 16

Melih Akdeniz was in his garden standing in front of the great swathe of material strung between his trees. When he saw İkmen he took a long swig from his ever-present medicine bottle and then wiped his mouth on the sleeve of his shirt.

'Have you come to see Reşad?' he said as the policeman and his assistant approached.

'No, Mr Akdeniz.'

'Haven't got the results from all those tests you made on his van?'

'No, sir.' İkmen, now level with the artist, smiled into the other's sick, bloodshot eyes. 'As I told Mr Kuran, these things take time. Sadly.'

'Mmm . . .' Melih Akdeniz looked up into the sky and squinted as he bathed his face in the rays of the midday sun. 'So what is it, İkmen?' he said huskily. 'Have you found my children?'

'Unfortunately no, sir,' İkmen said. 'No, my visit is just a courtesy.'

'Wanting to know why that car pulled into my drive this morning.' The artist looked back at İkmen again and smiled. 'I saw your little retard write it down in her little book,' he continued unpleasantly. 'You must try harder,

247

İkmen. Is it any wonder that my children are still missing when the İstanbul police are reduced to employing the mentally subnormal.'

İkmen, choosing to ignore this little tirade, said, 'And so the car, sir? What was that about?'

'It was about,' the artist mimicked both the depth and seriousness of İkmen's voice, 'some materials I need for my performance exhibit.'

'Ah . . .'

The clearing of a throat from over by the house signalled the appearance of Reşad Kuran at the back door. His hair tousled and his face unshaven, he looked as if he'd just fallen out of a very uncomfortable bed.

'I'm having a preview here tonight for the media,' Melih continued. Turning his gaze from İkmen to Ayşe Farsakoğlu, he added, 'It's at eight. Want to come?'

'Er . . .'

'Melih, I don't think that police people,' Reşad Kuran ladled the last two words with pure contempt, 'would either want to come or be capable of understanding.'

'The women police can come,' Melih laughed, swigging yet again from his bottle as he did so, 'all except that stupid girl.'

'Well then, maybe Sergeant Farsakoğlu might be prevailed upon to attend,' İkmen said, 'although if I were you, Mr Akdeniz, I would be careful about over-stretching myself at this time.'

'What do you mean?' the artist snapped.

'I mean that you appear to be needing rather a lot of your medication at this time, sir.'

'You think so?' the artist laughed. Bending down in

248

order to be level with İkmen's ear he said, 'How do you know I don't just take this stuff for fun?'

İkmen smiled. 'Because I have checked to discover whether it is prescribed for you, Mr Akdeniz,' he said, 'and because if it wasn't you'd currently be in one of my cells.'

'True.' The artist stood up straight again and looked through the trees at the sun.

'You're going ahead with your show despite everything that has happened?' Ayşe Farsakoğlu asked.

Still looking at the sun, Melih replied, 'Art is the only reality. My children know that. They are my works – I produced and own them.'

To İkmen the artist looked sicker by the minute, especially with the full rays of the sun on his thin, grey features. Skeletal – both his appearance and his words were unnerving. He seemed, İkmen felt, on the very rim of death. There was even some sort of smell, a decay on the air.

'The performance is based on Karagöz.'

'I'd gathered that.'

The artist looked down at İkmen once again, staring him now straight in the eyes. 'By which I mean that the piece is in shadow,' he said. 'The theme, if not the storyline, is contemporary.'

'Right.' İkmen cleared his throat. 'So these supplies, Mr Akdeniz . . .'

'Costumes,' Melih smiled. 'For my puppets.'

'Ah, so traditional Karagöz?'

'The puppets wear the traditional gear, in a way, yes,' Melih replied. 'It is, as I've said, the theme that is modern, in a way . . .' He looked vaguely distant again for a moment. 'Our relationship, as a society, to ourselves is flawed. Like Hacıvat, the Ottoman pedant, we live in a land of delusion. Only the simplicity of the common, foul man, the Karagöz, if you like, is real and has value, that and only that can be a permanent everlasting statement. You know that Karagöz corresponds to the 'Fool', Tarot card?' he smiled. 'The Fool is the most potent symbol in magic – good and bad he is the ultimate mage. Materials, my materials – blood, strongly pigmented paints, piss – reflect both magic and honesty. My themes of biological sex – it's not romantic, it shouldn't be kind, and death, neither good nor bad, are staring a man in the face from the hour of his birth. Take it, push it in the eyes of our people, give them that finality that is the only reality. Condense and preserve it—'

His tirade was cut off by the ringing of İkmen's mobile telephone. As the policeman turned aside in order to answer his call, Melih Akdeniz, who had now been joined by a somewhat anxious-looking Reşad Kuran, sat down on the ground.

Ayşe Farsakoğlu, alarmed by the trembling that had suddenly taken over the artist's body, went over to join the two men.

'Mr Akdeniz.'

'It's all right, I'm OK.' He took his medicine out of his pocket and took a long, deep draught from its neck.

'He'll be fine,' Reşad Kuran said as he looked, his eyes full of anxiety into Ayşe's face. 'He's OK.'

All three of them stayed like this, one watched the

others watching until İkmen, his face set and grave, returned.

'Mr Akdeniz,' he said as he approached the group, 'that was one of my colleagues, Inspector Suleyman. Your wife has—'

Yet again İkmen's mobile rang.

'Shit!' he muttered as he first held up a hand to indicate that Akdeniz should stay where he was and answered the call. 'Fatma?'

He moved quickly into one of the far corners of the garden, his deep voice muted by the abundant greenery that clung to every surface. Ayşe and the two men remained uncomfortably silent until he returned.

When he did, there was something different about him. Ayşe couldn't quite pinpoint what it was, but something his wife had said must have upset him. That, or he was suddenly in a hurry for some reason.

In one swift movement, he hunkered down beside the fallen artist. 'All right, Mr Akdeniz, I've had enough of this now. Your wife deliberately gave one of my officers the slip this morning. One of my colleagues has just seen her at the house of a Dr Keyder – a woman currently under investigation by some of my fellow officers.'

The artist, his eyes now heavy from the massive amount of medication he had taken that day, just looked blankly on.

'Now you're going to tell me why she was there and why she felt it necessary to keep her destination, apparently Sarıyer, where your children liked to go, from us.' He looked up into the face of Reşad Kuran. 'Or maybe you'd like to enlighten us, Mr Kuran. You deliver things.

251

Have you ever worked for Dr Keyder? Did you perhaps deliver one of Melih's paintings to her on that evening you seem to remember so little about? I haven't got much time now so I'd appreciate an answer from one of you.'

'My client is concerned,' Lütfü Güneş said as he poured himself yet another whiskey and water, 'that you may use the information he gave you about certain friends of his, fellow countrymen, to their detriment.'

İskender frowned. Rostov wasn't in the room with them, which was probably just as well, given the fury that seemed to have built up inside his colleague, Mehmet Suleyman. The latter, fresh from the private mortuary operated by Dr Keyder, sat brooding in the corner, his head in his hands, thinking no doubt rather unhelpful thoughts about that dead prostitute Masha.

İskender cleared his throat before replying. 'Well, sir,' he said, 'to be truthful I don't know whether or not that might be a possibility. The fact that Mr Rostov believes that some of his countrymen may have unburied corpses in their homes doesn't necessarily mean that we will approach them about that at this time. It is, further, a decision that someone far higher up will take, as opposed to myself.'

'My client is also worried,' Güneş continued, 'about the security of his own daughter—'

'That we cannot guarantee,' Suleyman cut in sharply. 'That *thing* down there—'

'What will happen to Tatiana is not yet decided, Mr Güneş,' İskender cut in with a very uncustomary smile on his face, 'but whatever is done, you can assure Mr

Rostov, will be performed with due regard to his fatherly feelings.'

Suleyman sniffed audibly.

İskender made his way over to where the lawyer was standing and placed a friendly hand on his shoulder. 'You may tell Mr Rostov that he has nothing to worry about at this time,' he said.

'Thank you.'

The lawyer threw what was left of his drink to the back of his throat and placed the empty glass down on one of Rostov's many occasional tables. 'I'll go up to him now.'

İskender bowed his head just slightly in recognition. Both officers watched Güneş' back as he left for the upper storey of the mansion.

When he'd gone, Suleyman rose to his feet. 'So Rostov's too prostrate with anxiety over his mummy to get out of his bed . . .'

'Now, look, Mehmet,' his colleague said as he walked over to stand in front of him, 'we have to tread very carefully now.'

'With a murderer?' Suleyman, a good head taller than İskender, laughed unpleasantly down into his face.

The smaller man raised a silencing finger. 'We don't know that he killed that girl, Mehmet.'

'But who else—'

'And furthermore, sad though each and every death might be, we shouldn't care.'

'What do you mean?'

İskender, moving in closer to his colleague, now lowered his voice to a whisper. 'Look, Mehmet,' he said, 'I know you fucked her. It's obvious. But—'

'How?' Incensed, his eyes blazing, Suleyman drew away from him. 'How do you know that?'

İskender raised his eyes upwards as if looking for inspiration from above. 'Oh, Mehmet, please,' he said wearily, 'every time you've seen her you've been like a teenager. You were in that room with her for a very long time.'

'I was . . .'

'Oh, don't keep on lying to me, Mehmet!' He moved away quickly and then threw himself down on to one of the large, gaudy settees. 'I'm not going to tell anyone!' Noting that his colleague hadn't moved out of his outraged pose, İskender leaned forward. 'The fact is, Mehmet, that if we want to make some sort of progress with the Eastern European mobs using what we know from Rostov we have to be careful. We can't just go tearing into people's houses looking for bodies and anything else we hope we might find using only Rostov as a lever. For a start Rostov could be lying. This Dr Keyder of yours wasn't very forthcoming with any actual names, was she? But then even if it is all true, so what? If we only find bodies and the mobsters can verify who the deceased once were, they'll just be taken away for burial. Unless we find drugs or arms, Malenkov and co. will be back on the streets very quickly. And they'll be angry and they may go looking for Rostov. If they do we've got a war. Think about it,' he said gravely, 'you know what the Russians are like. Do you want to have shoot-outs in the streets of Beyoğlu?'

'No.' Suleyman, temporarily deflated, looked down at the floor. 'But why would Rostov lie?'

'To buy a bit more time for Tatiana?' İskender shrugged. 'Maybe he thought he could prevail upon this embalmer woman to get on with the job while we looked into the activities of his friends. Who knows? That he's still got her dead body is beyond me.'

Suleyman moved forward and sat down. 'So how do we proceed?'

'You've spoken to Ardiç about what happened at the embalmers?'

'Yes.'

İskender took a cigarette out of his pocket and lit up. 'We'll wait and see what he decides,' he said. 'If he thinks this dead body angle is worth pursing I guess we'll go in. But he has to be considering the fact that Rostov's "friends" must know we've been here. If they put that together with our appearance at their houses and Rostov's boys are on the street . . .'

'Yes, I know. I know.' He sighed.

Suleyman's mobile phone started to ring. He took it out of his pocket and placed it against his ear.

'Suleyman.'

'Inspector.' The voice was female and familiar. 'It's Sergeant Farsakoğlu,' she said. 'Are you free to talk, sir?'

'Yes.'

She was very formal, considering that they had once, if briefly, been lovers. But that was as it should be and Suleyman was pleased that she had at last accepted the situation.

'Sir, I have a message from Inspector İkmen,' she said. 'Unfortunately one of his relatives has been taken ill and he's had to go over to the Taksim State Hospital.'

'Oh, I'm sorry.' This probably meant that his brother-in-law, Talaat, had taken a turn for the worse.

'İnşallah the inspector's relative will recover.'

'İnşallah.'

'But in the meantime, sir,' she continued, 'Inspector İkmen has asked, if you can, if you would meet him at the Taksim.'

Suleyman frowned. 'Why?'

'You contacted him earlier, about Mrs Akdeniz, Melih Akdeniz's wife . . .'

'Yes.'

'Inspector İkmen needs to talk to you about that, sir. Urgently. He feels there might be some sort of connection between his case and what you were doing out at Sarıyer.'

Suleyman looked at his watch, more out of habit than necessity. Until Ardiç made some sort of decision with regard to Rostov and his countrymen, he wasn't exactly needed anywhere. His appointment with Dr Krikor Sarkissian, something he didn't in any way relish, wasn't until 6 p.m. It was now two thirty.

'All right, Sergeant,' he said, 'I'll get over there as soon as I can.'

'Yes, sir. I'll get a message to him to let him know you're coming.'

'Thank you, Sergeant.'

They both cut the connection at the same time. Suleyman still frowning, put his phone back in his pocket. Metin İskender, who had only been privy to one side of the call, gave his colleague a quizzical look.

'Çetin İkmen wants to talk to me about some connection he might have made between his missing children case and

Dr Keyder,' he said as he made his way towards the door of the salon. 'The children's mother, Mrs Akdeniz, was over at Dr Keyder's yalı this morning.'

'What was she doing with an embalmer?' İskender asked.

'I have no idea,' Suleyman replied, 'which is why I'm going to see İkmen now. I'll keep you informed.'

'Please do.'

Suleyman left. Alone in Rostov's vast and tasteless salon, İskender found his thoughts, wandering back to that evening he had spent in that pavyon, watching Mehmet Suleyman through a thick carpet of smoke, alcohol and cheap females – looking at the other man looking at Masha. She had, even he had to admit, been stunning in an obvious sort of way. Ripe and tempting ... She had, they knew, worked for Rostov – all that stuff about Vladimir, one of Rostov's boys ...

Mehmet was probably right when he asserted that Rostov had killed Masha. If, as they suspected, he'd used her to draw the police into what had in truth almost become a public relations nightmare, then it had to make sense to get rid of her. It had really been fortuitous for the police when Suleyman discovered Tatiana's body in the freezer. If, indeed, it were fortuitous ...

İskender frowned. To follow Rostov and enter his house had been a police decision – one that Rostov could not possibly have influenced. But then, given that Masha's status as an informant was so obviously suspect, it was a logical, even a predictable, move. And when Suleyman did arrive he found nothing beyond Tatiana. When you broke it down like this ...

İskender sat down and then looked at the floor beneath his feet. Below in the kitchen was Rostov's daughter – or was she? As yet, no tests had been performed on the corpse; she hadn't even been seen by Dr Sarkissian. She could, in theory at least, be almost anyone. But why then did Rostov guard her so jealously? No, that didn't make sense. It didn't make sense but it did keep on representing itself in his mind. There was something else, about Tatiana, about the cleanliness of this house, something that failed to add up – something that İskender was not yet, to his frustration, able to see.

At three o'clock that afternoon, Eren Akdeniz arrived back at the great ochre house in Balat. As soon as she was in, Melih locked the back gates and closed all of the curtains at the windows. Effectively blinded with regard to activities inside the artist's house, Ayşe Farsakoğlu, now partnered with Hikmet Yıldız, and now ostensibly protecting the Akdeniz family, leaned back in her seat and lit a cigarette. Even with all the windows open, the inside of the car was unbearably hot and she was uncomfortably aware of the pace of her own pulse every time she moved.

The young constable, whose face still bore fresh and livid scars from Rostov's attack upon him, looked across at her a little nervously before he lit up a cigarette of his own. Perhaps he thought she might disapprove of his smoking in her presence. But then he didn't say a lot and so it was difficult to tell. Yıldız came, Ayşe understood, from one of the tower-block apartments near the airport. Not the most salubrious part of town – his parents were, in all likelihood, originally from the country. Maybe, she thought, his mother discourages him from associating with women.

'You're the beautiful girl with İkmen, aren't you?'

The depth and huskiness of the voice made Ayşe think, at first, that it had to belong to a man. However, the smiling face that had thrust itself into the open window was definitely female. It was also, Farsakoğlu noticed, extremely voluptuous and exotic.

'My name is Gonca,' the woman continued. 'I have met with Çetin Bey, he knows me. I'm an artist.'

'Oh.'

'I, like most of the district,' she said wryly, 'have noticed you and your very cute companion watching the Akdeniz house. Melih is exhibiting his work tonight. Are you going?'

Yıldız, in response to her words, blushed.

She was very direct – it wasn't something Ayşe Farsakoğlu was accustomed to or, in fact, that she liked.

'I am not at liberty to say,' she responded haughtily.

Gonca shrugged. 'Suit yourself,' she said lightly, 'but I think it will be worth a visit. His work, if you know how to look at it, always shines with magical energy. He's invited me and I'm going.' She smiled. 'But then I would.'

'Oh?'

'Melih Bey and I are old friends,' the gypsy continued. 'We do things for each other, you know . . .'

'I understand it's performance art, based on Karagöz,' Ayşe said.

'Yeah. Shadow play with a contemporary theme.'

'What theme?'

'I don't know,' she smiled. 'Just because Melih and I occasionally pleasure one another doesn't mean that he tells me anything about his professional plans. Artists don't.'

Now red to the hairline, Hikmet Yıldız cleared his throat in an obviously nervous fashion.

Gonca laughed. 'Has this old gypsy embarrassed you, little one?' she said, oozing sexuality as she did so.

'Er . . .'

'That poor little boy needs taking in hand,' Gonca said to Farsakoğlu, 'in my opinion.'

'Yes, well . . .' Ayşe too cleared her throat nervously. This gypsy was a little too rich for her blood. What on earth would İkmen have made of such a person? Probably had a good laugh with her. 'Do you know anything else about this performance, Miss . . . ?'

'Gonca. Just Gonca.' She pushed a thick lump of unruly black hair away from her face and said, 'Not much. I know he's been working in camel skin, which is the traditional material used for Karagöz puppets. I know he's been making costumes for them, something using designer labels. But then if you're going tonight . . .'

'If I'm going.'

'All will become clear, won't it?' Gonca said, and with that she started to move away from the car, her jewel-covered hips swaying as she moved.

'Er . . .' Ayşe Farsakoğlu, confused about why the gypsy had approached her, opened the car door and got out. 'Did you want something?'

Gonca turned, looking provocatively over one shoulder, 'No,' she said smiling, 'only to say that if you see Çetin

Bey you might like to tell him that I think the answer to the puzzle he has been trying to solve is at hand.'

'What puzzle?' Ayşe replied.

'The one about the two little children,' Gonca said, 'Melih's kids.'

'Yes, but how—'

'You can tell him that I know because I had a dream. Their torment is about to conclude. He will understand,' the gypsy said, and then, with one last pout at Yıldız she started to make her way down the steep stone steps that led to lower Balat.

Ayşe, her head shaking in disbelief, got back into the car. Just in time, Hikmet Yıldız turned his head away from the retreating gypsy and towards his superior.

'She's a bit . . . full on,' he said. 'A bit . . .'

'Anyone known to Inspector İkmen on that . . . that sort of witchcraft level, which is where I would place her, is odd,' Ayşe said with a sigh. 'Dreams, magic. Allah! But Çetin Bey will take her seriously. Modern police force but we still use soothsayers.'

'My mum always says that it's dangerous to ignore all the old what she calls countryside ways,' Yıldız replied in a rare moment of disclosure. 'She says that Allah in His great wisdom makes only those who can deal with such things aware of these mysteries.'

'Oh?' Ayşe, who was a woman who, though very respectful of İkmen and his ilk, was a very 'earthbound' person, raised a sceptical eyebrow. 'And what does your mother have to say about rapacious middle-aged women with an eye for young men?'

Yıldız blushed again. Ayşe, in order to hide the smile

that was spreading across her face, looked away. She
would tell İkmen about the encounter with the gypsy
as soon as she could. He laid great store by such things
and she, in spite of herself, felt that what Gonca had said
was important.

# CHAPTER 17

İkmen was, as Suleyman had suspected he would be, lurking disreputably outside the hospital entrance. Like Suleyman himself, being in hospitals tended to make the older man feel nervous. Not helped by the fact that smoking was now frowned upon inside.

After the two men had embraced, Suleyman said, 'How is Talaat?'

İkmen sighed. 'He was restless last night, with the pain,' he said wearily, 'but this morning, after I'd left for work, it became uncontrollable. Fatma called an ambulance.'

'She's inside?'

'Yes.' İkmen lit a new cigarette from the butt of the one he'd just finished. 'They're trying to get the pain under control now. It's like a nightmare in there, but she won't leave him.'

'Is anybody with her?'

'Çiçek was visiting this morning and so she's come along,' he said naming his eldest daughter, who worked as an air hostess. 'You know these women are far tougher than we are, Mehmet. I was in there, Talaat screaming, I was beside myself. But Fatma? She just held on to him, speaking softly into his ears while my daughter very calmly bathed his forehead. Doctors everywhere with

263

monitors, plunging hypodermics into Talaat's arms. But then I don't have to tell you about tough women, do I? You have Zelfa.'

'Yes.' Not that he wanted to discuss his wife, his *betrayed* wife now. Suleyman changed the subject. 'Ayşe Farsakoğlu said that you wanted to see me about my involvement with Dr Keyder.'

'The embalmer. Yes. Did you find out why Mrs Akdeniz went to see her?'

Suleyman lit a cigarette before replying. 'Dr Keyder told me that Mrs Akdeniz's visit was about art rather than embalming,' he said. 'The doctor is a great admirer of Melih Akdeniz's work and has a considerable collection of his art. It was something to do with that, I understand.'

'Yes, Melih told me the doctor wants to buy one of his old pieces,' İkmen sighed. 'Seems on the level, although I'm not sure about Mrs Akdeniz's brother.'

'Who?'

İkmen briefly outlined Reşad Kuran's involvement in his investigation and then said, 'He claims he's never met Dr Keyder and has never been to her yalı. However, mention of her name did prompt him to miraculously recall the address he delivered to in Yeniköy on that Friday night. I've got to check that out.'

'Do you want me to ask Dr Keyder about him?'

'Yes.'

'You know Dr Keyder is a very enthusiastic fan of Akdeniz's work – her yalı contains many examples,' Suleyman said. 'Like him, she's a Balat Jew, although she's a lot older than he is.'

'Mmm. The fact that she lives in Sarıyer I find interesting too,' İkmen said. 'Akdeniz had promised to take his children out to a restaurant in Sarıyer on the day they disappeared. Did that visit perhaps involve seeing Dr Keyder? She's a collector, he knows her. I also feel sure that Kuran has to know her too. He does all of Melih's deliveries, he must have come across her. Maybe Melih and Reşad don't want to be associated with something so grisly, although they're both so odd, I can't see why that would be. I know a bit about what's been going on, with regard to Çöktin's involvement with an embalmed body, but I don't know much about your investigation.' He frowned. 'One tends to develop tunnel vision when working on a missing children case. Tell me some more about it.'

At Suleyman's request they both sat down on a low wall to one side of the hospital entrance. The younger man then spoke at some length about Rostov, about the trade in body preservation and about the strange career of Dr Yeşim Keyder.

'I think it's possible she may have had some sort of romantic attachment to this Spaniard, Pedro Ara,' he said

İkmen visibly shuddered. 'How macabre,' he said, 'and also, I don't quite know why, but how very Latin. I remember some years ago, Çiçek flew to Palermo in Sicily and visited the catacombs of some monastery there. She said they embalm all their deceased initiates and place them standing up in this place. It gave me the creeps.'

Suleyman smiled. 'I know what you mean,' he said.

265

'I think that perhaps one has to be a Christian to really understand these things. Zelfa does.'

'Mmm. But you say this Dr Keyder is Jewish . . .'

'Yes, although she doesn't practise her religion. I get the feeling that Judaism belongs to a past that Dr Keyder would really rather forget.'

'Except maybe through her devotion to the works of Melih Akdeniz.' İkmen thoughtfully rubbed his chin. 'So you think she's working for various mobsters?'

'Yes. There were no records bearing significant names that we could find but . . .'

'So what are you going to do?' İkmen, his eye caught by a figure that was approaching the hospital gates, waved at it energetically. 'Orhan,' he said to Suleyman by way of explanation.

The younger man turned to look at the figure and smiled. Then he turned back to İkmen and said, 'I'd like to use these unburied bodies as levers to get into the homes of people like Vronsky. I know Ardiç does too, although he's holding back at the moment – afraid, I think, like we all are about how entering such homes might affect relations between mobsters and their men on the streets.'

'He's right to be cautious,' İkmen agreed. 'If you've nothing apart from Rostov's evidence your intervention could cause trouble for him.' And then seeing the look of disgust on his colleague's face he added, 'Not that you're bothered about Rostov's safety.'

'You know he killed Masha.'

'The girl you . . . ?'

'Yes.' Suleyman turned away just as the man İkmen had seen at the gate drew level with them.

'Orhan!' İkmen stood up and took the man, who was considerably taller and younger than he in his arms.

'Hello, Dad,' the man replied after he had kissed his father on both cheeks. 'How are things?'

'Not good.'

Suleyman, who had now risen to his feet, took one of Orhan's hands in his. 'Hello, Orhan,' he said. 'It's such a shame that we should meet under such unpleasant circumstances.'

Orhan İkmen smiled. Even though he didn't see him from one year's end to the next, he had a lot of affection for Mehmet Suleyman. When he'd been a poor medical student in Ankara some years before, it had been Mehmet who had kept him supplied with much-appreciated pairs of shoes. Ostensibly given because Mehmet had tired of them, Orhan and Fatma always believed that the far more financially secure Suleyman had bought the shoes for the young man out of the kindness of his heart.

'Mehmet.' He embraced him before turning back to his father. 'So is Mum inside?'

'Yes,' his father replied. 'Çiçek also. I'll take you in in a moment.'

He turned back to Suleyman and said, 'Listen, Mehmet, I think we must maintain contact over these matters. I'd like to talk to you again soon.'

'Of course.'

'The fact that this doctor lives in Sarıyer bothers me.' Once again he visibly shuddered. 'Oh, just out of interest, was she working on "anyone" when you went to her laboratory?'

Suleyman smiled. 'No,' he said, 'apparently the Nabaros

– a couple, I believe – had just "gone", been delivered or whatever.'

'Oh.' İkmen shook his head slowly. 'Unbelievable.' He started to walk away and then stopped. 'Nabaro, you say?'

Suleyman, who had started walking away from the hospital, turned. 'Yes. Why?'

Once again İkmen shook his head. 'I don't know,' he said as he raised one tired hand up to his brow. 'Just sounds familiar.'

'Give Ayşe Farsakoğlu a call,' Suleyman said. 'You work together, maybe she'll know.'

'Maybe.'

İkmen and his son went into the hospital while Suleyman went back to his car. No one had called him while he'd been with İkmen and so it was unlikely that Ardiç had come to any sort of decision with regard to the embalmed bodies. He was in all probability taking advice from higher up. But there were still tasks to be done in the meantime. Suleyman brought Dr Keyder's number up on his mobile phone and pressed the call button.

'You do know what this means, don't you, Valery?' Lütfü Güneş said as he lowered himself into the chair beside Rostov's bed. 'If the police raid the homes of your –' he hesitated to use the word 'rivals' to a client – 'friends, they won't be best pleased.'

Rostov shrugged.

'In fact, it could start a war—'

'Not if the police arrest them,' Rostov cut in coolly, 'which they will. Malenkov is a drug dealer, Vronsky busies himself with guns and Bulganin is a pervert. I'm on very friendly terms with all of them. They will know that I'm having a little trouble from the police at the moment. Russian businessmen do from time to time. They will all be very relieved it isn't them. They will carry on as usual. The police are bound to find a lot of illegal goodies as they search through their homes for – what do they call them? – unburied corpses.'

Güneş lit up a cigarette. 'They came here looking for things, Valery.'

'Ah, but I am an innocent man, aren't I, Lütfü?'

The twinkle in Rostov's nevertheless unsmiling eyes said it all.

'Oh, come on, Valery, you and I both know . . .'

'What?' Slowly Rostov rolled over on to one side so that he was directly facing his lawyer. 'What do we know about me, Lütfü?'

Under the hard and menacingly amused glare of Rostov's clear blue eyes, Güneş felt himself shrink. Instinctively he looked away.

'Valery, this place was totally clean when the police . . .'

'Well, that has to be because I'm not doing anything illegal then, doesn't it, Lütfü?' He reached over and took a cigarette from a box on top of his night table.

Güneş, who could now actually feel his blood pressure rising, turned back to look at his client. Very lucrative, Valery – not that that stopped him from being a cheap, tasteless Russian shit.

'You know that these friends of yours have these embalmed bodies?' he asked once he had managed to get the courage up to look Rostov in the eyes again.

'Yes. As I told you, Lütfü, I have seen them in their homes.'

Until the police had discovered what Rostov said was the body of his daughter in one of the kitchen freezers, Güneş hadn't known anything about either embalming or Tatiana. Like a lot of people, he had always assumed that the Russian was gay. OK, so mobsters, which was what Güneş knew Rostov to be, had to employ lots of hard young men in order to protect themselves and their investments. But they didn't have to employ so many beautiful men. They also didn't have to have the young men suck them off – something Güneş had just walked in on one evening. Rostov with some youngster called Vladimir. Someone who, like several of the boys, now he came to think about it, had left rather smartly.

'I don't know why you didn't tell me about your daughter, Valery,' Güneş said.

'Perhaps because Tatiana is none of your business.'

'But how did you get her into the country?'

'By plane.'

'But why now, Valery?' Güneş asked.

Rostov eyed him coldly. 'Because now is the right time, Lütfü,' he said. 'Now suits me.'

Temporarily bullied into silence, Güneş looked down at the floor. Although he'd been into this room several times during the course of his association with Rostov, it was only now that he noticed how gaudy the carpet was. Pink with thin skeins of gold threaded through the weave. It was dreadful. But then so was Rostov – with his cocaine parties, his boys and girls for sale all over the city, that greedy face of his, slavering with pleasure as that youngster gave him oral sex.

'So you don't fear a war . . .'

He looked up just in time to see Rostov smile. 'I'm an antiques dealer. My friends showed me their very unusual works of art. I didn't know that what they were doing was against the law, I'm not from this country.' And then, as he rearranged his features into a sad and regretful expression, he said, 'As long as Tatiana is preserved I will be happy. I will do anything to prevent anyone taking her away from me.'

Although he both looked and sounded sincere as he said it, Güneş couldn't find it within himself to believe Rostov. If the police were going to take Malenkov and the others' 'unusual art works' away, then why did Rostov think they would spare Tatiana?

İkmen eventually managed to slip away at just after 6 p.m. After what had seemed like for ever, the doctors had finally managed to deal with Talaat's pain. This had, however, meant putting him into what was effectively a morphine coma. Drugged beyond any ability to communicate he just lay there, attached to an alarming array of dials, drips and monitors, Fatma and Çiçek sitting one each side of him holding his hands.

As soon as he got outside the hospital building, İkmen switched his mobile phone back on. No one except for the person experiencing it could know what went on when a person entered a coma. The doctor had told Fatma and Çiçek to keep on talking to Talaat. 'He can hear you,' he had said, 'your voices will give him comfort'. Orhan,

271

although he'd said nothing to either his mother or his sister, disagreed – İkmen could see it on his face.

There was one message on his phone. It was from the Forensic Institute telling him that faint traces of blood had been found inside Reşad Kuran's van. The blood group was the same as that of the Akdeniz children. Not proof – yet – but İkmen was nevertheless pleased that he had detailed his men and women to keep on watching Kuran. He phoned Ayşe Farsakoğlu to let her know.

'Kuran is still at Akdeniz' house,' Ayşe said after İkmen had given her his news. 'The wife is back too.'

'On her own?'

'Yes. Three of them in the house, all preparing, I imagine, for this show tonight.' Then with a sigh she added, 'It's all beyond me, sir. I mean whether art is important or not, surely your parental feelings would dominate and effectively bring your life to a standstill at a time like this. If I had a child and he or she went missing I don't think I'd even be able to feed myself, much less organise a show.'

İkmen rubbed his bloodshot eyes with his fingers. 'I don't know,' he muttered. 'These artists ... The statements they feel compelled to make.' He then cleared his throat and stood up a little straighter. 'So, look, did anything else happen?'

'No, no movement here. The gates are closed at the moment, as are the curtains.' İkmen heard her light up a cigarette and then exhale smoke into her telephone. 'Oh, we did have a visit from some huge gypsy woman.'

'Gonca?'

'Yes.'

'What did she want?'

'She asked me whether I was going to Akdeniz's show tonight. She went on about how it was to be based on Karagöz – things we know.'

'Ah.'

'She and Akdeniz are sometime lovers, I think . . . She asked me to give you a message. She said that the solution to your puzzle about the Akdeniz children was at hand. She had this dream,' Ayşe said. 'I'm sorry, sir, I know you believe in and use this occult stuff yourself but . . .'

But the voice of his sergeant was a very long way away now. For the moment, İkmen was back in the gypsy's house, walking in through the spangled fabric doorway, looking down at the colourful cushions on the floor – the prim seated figure of Nilufer Cemal, the ceramicist. The bitter ceramicist who knew a thing or two about both Melih Akdeniz's artistic philosophy and his past.

'Ayşe,' İkmen cut in, 'stay where you are and keep Yıldız with you.'

'Sir?'

'Look, just do as I say, Ayşe. I can't explain, but I'm coming. Stay where you are.'

Then, his fingers trembling in time to his pounding heart, İkmen ended the call and punched another number into the keypad. If what had just shot into his head would or could be true, he'd need some sort of steadying influence, first, to organise what had to be a product of insanity, and then, if that idea proved to be true, stop him from killing Melih Akdeniz.

\* \* \*

Krikor Sarkissian was a thinner and rather more grave version of his brother Arto. A doctor by training, his speciality was addiction and the diseases associated with it. The man sitting opposite, who had been referred by his brother, was, in common with all of his patients, very nervous.

'Look, Mehmet,' Krikor said as he doodled his pen unthinkingly across the bottom of his blotter, 'these things happen. Men go with women that they shouldn't, women purchase gigolos of dubious provenance. There's no point punishing yourself for this. Dealing with the outfall is what should be exercising your mind.'

'But I betrayed her,' Mehmet Suleyman said miserably. 'Zelfa . . .'

Although immaculately dressed and perfumed, Krikor Sarkissian didn't possess the kind of office one would expect an expert to inhabit. Situated in a picturesque but tatty Ottoman building just off Divanyolu, Krikor's addiction centre was a place where people could obtain advice and assistance about giving up drugs and getting medical help. Funded by privately raised money, the centre was sometimes prey to raïds by overzealous police officers keen to raise their numbers of successful arrests. Çetin İkmen, who had been instrumental in helping Krikor to realise his dream, did try to prevent such actions taking place. Krikor owed İkmen much when it came to the centre, which was why he was happy to see Mehmet Suleyman now. There would, of course, be no fee for this consultation.

'You will have to tell your wife in order to protect her,' Krikor said. 'I don't know whether you practise protected sex with your wife . . .'

274

'I don't practise any sort of sex with her at the moment,' Suleyman responded miserably. 'We haven't had sex for months. If we had, I wouldn't have gone with that Russian.'

'You will still need to tell her, Inspector.'

'I know.'

Krikor looked through the notes he had already made on the pad in front of him and said, 'I can test you for hepatitis B and do the first test for HIV today. With the latter, however, as I think my brother explained, you will need to come back in three months, whatever this preliminary test shows.'

'What if this first test is negative?' Suleyman asked.

'That will be a good sign,' Krikor said, 'but it won't be conclusive, I'm afraid.'

'So there'll be no way of knowing whether I am definitely HIV positive?'

'No, but if what you've told me about this girl is correct, I wouldn't be too worried.' He looked down at his notes once again. 'She displayed no obvious lesions, no bleeding as far as you know, you have no genital wounds.' He looked up. 'You have to suffer exposure to your blood supply from the virus, which is passed in bodily fluids. From what you've told me this is unlikely.'

'But not impossible.'

'No.' They sat in silence for a few moments as Suleyman took in the information Krikor had given him. Now he was actually with the specialist, things didn't look quite as bleak as they had done. However, Krikor admitted that he still couldn't be certain and Suleyman would have to submit to the wretched HIV test come what may.

It was just a mercy that Dr Krikor knew him and, in addition, knew to keep his status a secret from Suleyman's employers. He wondered silently whether, in a fit of hurt and spite, Zelfa could be relied upon to do likewise.

Krikor leaned back in his chair and smiled. 'You know, most people I test for HIV prove negative,' he said. 'It's not an easy virus to catch, unless you routinely share your blood with others. Heroin addicts are the principal culprits, sharing needles. I've seen junkies as young as twelve who are HIV positive.'

Suleyman shook his head sadly.

'They come mainly,' Krikor continued, 'from the former Soviet Union. The girls are frequently on the streets. Most of the time I see them once or twice before they disappear. I know, as I'm sure you do too, that most of them end up butchered by their pimps or their punters in some hellhole . . .'

'Masha, this girl I . . . she was from Russia,' Suleyman said.

'Yes, well, that is the downside to your story, Inspector,' Krikor said with a sigh. 'So many of them are infected. But even if my brother discovers that she was infected, that doesn't mean that you are.'

'No.'

The silence rolled in once again, throwing an even heavier layer across the already thick late afternoon heat. But Krikor was accustomed to such reactions and knew that the only way forward was through action.

'Well, I think it's now time, provided you're clear about everything so far, Inspector, to take some of your blood for testing.'

'Yes . . .' His mobile telephone began to vibrate against his thigh. 'Oh, Doctor, my phone, I'm sorry,' he said as he took the instrument out of his trouser pocket and placed it against his ear.

'OK,' Krikor smiled. Big men and their little toys. Mobiles were, of course, useful but . . .

Suleyman, who had turned away to take the call, said, 'Yes, I'm sure . . . Nabaro, definitely . . . No, no I didn't see . . . She was out earlier. I'll try again now . . . No . . . No, if she isn't in I'll meet you at Akdeniz's house . . . No, I don't . . . Yes, all right I'll tell him to come too. Yes . . . Yes . . . Yes . . . OK, goodbye, goodbye.'

It all sounded very frenetic. When Suleyman turned to face him, Krikor raised a questioning eyebrow.

'Now, Dr Sarkissian, I want you to believe me when I say that I'm not doing this just to get out of giving you some of my blood,' Suleyman said, 'but that was Çetin İkmen and—'

'You don't have to say any more,' Krikor said as he held one silencing hand aloft. 'I grew up with Çetin, remember?'

'Then you know . . .'

'That when an idea strikes him, everybody has to jump? Yes,' he smiled. 'You know when we were children we used to sometimes go and play out on the land walls, Edirnekapı. Wasn't the mad place then that it is now. However, we were playing quite happily one day when Çetin suddenly gets it into his head that this very solid-looking section of one of the walls is going to fall down and crush us. He went mad, screaming for Arto, his brother and me to get out of the way.'

Suleyman, who had now slipped his jacket back on, checked his pockets for car keys. 'But it did fall down, didn't it, Doctor?' he said. 'The wall.'

'Of course it did,' Krikor replied, 'seconds after he pulled us out of the way.'

'Yes, I'm sorry I've got to go, make a call . . .' And with that he opened the door and rushed out into the corridor.

'Give me a call when you're free and we'll rearrange,' Krikor said to what was effectively thin air.

# CHAPTER 18

It was seven o'clock by the time İkmen got to Balat. He'd asked Ayşe Farsakoğlu to park her car away from the Akdeniz house, which she had done up on a piece of waste ground behind the Greek Boys' School. Shortly after İkmen arrived, Suleyman and Çöktin drove up in the latter's Toyota.

İkmen went straight up to Suleyman and said, 'She wasn't in, I take it, Dr Keyder?'

'No.'

'Right.'

Once everyone was together and quiet, İkmen spoke.

'I've brought you all here this evening,' he said, 'for reasons, I'll be honest, I don't want to give you.'

Yıldız and Çöktin, who were rather less accustomed to İkmen's ways than the others, looked confused.

'Because,' İkmen continued, 'if I tell you and I'm wrong you will all think that I'm a lunatic.'

'We won't,' Çöktin said.

İkmen smiled. 'You will, believe me,' he said. He lit a cigarette and then coughed wetly for a few moments. 'Now look, I want to gain access to Akdeniz's house before his performance begins at eight.'

'And if he doesn't want to let us in?' Suleyman asked.

'Then we force our way in.'

'But on what basis?' Suleyman continued. 'The man is, as far as I'm aware, a victim of crime. Are we searching for something or—'

'You can leave the explanations to me,' İkmen replied.

'But—'

'Come on,' İkmen said as he started to make his way down towards the Akdeniz house. 'We've got to get in there before the press or anyone else does. If I'm right about what has happened, the decent people of Balat will pull Akdeniz to pieces if they see what he's done.'

The four other officers followed in silence. Possibly forcing entrance into the house of a crime victim was not something any of them did every day. And if anyone apart from İkmen had asked them to join him in such an enterprise, they would have all walked off in the opposite direction. However, because it was İkmen, each and every one of them had a deep sense of foreboding about what they might be about to face inside Melih Akdeniz's great ochre house.

Balat houses were built to last. Surrounded by thick, high walls, every window ornately barred, the casual intruder thwarted by enormous wooden doors bolted through with iron – the people who had once lived in these hadn't wanted too many surprises. But then where they'd come from – mediaeval Spain and Portugal – had been nothing but surprises – the fire, the rack, the thumbscrews. And although the Ottoman Empire had been many thousands of kilometres away from the clutches of the Holy Inquisition, people like Melih Akdeniz's Jewish ancestors had taken no chances.

İkmen walked up the small flight of stone steps that led to the heavy front door and knocked. 'Mr Akdeniz!'

Both the knock and his words echoed hollowly through the building like retreating ghosts. It was early, and no one else had yet arrived to view Melih Akdeniz's performance. İkmen looked down at Suleyman and Çöktin, who just shrugged. Farsakoğlu and Yıldız were covering the back and side entrances. İkmen could see the boy, his face drawn with tension, but not Ayşe.

'Mr Akdeniz!'

Minutes rather than seconds passed. The two younger men looked at each other with raised eyebrows, wondering how long it was going to take to batter such a heavy door down.

'Mr—'

'We're not ready! Come back at eight!' It was a woman's voice – slightly slurred. Eren.

'Mrs Akdeniz, it's Inspector İkmen. Let me in please.'

'I've told you the performance doesn't start—'

'Mrs Akdeniz, I've come to see Yaşar and Nuray. Will you let me in please?'

A breathless silence followed and for just a moment, everything slowed: the looks of confusion on Suleyman and Çöktin's faces, spreading across their features like the slowly encroaching darkness; İkmen holding his breath as he listened to the almost imperceptible sounds of the woman beyond the door – her gentle drugged breathing, the imagined beat of her heart.

'Mrs Akdeniz,' İkmen said slowly, 'if you don't let me in, I'll have this door removed.'

'The show . . .'

281

'The show is over, Mrs Akdeniz,' he continued. 'Your husband—'

'I must go to him!'

The sound of her feet slapping as they ran on the cool tiled floor caused İkmen to shout, 'Mrs Akdeniz!'

He turned away from the door and looked down at Suleyman and Çöktin. 'We'll have to get this door down,' he said.

'But why?' Çöktin asked, 'I still don't—'

'Because the missing children are in there,' İkmen said.

'But . . .'

A loud click from inside the thick garden walls preceded the flooding of the area with light. Yıldız, who was nearer the garden than anyone else, peered through a gap between the metal coach house doors. 'There's a light,' he said, 'behind some sort of screen.'

'For the shadow play, yes,' İkmen said. 'Now how are we going to get this door—'

And then there was the unmistakable sound of a gunshot.

At first, because he sprang back from his vantage point in front of the gates, the three men thought that it was Yıldız that had been shot. But it wasn't. He had, however, seen it, or rather the outfall from it.

'The screen's covered with blood!' he said as he continued to move away from the gates.

İkmen and the others, who had now been joined by Ayşe Farsakoğlu, ran over to the young man.

'There's only a padlock on the gates,' Yıldız said as his face moved from tanned to green within the space of a second.

Without another word, Suleyman took his pistol out of its holster and shot the padlock to pieces.

'I don't know what any of this is about, Çetin,' he said as he pulled the chain that had held the padlock in place out on to the ground, 'but . . .'

İkmen roughly pushed Suleyman to one side. 'Someone's armed in there!'

Çöktin, Farsakoğlu and Yıldız drew their weapons.

'Cover me while I open these gates!' İkmen said.

As he stepped forward his whole body trembled. Safety catches clicked off all around him as he pushed the gates inward.

Inside the garden, standing on the path, the gun still smoking in her hands, stood Eren Akdeniz. The light from the powerful lamp behind the bloodied screen framed her head like a halo.

'Put the gun down, Eren,' İkmen's voice trembled as he spoke. The expression on the woman's face was so weird as to be completely indecipherable.

'Someone must be hurt,' he continued. 'We need to come in so that we can help.'

'He's dead,' she said dreamily.

'Who's dead?'

'Melih.'

From somewhere inside the house came the sound of a door slamming. Çöktin, who was currently at the back of the group, moved slowly backwards out of the garden.

'Please let us come and see Melih,' İkmen said. 'We may be able to help him.'

'He's dead . . .'

'I'd like to see for myself, Eren.' İkmen held out his hand towards her. 'Please give me the gun so that I can make it safe.'

She smiled as she gave it to him. Her face, just this once, struck İkmen as almost beautiful. Gently, for she was or appeared to be, in a different space from any of those present, he sat her down on one of the low garden walls and motioned for Ayşe to come and sit with her.

'Now look, Eren,' he said softly, lest he wake or disturb her from her fugue. 'I'm going to leave you here with Ayşe while my colleagues and I go and see what we can do for Melih.'

'The work is complete,' she said. She looked so happy.

'Yes. Yes.' İkmen straightened up and looked across at Suleyman and Yıldız. 'The brother-in-law, Kuran, should still be around,' he said nervously.

'There was a noise from inside the house,' Suleyman replied. 'I think Çöktin's gone off to investigate. What is all this, Çetin?'

The big white and now red screen was strung between two trees at the top of a small flight of steps. İkmen put his foot on to the first one and said, 'I fear we're about to see the place where art and science meet.'

And then before his nerve failed him he ran up the remaining steps and pulled the screen down with one adrenaline-fuelled tug.

It was obvious that Akdeniz was dead. Half his head had simply disintegrated. But İkmen felt for a pulse anyway – it was just something you did. It also gave him a few

284

# 20

**TUESDAY**

|  | S | M | T | W | T | F | S |
|---|---|---|---|---|---|---|---|
|  |  |  |  |  | 1 | 2 | 3 |
|  | 4 | 5 | 6 | 7 | 8 | 9 | 10 |
|  | 11 | 12 | 13 | 14 | 15 | 16 | 17 |
|  | 18 | 19 | 20 | 21 | 22 | 23 | 24 |
|  | 25 | 26 | 27 | 28 | 29 | 30 |  |

Hore Abbey, Cashel, Co. Tipperary

more seconds before he had to look at what else had been behind the shadow play screen.

Yıldız pushed past the Karagöz puppet and switched off the floodlight.

İkmen, looking now out of the corner of his eye, saw Suleyman approach one of the other traditional figures and say, 'Whatever one may think of Akdeniz's art, he was certainly a skilled craftsman. These are exquisite.'

İkmen felt a painful squeeze in the pit of his stomach as he very slowly stood up and looked into the face of Nuray Akdeniz. He recognised the costume from his youth. All the old shadow play men used to represent women like this. She wore a long red coat called a ferace, which covered her whole body. On her feet she wore little red velvet slippers, while her head was encased in a blue bonnet called a hotoz. The thin yaşmak that covered the lower half of her face did nothing to hide those familiar features from İkmen's gaze. But then the yaşmak in Karagöz had never been about modesty – it was about teasing, about the power women have over men and about the transparent nature of false modesty. İkmen extended a shaking arm towards the figure and took a corner of the ferace between his fingers. Up close he could see that the whole ensemble had been made up from red designer labels. It must have taken Akdeniz forever – which means he must have planned.

İkmen looked across at Karagöz, slumped in front of a picture of a hamam painted on to camel skin. The huge penis-like nose that had been attached to the lifeless face might have thrown anyone else, but İkmen had seen, studied so many photographs . . .

Somewhere, possibly from the Greek Boys' School, a clock struck the half-hour. Seven thirty, almost showtime.

'I wonder if he actually made them himself,' Suleyman said as he took one of Karagöz arms in his hands. 'I know not all artists do these days.'

'In a sense you could say that he did,' İkmen began.

'It was, however, myself,' an elderly female voice cut in, 'that transformed them into art.'

İkmen looked down to where she stood in front of a now motionless Eren Akdeniz.

'You've come to see the show, Dr Keyder?' he said.

The embalmer looked beyond İkmen into the shocked face of Suleyman.

'I take it from your expression,' she said to him, 'that you didn't make the necessary connection yourself.' She looked across at İkmen, 'But you did, er . . . ?'

'İkmen, Inspector Çetin İkmen.'

Seemingly oblivious to the presence of Melih's bloodied body on the ground she walked up the steps and towards the two shadow play figures. 'So how did you arrive at this place, Inspector İkmen?' she said.

İkmen stood in front of her, blocking her off from her goal. 'I was looking for your friend Melih's children,' he said. Now as the initial shock subsided he began to feel angry. His eyes blazed at her. 'I'd heard that his family were originally called Nabaro. You booked Yaşar and Nuray into your laboratory under that name. So did you actually kill them, Dr Keyder, or did you just embalm the bodies afterwards?'

Suleyman, who now that he'd finished looking at the figures, had joined İkmen at the top of the steps said, 'What?'

İkmen turned to look his colleague in the eyes. 'Karagöz and the lady aren't puppets or figures, Mehmet,' he said as his eyes, barely able to sustain his anger any longer, spilled hot tears down his cheeks, 'they are the embalmed bodies of Yaşar and Nuray Akdeniz.'

Suleyman, briefly looked behind him at *them* once again. When he looked back his mouth remained open and dry. From somewhere behind the darkened floodlight, Yıldız said, 'Allah!'

'Well, Dr Keyder?' İkmen hissed. 'Did you?'

A scuffling sound over by the open metal gates made İkmen look up. Çöktin was approaching with Reşad Kuran hopping and squinting in front of him, his arms pinned painfully to the top part of his back. As he passed the blankness that was his sister, he said, 'It was her, Eren, she killed Melih! She's fucking crazy!'

'Keep him there,' İkmen ordered Çöktin and then looking down at Farsakoğlu he said, 'Close the gates, will you, Ayşe? We don't want anyone else having access to this "performance". Please call the station for backup.' He looked around the beautiful garden with disgust. 'We'll need to get this place cleaned up.'

'If you're going to move my exhibits,' Dr Keyder began, 'I'd like to—'

'You're not in a position to do anything!' İkmen yelled.

'I bring the dead back to life!' she countered fiercely. 'I work and slave and pin their spirits back to their bodies, just like Ara! I am the only person in this world—'

'These were children!' İkmen said as he swung one arm backwards towards the Karagöz bodies. 'Human beings!'

'But now they are liquid suns!'

Everyone in the garden looked at Eren Akdeniz. Standing now and smiling, she looked up at what was left of the daylight and just very gently swayed from foot to foot.

'My children are immortal,' she said, 'they are a statement for all time. Death and decay can be separate. Art and science combine to produce beauty presented here as the immortal Fool Karagöz and his wife.' She looked at the sprawled body of her husband and frowned. 'Melih is the antithesis of the statement – the death in life,' she scowled. 'The flies were coming for what the cancer hadn't eaten months ago.'

'Is that when it was decided to kill the children?' İkmen asked softly least he wake her from what appeared to be a lucid reverie.

'It is the ultimate statement,' she said, 'to make life you have created into art. Melih gave the children poison. There's nowhere to go after this, he told me, no other artist on the planet can catch me now . . .'

The garden descended into silence. From the street outside İkmen and the others could hear voices, people, probably media types, knocking on the thick front door. And there was Gonca too, just to one side of a considerable group of elegantly dressed women. Her sequined skirts shimmering in what was left of the dying day, she stood by the silent wall of the Akdeniz house and looked down at the motionless waters of the Golden Horn below. For how many years had Jews and Gypsies shared this view? Not that she would be sharing it with her Jew any more.

A hole, just a small one, had opened up in her soul and she knew that Melih had gone. Someone had fired a shot – Eren, poor bitch, finally at the end of her long humiliation.

The policeman, İkmen, was in there now – the witch's child. He'd provide justice for whatever had gone on. Unlike the flawed and fatal Karagöz Melih had planned, İkmen the juggler, the foolish-looking high Magus of the tarot deck, would make it all tie together in the end. He'd come and see her too at some point, she thought as she began to walk back down the hill towards her own colourful little home. He'd tell her what he could, he liked her and, if she performed the right spells, he might even bring that very young and delicious officer with him. But then whether he did or not, it wouldn't make any difference to what was written. She'd make that boy a man because she'd seen it in the bottom of her soul, in the same place that İkmen had viewed the Akdeniz children descending from the Lightning-Struck Tower into hell. Struggling still, their agonies were not yet over, although she knew that they soon would be. Once they were returned to the earth they would be still again. Nature would take its course. It always did, in the end.

As she walked down the steps, Gonca heard what were three police cars pull up at the great ochre house behind her. But she didn't turn in order to see what was happening. Back there was death, but down the hill things were still very much alive. She thought that in lieu of having that young policeman constable in her bed tonight she might go and offer herself to her husband.

# CHAPTER 19

Dr Yeşim Keyder sat very primly behind the table in Interview Room No. 3, her large leather handbag perched on top of her knees.

'You took delivery of the children's bodies on the Friday night, didn't you?' İkmen asked. Both he and Suleyman sat opposite the old woman, both smoking heavily in the dense night-time heat – the old partnership temporarily back together again.

'You get a much better result if you can get hold of corpses when they are fresh,' she said matter-of-factly. 'Melih wanted his subjects to be as close to the perfection he had observed in the pictures I'd shown him of Evita as possible. Melih was very insistent that he administer the poison in the children's own home – he could have done it in mine – but he didn't want to alarm them.'

'How very thoughtful,' Suleyman said *sotto voce*.

'Reşad Kuran delivered them to you?' İkmen asked.

'Yes. Reşad had worked for me for a number of years . . .'

'Delivering dead bodies?'

'Yes,' she shrugged. 'He is a delivery man, he delivers things. I use him to fetch and carry corpses, what of it? Of course I didn't know for some time that he was Melih's brother-in-law for I didn't realise that Melih was related to Zelda and Moris Nabaro. They were his parents; I grew up with her. But I didn't know that until I'd been collecting his works for some years.' She smiled. 'I'd always liked his creations. He has a particularly Jewish style, much of which is based upon Kabbalistic theory, including the tarot, that appeals to my past.'

'Reşad Kuran put you in touch with Melih Akdeniz?'

Yeşim Keyder, seemingly amused by İkmen's flat, sepulchral style laughed. 'You make it sound as if we only met in order to work on his Karagöz project,' she said.

'You ended up killing his children.'

'No. No, I didn't kill the children, Inspector,' she said, suddenly stern-faced once again. 'If you recall, that was Melih. It was part of the statement. If I, as someone with no connection to them, had killed them, no new boundaries would have been set. Apart from the artistry inherent in my own expertise, the exhibit would have been devoid of any fresh philosophical base.'

'You believe that killing children, embalming their bodies and using them as puppets in a Karagöz show is art?'

The tone of Suleyman's voice raised her hackles.

'Art is all about statement,' she said haughtily. 'In Kabbalistic terms, Melih was the cosmic juggler, the Karagöz figure, if you like, at the very pinnacle of that magical system. Both creating and taking life which he and I then rendered immortal. Evita was Pedro's statement. That body told the world that it was possible for a life force to be pinned to a perfect corpse. A liquid sun is how Pedro described her, a thing of glorious immortality.

But my work with the Akdeniz children took this even further . . .'

'I always thought the cosmic juggler, the fool of the tarot, was supposed to be a balancing force,' İkmen said.

'Dr Keyder,' Suleyman cut in, 'did you, maybe guided by Ara, ever indulge in sexual acts with corpses?'

'Can we please stick to the Akdeniz case?' İkmen said.

He was very tired now, worn out by the tragedy and insanity inherent in two young corpses – worried about Fatma and about Talaat who, although beyond anyone's help now, deserved what Yaşar and Nuray had he felt been denied – dignity in death.

'The bodies were delivered to me at around midnight on the Friday,' Dr Keyder began, back again in her businesslike style. 'I started working on them straight away. I used a four per cent formaldehyde solution, via gravity injection . . .'

'Dr Keyder, we don't need the specifics of your trade,' İkmen said sharply. The woman, for all her years, looked as if she were getting some sort of gratification from her descriptions of processes. 'Mr Kuran delivered the victims to you, you preserved them and . . .'

'Melih was dying, as I'm sure you're aware, from cancer,' she said. 'The Karagöz performance was to be the pinnacle of his career, his final shattering statement. I worked hard for several days afterwards. I locked myself into my laboratory. I didn't want any distractions. I told my neighbours I'd gone away. But I could have done a better job had I had more time. I told him this. However with the inevitable investigation into the children's disappearance plus Rosita's death and all the questions about Miguel, as well as my usual maintenance practice . . .'

'Preserving the mothers of Russian gangsters . . .'

'The identity of my clients is private,' she snapped.

'With the exception of the Nabaros,' Suleyman said.

'How was I to know that name would come back from the dead?' she responded bitterly. 'Melih buried that years ago. How was I to know that you had any connection to the missing children investigation?'

'Have you ever met a man called Rostov?' Suleyman continued. 'Valery Rostov?'

'I don't know . . .'

'He says he's met you.'

'Yaşar and Nuray weren't present in your laboratory when Inspector Suleyman visited you this morning,' İkmen said as he yet again attempted to drag the interrogation back to the Akdeniz case. 'When did you move the bodies?'

'Last night,' she said, 'when I returned from meeting you,' she looked at Suleyman, 'at the mortuary. I knew I couldn't use Reşad; Melih had told me about his problems with yourselves. I called a client of mine, who offered to do the job for me.'

'The car that arrived at the Akdeniz house this morning,' İkmen said.

'Yes.'

Suleyman cleared his throat. 'Who was driving, Dr Keyder?'

'Someone totally innocent,' she replied. 'A foreigner.'

'A Russian.'

'A foreigner, yes,' she smiled.

293

'And yet if you hadn't willingly owned up to being the person responsible for the body of Miguel Arancibia, we wouldn't be in this room now,' Suleyman said with a frown, 'and you wouldn't be facing very serious charges. Why did you do that, Dr Keyder? Why did you turn up at the mortuary with that peculiar Spaniard?'

'Orontes?' Yeşim Keyder laughed. 'He was trying to break into my brother's apartment when I found him,' she said. 'He was under the impression that he might find some of Dr Ara's balm in there.'

'Was he right?'

'No.' Her face became grave again. 'That is made in only small quantities and had, I knew, been used up.' She looked down at her handbag. 'I engaged Orontes for my own purposes,' she said, 'but I claimed Miguel for myself because I had to have him buried with Rosita. If I didn't I couldn't take possession of Veli's apartment.'

'But surely you, with all your "clients", your yalı, can't need an apartment in Kuloğlu?' Suleyman said. After all, as he knew only too well, Yeşim Keyder lived in some style.

She turned upon him with fierce eyes. 'Have you ever been poor, Inspector?' He didn't so much as blink. 'No, I thought not,' she said, her voice thick with contempt. 'Well, I have. Veli and I worked every hour in the day to get out of Balat. My brother was a brilliant man – unappreciated here, which is why we went to South America. There were a lot of Jews in Buenos Aires back in those days. My brother rose very quickly – we entered the magic circle of Peron. I met Ara and, strangely he always said for a woman, I didn't back away from him when he told me what he did. He liked that and so he showed me his work – his perfect ballerina – frozen in mid-step, eternally beautiful. I have subsequently produced such a work myself, another dancer . . .' She smiled. 'You know, it was as if Ara were a god, imbued with the power of eternity. I saw through him a window into immortality as well as a way of ensuring I would never be poor again.'

Suleyman made as if he wanted to cut in but was prevented from doing so by one of İkmen's upheld hands.

Yeşim Keyder, now seemingly quite far away from them, continued, 'He let me work with him maintaining Miguel. It was electrifying.' She sighed. 'But then when Peron's regime fell apart Veli and I, together with Rosita, had to come back here. There was nowhere else to go. We brought Miguel, I maintained him, but we had no money. Veli got a poorly paid job in a department here. We all lived in one small room . . . But then one day Rosita came back from church and told me about a little old lady who wanted to have her husband embalmed but couldn't afford the outrageous prices the Greeks and the Armenians were charging.' She looked up. 'It grew from there. I made the money that funded my brother's famous experiments. I looked after Miguel and Rosita. And in answer to your question, no I don't need the Kuloğlu apartment, but who knows if I might do in the future? Besides, it's mine, I've earned it.'

İkmen spent a few moments in silent thought. It was, he felt, very fitting that Dr Keyder should be so fixated on what was hers. Preservation and just simply 'holding on', as she was with the apartment to what was hers, represented her entire life. Selfish. Not to let the dead go was selfish. Putting all of this effort into preserving what had gone had to be an act of desecration. Maybe, he thought, the old Turkish idea about the soul of the deceased being in pain until the body was buried had a more practical application that extended beyond mere superstition. Perhaps that custom had sprung, originally, from the desire of learned men to see people move on – to prevent that protracted fall from the Lightning-Struck Tower and to ease the soul's torment.

'You will be charged with aiding and abetting a murderer,' İkmen said dully, 'but then I imagine that, in view of the fact that Melih's "performance" was to be a public display, you always anticipated this possibility.'

'Yes,' she sniffed unpleasantly. 'My work has been in the shadows for too long. I'm old now, I need the world to see my genius before I die. And besides, I didn't kill those children, I have nothing—'

'But you knew what Akdeniz was going to do!' İkmen yelled.

'Yes, although he was going to shoot himself in front of the press . . .'

'You knew that one crime had been committed and that a suicide was about to take place, but you didn't report it did you?'

'No.'

'Then you must share in the responsibility for these three deaths!' İkmen, his hands shaking with both anger and tiredness, ran his fingers through his hair. 'Like Melih Akdeniz you are evil, Dr Keyder. Even human life is subsumed beneath this unhealthy passion you still possess and he did have for your "work".'

'Embalming isn't work,' Dr Keyder said contemptuously, 'embalming, as I learned it from Ara, is a magical art. Melih knew this. That Christian pathologist Sarkissian, for all his professional veneer, was staggered by Miguel.'

'Perhaps as a scientist, yes,' Suleyman said, 'but Dr Sarkissian didn't *like* what he saw. There was nothing pleasing . . .'

'Art isn't meant to be pleasing!' she laughed at him mirthlessly. 'Art is about making people think. It's about saying things we all want to say but are too afraid to do so. Nobody wants their loved ones to die, nobody actually wants to die themselves. My art is about the expression of those desires and, because Ara taught me to capture the very spirit of the subject, it's about re-establishing a mystical link with the deceased too. Every body is a unique work of art. Melih's death, my incarceration – these are such small prices to pay for the opportunity to make such a gigantic statement. For me to be able, at last, to show my unrivalled skills to the world.'

İkmen just shook his head in disbelief. He looked at Suleyman and said, 'I can't listen to any more of this now. Take her down to the cells, constable.'

They all thought that Dr Keyder would continue either to resist still further or carry on talking about her work. But she didn't. She just let the constable place the handcuffs around her wrists and lead her out of the room. As soon as she had gone, İkmen keyed a number into his phone and placed his head in his hands as he waited for someone to answer.

\* \* \*

Ayşe Farsakoğlu was standing in the corridor outside one of the cells when İsak Çöktin and one of his men approached with Reşad Kuran. As soon as the artist's brother-in-law had been pushed, silently, into what Çöktin knew to be one of the hotter station cells, he approached her.

'How are you?' he said. She looked very pale, her eyes were glassy and had a sore appearance. The discovery of Yaşar and Nuray's bodies had affected everyone very badly. What had been done to them had been so bizarre, the reasons behind it so mad, none could quite take it in.

'You know Inspector İkmen had one of his feelings about the children,' she said as she took a packet of cigarettes out of her handbag and offered it to Çöktin.

Çöktin took a cigarette from the packet and then lit up both for her and for himself. 'What are you doing here?'

'I've just put Eren Akdeniz away for the night,' she replied. 'You know she told me she killed her husband because he asked her to?'

'What do you mean?'

Ayşe drew on her cigarette before replying, 'She said that once she told Melih that we were outside and that Inspector İkmen knew that the children's bodies were inside, he told her to kill him.'

Çöktin frowned. 'But hadn't Akdeniz invited you to his performance anyway?'

'Yes.' She looked up into his eyes and shook her head just gently as if in disbelief. 'Apparently his final "statement" was always going to be to shoot himself. Standing between the two children at the end of the shadow performance. By arriving early we ruined his tableau. Infanticide and suicide as art. She also rambled on about the contrast between Melih's rotting body and the preserved bodies of the children – something about decomposition and permanence.' Tears sprang into her eyes. 'She must be insane.'

'I don't know,' Çöktin shrugged, 'I would think so. But legally it would depend upon what the psychiatrist says. Have you contacted Dr Sadri?'

They started walking together back towards the stairs.

'Yes,' she replied. 'He'll come in the morning.'

'She doesn't need to be sedated then?' Çöktin asked as he tipped his head back towards the grim row of cells behind them.

'No,' Ayşe responded with a sigh, 'no, she's quite happy in a strange sort of way.'

'Because her husband and little ones are all together in paradise?' Çöktin said acidly. He'd come across people like this before, those who killed their nearest and dearest in order to unite them in heaven.

'No,' Ayşe said frowning, 'because the statement, as she calls it, is now complete. Our photographers have taken hundreds of pictures of Melih's performance. It's been recorded as a crime, as a news item and, so she says, as a work of art. This "event", because we have recorded it, will live for ever.' She shook her head again, frowning. 'We've actually helped Melih and Eren. We've had no choice but to do so, but if I've got this right, we too are part of the performance, if you can understand . . .'

Çöktin didn't really understand anything she was saying, but he put a hand on her shoulder in order to provide her with a little comfort in her agitation.

'Do you think that such a thing can be art, İsak?' she

said as she looked up into his bright blue eyes. 'Can it really be something that hurts people? Can it really be anything an artist wants it to be?'

But Çöktin didn't have any answers. To him art was the statues of Atatürk in every town square, art was the graceful, soaring dome of the Süleymaniye Mosque, art was even the picture of a stag standing by a Scottish loch that hung on his mother's living-room wall. To him, art was something that people had to like. In that way it was similar, if not the same, as alcohol.

'I think we should go and have a beer,' he said, as he led her up the stairs and away from the cells.

'Yes, but . . .'

'And talk about something banal, like television,' he continued. 'You need to stop thinking, Ayşe,' he said gravely. 'We've had a long and very odd night. We've moved into the land of the sick. Now we need to heal ourselves.'

They'd never been close. In fact Çöktin didn't always feel that he could entirely trust Ayşe Farsakoğlu. She was, he'd sometimes thought, a rather arrogant woman. But for tonight he put that aside and took her for a drink.

Arto Sarkissian wasn't accustomed to being interrupted in his work. Post-mortem examinations, once begun, tended to proceed until they were complete. However, in view of the fact that the interrupter was none other than Commissioner Ardiç, Arto was left with little choice but to leave what he was doing and return to his office.

'Commissioner,' he said as he extended a hand he knew the other man would suspect of having recently left the inside of a corpse. Ardiç's expression confirmed this.

'So these mummies or whatever you like to call them and the artist from Balat are now in the building?' Ardiç said as he eased himself slowly into a chair opposite Arto's desk.

'Yes,' the Armenian replied. 'As yet, I've only looked at the external condition of the bodies. I'm currently working on what I'm coming to believe is a female suicide . . .'

'Vile business!'

Arto sat down. 'Suicide is always distressing.'

'I mean the mummies!' Ardiç shook his head and, the doctor observed, visibly shuddered. 'That anyone should think that murder and that abominable embalming practice is art, is beyond me. İkmen, as one would expect, is bending his mind to the deeper philosophies behind all of this, but then that is what he does.'

Arto smiled. However appalled his friend might be by the acts of violence and hatred that came his way, he always had to make some sense, however peculiar, out of them. Murder, he always said, had to have a reason, even if that reason was not anything that could be conventionally called real.

'So when,' Ardiç continued, 'will you be able to start work on the Akdeniz children, Doctor?'

'Tomorrow morning.' It was late now and both he and his team of assistants were already tired.

Ardiç nodded gravely. 'Mmm.'

'Is that a problem?'

'No,' the policeman looked up sharply, 'no it isn't. But

I do feel that I have to warn you, Doctor, that we are expecting some more of this type of corpse.'

'More embalmed bodies?'

'Possibly.'

Arto remembered what Suleyman had told him about the vogue for embalming that allegedly existed amongst Russian mobsters. But he knew better than to reveal his knowledge to Ardiç. Although he himself worked for the police he was aware of the fact that information like that, given to him by a serving officer, would be frowned upon.

'I came here because I feel that you deserve to know this,' Ardiç went on. 'Dealing with such bodies must be particularly abhorrent.'

'Yes, but when compared to a drowned body or one consumed by fire.'

'It's an abomination!' Ardiç blustered. 'Keeping the dead out of the ground! It's unnatural! What do they think they're doing? What do they do with them? I dread to think.'

The commissioner had, Arto felt, momentarily forgotten that he originated from a society where the preservation of the dead was considered to be normal. For Arto, the main difficulty was a scientific one. Establishing the cause of death was much harder in these cases.

When Ardiç spoke again it was in a calmer and more mollified fashion. 'But then whatever we may think,' he said, 'I feel it may be prudent for you to prepare your staff and your facilities for something of an influx.'

'Yes . . .'

'I can't, of course, give you any further details,' Ardiç

said as he held one silencing hand aloft, 'but I think that if you spend some time tonight making ready you will be glad that you did so in the very near future.'

It would appear that Ardiç was intent on finding some more embalmed corpses and since he knew only about the Russian connection it was in all likelihood that. Russian Mafiosi. Dangerous people. He wondered whether either İkmen or Suleyman might be involved, but again he knew better than to ask – either Ardiç now or his friends later. Besides, it was now well after midnight, and even if neither of them was yet in bed, they would be fully occupied – either with the outfall from the Akdeniz murder or, in İkmen's case, with his family. He'd called the İkmen household earlier in the day and had spoken to one of his friend's sons, Bülent. The boy had told him that Çetin's brother-in-law Talaat had been taken to hospital. Poor, yellow-skinned Talaat, finally dying . . .

All the lights were on when İkmen finally returned to his apartment at one thirty. And although the younger children were safely tucked up in their beds, all of the older ones, with the exception of the eldest, Sınan, had taken up residence in his living room. Also present, he noticed, sitting beside Hulya, was Berekiah Cohen.

After a brief cursory scan around the room, İkmen said, 'Where's your mother?'

His eldest daughter, Çiçek, replied, 'Still at the hospital. She refused to leave. We've only been back for a few minutes.' She walked over to kiss her father on the cheek. 'Would you like some tea?'

'Thanks,' he smiled. 'I appreciate how all of you children have rallied in support of your mother.'

'You know that Sınan would have been here too if he'd been in town,' Orhan said.

'I phoned and spoke to him a little earlier,' İkmen said as he lowered himself wearily into a chair. 'How are things with Uncle Talaat?'

Orhan shrugged. 'The same. There's no timescale when a person is in coma. He could go tonight, tomorrow, next week. In spite of everything, his heart is still strong.'

'Allah.'

'Mum hasn't been alone with him until now,' Çiçek said as she came back into the room holding a glass of tea. 'We've all been there all day.'

İkmen frowned. 'What, you left the kids?'

'No, no, Berekiah looked after them,' Çiçek said, glancing across at the tired-looking Jewish boy with a smile. 'We couldn't have managed without him.'

İkmen took the glass from his daughter's hand and drank a small sip of tea. 'Thank you, Berekiah.'

'I think that Mum now thinks Berekiah is some sort of saint,' Çiçek continued, accompanying her words with a nervous laugh.

İkmen looked up, quickly taking in the way that his two sons and two daughters all shared a brief, knowing look. They were nice children, Orhan, Çiçek and Bülent. They wanted their sister Hulya to be happy and were unanimously, for he knew that Sınan felt likewise, coming out in support of her union with the young man that she loved. He had, he felt with some satisfaction, taught his children well.

'You must have been busy to have to go, Dad?' Bülent said.

'Yes, I'm afraid that I ended up witnessing a most distressing incident,' İkmen said with what he alone in that room knew was massive understatement.

'Oh, not those poor children from Balat?' Hulya put her hands up to her face and shook her head slowly.

'You know I can't tell you anything about it,' İkmen replied.

'Have to wait for the news, I suppose,' Orhan observed.

'Yes.'

'Mmm.'

A moment of silence ensued during which everyone in the room, with the exception of İkmen, pondered upon just how odd his life actually was. Peppered with confidences, secrets and almost unimagined tensions, sometimes the İkmen children felt as if they were living on the edge of some sort of espionage – their father a grey and troubled spy.

'You know what upsets me most?' Bülent said. 'The look of him.'

'Who?'

The youngster looked down incredulously at his father. 'Uncle Talaat, of course. Laying on that bed, with the machines, all yellow . . .'

'Don't!' Çiçek put her hands over her eyes as if trying to block out the actual sight of their relative.

'He was always so cool, Uncle Talaat,' Bülent continued, smiling just a little at the memory. 'Young and out on the beach with lots of girls . . . He looks like an old man now, wrinkled up like a mummy.'

Or not, İkmen thought. Although technically mummified, what he had seen of the Akdeniz children had, even he had to admit, been more like the product of some artistic process than the result of scientific principles. What Dr Keyder had produced had been, well, beautiful. Smooth-skinned, clear- (if glass) eyed, stunning. Like great, gorgeous dolls . . . And yet Dr Keyder's assertion that she had pinned their spirits to them had been incorrect. There was something – İkmen always shied away from calling it a 'soul' – that irrevocably set the living and the dead apart. Even when people were very ill, in coma or close to death, there was always something alive about them. When it went a change took place that you knew not in your mind so much as in your gut. It was something very primitive, probably allied to self-preservation – the dead, after all, could host all manner of bacteria and parasites. Unless, of course, someone like Dr Keyder got to them first.

İkmen drained his tea glass in one gulp. 'I think we all need to rest,' he said as he rose stiffly from his chair. 'I know I do.'

'But what if Mum calls?' Çiçek asked anxiously.

'Then one of us will hear the phone and do whatever is appropriate,' İkmen replied. He looked across at Orhan and said, 'I'd be grateful if you'd take Berekiah and Çiçek home.'

'Yes, Dad.'

'But I want to stay!' Çiçek said, her eyes filling with overtired tears. 'I want to be here.'

'Well, if that's what you want of course you can,' İkmen said, and then with a wave of one exhausted hand he left the room.

He heard Orhan and Berekiah leave about ten minutes later, an event that was preceded by the sound of Hulya and the young Jewish boy kissing in the hall. Shortly afterwards Bülent went to what had been his, but had become Talaat's bedroom. And then there was silence – until he both heard and saw Çiçek at his bedroom door.

'Dad . . .'

'What?'

She walked into his bedroom and shut the door behind her. 'Dad, you know that Hulya has refused Berekiah's proposal of marriage.'

'No, I didn't know that.' İkmen pulled his duvet up round his neck as he sat up.

Çiçek sat down on her parents' bed and looked at her father with grave eyes. 'She told him she'll live with him, but she won't marry. He, Berekiah, thinks she's doing this because she wants to shock Mum and Mr Cohen.'

İkmen, who really didn't need any more problems in his life at this time, sighed.

'She told me,' Çiçek continued, 'that because of all the trouble she and Berekiah have had, she can't face marriage and all the heartbreak that will bring to everyone. But she also really loves Berekiah and she doesn't want to give him up.'

'Poor Hulya.' İkmen shook his head. 'Poor Berekiah.'

'You've got to do something, Dad,' Çiçek said as she leaned forward and stroked her father's face. 'You've got to get Mum and Mr Cohen to see sense and tell Hulya that if she marries Berekiah she'll be bringing this family so much joy. Allah knows but we need something happy in this family,' she said as her eyes filled with tears. 'What with Uncle Talaat, and Bülent going to the army. Oh, Dad, I've heard people at work talking about war.'

She started to cry so İkmen leaned forward and took her gently into his arms.

'Sssh, sssh,' he said as he rocked her to and fro in his arms, just like he'd done when she was little. 'It's going to be all right, Çiçek.' He kissed her on the top of her head. 'I'll make it all right, I promise.'

'Oh, Dad . . .'

'Sssh, sssh.'

He rocked her, as it happened in the end, until she eventually fell asleep in his arms. Just like the old days, İkmen thought as he lay back down, with his daughter, on his pillows. Çiçek was never a child to be easily put to bed – just like Hulya had never been a child to be easily pleased. But then in the current situation, being pleased didn't really cover what she wanted. This was about how much in love she was with someone who was, İkmen knew, a fine person. She would, he decided, marry Berekiah, and he would make it happen. And then suddenly and shatteringly he was asleep. Exhausted, İkmen's sleep was so deep it was thankfully even beyond the reach of dreams.

# CHAPTER 20

Three homes owned by men who had once been Russian nationals were raided at dawn. All three were, or had been suspected of, racketeering at some time since their arrival in the city. Wealthy beyond the imagination of most people Messrs Vronsky, Malenkov and Bulganin had, so Commissioner Ardiç, who headed one of the raids personally, thought, very strange tastes. Vronsky, who at fifty-five was quite elderly for an active mobster had his deceased mother of ten years sitting in his study, for Malenkov it was his child, a small daughter. Bulganin, the most ardent devotee of them all, had three examples of Dr Keyder's art in his possession and lived with the dead bodies of his wife, his mother and a cherished mistress. Obviously totally unprepared for a visit from the authorities, the gang bosses also provided the police with quantities of heroin, cocaine, crack, cannabis, guns, knives and even a small amount of the date rape drug, Rohypnol.

Ardiç, who had used only officers previously unconnected with this affair to lead these raids, was pleased. The unburied bodies had given him justification to go into the three properties. The drugs and arms – though fully expected – had been a bonus. And now with some very significant people in custody, possibly for quite some time, he felt that he had more than earned his wages for that day. True, there were still significant numbers of people who had worked for the three bosses at large in the city, many of whom were probably totally unknown to the police. Assuming they had formed a connection between their friend Rostov and the raids, the three bosses could get word out to their free cronies about him. But then if someone should take it into his head to shoot or stab Rostov, Ardiç certainly wouldn't lose any sleep, or express any sympathy over it. Provided the mobsters kept it amongst themselves and avoided all-out war, they could all kill each other with impunity for all he cared. Sometimes, as his superiors had told him when he'd sought their approval, risks had to be taken. And with a general election pending, the party currently in control of the city was keen for people to know that they were serious about fighting organised crime. A little late in the day as far as Ardiç was concerned, however . . . Rostov, in any event, would have to give up his 'mummy', willingly or by force – whatever it took.

Ardiç picked up his phone and called Metin İskender to tell him of these developments.

Suleyman met İkmen inside the cream- and coffee-scented Sultanahmet Pastane. Although İkmen wasn't really given to breakfast as such, he did occasionally like to partake of a cappuccino and a chocolate pastry courtesy of the elegant proprietress, the widow Suzan Şeker. Only a year ago, İkmen had been instrumental in bringing the gangsters who had terrorised Mrs Şeker's late husband

Hassan, to justice. She was still very fulsome in her gratitude.

'No payment,' she said as she placed coffee and cakes in front of İkmen and Suleyman.

'Mrs Şeker . . .'

She held up a stern, silencing hand. 'No, I insist. You either take my hospitality now or later,' she said as she started to make her way back over to the chilled cake cabinet, 'as you well know, Inspector.'

İkmen shrugged his shoulders helplessly. His daughter Hulya worked at the pastane six evenings a week. Last time he'd insisted upon paying for his coffee and cakes, the girl had come home with enough pastry for the whole İkmen family which, given the size of his brood, was not inconsiderable.

When the widow Şeker had gone, İkmen lit a cigarette while contemplating the mountain of chocolate on the table before him. Suleyman, looking on, lit up too.

'I would appreciate it if you would sit in on my interrogation of Eren Akdeniz,' İkmen said, coming straight to the point.

'I thought that Sergeant Farsakoğlu . . .'

'Ayşe will be there too – only as an observer,' İkmen said. 'She's already interviewed the woman once herself.'

'And so why do you need me?'

İkmen looked up, his face taut with what looked like anxiety. 'I would like you to watch me,' he said, 'ensure that I behave professionally, with humanity.'

'You feel tremendous anger.'

'That woman allowed her own children to be murdered,

311

embalmed and exhibited.' He looked up into his friend's face, his eyes dark with fury. 'I don't want to, but I need to understand that,' he said. 'I have to make some sort of sense out of it both for my own satisfaction and so that I can at least attempt to explain what has happened to those under my command.'

Suleyman took a sip from his coffee cup and leaned back into his seat. 'I understand Dr Sadrı is spending some time with Mrs Akdeniz this morning.'

İkmen shrugged. 'I'll see what he says. But personally I don't believe that Eren Akdeniz is insane.'

'Why not?'

'Because I don't believe that love is necessarily mad.' He drew heavily on his cigarette and smiled. 'Melih, for whatever reason – sexual, artistic, I don't know – was more important to Eren than her children.'

'Do you think that he had some sort of hold over her?' Suleyman asked.

'She was a lot younger than he – she was once his student, you know. I've seen him humiliate her and I've seen him respond with touching tenderness towards her. Whatever their relationship is, or rather was, it is far more complicated than we imagined.'

Suleyman smiled. 'Not long ago Zelfa would have been fascinated by such a challenge.'

İkmen leaned forward so that he could lower his voice. 'Have you told Zelfa about . . . ?'

'No,' Suleyman lowered his eyes, 'I've still got to go back and see Dr Krikor. I was interrupted, by all this business, before I had a chance to start the tests.' He looked up sharply. 'I feel OK.'

'That means nothing,' İkmen responded sharply, 'as well you know.'

'Yes.'

'You need to tell her now,' İkmen continued, 'get it over with and . . . I am not judging you, Mehmet. I just simply feel that . . .'

'When are you planning to interrogate Mrs Akdeniz?'

It was typical Suleyman behaviour. His private life entered the conversation, he became uncomfortable and brought the subject to a close. It was, İkmen always felt, one of those times when his friend's Ottoman ancestry showed very clearly through his veneer of modern openness and tolerance.

But the older man, accustomed now to the idea that sometimes Suleyman's private life was what the Ottomans had called 'walled', just simply shrugged and said, 'If we finish this and get over to the station, Dr Sadrı should be concluding his examination.' He leaned back and sighed. 'Do you know whether Dr Sarkissian has come up with anything to connect that Russian girl to our friend Rostov?'

Suleyman looked down at the table and dug his fork into the side of one of the cakes Mrs Şeker had placed before them.

'No . . .'

'Which means I suppose that almost anyone could have drowned her.'

'Yes.' Suleyman scraped some of the chocolate from the side of an éclair and smeared it bad-temperedly into his mouth. 'Except that I know that he, or one of his creatures, did it,' he said. 'What use was she once she'd attempted to set me up? An alcoholic, a junkie, HIV positive.'

İkmen leaned forward again. 'He's sure about that?'

'Yes. It was apparently quite well advanced.'

They both sat in silence for a few moments after this. İkmen had been aware of the possibility that the prostitute Masha might be HIV positive, but he hadn't known until this moment that it was a certainty. Looking across at his friend, the thought of it made his blood run cold. In his soul he was afraid for Suleyman. Perhaps this was how Rostov had intended his friend to be 'set up'? Perhaps it never had had anything to do with discrediting him in a professional sense at all? Maybe by the time İskender had come into contact with Father Alexei, by the time Suleyman had entered the gangster's unusually 'clean' house the damage had already been done? And yet, if that were the case, then what of the gangster's child, that poor cold little parcel Suleyman had seen nestling in the depths of Rostov's freezer? What of that?

Metin İskender didn't even attempt to introduce the small, sombrely dressed man at his side. There would be time for that soon enough. For the moment, however, there were other, more pressing concerns.

He looked up into Rostov's features with a grave expression on his face. 'Bulganin, Malenkov and Vronsky are all in custody,' he said.

'Oh.'

He watched as Rostov's lawyer, Lütfü Güneş shot the gangster a nervous glance.

'What for?' Rostov sat down on one of his considerable settees and lit a cigarette.

'For a variety of offences,' İskender replied, 'including in all cases the possession of unburied corpses, the identities of whom we have yet to verify.' He sat down opposite the Russian and lit a cigarette of his own. 'Your three "friends" don't yet know that it was you who informed us about the corpses, but I don't suppose it will take them too long to work that out.'

'You shouldn't have done that!' Güneş began. 'You've put my client in danger.'

'However,' İskender raised one hand in order to silence the lawyer, 'we do also have the embalmer in custody too. So perhaps your involvement isn't quite so obvious, Mr Rostov.' He looked down at his fingers curling around the end of his cigarette. 'Or at least it won't be, provided you allow Mr Livadanios and myself to take Tatiana away with us.'

'Why?'

'Mr Livadanios is an undertaker,' İskender said as he acknowledged the Greek with a slight incline of his head, 'well versed in the Christian Orthodox rites and traditions to which you adhere, Mr Rostov.'

'The law requires that we bury your daughter, sir,' Livadanios explained. 'We cannot leave her frozen.'

'But Valery,' Lütfü Güneş said as he turned to face his employer with a frown, 'you wanted to have her embalmed. You wanted to keep Tatiana.'

The Russian stubbed his cigarette out on a sigh. 'Yes, well . . .'

'If it's any consolation,' Yiannis Livadanios said with

that professionally kind edge such people were so good at giving their voices, 'embalming wouldn't have worked anyway.'

Lütfü Güneş looked shocked. 'What? Why not?' He looked down at Rostov and said, 'But, Valery, weren't you told—'

İskender, if no one else, saw the Russian's face change colour.

'Bodies that have been frozen respond badly to the embalming process,' Livadanios continued. 'Once the thaw is complete, deterioration begins rapidly. Bacterial decomposition deep within the body moves very quickly to overwhelm the subject. It's a most distressing thing to witness.'

'According to you, yes,' the lawyer, now leaning in towards the undertaker, said aggressively, 'but what about all the other bodies this embalmer has treated? Didn't they come from Russia in frozen—'

'Apparently not. Part of Mr Vronsky's defence is that his late mother was originally embalmed in Russia,' İskender said as he attempted to retain his concentration on to Rostov's seemingly ever-shifting features. 'He brought her here to be more expertly treated by the embalmer we currently have in custody. He maintains that she is still a Russian "citizen".'

'But she wasn't frozen?'

'No, Mr Güneş,' İskender said, 'none of the other bodies we have discovered, except Tatiana, has been frozen. Apparently the fact that frozen bodies cannot then be embalmed is well known.'

'Valery must have been wrongly advised.'

'Maybe.'

İskender knew it wasn't really possible. Although he had only met her in person once, he'd heard enough about Dr Yeşim Keyder to know that the last thing she would ever compromise would be her professionalism. If nothing else, his memory of that startling photograph of a dancer she'd had on display in her yalı had to be significant. Like her mentor Pedro Ara's famous dancer, Dr Keyder's performer had, he now knew, been quite dead. Petrified within a perfectly preserved moment of artistry, this – and the fabulous Akdeniz children – were the kinds of subjects Dr Keyder would want to be associated with as opposed to some half-rotted urchin from Moscow. Just what and why Rostov had started all of this business with Masha, with poor little 'Tatiana', with his stories of bodily preservation, began to worry, as it had done before, at Metin İskender's mind. This time, however, he came to a conclusion.

Rostov said no more about the removal of Tatiana from his premises. As the undertaker, Güneş and the two uniformed officers İskender had brought with him, disappeared downstairs to the freezers he just sat very still, looking sad.

İskender, still sitting opposite the Russian, crossed his legs. 'Of course,' he said after a pause, 'Malenkov, Vronsky and Bulganin still have their dealers, runners, girls and boys.'

'I'm a businessman, I don't know what you mean.'

'Out on the streets, waiting to either inherit their masters' empires or join forces with another master who will pay them just as well, if not better.'

He looked across at the Russian, who averted his eyes.

'You're a very clever man, Mr Rostov,' İskender said as he helped himself to a cocktail cigarette from one of the golden boxes on the coffee table in front of him. 'I've always considered myself to be bright, but you've beaten me.'

'I don't know what you mean.'

'No?' İskender lit up and smiled. 'Perhaps I ought to explain,' he said, 'although quite why I should do so to you.'

Rostov very pointedly looked out of a window and into his sunlit garden beyond.

'It's like this,' İskender said. 'You want to take over. Everything. Drugs, prostitution.'

'I don't.'

'Just hear me out, Mr Rostov,' İskender said with a smile. 'So how do you do that? You get something on your "friends" you know they won't be able to either defend or hide.' He leaned forward towards Rostov. 'The bodies. Their sainted dead, incorruptible in time, unacceptable in a Muslim country.'

'You're crazy.'

İskender ignored the remark and continued, 'It must have taken some planning,' he said. 'To get that body into this country just as we were beginning to take an interest in such things. How did it happen, Rostov? Did you read about Dr Keyder's sister-in-law in the paper? Did the good doctor even take you to see her greatest work, Miguel Arancibia, the unknown dead man of Kuloğlu? And then, of course, you also set my colleague up with your prostitute. I was impressed by the way you knew so much about his difficulties at home.'

Rostov turned back to face İskender. 'This is all pure conjecture,' he said. 'You have no proof.'

'I'd like to know who in my department sold Inspector Suleyman to you.'

'I don't know . . .'

'" . . . what you mean"?' İskender, still smiling, rose to his feet. 'I'm getting a little tired of that phrase, Mr Rostov.'

Suddenly, with one quick, deft movement, he leaned forward, took a portion of Rostov's hair between his fingers and pulled.

The Russian, outraged, bellowed, 'What!'

İskender pocketed the hair as he moved towards the door.

'If the DNA in the sample I've just taken from you matches that of "Tatiana", you will have nothing to worry about, will you, Mr Rostov?'

The Russian, still nursing the sore place on the top of his head, frowned. 'And if it doesn't?'

'Then I will come after you,' İskender said as he opened the door from the living room into the hall.

'And do what?' Rostov said.

'And—'

'And connect me to a prostitute to whom I have no connection?' he laughed. 'You seem to think I set up your Inspector Suleyman with such a woman for some reason.'

'Yes I do. I don't know what the original plan was, though,' İskender said. 'However, the result, that he found Tatiana and unwittingly assisted you in your mission against your countrymen, has worked to your advantage. Now you alone, if you want, can run this city.'

'Except that I don't want.' Rostov leaned back comfortably in his seat once again. 'Or rather there is no proof that I want,' he said. 'Just like there is no proof to connect me to this prostitute, there is no proof that any such plan existed. The body in my freezer is that of my daughter, as your tests will confirm.'

'I don't believe you.'

Rostov shrugged. 'That isn't my problem,' he said. 'Your tests will confirm that my daughter died a long time ago and that I brought her from Russia to be with me.'

'I still don't believe you,' İskender retorted. 'That corpse is frozen, there is no way it can be embalmed.'

'And yet within the ice,' Rostov smiled, 'she is perfect, Inspector. You should go and see for yourself. Go now before—'

'What about you?' İskender asked. 'Don't you want to see your "daughter" before . . .'

'No.' He turned back to the window once again. 'No, I've seen her many times.'

'And now you can dispense with her.'

'I can let her go, yes,' he smiled. 'That's healthy, isn't it?'

İskender, stung by the cruel irony in the Russian's voice, turned sharply on his heel and left. The Russian, smiling still, waited until the body had been removed from his house before he called his ex-wife to thank her for her understanding and assistance. Giving up Tatiana, and at such short notice, must have been a wrench. But then she had other children and he was going to reward her handsomely. If only he could thank Miguel Arancibia too. He owed him so much, that lovely – as he recalled so clearly – pride of Dr Keyder's life. But then as Bulganin had said when he'd taken him to Kuloğlu all those months ago, Miguel was the best example because Pedro Ara had, in truth, been far better than Yeşim Keyder.

So many people to thank. Dear Masha – ah, but she was dead now. Still, he couldn't have done it without her or without his friend in the police department who had known so much about Inspector Suleyman's private life. He'd have to employ that informant again . . .

What would be usual in a case such as this, Dr Sadrı the psychiatrist told İkmen, would be for Eren Akdeniz to place the blame entirely with her husband. He was, after all, dead and therefore incapable of either confirming or denying anything she said. But Eren wasn't like that. In fact as she sat down calmly opposite İkmen, Suleyman and Farsakoğlu, Eren Akdeniz looked more like a person at a job interview than someone facing life imprisonment.

'My husband was and still remains the greatest artist in the world,' she said. 'The Karagöz exhibit is exquisite. Don't you agree?'

İkmen found it hard to concur.

'I think I would find Yaşar and Nuray of more interest if they were alive, Mrs Akdeniz,' he said, 'but I suppose I'm coming from a rather different perspective.'

'You think it's weird, don't you?' She narrowed her eyes to peer into his. 'I expect you think that you just wake up one morning and do something like this?'

'No.'

'Yes, you do.' She leaned into the hard back of her chair and looked across at Suleyman. 'But it isn't like that. There is pain. I felt their loss. I took drugs to dull the pain. But there are bigger things in life. Something like Karagöz, someone like Melih takes years of development, planning, preparation.'

Briefly robbed of energy, she stopped what she was saying and stared blankly beyond the officers at the stained walls behind their heads.

İkmen, after a brief glance across at Suleyman, said, 'So why don't you tell us about that then, Eren? Make us understand.'

For just a moment she didn't appear to have heard what he said. Suleyman lit a cigarette and thought about Masha and what Metin İskender had told him about Rostov. Now, İskender had said, Rostov would be making calls to the other bosses' henchmen; soon he would control them all, plus a lot more lawyers like Güneş, a lot more dying girls like Masha.

'My parents didn't want me to marry Melih,' Eren said, brightly now that she appeared to have moved out of her trance-like state. 'I was very young and he was a Jew originally. Nabaro.'

'Yes,' İkmen said, recalling that it was just this name that had finally alerted him to what Melih had in mind.

'But I married him anyway,' Eren said. 'I loved him.'

'Even when he went with other women?'

Suleyman looked across at İkmen and noted that his face possessed that taut quality it assumed when he was really, truly furious.

'Yes,' she smiled.

'How?'

'Because my husband was always working,' she said,

'having sex, taking drugs – it was all an act of creation. He taught me that. He taught me that observation could be creative in itself, that jealousy has an artistic purpose. He was a magician, you know.'

'He conned you into believing that everything he did was a statement.'

'No,' she paused to look İkmen deeply in the eyes once again, 'because everything that he did *was* a statement.'

'And you just came to that conclusion?'

'No. No, over time as I learned more.'

'As Melih desensitised you to the unacceptable,' İkmen snapped, 'as he made you into something that could take the lives of your own children.'

Suleyman, in line with previous instructions, placed what he hoped was a calming hand on İkmen's arm.

'I'd like to know, Mrs Akdeniz,' he said, 'how Dr Keyder entered into your husband's plans.'

Temporarily mollified, İkmen just sat quietly with his head down.

'Dr Keyder had always admired Melih's work,' Eren said. 'She and her brother were originally from Balat. She's a very clever woman, Dr Keyder.' She dropped her gaze. 'She understood all the Kabbalistic stuff that lies at the heart of Melih's work. I never really did. Melih was far above me. She could talk to him for hours about what it all meant.'

'When did they first meet?'

'A couple of years ago. My brother Reşad works for Dr Keyder, transporting subjects.'

'Do you know why your brother would want to perform such a grisly task?' İkmen asked.

Eren very pointedly looked away.

'Was it possible,' İkmen said, 'because corpses, like little girls, are essentially helpless?'

Once again, Eren did not reply.

'You know one of my colleagues spoke to this Bursa woman Reşad is friends with?' İkmen continued. 'Very interesting. They met only recently and she is very taken with him. It's very sad for her that your brother can't get an erection when he's with her.'

'I don't want to hear this!'

'As you wish. And so how did,' İkmen, raising his head, said acidly, 'the idea to murder and embalm your children evolve? It is not, after all, something that occurs to most people.'

Ignoring his tone entirely, she said, 'Melih was impressed and fascinated by Dr Keyder's work. Her connection through Pedro Ara to Eva Peron was he felt, a work of art in its own right. When he first discovered, last year, that he had cancer, he asked Dr Keyder to embalm him. She said that she'd do it but that she couldn't guarantee to get a good result. Even without all the cancer treatment, he'd already messed his body up with drugs. Melih felt that it could stand as a work of art anyway, but Dr Keyder wasn't happy.'

'So was it Dr Keyder who suggested the use of your pristine little children?'

Eren frowned. 'Not exactly.'

'What do you mean?'

She looked up. 'I mean that Melih was already wondering how he was going to do without the children when Dr Keyder suggested a way in which he could take them with him and create the most challenging piece of art in the world.'

'By doing without the children,' İkmen said, 'I take it you mean—'

'Dying without them, yes.' She smiled. 'He couldn't bear it. But then if he could incorporate them into his own death, as art, well . . .'

'What do you mean "as art"?' said Suleyman, who was also, he now felt, beginning to experience considerable barely controlled anger.

'I mean that Melih, as you saw yourselves, finally achieved it all,' she said, 'the ultimate statement featuring multiple ultimate taboos – infanticide, suicide, the petrification of the flesh that is so well preserved one can actually see the soul pinned to the skin. That he expressed this in what is an essentially Turkish form, Karagöz, is consistent with what he has been producing for the whole of his life. It all fits. You know that all the greatest Karagöz masters were either gypsies or Jews – just like Melih. Karagöz therefore concluded his work in a cohesive—'

'Your husband poisoned your children!'

'Yes, but—'

'No "buts".' İkmen held a warning finger up to Eren's face. 'Your husband killed them with your own and Dr Keyder's knowledge.'

'But they, like he,' Eren said, her eyes now bright with what could have either been tears or emotion, 'still exist within the moving shadows of Karagöz. The show is, Melih always said, littered with Kabbalistic references, these universal archetypes as exemplified by Karagöz and, by extension, through Melih, don't die. My family is immortal.'

'Except for you, and your brother,' İkmen said, 'who remain to take the punishment the state deems appropriate to the crimes your husband committed in the name of art.'

Eren leaned across the table at the two men, 'Which, just like all of the reporting around our event, all of the photographs taken by you of the exhibit, is just a continuation of the performance. I spoke of these things to Sergeant Farsakoğlu,' she said, as she shot one of her now customary smiles at the female officer. 'The performance began the second Melih was conceived – it will continue for as long as our event lives in the memories and the archives of people across the world. It is immortal and because Reşad and myself are part of it, we are immortal too. Art cannot be killed.'

'I've ordered post-mortem examinations on both your children and your husband,' İkmen said. 'This means, Mrs Akdeniz, that your relatives will be cut up in order to establish cause of death. In the case of your children, the maintenance programme that follows embalming will be curtailed and once our doctor's investigations are at an end, the bodies will be released to your mother for burial.'

'Yes, but—'

'What I'm saying, Mrs Akdeniz,' İkmen said tightly, 'is that I am finishing your "performance".' He cleared his throat before continuing, 'You and your brother, who claims your husband blackmailed him into this, and Dr Keyder will eventually be sent for trial. Then when the bodies of your husband and your children are buried and you and your cohorts are safely in prison the world will move on.'

'No . . .'

'Oh, yes,' İkmen said, 'it will, Mrs Akdeniz.' He leaned across the table towards her. 'And do you know why that is, Eren? It's because everything dies: people, animals, ideologies, faith, even art. Everything has its time in the sun and then,' he clapped his hands together, making Eren jump in the process, 'like Karagöz shows, like the midgets and mimes who used to entertain our old Ottoman rulers, things go. Things give way to other things, it's called progress.'

'Yes, but some things are immortal, like the architectural work of the great Sınan. I mean everyone still admires the Süleymaniye, the Sokollu Mehmet Paşa Mosque . . .'

'Yes,' İkmen agreed, 'they do. And do you know why that is, Mrs Akdeniz?'

Before she could even draw breath, Suleyman who could now see very clearly where this conversation was going, put in, 'It's because the work of great artists needs no explanation,' he said. 'Whatever one may think of either the religion or the monarchy that patronised Sınan's work, there is no denying the beauty and artistry inherent in his buildings. His skill and the loveliness of his creations speak directly to our senses. They help us to experience the higher emotions of spirituality, the glory of Allah . . .'

'My husband's work reached the divine in a far more profound way!' Eren stood up. İkmen too rose from his chair. 'Your husband's "work" will live in the annals of crime! Your husband was a monster! Your husband created only ugliness! I know your children were beautiful, Mrs Akdeniz, but when Melih killed them and then gave them over for embalming, he didn't have their spirits nailed to their bodies, he robbed them of everything! Of life, of choice, of dignity. He left their poor spirits untended, ugly and uncared for . . .'

'That old Turkish nonsense!'

'Which, whether you believe it or not, does give the dead some dignity!' İkmen said. 'I too, Mrs Akdeniz, have some if you like magical knowledge. I've seen the torment he subjected your children to. Even now they are not at peace. How can you condone that? Bury a man soon and give that man, and his family, some peace!'

'Oh, if you choose to believe that, yes,' she replied, 'but that isn't the case with Melih. Melih's just going on and on,' she smiled, 'continuing the performance. The work is complete but the performance continues.' She raised her arms high in the air, artfully like an actress, as she looked at the two men and one woman before her. 'When one is an artist, even when one just simply lives and loves with an artist, the creation, the magic never stops. Even in prison I will continue to evolve, the work will always and forever endure . . .'

İkmen looked across at Suleyman and then, seeing the same lack of connection to this woman in his eyes, he shook his head. Whatever she might have been prior to Melih's death – wife, acolyte, humiliated slave, even a concerned mother at one time – she was something quite different now. Now she was the artist – finally and seemingly joyously the inheritor of her husband's artistic legacy.

# CHAPTER 21

Talaat Erteğrül died later that afternoon. Two of his sisters, one of whom was Fatma İkmen, were with him when he took his last breath. Almost unrecognisable from the man he had been even at the beginning of the week, Talaat's corpse looked so small and pathetic as Fatma bade him a last, tearful farewell. Not that she could allow herself the luxury of mourning for very long. Although not pious himself, Talaat had been part of what was largely a religious family and so a speedy funeral was essential. For a while Fatma and everyone around her existed in a kind of whirling vortex of tear-soaked activity. When the funeral did start, it almost, as is common with the hastily organised Muslim rite, came as a shock to those who had been most intimately involved with it. This, fortunately, didn't include İkmen.

Although, especially towards the end of his life, İkmen had developed an affection for Talaat, his death only really touched him in relation to how it made Fatma and the children feel. He helped where he could; making arrangements, informing relatives who lived out of town and, of course, comforting his wife when she wanted to be soothed. But there was little he could do beyond that. Fatma's family were a little too pious for his taste, and so the sight of two of his wife's nieces wearing headscarves was all the excuse he needed to get away from the family Erteğrül and head for a quite other type of ceremony.

'It's very good of you to come,' Father Giovanni Vetra said as he shook hands with İkmen and Çöktin at the graveside.

'It's nothing,' the older man replied with a shrug.

All of Rosita Keyder's friends had gone from the site some time ago. All, without exception, elderly people, it had been difficult for the priest to try and explain to them why she was not being buried alone.

Father Giovanni took a handful of sandy soil between his fingers and threw it down on to the top of the coffin, that of Miguel Arancibia.

'You know when I was preparing for this service last night,' the priest said, 'I thought how dreadful and bizarre it must have been, living with this corpse for so long. That Veli Keyder allowed it . . .' He shrugged. 'But then my mind drifted from this situation to the holy relics phenomenon and, you know, the more I thought about those the more I could appreciate the preservation of Miguel Arancibia. After all, he was young, his death was cruel and he was beautiful. Just like Evita Peron,' he smiled. 'And so we make saints from the young, beautiful dead because we cannot and will not let them go.'

'My understanding of Catholicism is that that's OK,' İkmen said. 'Forgive me if I'm wrong, Father, but from what I have observed, some elements of your worship are very dependent upon physical images.'

Father Giovanni smiled. 'You must think us heathens

when you see us standing and praying in front of statues and pictures.'

'Oh, I don't think anything myself, Father,' İkmen replied with a smile. 'I espouse no religion.'

'Oh?'

'No, I have my own ideas, if you know what I mean.'

'Do you, Inspector, subscribe to the Turkish belief that the dead are in torment until their bodies are buried?' the priest asked as he moved to one side in order to allow the grave diggers to begin their job of filling the site.

'Yes,' he answered simply, 'and I do feel easier now that Mrs Keyder and her brother are in their graves.'

'Such a strange business with Rosita's sister-in-law,' Father Giovanni said, as he shook his head at the memory of what he had been told about the affair. 'And to actually kill those poor children . . .'

'Sir . . .' Çöktin reached across in front of the priest to touch İkmen lightly on the arm.

'What?'

'Over there,' the young man said as he tilted his head in the direction of a particularly gnarled cypress tree at the far end of the small cemetery.

İkmen narrowed his eyes against both the high mid-afternoon sun and his own occasionally blurry eyesight. When the figure in front of the tree did eventually come into focus it was instantly familiar. Unfortunately.

After giving instructions to Çöktin and the priest about keeping back from what was about to take place, İkmen first lit up a cigarette and then approached the man.

'Señor Orontes?'

The little man turned sharply and with a gasp.

'What are you doing here, señor?' İkmen asked.

'I am, er . . .'

'Because if you've come to disturb or in any way desecrate the last resting place of Miguel Arancibia then I think you should know that we bury them very deep here in the Republic. As well as needing to hire some quite serious digging equipment,' İkmen smiled, 'you will also need to get past my officers, who will be guarding this site.'

Orontes, seemingly offended, pulled himself up to his full, small height. 'I came here only out of respect,' he said, 'for the young man and for the artistry that went into his preservation.'

'Not because you thought you might salvage something of what remains of Dr Ara's work?' İkmen said as he placed a firm hand on to the Spaniard's shoulder. 'Not because Dr Keyder promised him to you – or rather she wanted you to keep him for her.'

'No!'

'Well, that's very good,' İkmen said, 'very good. Because I would hate to think that your devotion to your craft might be leading you into committing an offence.'

'No.' Orontes looked down at the ground. 'Even if I sincerely believe that to bury such beauty, such exquisite art is—'

'Natural, right and respectful,' İkmen interrupted, 'qualities, I am sure that you possess, Señor Orontes.'

The Spaniard looked up with such an expression of hatred on his face that İkmen, for a moment, was entirely lost for words. When he did finally get around to speaking it was with an entirely different tone. He moved his hand up the Spaniard's back, towards his neck, moving the little man away from Father Giovanni and Çöktin's line of sight as he did so.

'Now listen to me, you little shit,' he said. 'If a dog so much as sniffs around the edge of Miguel Arancibia's grave, I will come for you.'

'But—'

'You want the secret of Dr Ara's balm, you go and dig him up,' İkmen sneered, 'or, better still, why don't you go and visit Dr Keyder in her cell? Once she's been inside for a few years, she'll tell you her secret. She'll probably also tell you where the djinn who torment her nightly come from too.'

'You shouldn't be incarcerating a woman like Dr Keyder!'

'I agree,' İkmen said, now no longer smiling. 'Quite right, Señor Orontes. We should be executing her,' İkmen said. 'Even though I don't believe in capital punishment myself, it's what we should be doing.' He bent down low in order to whisper into the other man's ear. 'She colluded in the killing of children,' he said, 'an inhuman act – an offence beyond mercy.'

'She is a genius!'

İkmen, shaking his head in disbelief, let go of the Spaniard's neck and started to walk up towards Çöktin and the priest. He didn't look back at Orontes as he left although he did speak to him once more before he'd finished.

'I will ask Father Giovanni to pray for you, Señor Orontes,' he said. 'Such a good man may have some influence with your God. Your twisted soul will need all the help it can get.'

\*    \*    \*

She was a good-looking woman in the same way that his wife was a good-looking woman. Large-boned and luscious, she was a lot darker than Zelfa, probably a few years younger and definitely, by her style of dress and demeanour, a gypsy. Not that Mehmet Suleyman had come to spy on Gonca the gypsy artist – he didn't even know her. What had made him drift back to Balat he didn't really know. Years before, when he was İkmen's sergeant, the two of them had worked a very complicated case in the district, which was when he had first become familiar with the place. But it wasn't memories of that time that had called him back. No, it was more to do with what he and his colleagues had all too recently been through, namely Melih Akdeniz and his now empty great ochre house of death. Suleyman looked up into its blank windows and frowned. A place, he recalled, that had once, together with so many other properties in this area, served as a safe haven to those persecuted for their race and religion. So awful that this particular example had been despoiled by Melih and his artistic insanity. But maybe that sense of difference that Balat could bring had contributed to the artist's descent into darkness. Maybe the majority, by their lack of understanding, did indeed set small groups up to be odd, different and even dysfunctional?

But then if that were so, why weren't more people disordered and deranged? Why wasn't he? After all, as an Ottoman he was as much a member of a minority group as the Jew Melih Akdeniz? No, one could only take difference so far – after that it was all down to personal agency, and to what fate threw out towards you.

The gypsy, who was swathed from head to foot in metres of almost transparent gold and purple chiffon, watched him through a filter of the smoke from her cigar. She was standing in front of the gateway to the artist's garden, the one through which İkmen and Suleyman had run in order to get to the dead Akdeniz and the luminescent bodies of his children. She appeared to be waiting for someone, although quite who that might be in what was an entirely deserted street he couldn't imagine. It certainly wasn't him. Women, however lovely, were not on his agenda at the present time. He still had to make another appointment for tests with Krikor Sarkissian and the problem remained about how and when he was going to tell Zelfa about Masha and what he had done with her. How stupid it all seemed now, stupid and weak and ultimately destructive too. Masha was dead, killed almost certainly by the man who was now possibly planning to exert his malignant influence over the city as never before, Valery Rostov. Suleyman himself could have hepatitis, be HIV positive – almost anything. And then there was still the issue about who had told Rostov about his private life. Someone, so Metin İskender felt, in the department, someone close and well hidden from view . . .

Now, metaphorically, out of his box, Rostov would have to be dealt with. Maybe when those tests on the body of 'Tatiana' came through? But then maybe not. Suleyman brushed some of the sweat that had gathered on his forehead away from his eyes and then lit a cigarette. If Rostov could buy people in the department then he could buy other people at the Forensic Institute too. But then did that particular aspect of the case matter anyway? Some very bad gangsters were currently awaiting trial for the possession of guns and drugs. People like Vronsky were known killers. That he was out of circulation had to be good. And yet the thought that possibly he, Suleyman, and his colleagues had actually helped Rostov to gain more power still rankled. Rostov was, and would remain, unfinished business, until, that is, Suleyman himself chose to deal with him. That would, he knew, have to come one fine day. And in his heart of hearts, Suleyman knew that his revenge could and would take only one form.

As he watched the gypsy turn to smile at a young man who was now huffing and puffing his way up the hill, Mehmet Suleyman wondered how long it might take him to plan and execute Rostov's death without pointing the finger of suspicion at himself. The perfect crime was, of course, a largely illusory concept but then people like Rostov got away with murder all the time . . .

The young man, on seeing first the gypsy and then Suleyman, reddened. This was, the latter reasoned, his cue to leave Balat and go and have a serious and difficult conversation with his wife. He did not, after all, have any interest in embarrassing the young man. By her sensual demeanour and her provocative clothes, the gypsy was obviously signalling that her appearance on the young man's route home was no accident. It was also quite apparent that she hadn't intercepted him in order to just offer him conversation and tea. And indeed, as he turned away from the couple to make his way back down to the shores of the Golden Horn, he heard the moist sound of their kissing.

So young Hikmet Yıldız was being seduced by a gypsy.

Suleyman smiled. That was good. She was beautiful, the boy was young and it was a hot, sultry afternoon. The sex could go on for hours. Maybe one day he and his wife would do such things again. But then if they didn't there was always his hatred to get him through the sticky ennui-filled summer afternoons to come. One is never, he thought, alone with thoughts of death . . .

Because he knew that his daughter Hulya and her boyfriend, Berekiah, would still be at his apartment with his grieving wife, İkmen took the opportunity to go and see Berekiah's father. And although he knew that Balthazar Cohen wouldn't be alone, he was also aware of the fact that his old colleague's wife, Estelle, was essentially on his side. It was she who let him into the apartment and who disappeared quickly once she had settled her guest, who hadn't actually spoken to her husband for some months, opposite what remained of Balthazar.

Although the great earthquake of 1999 had only robbed Balthazar of his legs from the knees downwards, his body as a whole had shrunk considerably since that time. Lack of exercise, as well as a disregard for food and strong addictions to both painkillers and tobacco had rendered him small, bitter and ill. However, İkmen knew from Berekiah that there was at least the possibility for change on the horizon because Balthazar had, apparently, agreed to try prosthetic limbs. Not that he had come to speak about such limbs now, although he did use this topic in order to open up conversation with this man who had flatly refused to speak to him for some months.

'I'm told they'll hurt,' he said in answer to İkmen's question about the limbs, 'but then—'

'You're a strong man,' İkmen put in, 'you're tough.'

Cohen turned to look at İkmen with hard eyes. 'I will never approve of a marriage between your daughter and my son,' he said bluntly, 'so you might as well leave now.'

'Yes,' İkmen shrugged, 'that's true. But they're going to do it anyway.'

'And you are going to give them your blessing, Çetin Bey.'

'Yes.' İkmen watched as Balthazar lit a cigarette and then lit one of his own. 'I can't think of any young man I would rather have join my family than Berekiah.'

'And your wife?'

İkmen smiled. 'My wife is at bottom a realist, Balthazar,' he said. 'She sees, as I do, the very genuine love that exists between our children, even if she cannot actually approve of it.'

Estelle Cohen came into the room bearing glasses of tea for the two men. Her husband eyed her suspiciously as she placed his glass down beside him.

'And you?' he said harshly as her face drew level with his own. 'What do you think about your son and this man's daughter?'

Estelle first looked across at İkmen before replying.

'I think that love is a rare thing and that one must grasp it tightly before it passes,' she said.

'So five hundred years of Jewish life in this city means nothing to you?'

Estelle, her mind as it always did when this subject

arose, flew back across the years to her old life in Balat and that shining Turkish boy who had once kissed her. Ersin.

'No,' she said, 'but I think that I love my son more . . .'

'Then if you love him so much, why don't you stop him?' Balthazar fixed his wife with a harsh gaze. 'Look what goes on in Israel. Jews and Muslims always at each other's throats! Look at how Jews are still, even now, thrown out of countries like Iraq and Iran, Muslim countries where we are hated.'

'And look at how safe we are here, Balthazar!' his wife responded passionately. 'Look at how our synagogues are protected! Look at how we come and we go from this country as we please! Look at the reality of how none of the things you have mentioned apply to where we are!'

'Yes, but that can change!' Balthazar spat. 'My uncle went to South America because he—'

Estelle flung her arms up into the air. 'That was decades ago!' she cried. 'Jews went from all over the world to South America at that time! There were opportunities in those countries – for a while – until people started to realise how many Nazis lived over there! Until the most appalling people came to power in places like Chile and Argentina!'

'Yes, and we're going to have an election here soon, aren't we?' Balthazar said as he puffed furiously on his cigarette. 'And so how do we know who is going to govern us? Maybe fundamentalist Muslims? Who knows?'

'Yes, right, who knows?'

'Agreed. But if our new government does enact Sharia law then what about couples like Berekiah and Hulya? What do you think people will think of them? What will happen to them? What will happen to their children?'

'I don't know!' Estelle now close to tears, sat down. 'I don't know.'

İkmen, who had been listening carefully to everything that had been said, leaned forward and looked at both the Cohens with a grave expression on his face.

'And neither do I know,' he said. 'No one does. The world could be at war in a few months' time if some are to be believed. Wherever one is in the world, the fact is that regimes and opinions can change. We have to accept that as a possibility, but what we don't have to do is like it or approve of it.' He sighed. 'I know that marriage like this can cause problems for people. But these problems are often caused not by the couple but by others who wish to put obstacles in their way and raise barriers of difference up in their minds.'

If Melih Akdeniz had not been so aware of his own difference, would his 'art' have been so very disordered? Had he, by being so extreme, sought to prove something to 'the Establishment' that hadn't needed proving anyway? Although, of course, he had painted and sculpted before, had the disapproval of Eren's parents provided the final push to tip his unstable psyche over the edge into madness? Fear had made his parents take the decision to hide what they were. But fear of what? Balat was and always had been a safe place for Jewish people to live. Even when the district started to change character . . . But then maybe it was the same fear that Balthazar was exhibiting now, fear of the future, the unknown, shadowed by a past İkmen knew he could barely imagine. After all, as the Greek monk Brother Constantine had told him when they both stood outside Melih's house and had talked of such things, the Balat Jews had been tortured almost to extinction before they left Spain and Portugal. Maybe that pain was stuck somehow in some primitive area of their brains, a defence mechanism that came into play whenever their solidarity was threatened.

But İkmen hadn't come to explore issues allied to the case he had just completed. Relevant or not, the only real fact here was that his daughter and Balthazar's son were in love and whatever waited for them in the future was as uncertain and nebulous as sea mist. In that they were just like every other couple in the world.

'My brother-in-law Talaat died yesterday,' İkmen said.

'May your head be alive.' Estelle murmured the standard response to this news.

İkmen smiled his reply to her. 'And so when the mourning period is at an end, I am going to arrange a wedding,' he said. 'In spite of death, elections, religion, war and an almost complete lack of money, I am going to give my family, and yours, if you want it, a party.'

'But—'

'Because if I don't they will just live together and really scandalise our wives and because, Balthazar, life must and will go on,' İkmen said. 'And although I know in my heart that fate will do whatever it wishes with us in the end, sometimes it's important to have what you want first and then take the consequences. I'm giving those young people to each other . . .'

'With my blessing,' Estelle put in softly.

They both saw the tears begin in the crippled man's eyes.

'Balthazar . . .'

'And so at the bottom of my life, you take my honour away from me Çetin Bey?' He looked up furiously into İkmen's face.

'No.'

'Yes! You take my child and . . .' His tears overwhelmed him, robbing him of speech.

Estelle, with one eye still on İkmen, went over to her husband and placed her arms around his shoulders. Strangely, in view of the fact that she had effectively defied him, he didn't resist. Great screaming sobs came out of him then, the result İkmen knew of years of misery that went quite beyond the situation with Berekiah.

However, misery of this depth should, İkmen knew, only be exhibited to those closest to a person and so, with a small smile at Estelle, he left. He had hoped that Balthazar would willingly come round to his point of view in the way that Fatma had, but then, thinking about it as he walked down the steep streets of Karaköy, he knew that hadn't really been very realistic. Change, even of the welcome variety, hurt. Maybe over time Balthazar would come round . . .

But maybe not. What was and had to remain important was the future. Hulya, Berekiah, all of his other children. What was in the past was just that – in the past – important but gone. Old concepts, like old bodies, rotted and dissolved for a reason. He'd watched Fatma let go of Talaat with tears of pain in her deepest heart, but he knew that what she was doing was right. Now that

Talaat's body was buried they could start planning for the wedding. Fatma and his girls would enjoy planning the food and choosing their clothes. As for him, İkmen thought that perhaps he might enjoy getting involved in the organisation of the entertainment. Gypsy musicians and fortune-tellers – just like the old days. İkmen smiled, perhaps he'd go and see Gonca, maybe she'd decorate the apartment for the occasion – with tarot cards and horse tails. Maybe he'd even ask her or one of her relatives to perform spells to prevent war, to protect Bülent and all his young friends too. With people like George W. Bush and Saddam Hussein loose in the world, ordinary boys like his son needed all the protection they could get.

But all of that was for the future. Now was not the time to go wandering up the hill towards Gonca's rackety place. If anyone had asked him why it wasn't the right time, İkmen wouldn't have been able to answer them. He just knew. Gonca, whether with reality or with dreams, was otherwise engaged. He also knew that whenever he saw her again, she would tell him all about it. İkmen smiled. Neither black nor white, good nor bad, the gypsy was always and shamelessly herself. He liked that about her.

İkmen walked down the Galata Hill, across the Galata Bridge and up into Sultan Ahmet. The unaccustomed exercise made him puff, and pulled at his muscles, but it reminded him that he was alive, which was good. And as he entered his apartment other live bodies came forward to greet him. Every one of them touched him with affection.

# Deep Waters

## Barbara Nadel

'Intelligent and captivating . . . recalls Michael Dibdin's
Aurelio Zen' *Sunday Times*

On a foggy night, by the banks of the Bosphorus, a man's
corpse is dumped, his head almost severed from his
body. His identity card names him as Rifat Berisha, a
twenty-five-year-old Albanian. His family, resident in
Turkey for decades, is stoic and impenetrable. But when
Inspector İkmen, whose mother was Albanian, consults
his cousin Samsun he's left in little doubt as to the cause
of the man's death. For the Berishas are embroiled in a
terrifying, implacable, self-perpetuating blood feud with
a rival clan. And, as Samsun points out, if either of the
warring families discovers who İkmen's mother was, he
himself will be pulled into their murderous vendetta.

Determined not to be swayed by Samsun's assumptions,
İkmen finds himself journeying into his own past, forced
to confront what the dimly remembered death of his
magical, passionate and mysterious mother really
meant . . .

'The delight of Nadel's İkmen books is the sense of being
taken beneath the surface of an ancient city' *Independent*

'A first-rate author' *Good Housekeeping*

'Nadel goes from strength to strength . . . a gallery of
richly created characters, along with superb scene-
setting' *Good Book Guide*

0 7472 6719 7

## headline

# Harem

## Barbara Nadel

The body of a teenage girl is discovered in a cistern deep below the city of Istanbul. For the Turkish police force's most idiosyncratic and talented officer, Çetin İkmen, this is a difficult case. The girl was his daughter's friend and her attire, that of a nineteenth-century Ottoman, offers no easy explanation.

With his promise of justice to the dead girl's mother still fresh on his lips, İkmen is taken off the case. He's reassigned to the kidnapping of an ageing movie star's wife. The star is hiding something and so, İkmen fears, are his superiors. A powerful secret exists in the labyrinthine city, one which those on either side of the law will do anything to prevent escaping. But for İkmen, there's no choice, only the truth.

Praise for Barbara Nadel's İkmen series

'Really refreshing to encounter something as idio-syncratic and evocative . . . as Barbara Nadel's Istanbul-set thriller' *The Times*

'Unusual and very well-written' *Sunday Telegraph*

'Intriguing, exotic . . . exciting, accomplished and original' *Literary Review*

'Full of complex characters and louche atmosphere' *Independent*

'My reader rates this atuhor higher than Donna Leon' *Bookseller*

0 7472 6720 0

## headline

Now you can buy any of these other bestselling Headline books from your bookshop or *direct from the publisher.*

FREE P&P AND UK DELIVERY
(Overseas and Ireland £3.50 per book)

| | | |
|---|---|---|
| Murphy's Law | Colin Bateman | £6.99 |
| Mandrake | Paul Eddy | £6.99 |
| Seven Up | Janet Evanovich | £5.99 |
| A Place of Safety | Caroline Graham | £6.99 |
| A Restless Evil | Ann Granger | £6.99 |
| Dead Weight | John Francome | £6.99 |
| The Cat Who Went Up the Creek | Lilian Jackson Braun | £6.99 |
| On Honeymoon with Death | Quintin Jardine | £6.99 |
| Deep Waters | Barbara Nadel | £5.99 |
| No Good Deed | Manda Scott | £5.99 |
| Oxford Double | Veronica Stallwood | £5.99 |
| Bubbles Unbound | Sarah Strohmeyer | £5.99 |

TO ORDER SIMPLY CALL THIS NUMBER

**01235 400 414**

or visit our website: www.madaboutbooks.com

Prices and availability subject to change without notice.